BOUND TO DIE

LAURIE ROCKENBECK

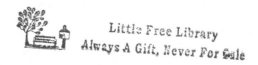

BANE BODKIN
P R E S S

BANE BODKIN
PRESS

Bane and Bodkin Press
16625 Redmond Way, M-229
Redmond, WA 98052

This is a work of fiction. Any resemblance to persons living or dead is entirely coincidental.

Cover Design by Mariah Sinclair

ISBN: 978-1-947234-03-1 (paperback)

ISBN: 978-1-47234-02-4 (hardcover)

ISBN: 978-1-947234-01-7 (ebook)

—to my darling hubby. I'm really glad you've stopped looking at me funny when I talk about where to hide the bodies.

1

SWEAT. FEAR. PISS. SHIT. DEAD BODY.

Court breathed in the foul air, recognizing it as part of the job and hating its familiarity at the same time. He fingered the jar of menthol rub he kept in his pocket. The elevator door swished shut behind him, giving him only one direction to move. Toward the smell.

Yellow crime-scene tape marked an expansive area beyond the only open door of the six rooms in the office suite. All were dark except for one.

Ivy gagged next to him, raising her wrist to her nose as if her scant perfume might cover the smell of death. "I hate this part."

Court opened the jar, tilting it toward her in invitation. She hesitated, looking around before dabbing her finger into the paste.

"It helps," he said as he dabbed menthol at each of his nostrils.

She sniffed loudly, wrinkling her nose at the menthol. "I thought people got used to the odor after a while."

"I never have. Don't care if people think I'm a wimp." He held up the little jar. "I prefer this to dead-body any day."

In the foyer, a woman sat upright on an oversized circular ottoman. Her long hair curled into wide, dark rings with a glowing smoothness straight out of a shampoo commercial. A thin gold chain with a sparkly heart dangled from her throat. Matching glints on each ear twinkled in unison as she moved her head. She looked like a banker, with the exception of her bare feet. And her nose, which was red, wiped raw. Her eyes met Court's and her lips faded into a tight white line.

A uniformed officer checked their badges and handed Court the clipboard to sign in. "Detective Pearson, I thought you guys would be here sooner." He dipped his head and smiled broadly at Ivy. "Detective Langston, congrats on the move to Homicide."

Court checked his watch. Five forty-five p.m. "It's rush hour and a Friday."

Ivy reached for the clipboard. "Thanks. Glad to see my first week is finally getting interesting."

A fresh case was always more interesting than slogging through cold files, but Court had never delighted in news about a death. Court recalibrated his plans for the weekend. A dead body didn't necessarily mean there was a murder to investigate. Maybe they'd luck out, and the woman with glowing hair would confess to whatever they were about to find inside. He raised his chin toward the open door. "Who's running the scene?"

"Maclean. He's inside." The officer pointed his pen at the woman in the chair. "He's already interviewed her. She called it in." He lifted the tape as they passed underneath.

"Maclean's the guy who writes mystery shorts under a pen name, right? Got in trouble for not changing all the names on something last year?" Ivy asked.

"Yeah, he's not a bad guy. Good cop. He likes to get chatty, especially when he's fresh on first watch." Court turned back to the officer. "Tell Miss Tension over there we'll talk to her after we get a look inside."

They crossed the common area toward the office in the corner. The sign next to the door said ALLEGIANCE INVEST-MENTS. Right on cue, Colby Maclean appeared from within, holding out his hands, barring them from entering. He pointed to a box on the floor. "About time, detectives."

Court grabbed four of blue paper shoe-wraps, handing Ivy a pair before covering his feet.

Maclean led them through the scene. "The 911 came in at four forty p.m. I got here at four forty-five…"

"It only took you five minutes?"

"Yeah. Happened to be on a call at the convenience store across the street. Some kids making trouble. Didn't even have to move the car. How funny is that? Anyway, so I get here and the door is open. Caller's in there, pacing around in her bare feet." He circled his finger around his temple. "I don't think she's all there, if you get my drift." Maclean swished his arm back and forth in front of a large wooden desk, tracing her path.

Small artsy crap and a bunch of leather-bound books decorated a bookshelf lining the wall behind a large mahogany desk directly across from the door. Two squat polished-chrome and pleather chairs sat across from the desk. It sported a green blotter with an iPad and a pile of unopened mail strewn across it. An old-style computer with a monitor the size of a moving box filled a corner.

A single shoe—a dozen buckled leather straps on a six-inch heel—lay next to the desk. Stilettos stuck out in a city where Birkenstocks were accepted as fashionable. It would match the outfit the woman outside was wearing.

"So," Maclean was saying, "she stops when she sees me, points to this other door and says, 'He's inside.' The smell was bad, so I knew without checking there had to be a body in there. Can't miss that smell, you know? I go inside, and holy shit, you aren't gonna believe this one. This is one for the books. I'm telling you. Hunter, the woman in the chair out there. She's the caller, her name is Karen Hunter? Anyway, she calls this her *therapy room*." He laughed, repeated the phrase, jabbing two fingers of each hand at the air for emphasis. "You ask me? I'd call it a dungeon."

Maclean led them into the room, indicating the path of approach to the body as he went. Court followed, grateful that the officer was competent with procedure. The designated path had been ignored in · plenty of death scenes, mucking them up with trace evidence. He wished Maclean would stop talking, though.

What would it be this time? Brains all over the wall? Blood spatter everywhere? He swallowed, working his tongue over his teeth and lips, trying to get some moisture back in his mouth, breathing in the menthol to steel himself against whatever was to come.

In the center of the room, a man's body hung amid a tangle of ropes. His arms were pulled behind his back.

Purple rope was wrapped around them in a long neat coil, punctuated with a decorative knot every three inches. Black rope crisscrossed his waist, hips, and upper thighs, and supported the bulk of his weight. A metal bar attached to his ankles by thick metal cuffs spread his legs obscenely wide, giving them an intimate view up his backside. More rope pulled his ankles up toward the ceiling. One final rope cut into his neck. Each section of rope was attached to a Frisbee-sized metal ring hanging from a giant hook in the center of the ceiling. A pulley system anchored the whole assembly to the wall opposite the door. His genitals were distended and bloated, forming a deep splotchy purple along the bottom of the arc of his body. A mass of what was probably dried urine and feces stained the bamboo floor below.

Ivy let out a long, slow whistle. "Holy….what is this place?"

Court's stomach flipped and settled into a slow burn. He'd never seen a person trussed up like a pig before. "Not an investment firm, that's for sure."

2

COURT STAYED ROOTED TO HIS SPOT NEAR THE DOOR AS
he worked gloves onto his hands. The latex snagged on his
hair, prickling his skin. His sweat was already beading up,
making his hands clammy. He forced himself to stand still, to
take in details before moving forward.

He approached the body hanging in the center of the
room. He had been someone. Someone's son. Someone's
lover?

A massage table sat underneath a series of large
eyehooks. A shoe matching the one in the front office lay
under the table. A counter with overhead cabinets filled one
wall. A tray on the counter held the biggest clue to what the
space was used for—an assortment of sex toys that rivaled
the inventory of a Lover's Pantry.

Thick blocks of fabric-covered foam filled in the only
windows. To keep light out or noise in? Both? The room
itself had a deadening lack of sound, as if it had been soundproofed. Two doors stood open. Through the first, a modern

square sink with shiny chrome fixtures out of *Architectural Digest* was centered beneath a simple round mirror. The second door opened onto custom-made walnut shelving stuffed with clothing.

The walls were painted in calming greens, and the lights were all fixed in the ceiling. A control box with a mini touch-screen indicated they were customizable. Mood lighting? A number of tracks with lights pointed at various parts of the room, including four obvious spotlights aimed dead center. A simple clock with large numbers hung on the wall facing the victim. Had he hung there watching the red hand sweeping the seconds by as he died? Court shuddered.

"Man, it's hot in here, any way we can turn down the heat?" Ivy asked.

Maclean pointed to the thermostat. "It was set at ninety-eight when I got here, but I didn't want to touch it."

Opening the door had already compromised the temperature of the room, but Court didn't point it out to Maclean. The switch was set to manual. He changed it to the automatic program and the screen flashed a reasonable seventy-one degrees. The heater clicked off as the system switched to air conditioning. He shut it down entirely. He'd already be in trouble with the ME for turning the heat off, and he didn't want to risk adding cold air to his offense.

"Any idea who he is?" Ivy asked.

They circled the body, careful to follow in Maclean's steps. "Yeah," he said. "Take a look for yourself."

Court dropped to his haunches so he could see the face of the man hanging from the tangle of flesh and rope. It was Berkeley Drummond—local entrepreneur, big supporter of the current mayor and the Seattle Police Department. Court had shaken hands with him once, at a political fundraiser.

Court didn't remember anything on the local news or the blotter update about the famous man going missing. How long could someone like Berkeley Drummond be gone before it got reported? Did anyone in his privileged world go anywhere for more than a couple of hours before someone demanded—*needed*—to know where they were? The state and smell of the body made it appear like he'd been here for days. The high temp had fucked them over in regards to actual time of death.

Ivy squatted next to him. Her cheeks paled. "Oh, my god. Is that really him? How long has he been here? This is big. Really big."

That was an understatement. "A couple days at most, I'd guess. But I'm not the medical examiner."

They stood. He pointed to the ropes holding the body in mid-air, indicating their path to the center of the ceiling and out to where the rope anchored everything to the wall. "We can probably rule out suicide."

"Probably? You think?"

"Sarcasm, much? Langston, this is your first gig. You can't assume murder without considering the alternatives."

"Oh, come on. It's obvious he didn't do this to himself. Someone else *had* to do that." She thrust an accusatory finger toward the mess of ropes. "That says murder to me."

"Homicide, *probably*. We still don't know for certain. And, if it was homicide, we still don't know if it was murder." Court's tone had taken on that of someone lecturing a child. He checked himself, shifted gears. "Maybe his death was an accident."

"It might have started off as an accident, but someone tied him, left him for dead. They even turned up the heat to mess with the time of death."

"It's possible it started out as consensual BDSM shit, and the guy died of a heart attack. The person tying him up ran scared." Court studied the mechanism holding up the body. He couldn't imagine how Berkeley Drummond could have done this to himself.

3

"LET'S CHECK THE PLACE OUT WHILE WE WAIT FOR THE ME to show up. Maclean, what's the ETA from the ME's office?" Court asked.

"Didn't get one. Said they'd send someone over. You want me to call them for a status update?"

It was already six o'clock. The King County Medical Examiner's office was less than half a mile away. The docs had probably all left for the evening when the call came in, so they probably had to get the on-call doc in from wherever. "No, they'll get here when they get here. Thanks, Maclean, we'll take it from here. Make sure someone's taping outside."

Maclean tapped two fingers to his forehead and left.

Court waved Ivy toward the other rooms. The bathroom was sandwiched Jack-and-Jill style between a small dressing-bedroom and the closet. Drummond's clothing, even his underwear, was neatly folded on a bench. The ID in his wallet made it official. A shit storm of attention was sure to follow.

It had been three years since Court had been on anything that garnered much press attention. Multiple homicides and the Chinese mob were always great fodder for those vultures. They'd waited outside his building for weeks, circling him as he stepped outside, microphones shoved at his face, demanding answers and details. He fumbled in his pocket for a piece of gum.

Court held the wallet open wide for Ivy to look at. Five crisp one-hundred-dollar bills were nestled against the same number of twenties. Behind the hundreds were ten cashier's checks, each made out to Allegiance Investments for ten thousand dollars. They were all drawn from the same bank on the same date, Wednesday.

"A hundred thousand?" Ivy let out a long slow whistle. "I'm in the wrong business."

"Transactions over ten K get more scrutiny." Court slid the checks into their own evidence bag, placing it in a box with Drummond's bagged clothes. Everything would be checked at the crime lab for trace evidence.

Both rooms were orderly without anything obviously out of place. Whoever had been here had either been meticulous in a search, or hadn't messed with anything at all. Initial search done, Court decided to interview their only known witness, at least until the other teams arrived. As they approached Karen Hunter, Court leaned toward Ivy. "I'll take the lead on this."

Ivy paused in her stride, offering an eye-roll worthy of a teenager. "Of course."

It hadn't been obvious to him that she wasn't going to jump in with questions. Maybe he hadn't needed to remind her he was in charge, but they hadn't worked together yet and had no established rhythm.

Hunter watched their approach with a Mona Lisa-like expression. She stood only when Court and Ivy introduced themselves.

"You're the one who called this in? This is your...?" He waved his hand toward the door, wondering what word she would use. Office? Play space? Studio? Dungeon? He'd heard them all used more than once.

She opened her mouth, then closed it. She crossed her arms and tapped her watch. "When can I leave?"

This was going to be interesting. No, *she* was interesting. "Soon. You can go after you've finished answering our questions."

Hunter glanced toward the elevator. "You can ask. I might answer. My attorney should be here any minute."

She'd already called her attorney? Then why even ask when she could leave? What the hell? "I'm merely trying to get a clear picture of all this. Getting your lawyer here will take time. Traffic is a bitch tonight."

"As I said before, you can ask. I'll answer what I feel I can."

Her voice was firm and confident, but she grasped her arms tight against herself. Maclean had said she referred to the room containing the body as her therapy room. It was clear she'd talked to Maclean, but had gotten control of herself since then. "Well, all right then, Ms. Hunter. We were told you found the body and called 911."

"I did."

Hunter's dark brown eyes met his with a cool aloofness

that betrayed her body language. She kept glancing toward the elevator.

"This your office?"

"Yes."

Ask a closed-ended question, and you get monosyllabic answers. Court chewed on his lip for a second before continuing. "Who all has access?"

"My clients."

She said the word 'clients' with deliberate care. "You're saying your clients can come and go as they please?"

The look she gave him reminded him of a disappointed kindergarten teacher. "No. They have key cards that let them come into the office right before an appointment. A limited, ten-minute window of opportunity."

In a town where computer programmers were barely outnumbered by MBA's, Court bet there would be a way to hack her entry system. Going through her whole client list was going to be a bitch, and it would require a warrant to get it in the first place. If he couldn't get her to offer it up voluntarily. "What kind of service do you perform? The sign on the door says financial, but the inside says something different."

"I'd rather not answer that until my attorney is here."

"Ms. Hunter, I can assure you, all I am interested in is finding out what happened here. What you do probably has something to do with how Berkeley Drummond died in there."

Hunter lifted a hand to her necklace, sliding the diamond back and forth along the chain. "I've been told to wait to speak to you."

It took a lot of effort to keep himself from rubbing at his

temples. His head was beginning to throb a slow, steady beat. "Okay, let's try this. Why is one of your shoes next to the desk in the front office and the other in the room with the body?"

"Oh." She raised a hand to her mouth. "Hmmm. That."

Court was sure she was hedging for time, trying to figure out what she could say. Before he could press her for an answer, the elevator door opened and a woman rushed out. Everything—from her neatly coiffed all-white hair, her hand-tailored suit, her leather briefcase slung from her shoulder to the tips of her Louboutins—screamed *attorney*. A pricey one.

Court nodded at the officer to let him know that she could come inside.

The attorney put a hand on Hunter's forearm, squeezing it gently but addressed herself to Court, then Ivy. "I hope you haven't asked my client too many questions, detectives."

She offered her card. BERNICE WAGNER, ATTORNEY-AT-LAW. Court was pretty sure she was involved in a bunch of cases recently with the ACLU, but he couldn't name any of them. They were all civil-rights issues. A high-powered lawyer for a high-powered domme?

4

—————

"WHAT'S A CIVIL RIGHTS ATTORNEY DOING HERE?" COURT said in a low voice, watching as the attorney consulted with her client a few feet away. "Even if Hunter was worried about being charged with something vice-related, she'd want a criminal defense attorney."

Ivy shrugged. "Could be the only one she knows. My guess is that Wagner can handle the basic questions, but would give her a referral for anything further."

"And you think working as a rich guy's dominatrix would be enough to cover the costs of an attorney like her?" He bet her retainer alone would take most of his annual salary.

"I don't know. She probably makes huge bucks as a dominatrix. Think about the checks we found."

"Prices have risen since I worked vice. There's no way he was paying her ten K a pop."

Ivy nodded. "This setup is pretty high-end, but nothing is that high-end."

Court opened his phone's browser, searched Karen

Hunter, and found nothing. Bernice Wagner, on the other hand, brought up hundreds of hits. He scanned the links until Hunter and her lawyer turned back toward them. Of interest was Wagner's representation of a class action on behalf of several thousand women and men seeking to legitimize many kinds of sex work—prostitution, professional handicap companionship, domination among them. He held the phone's screen toward Ivy. "I bet they know each other from this."

Wagner approached them. "Detectives, we know how things work. Get my client full immunity on anything vice-related, and I'll let her answer your questions."

Court had already figured this was the main issue. All they had in the other room were a bunch of perfectly legal sex toys. The cashier's checks could be payment to Hunter for a car she was selling him, could be for anything. Bending the rules a little bit might go a long way in this case. "You know we don't have that kind of authority. But, we're here to figure out what happened to the deceased, not ding her for her profession."

"Ms. Hunter is very upset about this. She wants to cooperate, but can't until certain assurances are made."

Court knew that the only way Wagner would make this kind of offer was if Hunter had given her enough information to make it clear that anything she said wouldn't lead to her arrest. "We'll talk to the D.A. about a deal. You get your client to answer our questions for us, first. Establish some basic facts. We can see where things go from there."

Wagner studied him for an uncomfortable length of time before nodding. "Do you have a time frame for the death?"

"Nope. No idea." Even if he did have a clear idea at this

point, he would want to hear what Hunter had to say before telling them.

Wagner's lips twitched. "Let's take it question by question then. You ask, I tell her whether or not to answer."

"How about I ask her the obvious... Did she kill or somehow cause the death of Berkeley Drummond? Could save us a lot of time."

Wagner shook her head, rolling her eyes with a lazy, maternal grace. "Nice try, Detective. Go ahead, read Ms. Hunter her rights, and we'll go one by one. Maybe you can question her while your partner can call someone at the D.A.'s office and get a basic deal hammered out so we can expedite this. I have no desire to meet with you again this weekend."

Court glanced at Ivy, who was already pulling up her contact list on the phone. "Verbal preliminary work for you?"

Wagner swung her briefcase around so she held it in both hands, letting it bounce against her knees. "Sure does. For the basics. Gotta give a little trust to get a little trust, eh, Detective?"

Ivy turned away from them to make the call. Court activated his phone's recording app, read Hunter her rights, and stated the names of everyone present, along with the date, time, and the location. Hunter stated that she understood what was happening.

"Okay, let's get back to the facts," Court said. "Are you the Karen Hunter who called 911 at four forty this afternoon to report the body in the other room?"

"Yes."

"Do you know who it is?"

Hunter waited for Wagner's go-ahead. "Yes."

Anyone who had picked up a paper in the last four months would have recognized the philanthropist businessman, but he wanted everything on tape. "Could you state his name for the record, please?"

"Berkeley Drummond."

"How did you know him?"

Another quick glance at the attorney. Another nod. "He was a client."

"Can you be more specific about what kind of client?"

She smiled. "A private one."

Court shook his head. "Okay, when was the last time you saw Berkeley Drummond alive?"

Wagner placed a hand on Hunter's forearm. "Detectives, we're done for now." She turned to her client. "I advise you to not talk to him further until he has a signed deal offering you all immunity from any vice-related charges."

Hunter squeezed Wagner's hand. "I know. But they said they would get the deal taken care of. I want to answer their questions and get home. Okay?"

Wagner withdrew her hand and shook her head. "Why am I even here?" She raised a carefully manicured finger in front of Court's face. "I'm watching you, Detective."

Court wondered what it would mean to have such a high-powered attorney watching him, in addition to the inevitable press and SPD brass. "Okay, Ms. Hunter. Berkeley Drummond is dead. In *your* 'therapy room.' I would like you tell me exactly what happened here."

Hunter swallowed, taking in a huge gulp of air and releasing it before answering. "Berkeley has… I mean had, a standing appointment every Wednesday evening. This week,

I canceled because of an emergency. I arrived here at three o'clock Wednesday afternoon. I left around four, maybe four-fifteen. I was at the doctor's office in Redmond by four forty-five and then at the hospital with my son. I spent the rest of the night at Evergreen Hospital. I was there until noon yesterday when my son was discharged, and I took him home." She closed her eyes for a second. "Then, today, I realized I'd left my iPad here, so I decided to come in and get it after my daughter got home from school. She's old enough to babysit her brother."

Women in the sex trade often had kids. A disconcerting thought. Maybe it was because Hunter lived on the Eastside. The long commute over the bridge across the lake into Seattle would drive Court batty. "Your daughter. Where was she while you were at the hospital?"

"She was at home, with her dad. She's okay babysitting into the evening every once in a while, but she doesn't like spending the night alone."

Her alibi would be easy enough to check out. He took down the doctor and hospital information, then opened a HIPAA boilerplate on his phone. Getting her to consent to access the information was much faster and easier than a search warrant.

She signed without hesitation and with her lawyer's approval. It was surreal. They were both being awfully cooperative. Maybe too cooperative. Had he missed an angle here?

"Ms. Hunter, can you tell me what you charged for a session with Mr. Drummond?"

"I … don't charge for my services. My clients leave me a tip or gifts when they leave. It varies."

"What kind of *gift* did Mr. Drummond leave each week?" Court asked.

"Berkeley usually left me a cashier's check for five thousand dollars. At Christmas, and on my birthday, he would give me as much as ten thousand."

"Any idea why he would have ten cashier's checks made out to you, each for ten thousand dollars in his wallet?"

Hunter's eyes went wide as her eyebrows drew together. "What? No. I have … no idea." She turned to her attorney, mouth open.

Ivy returned to the huddle, interrupting them. "You have a deal, Ms. Hunter. No charges on anything vice-related, if you answer all our questions about Mr. Drummond to the best of your knowledge and cooperate fully with our investigation. Of course, this does not clear you of the murder charges if we end up going there…"

While Ivy spoke, Court watched Hunter carefully for signs or tells. She looked back and forth between Court, Ivy and her attorney. "But the money? I don't understand all those checks."

Wagner put a hand on Hunter's forearm, stopping her, while addressing Court. "I want the written agreement. Ms. Hunter can answer any other questions you might have tomorrow, once we have the signed deal in hand."

Court bit back a snarky reply.

5

THEY CUT HUNTER LOOSE FOR THE EVENING AT THE SAME time one of the county's Medical Examiners made her appearance, followed closely by two assistant investigators and the CSI unit. Mary Coleridge was the ME on call. Court enjoyed working with her in spite of her somewhat creepy personality, though he'd never met a forensics expert who wasn't sort of odd. It must come with choosing a profession in which you cut up dead people all day long. Things that sent him over the edge and running for a toilet didn't faze her. And he had a pretty strong stomach. She would be just as happy picking apart a room filled with slaughtered children as she was an alley with a single bludgeoned drunk.

Mary had been a study in contrast from the get-go. Her elfin features and large eyes, coupled with her short pixie cut, made her look more like a blonde anime heroine than a geeked-out forensics nerd. It took him only a few minutes on their first scene together to learn that her appearance was utterly at odds with her personality.

"This better be good. I had tickets to a show tonight."

"Nice to see you too, Mary," Court said. "I think you'll find this one pretty interesting."

He put Ivy in charge of the front office area, leaving her to work with the CSI team there while he led Mary and her assistant to check out the body.

Mary raised her gloved hands. "Don't say anything. Let me do my thing." She circled the body twice, dropping to a deep squat to examine his underside several times during her inspection. At length, she stood up to contemplate the tangled mess before them.

Court hoped—maybe even prayed a little bit—that he'd never end up like this, hanging on display, all vulnerable and naked. In all the ways he'd seen people die, this had to be the most humiliating. He wanted to throw a towel over the poor guy.

Mary tilted her head. "The room is soundproofed, isn't it?"

Court pointed to the funky foam on the windows. "We still need to check and see if the walls are also insulated. But yeah. So, what do you think?"

Mary clapped her hands, rubbing them with the exuberance of a five-year-old opening a birthday present. She bobbed up onto her toes and rolled back down on her heels before answering. "He's dead, all right."

"Thanks, that helps tons."

She pointed at the thermostat. "What was it set at?"

"It was too hot in here to think. It was at ninety-eight. The thermostat was on manual override, so it had to have been cranked up the entire time. Maybe I shouldn't have touched it."

She shrugged. "On-scene temperature is highly over-rated, anyway." She turned to her assistant. "Martin, go ahead and take a liver temp. Note that the surrounding temp has been messed with." The look she gave Court as she spoke made him want to crawl under a rock, in spite of her blasé response.

"So, you think it was the rope around his neck?" Court hoped she'd confirm the obvious.

Mary indicated the mess on the floor beneath the body with the sweeping gesture a maître d' might use to seat someone at a fine restaurant. "Bowels often evacuate during asphyxiation. I will venture an educated guess that this is urine and excrement. I can't be certain about that until we get the analysis back from the lab."

Another evasive answer. Mary at her finest, saying nothing with a bunch of words. "Okay, let's theorize that maybe the rope around his neck had to do with his death. Would that be a bad working theory?"

Mary leaned forward and carefully lifted Drummond's head while watching the rope. She sucked in her lower lip and nodded. "The rope around his neck. Tied brilliantly. If he got tired and slumped, it would constrict. Not that I can tell you with certainty that is the cause of death. Won't know anything for sure until I do the autopsy."

Of course. "So, by what you see here, what are the possible causes of death?"

"Really? You want me to list all possible causes? He could have been poisoned and brought here by six large men who tied him up and left him to die. He could have been tied up having a good time and had a heart attack."

Court raised his hands, willing her to stop. "Okay. So,

how long can someone hang like that, the arms and all the other ropes. Pretend the rope around the neck wasn't there."

Mary let out an exasperated sigh. "Well. It's a bad position. Not good for anyone. Not long. Certainly not days. Hours, maybe."

Human beings aren't built to have their entire weight supported primarily by their arm sockets. It had to be an excruciating position. Court put his arms behind his back and pushed them upward. He imagined being lifted in the same position as Drummond. The pain in his shoulder would have him crying like a baby for release in a couple of minutes. The few videos he'd watched with this kind of shit weren't instructional or realistic.

Ivy suddenly appeared at his side. "You thinking of trying it out, Pearson?"

He straightened up, shaking his arms out. "Shit, Langston. I'm trying to imagine what it must have been like for him."

"Yeah, right." Her tone dripped with sarcasm. "They're boxing up her computer and iPad. I'm sending it over to tech." She tucked a straying curl behind her ear and turned to Mary. "Could someone be left there, hanging, for a while and still be okay?"

"'A while?' That's pretty vague," Mary said.

Court had learned long ago that Mary had semi-autistic tendencies toward precision. "Okay, you think they could last an hour?"

Mary considered the ropes and the angle of the body. "Hypothetically, someone hanging like that for an hour would be in pain, but would survive. Most likely." Mary lifted Drummond's head by the hair, and showed them the slack in the rope. "The rope is not even against his neck when in this position. But, when it drops, it binds the neck tightly."

Court brought his hand to his neck, pressing the open L of his thumb and forefinger against his skin. "So, when he got tired…"

Mary let go of the head. Court took a step back as the head dropped downward. His late-afternoon latte burned in the back of his throat. Court had seen hundreds of bodies. Cut-up flesh, blood, smashed brains, burnt flesh, crushed bone? No problem. When a body sat there with its parts all dead and with no motion, he was fine. Put a little movement in it, and it was a different story. He raised his hands as if to ward off an attack. "Please don't do that again."

Mary lifted Drummond's head again as if Court had not said anything, but this time she pointed out the marks the rope had left. "Definitely in place at time of death—either before or during." This time, she guided the head back down slowly. "Poor guy." She put her hands behind her back as if to keep herself from playing with a new toy.

Court swallowed the bile and forced himself to get over it. He was looking at another body in a long line of bodies. Mary had said it. *Poor guy.* Whoever had done this was a sick bastard. And now it was Court's job to find him. His and Ivy's. He wasn't used to Ivy yet, hardly knew her. He had gotten to the point where he could finish Sean's sentences, or they would exchange a glance and know what the other was thinking. Everyone had to retire eventually, but Court was wishing Sean had stuck it out another year or two. He'd been a great partner.

Ivy though? It was too soon to tell. She didn't seem to

like him all that much, but it could be that he was overly sensitive.

Ivy turned toward the tray on the counter running the length of the wall. "Check this out."

An anal plug, a large dildo, nipple clamps, a ball gag, and a crop were as neatly arranged as a surgeon's instruments might be. Court eyed the collection wearily. When he was a rookie, he'd never envisioned his job description would include such an intimate knowledge of BDSM and some of the so-called 'toys of the trade.' When he was an innocent twenty-two year old, he'd never heard of a ball gag let alone been able to identify one.

Ivy leaned over the tray and examined the items from various angles without touching them. "Sick fucks."

Oh, so she did swear. Court was learning a lot about his new partner. It wasn't like they'd ever had a conversation about sex in the week they'd been working together, and certainly not about kinky stuff like this. Was she naive or grossed out? It had to be the latter. After being in vice for five years, she must have been exposed to every sexual deviancy on the planet. Maybe she was sick of seeing it.

She turned her back on the tray. "So, maybe Hunter lied. Drummond shows up as usual and things went wrong? She leaves him here with the temperature turned up to mess up the timing, and makes up a story."

"Or, her alibi checks out. Drummond shows up for his appointment and someone is here waiting for him. Or he brings someone with him knowing his domme would be gone." He pointed to the shoe on the floor. "She didn't answer my question about the shoes. Why one in here and one out there."

Ivy eyed the shoe and shrugged. "Huh. I'm having a hard time believing he liked being tied up like this. He came across as so vanilla."

Court donned a fresh pair of gloves, and opened a cupboard door to reveal several plastic bins, each one neatly labeled: DAPHNE, IRIS, DAHLIA, ROSIE, DAISY. "I am thinking this is the one she used for Drummond." He tapped on a bin that was pulled forward from the others by a few inches. Its position gave him the sense it had been the one most recently used.

"Each client gets his own bin?" The word "john" was too crude a term to use. Someone seeing Berkeley Drummond had to be a few steps up the scale from someone working the streets.

Ivy opened the other cupboards. "There are eight more over here. Same situation. So, that's, what, sixteen total? Plus a couple that are unmarked."

Court tapped the tray with the back of a knuckle. "We'll inventory it all into evidence. Honestly, I don't think they'll find much on any of it. I think Drummond was bound and left to die."

Ivy turned to Mary. "Any signs any of these were used on him?"

Mary looked at Ivy as if she'd never noticed her before. Had Court remembered to introduce them? Mary addressed her answer to Court. "Can't tell for sure until…"

"I know. I know. You can't tell until the crime lab runs all their tests, and you've done the autopsy."

They all turned back to the body. Ivy pointed to where the rope held everything together at the anchor on the wall.

"Do you think *anyone* could lift him with this? A man *or* a woman?"

"It is a simple pulley system. Almost any adult would be able to haul his body weight like that."

"Is there a sign of *any* struggle?" Court asked.

Mary laced her fingers together and held her hands in front of her chest, her thumbs pointing upward. "There aren't many abrasions around the rope areas. No more than what his weight would have caused. I think he got there because he wanted to be there."

"Any possible way he did this to himself?"

Mary tilted her head side-ways as if looking at it from a new angle might give her a new insight. "I don't see how anyone could get into this position by themselves."

"Okay, so accident or murder?" Ivy asked.

"Could be either." Court got the sense that the domme would have handled an accident differently. She came across as serious and intense, but responsible. "Why would someone want to murder Berkeley Drummond?"

Mary threw her arms upward, palms toward the ceiling, a broad gesture either beckoning to The Powers That Be or showing she could not care less. "My job is to figure out how he died, not why. And, for that little distinction, I am eternally grateful."

6

COURT KEPT AN EYE ON EVERYONE WORKING THE SCENE through the rest of the evening. Someone would break under the temptation of a bribe and leak the details to the press. If not one of the people in this room, it would be someone working the case. He'd be assigning dozens of uniformed officers to take statements in the building and neighborhood. Someone would give in and talk. What a scoop it would be to let the whole world know about Drummond's hidden, kinky side. Assuming he really had one. They only had the domme's word that he was a client. It would be a coup if they could keep a lid on these details until after they had made an arrest. One thing working in their favor was that Hunter hadn't identified Drummond during her 911 call. A death like this was going to have the press jumping down their throats as soon as it was public.

The scene wrapped at ten p.m. Quick as these things go. They chased Audrey Drummond down at a fundraising gala at the Woodland Park Zoo. Court discreetly flashed his badge, explained that her husband had been found dead, and asked her to come to the morgue for a formal ID.

She closed her eyes, drawing her lips in around her teeth. She let out the tiniest gasp of air before opening them again. "Must I ride with you? I have a car and driver."

"He can pick you up from the morgue when we're done. We'll take you over there."

Court sat in the back seat and let Mrs. Drummond take the front next to Ivy. "You're not surprised your husband is dead, Mrs. Drummond."

She gave an imperious wave of her hand. "It's too late, Detective. We can do the identification tonight and discuss the details tomorrow."

She was used to being in control. Court sank back into the seat, exhausted by the day. He'd get more from her later. He closed his eyes and relaxed the rest of the way.

They arrived at the morgue at eleven thirty. Her attorney was waiting for them in the lobby. Harley? No, Harlan. Harlan Eccles. He was famous, known for getting a local music icon off a murder rap a couple of years prior. Huge case, with this guy's confident mug all over the TV for months. Big, beefy, smiling guy. Not a genuine smile, but one of those reassuring things that people plastered on their face out of habit when they didn't know how else to look.

Eccles wore gel to keep his hair in a wavy but firm hold on his head. Even late on a Friday night. Who the hell put V-5 in their hair anymore? Eccles didn't look a day over fifty in spite of the white stripe of hair swooshing into a loop above his forehead. His suit was cut close to his body to make it clear he wasn't the kind of guy who sat at his desk all day.

They followed a tech past the records office and the large

autopsy suite to the private viewing room where family members were asked to identify loved ones. It wasn't like on TV where they pulled a drawer open. The window provided a visual while protecting loved ones from the smell and other nasty realities of death. It also kept them from touching the deceased, preventing them from introducing new trace evidence onto the body. Court was pretty sure people would be upset if they could see the inside of the morgue's giant fridge where bodies lay lined up on gurneys, limbs sticking up in rigor, faces only partially obscured by covers thrown casually on the unprocessed bodies.

The tech tapped the window and the curtain parted. A second tech, covered in a Tyvek bunny suit, peeled the cover away from Drummond's face. He went a little too far with it, revealing the marks left by the rope around Drummond's neck.

Court made a circling motion at his own neck and pointed to Drummond. The tech caught the frantic motion and rolled the cloth back up to the chin, tucking it behind the ears, but it was too late. Everyone had seen the embossed pattern of rope.

Audrey Drummond's brow creased as she approached the window. "Yes. This is my husband, Berkeley Drummond." She placed her hand up against the glass, the diamond on her wedding ring slipping around so it fell in the V between her spread fingers.

No tears. No questions. No surprise. Only a calm poise. There was a lot more to the Drummond story than what he would find via internet search. Their charitable foundation had given a million-dollar grant to the Seattle Police Department's community-policing initiative. Politics and personality would influence the case as much as the facts. If she had killed her husband, any prosecuting attorney would be looking at a career-ending case. It might prove to be the end of his, too. Being objective about it all was going to be challenging.

Harlan Eccles put an arm around Audrey Drummond. "We're done for this evening, detectives. You can come to the house tomorrow at ten o'clock to talk to Audrey. I'll take her home now."

IVY WAS all hyped up as they left the morgue, speaking with more animation than he'd seen from her all week, making verbal lists of what to do next in the investigation. It had been a long time since he'd been that pumped up about a case. This case made him nervous. Anxious. Wary. Excited? Okay, maybe a little bit.

He dropped himself into the car and checked his phone. Four messages from Cami. He'd forgotten to text her to let her know he couldn't make it to their regular Friday night watering hole. If he was lucky, they'd get back to the station, get their reports in, and he might still have time to connect with her. He texted Cami he would be there late, if at all. When she asked if he was on a new case, he replied with, "Yeah. Big one."

He ached to climb into his bed and pull his comforter over his head. It was going to be a nasty case. The press would be circling as soon as word about Berkeley Drummond's death was made public. Reporters would be stepping all over official toes, getting in his way.

He snagged five minutes to update Lieutenant Stensland before the scene was closed off for the night. He closed his eyes and ignored Ivy as she drove them back to the station. This late at night, it took them less than a third of the time it had taken for them to get there.

The main floor of the station was bustling with activity. Late Friday was always like this. Ivy went to a computer, setting up a table of what they had learned and what they needed to do.

Given what Hunter had told them, Drummond had probably been dead since Wednesday evening. The forty-eight-hour window thought to be so critical to investigation was not as solid as television made it seem. They were well past the magical hour. It irked him that Stensland didn't see it the same way. He always started the clock at the discovery of the body, even if the death occurred twenty years before. They'd be expected to work through the weekend.

While Ivy was working on logistics for tomorrow, Court summarized everything for their report. When he was done, he spun to face Ivy. "Let's start with a web search on Drummond. Get a handle on his public image, anything on his business. Figure out who we need to talk to at work, and get working on finding them. It's too late tonight to get out there, and they might be hard to find on the weekend."

Ivy was nodding along. "Okay, right." She paused, appearing confused for a minute and then checked the time on her watch. "Man, it's late."

"Let's put on a fresh pot of coffee and see what we can figure out about our dead guy."

An hour later, Court found Ivy with her head slumped against her chair. Reading online articles about a man who made it big by manufacturing sleeping bags and down-filled vests wasn't exactly thriller material. Besides, nothing was more boring than studying the rich being rich.

Court squeezed her shoulder and she startled, blinked and rolled her head around to stretch her neck. "Sorry. What did I miss?"

"Nothing. Why don't you go take a nap? I'll keep on with the research."

She glanced at the clock and nodded. She shambled over to the little bunk room reserved for detectives working around the clock.

Court was settling into his chair when Cami texted him. *Come on, dude. Look at the time. No one will miss you.*

Court considered the text for a while before answering. He got up and hovered by the bunk room door and listened to Ivy's steady snoring for half a minute. He put a sticky note on her computer, telling her he'd be back in the morning.

7

COURT LEANED ON HIS ELBOWS, HIS DRINK DANGLING between his hands. Half an order of satay sat on the table between them, the peanut sauce congealing into an unpleasant cold mass. Maybe he should have climbed into one of the other bunks instead of sneaking out.

Hanging out with Cami was usually easy. Fun. She wasn't his type, and he wasn't hers. It had taken them about three minutes together to figure it out on a blind date set up by his sister, Britt. She kept missing the target. Sometimes by miles. Britt had gotten it half-right with Cami. They both liked the exact same kind of women—feminine, soft, girly-girls.

Cami picked up a skewer of chicken, swiped it through the sauce, and bit into it. She made a face and dropped the rest on her plate. "Court, I honestly think you're lucky."

"Lucky," he said, repeating the word slowly, as if he'd never heard it before. He drank down the remnants of his lager. His half-hour grousing about Ivy had gotten them to his being lucky? "I don't get her. One second she's interactive and working with me, the next. I don't know… She's a wall. It's weird. The guys in Vice have only good things to say about her. Not what I'm seeing firsthand. If we're on task, it's fine, but being alone with her without a specific focus is extra chilly. As soon as we got this case, it was like a switch was thrown."

Cami stabbed at the cherry on the bottom of her glass with her straw, piercing it through the middle and sliding it to the top. The progress of the red blob moving along, smooshed into a half-flat dome was a visible metaphor of Court's life—upwardly mobile and sweet in some ways, but with his back firmly against the wall in so many others. She lifted her prey to her mouth and stirred the dregs of her drink until the little bits of fruit and mint swirled to life in a tornado of gooey, boozy slush.

She sat back, pushing the sticky glass away from her. "Dude, you need to talk to her about it. Maybe she's trying to figure you out, too."

Court had watched Ivy kick ass taking someone down on a vice bust the year before. He trusted her physically, and she knew how to read email—some of the old farts in the department would still be using typewriters if they could.

"You've got a point," he said.

Cami fiddled with the skewer on her plate, turning the chicken over. "So, this new case you're on? Anything interesting? What's got her all fired up about it?"

If anyone would understand the case, it would be Cami. Her connection to the kink community meant she might even know Karen Hunter. Talking to her about it would be risky, though. She was a reporter and, while the Seattle

Police Department wasn't her beat, this kind of story was too provocative not to pique her interest. Time to divert. "It's new. Barely getting started. We didn't even have an official ID by the time the news was airing. We aren't even classifying it yet. It's Ivy's first official death investigation, so I can see why she's switched into eager-puppy mode."

"Anything you can share? Off the record, of course."

She sure was being persistent. "Nope. Definitely not looking forward to the media shit storm heading my way." Had he tipped his hand admitting to the fact he was working something high-profile?

"Well, whatever it is, it can't get as bad as the thing with the Chinese mob."

She always had a way of putting things in perspective. "Hell no. I'm thinking this is a probably a murder. Maybe accidental death. Hard to say for sure. But, I'll tell you what, I'll take this over human-trafficking shit any day." He picked up one of the chicken skewers, twisted it around before taking a bite. He caught the eye of the bartender and pointed at his glass to order a second beer. "Hey, you know, Cami, I can't get into this with you, all right?"

She waggled her eyebrows, the diamond in her brow-piercing twinkling bright with the movement. "So, what's she like. This lady detective. Gets me kinda tingly thinking about it … you know, a woman with handcuffs?"

Court relaxed back against his seat, reaching for the fresh drink that appeared in front of him. Back to women and sex, his favorite topic with Cami. "Not your type. She's married with children, and she doesn't eat pork. You'd never agree on dinner." Cami's love for barbecue had ended more than one relationship.

She scrunched up her face. "Hmm. Fair enough. So, married with kids, not your type either? So, my friend, when was the last time you were laid?"

Court shuddered visibly. Dating a fellow detective was one the worst things he could imagine—married or not. "It's been so long I can't remember."

"Oh, man … that is about the saddest thing I've ever heard." Cami's shoulders slumped downward along with her entire upper body as she leaned back against her chair. "You're kidding."

"Duh. It's only been a couple weeks." He usually shared everything with her. When was the last time they'd hung out? Used to be they got together three or four times a week, but Cami had been the one full of excuses lately.

Cami leaned forward, full of attention now. She liked the nitty-gritty. "Still too long. Another of Britt's candidates?"

"Yep. Now, get this. We went to a Renaissance faire. She dressed me up with elf ears and made me wear a long blond wig."

"Ohhhh. Did she wear one of those costumes with a corset?" Cami pushed her breasts up through her shirt, shimmying seductively.

Court chuckled at the attempt. "Okay, that part wasn't so bad. "

"Don't suppose you got any pictures of you with pointy ears and long hair."

Court laughed and leaned over his phone. The beer was making him a little tipsy and it took him three tries to get his PIN. He barely remembered to cover the screen when he opened his album. Didn't want Cami to see the photos he'd taken at the scene. He scrolled up to the one of him in the ridiculous get up, spinning the phone around for her. The condensation from his beer made the surface slippery. It skittered out of control so Cami had to catch it before it flew off the table. She examined the photo of Court with his arm draped casually over the naked shoulders of his date.

Her jaw dropped open for a second. "Yowsa. How did I miss her? She's hot, Court. What happened?" Cami slid his phone back over the slick surface.

He caught it, shrugging. "The physical chemistry was good, but I wasn't a fan of dressing up all the time. And I mean, *all the time*. Renaissance faires, comic book conventions, fantasy conventions, *Star Trek*, *Star Wars*. You name it, she had a costume for me. She wasn't my type for long-term."

Cami's face shifted into serious mode. "Is anyone, Court?"

Court dropped his gaze to the foamy ring at the bottom of his glass, wondering how it was already empty. It would have been easier if she'd asked for details about elf sex.

Cami drummed the table with her fingers. "Okay then. So … you think Britt will have someone new on tap for you tomorrow?" Cami had been babysitting his niece and nephew for years and was pretty close to them. As a consequence, she was invited to all their family gatherings.

Crap. Court had forgotten about the birthday party. It would be a madhouse, with kids running everywhere. Britt would use it to introduce a new candidate. He pushed his empty beer glass aside, dropping his head onto crossed arms. "Probably. I'll be working all day. Maybe I'll be into something and have to skip the party. Only go to the family thing on Monday."

Cami stood up, stretching. "Hot new case makes Court a dull boy."

Court shrugged, annoyed at himself for opening that avenue again. "I'm kidding. I would hate to miss the twins' party. I already have their present."

Cami leaned over to kiss his cheek. "You'll be there. Besides, deep down, you know you can't help but wonder who Britt is going to throw at you next."

8

A NEW INVESTIGATION OFTEN KEPT COURT AWAKE. IT WAS worse at the beginning of the case when the field was wide open, and his imagination ran wild with possibilities. He'd managed to crash into sleep only after he'd written everything flooding his head down in his tiny notebook. He was in the middle of a dream when his phone rang.

He rolled into a sitting position, wiping sleep from his eyes. Five o'clock in the morning phone calls were never social engagements. "Pearson."

"Court, this is Mary. Mary Coleridge."

All fragments of sleep skittered away. Court stood up. She'd never called him at such an ungodly hour before. "Mary? What's up?

"Bad news. We have a train derailment with multiple deaths five miles west of Wenatchee. Something about a tunnel door not functioning. I don't have the details yet, but, the number of bodies is too high for the local coroner to handle."

Court flopped back onto the bed. "Holy crap. Do you have a count yet?"

"Eighteen. So far. First responders are still at it. There's no way we'll get to Drummond's autopsy today. It'll have to wait."

All those people. No doubt it would be a mess. His stomach churned. Court did the math in his head. Most county offices can manage one to four bodies at a time. Even King County could only handle about twenty before getting backed up. A gigantic landslide the previous year had required a similar shared response, pulling in agencies from across the state. Autopsies at King County had been backed up for six days before getting back into a regular rhythm again. "Everyone has to go? Any chance you can do Drummond now, before you head out?"

"No. Too many people are on the invite for this autopsy. Stensland, you. Hell, the DA wants one of his prosecutors in there. Even the Chief wants in on it, too. Besides, you know how few deaths like this we see? I've got a couple of newbies on staff who need to be there."

He rubbed at his eyes. He wouldn't push harder. The *actual* cause of death wasn't likely to matter much in the investigation as a whole. And, it wasn't like the big deep rope marks around his neck left much to question. "Any idea when you'll be back?"

"No. I've got to go. We're all heading out to the scene now. I'll try to keep you updated."

She hung up. He stared at his phone for a long time before texting Ivy with the news.

Court had told Ivy he'd be back by 6:30 a.m. With the

autopsy delayed, he would have time to hit the early-Saturday Krav Maga class in the basement gym of the department before they needed to get to the Drummond house at ten.

He scoured the *Seattle Times* website during his bus ride, and only found one small article about Drummond's death. It gave only the basics: that Drummond had been found dead the night before and there was an active investigation into his death. Nothing about murder, yet anyway. The final line promised a full in-depth article in the Sunday *Times*. Great. How much more did they think they were going to get by tomorrow? He changed into his scruffy sweats and headed into his Krav class.

Gilad Agbaria was a crusty retired Israeli general who stood maybe five-three with shoes on. He was an old dude who could kill someone in hundreds of ways, but came across as a lovable grandpa. When he smiled, his face erupted into dozens of smile lines, and he moved with catlike grace. Court hoped he would get around half as well by the time he hit seventy-nine.

Agbaria had an easy, patient way about him, which made training with him a pleasure. Krav Maga was so much more fun than a traditional Karate setting. There was no bowing and scraping on one's knees to a Sensei. Instead, there was mutual respect and a sense they were in the fight together. And, there were no katas. Court understood the theory behind the form movements, but he'd never been in a fight in which he had to deal with four opponents coming at him from all directions with exactly the specified moves.

Working out in sweats and a t-shirt instead of the traditional heavy gi was an added bonus. The class was more crowded than he would have suspected. Russell Flanagan, one of three homicide detectives who had shown an active disdain for Court, was warming up by punching the hell out of a freestanding bag. He looked up from his target and gave Court a smile that promised a difficult workout. Court had made a fine art of avoiding Flanagan, but in a tight department like theirs, he could never be one-hundred-percent successful.

Sure enough, as soon as they were through their warm-up and asked to pair off, Flanagan squared off in front of Court.

"Don't recall seeing you in this class before, Pearson. Decided to take on the big boys?"

Court's usual classmates were the younger generation of street cops who slept in on Saturday mornings when they got the chance. Flanagan was close to retirement with the beginnings of a bulge dipping over his pants. Come to think of it, most of the guys in this room were over forty, Court included. "Exactly. I figured I could learn something from people who've been around a long, long time."

Flanagan clenched and released his fists. "Heard you got a new case last night. Think you can handle it with that pretty piece of fluff they gave you for a partner?"

Did anyone really think Ivy was a piece of fluff? Fluff? Fuck that. He stepped in close to the other man's face, dropping his voice to a throaty growl. "Don't talk that way about Langston. She's put in her dues." He wasn't even sure he liked Ivy, and here he was defending her honor?

Flanagan held his ground, a slow smile forming on his lips.

Agbaria cut into their tête-a-tête with a curt intensity, moving them through drills at breakneck speed. Talking would only get him hurt during this kind of workout. Court ignored Flanagan and fell into a near-meditative state, totally focused on the moves.

The class moved quickly from basic warmup before focusing on a review of close-up knife attacks. Court landed several nice kicks to Flanagan's groin in the process. He was savoring the latest blow when Agbaria pulled out the weighted plastic guns. They were as heavy as a regular gun, but a lot safer to toss around than a loaded Glock.

Court wiped the sweat from his face with his t-shirt, inadvertently pulling it up so it bared his chest to the group. People tried to pretend they didn't think about what was underneath his clothing, but whenever they got a chance, they couldn't keep themselves from peeking. He ignored them as best he could, knowing his six-pack abs were as hard and chiseled as any of theirs. Maybe more so. Early hormone therapy had prevented him from ever having breasts, but they didn't know that. They were looking for scars. Some sort of proof.

The pairings had made the rounds and he found himself up against Flanagan again. The other man took a too-gleeful approach at pointing the fake gun at Court's head. Court sidestepped trying to loop the gun out of Flanagan's hand, but the older man managed to pull out of it, flipping Court onto his back with the gun pointed between Court's eyes. How had he let *that* happen? The warmth of embarrassment crept up his neck and cheeks.

Flanagan reached down with a hand to assist Court to

his feet. Court took it warily. The yank would have been painful if he hadn't been expecting it.

Flanagan used the momentum to pull Court in close. Closer than Court liked to be to another guy. He whispered so no one else could hear him. "Nice try, Courtneeeee."

Court held back his hot anger, refusing a verbal sparring match. This time, Flanagan was going down.

9

ONLY A HANDFUL OF PEOPLE WERE WORKING WHEN COURT made it to the squad room. Part of him wished someone else had been on call last night, but another part of him wanted to dive in deep and ignore the world. It was the luck of the draw. While the official response was to treat every victim equally, there was no denying that politics would influence the handling of this case. Everything he did would be scrutinized under a microscope. He'd have to play this one hundred percent by the book. No shortcuts.

He and Ivy had cubicles directly across from each other. His was neat and orderly, but had nothing personal in it aside from a few helpful books on psychology and investigative techniques. No photos, no plants, no artwork. He used to keep a photo of Amanda and Bailey next to his monitor, but had removed it. It wasn't so much that it pained him to see them every day. He hated the undying pity oozing from those around him when they noticed the picture and put it together with what they knew about him.

Ivy sat with her back to him, typing with a quick efficiency he could only dream of. Her cubicle had one potted fern and three photographs adorning a corner. One was of Ivy and her husband at their wedding, ankle deep in shallow waves on a Hawaiian beach under a traditional canopy. In the second, Ivy leaned against her husband in front of a trippy sixties-modern style house, each holding a child. They were all smiles. The third was a family photo taken at her son's recent bar mitzvah, two kids standing in between the parents.

Court leaned over her shoulder and checked out the report she was finishing. There were no typos, and she had hit all the key points in a more thorough way than he would have. He usually kept his reports as short as possible and used lots of bullet points. Hers read like a rough draft of a novel. She'd gotten the deal with Hunter cleared and forwarded to Wagner, called the hospital on Hunter's alibi, and made a long to-do list.

He pulled out his phone and double-checked his email. "Why wasn't I copied on the deal with Hunter?"

She glanced over her shoulder at him, her face impassive. She saved the report and hit send. "Guess I forgot. Where'd you go? I woke up at five and you were nowhere around."

Court pointed to the screen. "I want a copy of everything you do on this case. Partners copy each other on everything."

She pushed back from the computer, edging him away from the space with her movement. "I'll try to remember that. Partners also check in when they take off."

Court bristled at her tone. He searched her monitor for

the note he'd left her, but it was gone. She probably wouldn't believe him if he tried to explain.

She stood up and tilted her head toward the squad's technical division. "Ashena's been working like an angry bee for a couple hours already. What'd you do to get her here so early?"

Court held out his hand to let her go ahead of him. "I called her last night and sweet-talked her into some Saturday hours. I asked her to get the information off the entry system to Hunter's office. Those things record key swipes and door openings. At the very least, we'll know when the door was opened and closed." It was stretching things a bit. In truth, Ashena Williams had owed him a huge favor for his discretion on a screw-up she'd made a few months prior. But he'd have to call in more than one favor to get traction on the case while working around closed businesses on the weekend.

As they approached, Ashena stood up from behind her warren of wires and terminals with a half-inch thick stack of papers held together by a black binder clip in her hands. She reached past Ivy, placing the papers directly into Court's hands, her spicy scent flowing past him. "There's definitely something hinky going on with the card keys," she said.

Court wondered how a goddess like Ashena had ended up geeking out. Her prominent cheekbones and glossy brown skin were more runway model than computer nerd. "What'd you find?"

"First, I did as you asked and pulled up the history from last week. Go to the first green sticky."

Court flipped it open and held it up so Ivy could see.

"That's the list of activity starting Wednesday. One swipe

from Hunter's key at 3:03 p.m. The door opened again at 4:15, presumably someone leaving. Fifteen minutes later, Hunter's key opens the door again. The next activity is at 6:55 when a key labeled 'Rosie' opens the door. Finally, the door opens, again someone leaving, at 7:30. No more activity until yesterday at 4:02 p.m., when Hunter's key unlocks the door."

Everything fit Hunter's story about leaving at 4:15 on Wednesday, except her return at 4:30.

"But, I checked her story with the hospital first thing this morning. Her alibi for Wednesday afternoon and evening is solid. She couldn't have been in both places at the same time," Ivy said.

"She couldn't, but she could have left her card behind for someone else to use," Court said. "And what about the Friday 4:02 stamp? Why did she wait almost forty minutes before making the 911 call?"

Ashena put her hand on the book. "Wait. I'm not done yet. I thought it would be a good idea to go back a few weeks and compare the regular usage of the keys to more recent. You know, see what the baseline activity is. And that's where things got a little strange."

"Come on, Ashena, get to it. Please," he said.

Ashena crossed her arms and glared at him over the rim of her glasses. "I'm getting there. Be a little patient, will you? So, I pulled the logs starting from July to obtain a good bit of data. What I found is this."

She flipped through the papers to the purple tab. "Hunter's activity is pretty consistent from July through mid-September. What you need to get from this, is she arrived pretty much the same time every day. Her arrival is followed by another key swipe entry. She issued every client their own card, programmed to work only for certain times. Then, Hunter and her client leave within a few minutes of each other a few hours later. For the most part. Sometimes, the Wednesday night shifts, and the person with the key labeled as 'Rosie' stays until the next morning."

"So, I highlighted the times where people had entered with a card key. Hunter's swipes are highlighted in blue, and each codename has a different color. A pattern emerged in the first few pages."

Court followed her fingers as she spoke, repeating her words to himself to get it straight.

Ashena flipped to another tab. "So, here's something you need to check out. Eight weeks ago, there was a reboot of the entire system. The installer, Haubek Inc., came out and wiped the system. All the previous cards were rendered invalid. Over the next week, the records show new cards being made, starting with Hunter's after the reboot. For two weeks, the pattern returns to normal. Then, six weeks ago, the system shows her coming back in at odd hours—out of her usual pattern. Sometimes in the middle of the night, but almost always on Wednesday nights. I thought this was kind of strange, so I dove into the code on the entry system."

Her speech picked up speed. Court's head spun with the information she was doling out. "Hold on," he said, lifting both palms up to stem the flow of information. "If they rebooted the system, wiped it, how do you know what happened before the reboot?"

"There was a backup on Hunter's computer. They

rebooted the card-key reader and the logs, but they didn't *delete* everything off her system." She waved her hand in the air as if she were brushing away a pesky fly. "There's a second key issued under Hunter's name. I was able to figure out which entries were made by the original key and this second key. All the new-pattern entries, and the late-night entries were made by the second key. I highlighted them in yellow."

Court let this sink in for a minute. "But there's no way of telling who actually has this key, right? It could be Hunter, or it could be someone else? When was the second key made?"

"There's the kicker. There is no record of it even being issued. I'd say it probably happened after the reboot." Ashena held up both hands in excitement. "And, more importantly, the four-thirty swipe on Wednesday was made with the *second key*."

"And when did Drummond enter?" Court asked.

"Turns out, he was 'Rosie', and he swiped in at six-fifty-five."

If Hunter was on the Eastside by 4:30 on Wednesday, then someone using the second key issued in Hunter's name had been there for almost two hours before Drummond showed up. There were dozens of yellow lines going back six weeks at various hours of the day and night. Whoever had the second key had been doing some serious reconnaissance.

Court rubbed at his eyes. He was going to have to chart this out. "Okay, let's say someone figured out where Drummond was going every Wednesday night. They stalk him for a while, then figure out how to get a card key into the domme's studio. They watch and wait for their opportunity?"

Ivy took the log from Court and examined it closely, as if by closing the distance she might get more information from it. "Maybe. But why? We need to figure out who would've wanted him dead."

"You think the reboot eight weeks ago has anything to do with the killing?" he asked. "Could it be coincidence?"

"Hard to tell. There was a reboot of the system, All I can tell you is everything was wiped during the re-boot and a second key appears under the owner's name along with all the new card-keys, but there is no trace of it being made on the system.

Court added Haubek to the to-call list. At the very least, someone there would be able to explain the technical aspects of the reboot and how keys are issued. They were seeing Hunter back at the scene later in the day as well. Maybe she could enlighten them.

Court turned back to Ashena. "What about her computer? Any emails? Any useful documents?"

Ashena tapped the computer they'd taken from Hunter's office. "As far as I can tell, the only thing she used it for is the card-key log—which appears to be something she ignored completely—and an occasional web search. She might have another computer at home, but she didn't have any email accounts on the system at all." She reached around and picked up an iPad in a plastic evidence bag. "This … this is what she used for her business and email. It's linked to her iPhone, so her texts are still coming across the device. Today, she's been canceling appointments across the board. Did she have a clue what she was signing over when giving you permission to look at this?"

Court had asked Hunter to sign a release that had been

intentionally vague, but gave them access to everything Ashena had been working on. Her attorney was either tired or unaware that Hunter's iPad had been left in the office, and she had approved Hunter's signing the release for them to search "all electronic equipment, computers, and the like." Court went to reach for it, eager to see what was on it.

Ashena pulled it away from him, holding it up over and behind her head and out of his reach, her other hand coming up with an accusative index finger to tap his chest. "I think this means I'm done owing you, Detective."

Court eyed the tablet. She'd been at his beck and call for a couple of months now. It was time to call things even. "Sure, Ashena. Now, spill it."

"All right, Mr. Antsy Pants." She put the iPad back down on her desk. "I printed you a transcript of her text conversation with Berkeley Drummond going back a month. It's as racy and hot as any erotica I've ever read."

"You read a lot of that stuff, Ashena?" Court asked.

She laughed. "Me? Nu-uh. But I have to say, this is certainly interesting."

Court skimmed the texts, feeling voyeuristic, and quickly found himself wishing he hadn't seen most of it. Their interaction had a playful, friendly intimacy combined with a fiercely direct sexuality. Hunter gave Dummond directions, and he responded. At least there were no naked photos of either of them. Several times, Drummond was directed to do specific sexual acts with his wife. Court wondered if the Widow Drummond knew her husband was coming to her bed at the behest of his dominatrix.

Reading these intimate texts felt intrusive. Even though

he'd already seen the man naked, dead and in a vulnerable position, the platitudes and promises of the texts were more personal. He skipped to the last entries, wishing he'd started there instead.

Hunter had sent Drummond only two texts on Wednesday, the first at 4:30 telling him she was going to be "a little late.' She told him he should get into his harness and wait on his knees until she got there. The second, at 6:45 p.m., was an apology as she cancelled entirely. Drummond had only responded to the first, saying he would wait for her as told. The second message was left unanswered.

"His phone was off from about six thirty onward. He never got the message she was canceling," Ashena said.

"You were able to get past his phone pass code?" Court asked.

"As weird as this sounds, Drummond didn't have a lock on his phone."

Court handed Ivy the package of papers to give her free rein with it as he digested this last bit of information. Why someone of Drummond's status wouldn't have a security code on his phone was beyond him. "Well, since you had access to his phone, did you find anything pointing us to someone in particular? Any chance someone texted him with a threat or anything?"

"That would make your day a lot easier, wouldn't it? But, no. And, oddly, he didn't have much email on his phone. Everything on there is new and unread, so I'm thinking he read and deleted as he went."

"Anything else on Hunter's phone? In her email? Anything useful?" Court asked.

"Like her client list?"

"Well, yes, actually," Court said. "Are you saying you have a client list?

"Sort of. She used codenames for all her clients, so I have to do a back-trace on the phones. I had barely started when you walked up."

Court checked his watch. They had to get a move on if they were going to make it out to the Drummond household. "Okay. Anything else in her texts or email?"

"Skimmed a few. Most of the rest of her texts and emails are pretty much about appointment times and requests. Surprising what some of these guys were into. I haven't had time to do more than skim her active mail folder—there's a shitload of it. There are several hundred emails in a folder called WHEN HELL FREEZES OVER. I read through a couple, and they're mostly creepy fan letters or desperate guys begging her to be their mistress, promising undying and everlasting devotion."

Court liked the way Ashena's voice parodied a gospel-preacher cadence.

Ashena reverted to her regular soft and melodious voice. "She has a bunch of rules set on her email so messages with key phrases in the subject line go directly to the HELL folder. She never even opened or read any of them."

"Can you get us a print-out of all her emails?"

Ashena's eyes dropped to half mast, her head lolling toward her shoulder. "Seriously? You want me to kill a tree on this?"

Court admired Ashena's ethics, but reading a few hundred pages of emails on the screen was too much. It would kill his eyes. "Two, if you have to." Ashena would print them all, put them in some sort of order in a three-ring binder, and use up a whole package of those little sticky tab things.

She slumped backward into her chair. "We are so even, Pearson. So even."

10

THEIR BUSINESS WITH ASHENA DONE FOR THE TIME BEING, Court and Ivy made their way to the motor pool. The guy in the booth set his paperback open and face down when they approached, and pointed to the row of available cars. Ivy picked the Ford Taurus, grabbing the keys before he had a chance to. She held them up with a smug grin. "I'll drive."

"Works for me. I'm happy to navigate."

She looked him over from head to toe. "Figures."

Court was used to the whole body sweep but, what, exactly, was her 'figures' thing about? Was it some sort of passive-aggressive bullshit?

"What figures?"

She glanced over her shoulder at him as she pointed the keys at the car and the tail-lights flashed, signaling it was unlocked. "Nothing. Just get in the car." She yanked her door open and flung herself into her seat.

Court paused at the passenger door, and shrugged away the feeling of being jerked around before climbing in. A little consistency from her would be nice. Court settled in and typed the address into his map as Ivy adjusted all the mirrors.

"The house is in Medina. Do you think it's even on the GPS? Or will it be all fuzzy like a secret air base?"

She rolled her eyes with a half-smile. Did she have a sense of humor after all?

"I know Medina pretty well. What's the address?" Court held out his phone so she could see the routes already plotted out on his map. She sucked in a quick breath of air. "Oh. I can get us there without help."

"Awesome, I can sit back and enjoy the view."

Ivy eased out of the parking space. "Why would Drummond even be coming over to Seattle to see Hunter, anyway? A guy with his money should be able to pay for someone to come to him, or put up someone closer to home."

And now, she was suddenly all talkative. It was time to track her responses. If she continued being short with him on every personal point, he'd have to talk to her about the attitude directly. He picked a neutral, teaching tone. "Think about it. You're super rich, and your face is well known. Better to hang out and do your dirty stuff away from home."

Ivy almost hit a scruffy old guy with a worn back-pack and tattered clothing as they pulled out of the parking garage. She held up a hand in vague apology as he stared at her the whole time he crossed the driveway. Court was pretty sure he slowed down on purpose and added a slight drag to his left leg for effect.

"A man like Drummond should be able to get whatever he wanted ordered in," she said as she pulled out onto the street.

Traffic was light, and it only took a couple of minutes to get from the garage and onto the freeway heading north. Court toyed with the glove compartment. Bits of garbage from someone's surveillance tumbled out. He picked up the pieces and crammed them back inside. *How hard is it to take your trash with you when you leave?* He wiped his hands against his pants.

"Hard to order in what she offers. Think about the hook in the ceiling. It's not like you can casually toss a rope around a light fixture and hope it holds the weight. Besides, she had, what, sixteen clients? A single location makes sense." Court grabbed the handle above his head as Ivy swerved around a slower vehicle. Her eyes were fixed on the road, completely focused. "Christ, Langston, we're not on a racetrack."

"I'm under the speed limit." She rolled her shoulders back into her seat, loosened her grip a bit. "I suppose it makes sense for him to go to her with all the hardware and toys involved. Still, it seems like he could have set up something more private."

"Nah. I think she's totally in charge. She set up her business and didn't want to travel to her customers. They came to her."

Ivy kept her eyes on the road, but waggled her head from side to side like a bobble-head doll as she weighed the idea. "Okay, okay. I can buy that."

They slowed to a near standstill as they hit the middle of the bridge. It was the northernmost of two floating bridges connecting Seattle and the Eastside over Lake Washington. Court checked to see if the mountain *was out*—a phrase locals used as an overall descriptor for the weather as well as their passion for Mount Rainier, the most prominent feature around. After a few seasons of living in Seattle, he'd learned how deceptive the clouds made the landscape. Months could go by when the rain and low-lying clouds completely hid Rainier—a fourteen-thousand-foot glacier-covered volcano sticking up out of nowhere. When the weather cleared, and you could see the mountain, it was like a goddess appearing to the world, its foothills her arms spread out for an embrace.

The mountain top glistened sparkly white against the cloudless blue sky, the single biggest feature in the landscape even though it was eighty miles away. He turned back to Ivy, a smile on his face. "I love the view of Rainier with the water in front of it like this."

Ivy kept her eyes on the road as the traffic regained speed. "Yeah, it's pretty cool."

Court wondered if growing up in the area made locals immune to the view. He didn't think he'd ever get bored with it. "Mrs. Drummond seemed pretty composed last night."

Ivy nodded. "People like her go through public-image training, don't they? I mean, she's the face on this huge charitable foundation. She's had lots of practice staying calm in front of people."

And people acted weird around death. "Hard to know what to think. One time, we had this case where the wife looked at her dead husband and didn't move for a long time. It was probably only ten seconds, but it seemed way longer. Then, she laughed. Loud, body shaking laughter. It was kinda freaky."

"Did she kill him?"

"No. He had been killed in an accident at work. Later, she was mortified by her response. She was in shock or something. Point is, people put a lot of stock in how someone reacts when they look at a dead loved one. It's not necessarily cut-and-dried."

"What you're saying is Audrey Drummond might have been calm on the outside but a mess internally."

"Exactly. I want to get beyond her public facade."

"In other words, you want to take lead on this."

"Yes."

She stayed focused on the road ahead, her knuckles turning white as she gripped the wheel. "Look, I get we're supposed to get them talking. Get them to trip themselves up by filling in holes in their story as they make things up. I can do this, too. It's not like I haven't been a cop for twenty years."

"It's your first case."

"My first death investigation. In Homicide. It's not like I haven't been a cop for twenty years."

Court cracked the window for some fresh air. Beat cops spent most of their time talking to people, interviewing witnesses. Maybe by giving on this, she'd be a little less prickly around him. "Fine. Tell you what. Let me start. It might be she clicks with women more than men. If I'm not getting anywhere, I'll find a way to hand it over to you. Wait for my lead, okay?"

She weaved in and out between half a dozen cars and took the first exit after the bridge. "Fine."

How was it that no one had ever mentioned Ivy drove like a maniac? True, he had taken to coming and going to work with minimum outside interaction with other cops. He hung with a couple of people after Krav on Saturdays, but they were beat cops and all a lot younger. He pointedly ignored the gossip rampaging its way through the department, especially since he was the focus of a lot of it. It could very well be he was not in the loop. Maybe no one else cared she was a danger on wheels. Maybe no one else let her drive.

The first exit off the freeway landed them at the north end of Medina, a little city comprising mostly big homes owned by rich Microsofties and other techies. He was impressed by Ivy's ability to navigate the area without aid. He would be lost without GPS.

The streets dwindled from four lanes down to two. They turned onto a winding downhill street barely wide enough for two cars to pass each other. The houses were an interesting mix of old and new, each hidden to some degree by varying levels of shrubbery. They were oriented to take advantage of the spectacular views of Lake Washington. The sunset view from the western decks must be mesmerizing.

Ivy slowed to a stop and peered up the hill toward an older house. Mature arboretum-quality plantings filled the terraces in a profusion of early fall color. The architect must have visited Tomorrowland when designing the house, in which every curve and line of the structure echoed Disney's imagined future.

"Is this it?" he asked. He expected the Drummonds to live in a modern marvel closer to the lake, not a spaceship embedded into the hill.

Ivy eased the car forward a little bit, slowing for a better view of the virtual time-capsule. "No. They're closer to the lake. My grandparents built this place in 1960 as a weekend house, then moved here permanently after the bridge was built."

Her face softened a little bit, and Court got a glimpse of

the Ivy other cops talked about—the Ivy Langston that was a good and easygoing partner.

"They sold it for a fortune ten years ago." She sounded bitter. "My husband and I wanted to buy it. Keep it in the family. But we didn't have the money. You know what the pay grade is like, and he doesn't make much more than me."

Court hadn't realized Ivy's family had been in the area for so long. Something in common, then, except he had moved away from his family. "The only reason I have the place I do is that my dad sold the house my great-grandparents built in the twenties," he said. "He didn't have the heart to stay in it after my mom died last year, and he split the proceeds between us kids. We were on the edge of Chinatown. Almost a hundred years old. The developer bought up the block and tore everything down to put in apartments."

Ivy took her foot off the brake, letting the car get up to speed on its own as they went further downhill. She kept her eyes on the house until it was out of sight. "I get why they sold it, but I wish it could have stayed in the family."

The Drummond house wasn't one of the largest houses on the street, but it was newer than most. It had a gate, and the view of the house was unimpeded by shrubs and trees. They were buzzed in at the gate when they identified themselves, and a driveway wider than the road they were on led them around a landscaped circle with a tall red metal sculpture in the center. He recognized it immediately.

Ivy paused as they drove past. "Looks like that thing at Seattle Center. Near the Space Needle."

"Same artist. I think this one is called Spider. One of Calder's smaller pieces."

Ivy turned to him, eyes narrowing on him. "You're into art?"

Wanting to cultivate the friendly Ivy, Court needed to give a little more than he got. So, he gave. "My dad was a curator at the Fine Arts Museum of San Francisco for thirty years. Our vacations always included trips to museums. I picked up a lot of art-talk and info along the way."

"You're full of surprises, aren't you, Pearson?"

11

THEY PARKED AT THE FRONT DOOR NEXT TO A BURGUNDY Tesla. The house itself was a modern architectural dream with exposed wood beams, poured concrete walls, and a metal shed roof slanting in one direction toward them. The solar panels tucked inside the roof framework were well camouflaged, definitely much more attractive than the blue and silver monstrosities he'd seen elsewhere.

"This is how the other half lives," Court said.

"More like how the one-percent lives." She pointed at the Tesla as they climbed out of the car. "Looks like Eccles is here already."

An unsmiling woman, dressed in black slacks and white button-down blouse, opened the door as they stepped onto the stairs leading up to it. "I'm Mrs. Drummond's personal assistant, Carina Simpson. She'll be ready for you in a few minutes."

She led them through the formal entry and past two large rooms, clearly designed to impress and entertain, to a smaller room. Court wasn't sure what to call it. He'd never lived in anything but the most conventional of homes. Nothing like this. He imagined it was "the morning room" where the owners might sit to write letters with fountain pens. The room's western exposure gave them an incredible view of the lake. If this were his place, he'd spend his afternoons here. The sunsets must be stunning. The room was an odd assortment of old and new. Old furniture, old art, new architecture, new lighting. Every fixture was modern and most likely all LEDs.

"Please have a seat. I'll be back in a few minutes with coffee."

Court tore his eyes away from the lake view to focus on the rest of the room. A painting of a basket with six oranges on a vivid yellow-and-blue background hung on the south wall. Even though he recognized it, he leaned in close to check the signature and let out a slow whistle—Vincent. It hung in a recessed alcove to protect it from sun exposure. Turning around, he spotted Ivy with her nose almost touching a bronze sculpture of a ballerina on a pedestal in the corner. It had to be a Degas. A Renoir hung in another alcove opposite the Van Gogh. He wondered who the collector was. The dead man or his widow?

There were no personal photographs, no small mementos or trinkets, nothing indicating a family lived here. Everything was neatly arranged, as if the house was a hotel or small private museum. But the furniture was worn and used. Court had heard the rich let things fall into near ruin. They didn't need to impress anyone.

When the door handle turned they both jumped, like children caught with their hands in the cookie jar.

Audrey Drummond strode into the room, followed closely by her lawyer. She let him close the door behind them as she reached out a steady hand in greeting. "I'm sorry, I didn't catch your names last night?"

Court responded by thrusting his hand into hers before Ivy could, re-introducing them both. He pulled a card out of his pocket and handed it to her as Ivy did the same. Mrs. Drummond took them, and barely glanced at them before passing them to Eccles.

She wore a classic dark blue Chanel suit with a triple string of pearls at her neck, pinning her champagne-colored silk blouse to her skin. Her pumps were elegant but short-heeled. Her eyes were clear, she was wearing makeup, and her hair was neat and tidy.

She gestured them to the small brocade sofa and slid into an armchair with a poise implying many hours of ballet or, maybe, Pilates. Eccles settled onto an ottoman next to Drummond, his knees bending up toward his chest because of its low height. The overall effect was one of Mrs. Drummond sitting on a throne with a lapdog perched nearby.

Court's late-night internet search had netted him some basics. Audrey Drummond was fifty-six and Drummond's only wife of thirty-two years. Their three children were grown and out of the house living their own lives. Audrey Drummond spent her time fundraising and volunteering for local charities. She split most of her time between the zoo in Seattle, and a foundation serving homeless youth that the Drummonds had started after their youngest son had been beaten into a coma while he was a street runaway.

As they settled in, Mrs. Drummond's assistant returned with a tray and placed it on the low coffee table between them, disappearing as quickly and silently as she had appeared.

Court sipped at a cup briefly before putting it back on the table. It was kind of hard to take notes and drink coffee. "You have quite an amazing art collection. The Calder out front surprised me. Every Calder I've seen has been in public settings."

Audrey Drummond turned her head toward the front of the house as if she was trying to remember what was out there. Her shoulders lifted and she shuddered. "Oh? I hate that monstrosity. Berkeley thought it was heavenly, but it will be one of the first things I get rid of."

It had taken him almost a year before he could get rid of any of Amanda's things. He still had a box of Bailey's baby and toddler clothes. What else is she looking forward to *getting rid of?* "I take it your husband was the collector, then?"

She waved her hand in a sweeping gesture to include the Degas, the Van Gogh, and the Renoir. "Yes. All of them. We have pieces of major art in almost every room. I thought it was a waste of money. Money we could spend in better ways. More useful ways. But Berkeley, well, he loved art, and he kept reminding me we had plenty of money. I plan on donating every last one of them to the Seattle Art Museum in Berkeley's memory."

An icy chill shimmied down Court's back. She had seen her dead husband less than twelve hours before, and she's already decided what to do with his art? "That's very generous of you, Mrs. Drummond."

"Yes. I suppose it is. I don't like living with the over-head. It's too much." She held out her hands, palms upward. Her voice took on a business-like tone. "Detectives, tell me what you came to tell me, so we can all get about our days?"

Court had no idea what Audrey Drummond was talking about. From the look on Ivy's face, she was equally dumbfounded. "What do you mean, Mrs. Drummond?" Court asked. "Why do you think we're here?"

Audrey Drummond clasped her hands together and tightened her lips. "I know how these things work. Any suspicious death is investigated to be determined whether it is homicide, an accident, or a suicide. So, please, get on with it, and I'll tell you *why* Berkeley killed himself."

COURT RUBBED the back of his neck, the mention of suicide sending his train of thought off the rails. Come to think of it, they hadn't even discussed the circumstances of Drummond's death when talking to her last night. "What makes you think we're here to tell you your husband committed suicide?"

The first flicker of doubt crossed the woman's face. "Why else would you be here?" She cast a quick glance at her attorney.

"Are you saying this is a homicide, detectives?" Eccles sat up at attention. He had gone from lap dog to guard dog.

Court kept his eyes on Mrs. Drummond. "His death is suspicious. We're investigating every possibility, but we're certain it's not suicide."

She flinched. Her hand fluttered up to her pearls, fingers twisted around them until her knuckles were pressed against the hollow of her neck. "No. That can't be. I saw the marks around his neck. He hung himself." Her voice took on a strident urgency.

Court leaned forward, putting his elbows on his knees. "You thought he had killed himself, why?"

Her jaw dropped open for a second, her brow wrinkling in confusion. Her fingers relaxed their grip on her pearls and dropped to her lap. She pulled at the hem of her skirt, smoothing it across her knees. "But, the marks. He didn't hang himself? How ... how did he die?"

Court noted the transformation from self-assured, to confused, to dumbfounded. "I'll be happy to explain, but first, what made you assume it was suicide? When you saw your husband last night at the morgue, what did you think had happened?"

Audrey Drummond's lips twisted before she pulled them in tight over her teeth. She dropped her head and focused on her hands, twisting her simple gold wedding band in circles around her finger. "I assumed he had committed suicide." Her voice was barely audible. "The lines on his neck...."

The way she said it sent fresh shivers down Court's spine. The only thing hinting at any emotion was the way her eyes shimmered from pooling tears. The first real sign of emotion.

Court dropped his voice low. Comforting, Soothing. Inviting. "Why would your husband want to kill himself, Mrs. Drummond?" A whisper, an echo from his past. *Why would anyone want to commit suicide?* He brushed it away. Forced himself to focus on the woman in front of him.

"My husband was dying. He had an inoperable brain tumor. He'd been trying crazy alternative therapies, but they were ineffective. Useless. The pain was beginning to be crippling. He was getting excruciating headaches. We knew it was about time…time to…" She broke off and covered her mouth with both hands.

Inoperable brain tumor? It sure would have been nice if Mary had been able to do the autopsy before heading out to the accident before they'd come over here. Now they'd have to wait until Monday, maybe Tuesday before knowing for sure. Court rubbed at his chin, running through what it meant. He didn't like to be blindsided like this in the midst of an interview, either. The whole "spouse as prime suspect" theory pretty much went poof.

Ivy cut in before she could continue, but her voice was soft, understanding. "Was that the plan, Mrs. Drummond? For him to kill himself when he couldn't stand it anymore?"

Court turned to look at Ivy, mouth dropping open for half a second. He hadn't given her any sort of signal for her to take over. He slammed his mouth shut, jaw clenched tight, and returned his attention to Mrs. Drummond.

She dropped her hands from her face. "Yes. He said he would do it without telling me exactly when. We always said goodbye as if we would never see each other again. When it happened … I assumed…and I felt okay with it. I've been grieving ever since he was diagnosed."

Court leaned back against the soft curve of the sofa. Every signal from Mrs. Drummond was genuine. Cancer and suicide. A tragic combination. He didn't need to hear this story. He had already lived it once.

Eccles handed Drummond a pristine white handkerchief. She took it, dabbing at the corners of her eyes to collect tears tipping out of their confines, not even smudging her makeup. She took several deep breaths, clearing her throat before continuing. "However, I am not okay with someone killing him. I want you to find whoever did this."

Ivy nodded. "We totally understand, Mrs. Drummond. Anything you can tell us will be helpful."

Court decided to let Ivy continue with the questions and only jump in if he felt she was leaving something out or missing something obvious. Trying to take back the interview now would look peevish on his part.

"I don't think anything I know would be of use to you."

"We need details about your relationship, your husband's company, your family. You need to let us figure out what's relevant."

Backtracking was a good idea. The way Ivy leaned forward invited Mrs. Drummond in, nodding as Mrs. Drummond spoke, was a technique he'd seen plenty of times; Ivy pulled it off with a natural grace he had not expected.

Court catalogued the way Mrs. Drummond tilted her head, when she nodded, when she waved her fingers around. Her hands were in constant motion, adding expression to her words.

The groundwork laid, Ivy got to last night. "When we picked you up at the zoo fundraiser, you weren't surprised to see us."

"No. I had texted Berkeley to check on him earlier in the day. He didn't answer. I had assumed by the dinner, he had decided it was time. Then, at the morgue, I assumed he hanged himself. Those horrible marks around his neck. He would never tell me what kind of suicide he had planned. I should have known hanging would not have been his style."

Court kept his eyes on Mrs. Drummond, looking for any signs she was lying or otherwise evading the questions. She was unflappable. If she had killed him, faking a suicide, she would have pressed it further. Pushed for a suicide determination.

Ivy clasped her hands together, holding her notebook closed over a finger and leaned in close. "And what would his style have been, do you think?"

Drummond shuddered and raised delicate long fingers to her lips. Several brown spots on the back of her hand told a different story than her unwrinkled face. "For a while, I thought he'd jump. Into the ocean. I imagined him driving up to Deception Pass and jumping into the churning waters there. Then, I realized he wouldn't leave us in any doubt about his death. Somewhere like Deception Pass might mean we'd never find his body."

Drummond paused to pick up the coffee cup she'd been ignoring until then. She swirled the contents around without drinking any, grimaced and put the cup down. She stood up and walked to the Van Gogh, running a finger along the frame as if she were testing for dust along the ridge. "He wouldn't have done anything to put others at risk, like driving off a bridge or into oncoming traffic. Then, he bought a handgun a couple of weeks ago. I caught him with it one day. Sitting at his desk in the office upstairs. He didn't see me."

Her eyes glazed over as she went through the inventory of her imagination, and her voice grew slow and dulled, like she was hypnotized. "He put it in his mouth, and I thought he might do it then, not knowing I was watching. Then he lifted it to his temple." She held up a finger like a fake gun and put it against the side of her head. "Then he put it back in his mouth. He did this about ten times. He squeezed the trigger and flinched. He had never loaded the gun. He was ... practicing. He did this over and over. Mouth, forehead, mouth, forehead. Pulling the trigger every now and then until he stopped flinching."

Court watched her finger moving back and forth from her mouth to her forehead in silent, unmoving horror. How could anyone stand there and watch another person point a gun at their own head? Repeatedly. Maybe she had wanted him to do it. For him to end things.

The warmth drifted out of his face and dropped into his stomach, causing a burning churn. A rushing sound filled his ears threatening to crash the world around him. He breathed in through his nose, counted to ten and exhaled slowly through his mouth. He needed to stay focused on what Drummond was saying. What was happening in the here and now. But he couldn't shake the question he'd never considered before.

Had Amanda *practiced*?

IVY JABBED his side with her elbow. What had he missed? Damn. *Voices.* Their words were suddenly clear and distinct. He'd have to get Ivy to fill him in. *Focus. Focus. Focus.*

Ivy flipped to a new page in her notebook. "When was the last time you saw your husband?"

"You mean, when was the last time I saw him *alive*? I did see him at the morgue last night." She had glided over to a small wet bar underneath the Renoir. She poured something brown out of a carafe into a cut crystal glass and returned to her seat.

Stupid semantics. What kind of person comes back with that kind of quip when their spouse was freshly laid out in the morgue? Someone who also drank at ten in the morning? Court clenched his jaw shut. Ivy's head jerked a little to her left, as if her neck had a kink or something. He'd seen it before, and now recorded it as a tell he could count on from his partner. Was she annoyed at herself for her sloppy question or at Audrey Drummond for her snide reply?

"Yes. I'm sorry if I wasn't clear. When was the last time you saw, or spoke to your husband, or had any sort of communication with him, *when he was alive?*" Ivy spoke through clenched teeth.

Audrey Drummond downed the drink in a single movement and set the empty glass on the coffee tray. "Wednesday. We spent the morning on the boat together. Had lunch up in Kirkland. I went off to a hair appointment in the early afternoon."

"You didn't see or speak to him since early Wednesday afternoon?" Ivy asked.

"That's what I just said, Detective. We didn't speak. He texted me a couple of times Wednesday … logistics for his plans. He told me he was going to spend the night after his session with his…" She paused for a long moment. But then squared her shoulders, sucked in a deep breath, and spoke firmly. "He told me he was going to spend the night in Seattle after his session with his dominatrix. I wasn't even expecting him home Wednesday night."

Court sat back against the seat of his chair, stunned. He exchanged a look with Ivy, and knew, for the first time, they were both thinking the same thing. What kind of guy told his wife he was seeing a domme? What kind of wife would put up with it?

Ivy's jaw dropped open for half a second before she spoke again. "You knew he was seeing a dominatrix?"

"Of course I did. I'm his wife. He told me everything."

12

COURT HAD HEARD OF OPEN MARRIAGES, BUT THIS WAS something else entirely. Could it be Audrey Drummond was feigning nonchalance? Or was she naive enough to believe her husband had been completely honest with her? Was anyone ever truly open and honest with anyone else?

It was possible Audrey Drummond only knew part of the story.

Court cleared his throat to draw her attention toward him. "And you were okay with your husband seeing a dominatrix?"

Drummond met his eyes with an uncompromising stare, her lips twitching upward at the corners. "I was more than okay with it. I was thrilled he was seeing her. Whatever they did together, and no, I don't know the gritty details, made him relaxed and happy. He would return from his sessions calm and serene. He was better for it."

Court digested this bit of information for a second before continuing. Sessions. She used the word with the same casualness as she might have used referring to a shrink. "And you had no jealousy over this other woman being with your husband?"

Drummond flicked her hand as if brushing a fly away and shrugged. "As long as he did whatever it was they did away from me, and out of my sight, I didn't need to think about it much." She clasped her hands together and pushed a knuckle against her chin, a prayer-like gesture. "I put that part of his life in a box, detectives. I didn't want to know the details. He became a better man after he started seeing her."

"In what way, better?" Ivy asked.

"More patient. He drank less. He was more assertive with me, in a good way. Whatever they did together gave him a whole new virility."

Court glanced at the lawyer, who smiled weakly. It was sort of strange that Eccles didn't object to Audrey Drummond speaking with such candor. Maybe he had complete confidence in his client's innocence?

"Would you say his relationship with the dominatrix was a positive one?" Court asked.

"Wait a minute," Drummond said, her voice rising in pitch and volume. "You're not surprised by this. Is that where he died? With her? Did she kill him?"

"He died in her office," Ivy said. "But she has a pretty strong alibi."

Drummond's shoulders slumped and her eyes went wide. She held out her hands in supplication. "Oh. Dear lord. Would you please do me the favor of laying it all out for me? When and how, *exactly* did my husband die?"

Everything about her was screaming surprise. She had been convinced her husband had committed suicide.

"The autopsy will confirm the exact nature and time of his death, Mrs. Drummond," Ivy said. "But we're thinking sometime Wednesday evening."

Drummond stood up again, reaching for her glass as she rose. She added another shot to her glass and paced around the room like a caged animal, swirling the liquid around and around. "He was found at her … place?"

"Yes. Yesterday afternoon."

She stopped in front of the Van Gogh with her back to them. "When will the media be all over this? Can you keep it from them?"

"Are you concerned about his reputation?" Ivy asked.

She spun back around. Her face had gone a pasty white. "Of course I am. Can you keep the dominatrix thing out of this?"

"It's bound to get out, Mrs. Drummond. You should prepare yourself. The photos, the details… if it goes to trial. They'll be made public at some point." Ivy's voice was soothing, apologetic.

Drummond tossed the remaining contents of her glass back in one gulp. No one spoke for a long time. Court willed Ivy to stay quiet, wait for Drummond to talk.

Finally, Drummond let out a long slow sigh. "What now, detectives?"

Ivy tapped her notebook, the dull thud of her eraser making an erratic drumbeat. "Mrs. Drummond, do you happen to know how and what your husband paid his dominatrix?"

She looked up. "Too much, I'm sure. He was always generous, even tipping at restaurants and other services. But, no. I never asked what he spent. On anything."

"Knowing your husband's habits, can you explain why he would have several cashier's checks made out to her in his possession?" Ivy asked.

"I'm guessing he was planning on ending things with her. It sounds like him. Leaving her extra money. He'd want her to get by for a while without him."

Could it be that simple? If Drummond had been planning on a suicide sometime soon, maybe he was leaving extra money for the domme he loved and didn't want to leave high and dry. Was a hundred K merely "getting by"?

"Mrs. Drummond, can you tell us where you were Wednesday afternoon and evening?"

Drummond returned to her seat, sagging against the back before she spoke. "I already told you. Are you seriously considering me as a suspect?"

Didn't everyone on the planet know the spouse is always considered a prime suspect? Maybe this lady didn't pay close attention. "Mrs. Drummond, answering our questions is the only way to ensure that we cross you off our list."

Eccles put a hand on her arm. "I think we're done for the day, detectives. If you have further questions for Mrs. Drummond, you can ask them another day."

He rose and extended a hand to help her up. She brushed his hand aside as her color returned to normal. "No, Harlan. Let's get this over with. I have nothing to hide."

Ivy leaned forward. "We need to know what you were doing Wednesday evening."

Drummond slipped her hands under her legs, pinning them between her thighs and the seat cushion. "I was home all evening. I got home after my hair appointment and stayed in for the rest of the evening." She looked down at her knees. "That's it."

"Was there anything unusual about not hearing from him on Thursday?" Ivy asked.

"He had told me he would spend all day Thursday at the office. He'd cut his time there to one day a week, and it was usually Thursday. When he didn't come home on Thursday night, I suspected he'd carried out his plan. By Friday morning, I was wondering when he would be found."

"Why didn't you report him missing?" Ivy asked.

"Honestly? I think I was hoping he'd show up, tell me he would put up with whatever was going on in his head so he'd be with us a little longer. If I called the police, there would be a media frenzy and man-hunt for him. I knew he wasn't kidnapped. The only reason he'd be missing would be because he'd killed himself."

She made it sound so rational. So normal. Court breathed in slowly through his nose, concentrated on his notes.

"Do you have any idea who might want to murder your husband?" Ivy asked.

She flinched. "Such an ugly word. *Murder.* But, no. I can't think of anyone who would want to have killed my husband. He was one of those men who come across as too good to be true. He was equal and fair in business dealings. He never cheated on me—not in any *real* sense. His children loved him. He changed their diapers while other men of his stature hired twenty-four-hour nannies."

Court's earlier assessment of the woman's innocence was drifting away again. Was she delusional? Or was Berkeley Drummond the near saint she claimed?

"Are you involved in the business?" Ivy asked.

"No. I didn't have anything to do with the business once the children came."

"How were you involved before the kids?" Court asked.

"We met in college. Me, Berkeley, and Henri. We all brainstormed the concept of the company together. The boys managed the technical and business ends. I handled the marketing. I came up with the name, designed the logo." Her fingers fiddled with her pearls again.

Nothing in last night's search detailed the company's origin. "Colchuck Down?" Court asked. "What does the name come from?"

"Colchuck Lake is up in the Alpine Lakes area. In the Cascades. We used to hike up there when we were younger. All four of us. Me, Berkeley, Henri and Monica." She shrugged. "I liked the way it sounded. Colchuck Down."

"And, to be clear, you're talking about Henri Montpelier?" he asked. Last night's internet search hadn't told him much beyond the fact there'd been a falling out, a lawsuit ending in an undisclosed settlement, and a fistfight between the two men at a Mariners game.

She nodded.

"You think he could have had something to do with this?" Court asked.

Mrs. Drummond made a face and let out an astonished laugh. "Heavens no. Henri? Kill Berkeley? Absolutely not."

The emphasis she gave those last two words were pretty full of conviction. "They had a pretty public fight."

"That was six years ago, Detective. They've long since made up."

Court let it go for now. They had other ways of following

up on Montpelier. "Did he say anything about any problems he was having with the business? Any problems with anyone at work at all?"

"I suppose there could be. He worried out loud, and I learned years ago that I didn't need to worry with him. Saying things out loud helped him work through things whether there was anyone listening or not. I usually tuned out work-related issues."

She tilted her head to one side as if hearing a ghost of one of those worry sessions. She closed her eyes and leaned forward, moving her head slowly back and forth as if considering the possibilities. She opened her eyes after a few moments of careful consideration. "No. There's nothing. I guess I must have stopped listening."

THEY SPENT another half hour getting a list of people from Audrey Drummond. Known associates, business contacts, employees, past employees, relatives.

They emerged from the interview into clear weather. The sunshine glinted off the Calder out front, giving the sculpture a different character than before. From this angle, and in his light, it looked like a gigantic spider about to jump onto the house. He could see why Mrs. Drummond might not want to keep it there.

Court slumped into the seat and shut his eyes. He'd investigated at least a dozen suicides since Amanda's, and he'd never wondered if she'd ever *practiced* before. Flashes of Amanda slumped against the dark mahogany of their bed, holding the only stuffed animal of Bailey's they'd kept.

Amanda not quite dead, the lower half of her face a gaping maw. Blood on the headboard. Blood on the green sheets. Blood everywhere. Her eyes wide in confusion, shifting into sorrow, apology or regret. He never knew which in the end.

Ivy waited until they were on the freeway before saying anything. "So, what's going on? You went blank for a while in there."

He wasn't ready to talk to Ivy about Amanda. Not yet. "Yeah, sorry about that."

"Seriously. I need to know what is going on with you. Is this some PTSD thing going on? Are you going to go all la-la every time the word suicide gets mentioned?"

PTSD? No. Maybe? Was he ready to talk to Ivy about Amanda yet? "No."

"Your face went white. Totally pale. I thought you were going to pass out on me."

"Was it obvious?"

"They might not have noticed, but I sure as hell did. I got them to focus on me instead of you."

Court leaned into the shelf of the car door, pressing his forehead against the cool glass. He stared out at the lake. This time he had a good view of the new bridge under construction. Little sail boats fluffed across the gently waving water. Happy boats filled with happy people.

Suddenly, Ivy hit the dashboard with a hand. "Oh, crap. Pearson… I'd completely forgot about your wife. I was so intent on the interview."

Her knowing about Amanda was simple proof of the way things get around in the department. How people talk and talk and talk. Cops were the worst gossips on the planet. This was nothing new. He counted on the gossip to keep from having to discuss things. He'd never had a direct conversation with anyone in the SPD about Amanda.

There was some unspoken rule to not talk to him about family while he was around. No one talked about their kids, their wives, or their happy lives. The typical gallows humor that filled a homicide squad around particularly gruesome deaths quieted when he came into the room. Not all the time, but certainly when suicide was on the table.

Court focused on a wooden boat, its sails full and puffed out. He tried to block out the image of Amanda holding the gun in her hand and moving it back and forth, trying to decide between mouth and temple. "I'd never thought she might have made a choice. When Audrey Drummond went on about it… I don't know, I'd never imagined her practicing." Maybe she had. He didn't even know why he said it aloud. Why now? Why pick Ivy?

Ivy's jaw dropped open and shut. At length she let out a very long, slow, "Ooooh." She kept her eyes fixed on the road, with a dogged determination, the way people avoid crazy street people or the homeless. As if acknowledging their existence makes them contagious.

13

COURT'S STOMACH GROWLED LOUDLY INTO THE SILENCE that had fallen between them. They stopped for a slice of pizza at the Pagliacci on Tenth before they headed south across Capitol Hill toward the scene of the crime and their second interview with Karen Hunter.

"So, did you buy the whole 'my husband was a perfect man' line?" Court used a finger to move a devilishly hot red pepper to line up with the point of his slice of pizza and bit down. The fiery pickled pepper stung his lips, filled his mouth and cleared his sinuses with its pungent spice and heat. He chewed it slowly, relishing the sensation.

Ivy put down her slice of chicken and pesto pizza and leaned forward, dropping her voice to a conspiratorial whisper. "No, I didn't. I don't buy the fact she was totally fine with her husband seeing a dominatrix, either. I've never met a wife who was cool with her husband seeing a domme. It just doesn't happen."

"I can see a compromise. Maybe she knew about the

domme, but wasn't as relaxed or easy about it as she told us. You know, telling a lie around a truth works better if you tell it as close to the truth as possible."

"Can't put my finger on it, but there was something about her I didn't like." Ivy picked up her pizza and took a healthy bite.

"The autopsy will show us if he had a tumor and how far it had spread. But I totally get the planned suicide. That part hit painfully close to home, but I believe it."

Ivy finished chewing and wiped her lips with a napkin before answering. "She wasn't lying about the tumor and the fact he was going to die. That stuff can easily be proven, so there'd be no reason to lie about it. Add in she was expecting him to die soon, there'd be no reason for her to kill him. Let him die of the tumor and be done with him."

Killing a dying man made absolutely no sense. Court was with Ivy on this one. They sat alone with their thoughts for a couple of minutes while finishing their pizza.

"Did you notice how she shoved her hands under her legs when she was telling us about Wednesday night? The rest of the time they were in full-out Italian mode," he said.

"Huh," she said, her eyes narrowing. "maybe that's what I couldn't put my finger on. I hadn't noticed. But yeah." Ivy crumpled her napkin and tossed it onto the empty paper plate in front of her. "The domme has an alibi, the wife is unlikely, we have bupkis."

"Not true, we have the extra key. The other person getting in at four thirty. And the list of friends, family and business associates Mrs. Drummond gave us. Don't forget about all those juicy leads. Plus all of the domme's clients."

Ivy grimaced. "Fine. I doubt her client list is worth

much. Not unless we can link one of them to Drummond directly. It will make a huge difference if Hunter knows about the extra key. You think she did it with an accomplice?"

Court shook his head. He didn't like to think Karen Hunter was involved either. Why kill such an important client? Some sort of misguided sense of euthanasia? Still, an accomplice would make for a convincing scenario. She was one of the few people who could issue the second key and remove data from the system.

"And the money? That would be one hell of a goodbye present. Or was she maybe blackmailing Drummond?" Ivy asked.

"If that were the case, he would have been more likely to kill her, don't you think?"

"Maybe. I don't know. I can't see someone laying out a hundred thousand like that."

Rich people did things Court didn't understand all the time. Why not give someone you love a hundred thousand when you have billions? It's just a drop in the bucket.

Hunter's response to the second key and how and when it was used would be critical. Court would, again, take the lead in questioning.

The pizza re-energized Court's senses, knocking away his funk. There was something about Audrey Drummond he didn't get. She had been too calm and collected. Too passive. Not angry enough. Not sad enough. Not *anything* enough.

The weekend traffic made Capitol Hill even more slow moving than usual. It was the main reason Court didn't bother with a car. His little house, a bungalow not far off the main drag, was in an area with a very high "walkability" rating. Coffee houses, bookstores, restaurants, grocery stores and bars were all within easy walking distance.

They pulled into the parking garage under Hunter's office building, a newish modern affair. Architecturally bereft buildings erected after the Second World War were being methodically replaced by the modern idea of community-style structures. The trendy new combination of restaurants and retail on the ground floor, small business offices on the next floor and apartments above was gaining in popularity throughout the region. It had to be at least three years old, though, because Court remembered it being there when he moved up from San Francisco. It was in his memory bank even if he hadn't paid much attention to it.

There weren't any lookie-loos or lurking journalists hanging around. There had been a small crowd outside when the ME and CSI cars had parked out front last night, drawing attention to the scene. They had dispersed by the time Court and Ivy had left to collect Audrey Drummond, and now, everything had returned to normal.

Large signs reading FOR PATRONS OF PRATCHETT BUILDING ONLY kept the casual parker at bay. A metal gate separated the private garage for residents. How many people enjoying their croissant and lattes inside Gerard's Cafe were aware there had been a murder above their heads?

The two security cameras, set across from each other kitty-corner in the garage, would have caught anyone coming or going. "What about Drummond's car?"

"They towed it to the crime lab to go over it. It was parked across the street, about where the beat up Honda is now." Ivy pointed at a dented, 1990s maroon Accord.

"Why park on the street? The garage is connected to the building."

"Avoiding security cameras?" Ivy asked.

"Maybe, but the lobby is probably wired, too. Why avoid one and not the other?"

It was unlikely the car would tell them anything. He doubted Drummond would leave anything of value inside a parked car on a street this busy. The area teemed with the colorful life he expected here. Couples, straight and gay, strolled by arm in arm. Punks or Goths or whatever they called themselves these days walked by without people craning their heads to stare. Their dark clothing and pierced noses fit in with the other leather-clad, tattooed, animal-print-wearing, and otherwise modified people who populated the area.

Court waved a hand to the corner across the street, where a teenaged girl leaned into a car window, chatting with an older man. "We'll probably be done by four, maybe we can catch up with some regulars who were around Wednesday when Hunter left and when the mystery key holder showed up."

The girl stood and backed away, disgust twisting her face. The car pulled away and disappeared down the street. The girl threw back her shoulders, dragging herself back to the group of other kids standing outside the mini-mart.

Ivy followed his gaze. "Any time of day, any time of night."

She almost sounded sympathetic.

14

HUNTER WAS WAITING FOR THEM INSIDE THE MAIN DOOR of the building. She was dressed more like Court expected an Eastside housewife to dress—jeans, button-down shirt, striped Toms.

It wasn't until he saw her that Court realized how much he had been anticipating seeing her again. They would have hit it off in a normal setting. He found her attractive and intriguing, if a little scary. Scary in a compelling way. It was too bad they had met over a dead body and not at a party or the gym. Add in that she was a suspect in the murder he was investigating, was probably married with two kids—though, curiously, she hadn't mentioned a husband during their first interview—and he had no right to even be thinking along those lines.

Hunter strode to the elevator and pushed the *up* button. She tapped her watch like a school teacher herding children into class. "You know, these things exist for a reason. You're ten minutes late." The elevator opened with a gentle swishing sound. Hunter pushed the floor button and turned to face them. "My attorney told me the paperwork came through, so we have a deal."

Ivy reached into her tote and pulled out a sheaf of papers. "Here's your copy. It's all in order, Ms. Hunter."

"Detective Langston had the docs all signed, sealed and delivered to your lawyer earlier. And, honestly? We're only interested in the murder. Anything you have going on inside is your business. As long as you didn't kill the guy, you won't get any trouble from us."

"Your word, Detective, is only so good. I prefer the paper." Hunter rolled the paper into a tight round and shoved it into her purse.

The elevator glided to a stop. The scene had been reduced to the office suite. Crime scene tape marked her door with a big yellow X. Two long strips along the door cracks served as official seals.

Hunter fingered a piece of the plastic and wrinkled her nose before looking down the hallway, past the other offices on the floor and toward the elevator. "How long until this goes away? Until I can get back in on my own?"

Was she worried about what her neighbors would think? Or was she anxious to get back to business? He couldn't imagine she'd ever see another client in there again, though she didn't seem too broken up over the death of Berkeley Drummond. Court cut through the tape along the edges of the door with his pen knife. Then he tapped the code into the security lock and pushed the door open. The stench was greatly subdued now that the body was gone.

"We'll need it closed up until we're done," Court said. "Could be a week. Could be longer. You know, this smell won't completely go away. Not until you rip out the floor and subfloor and replace it. Probably have to repaint and have all the fabric items replaced. Maybe the insulation. All that soundproofing? They're like massive sponges for the smell."

Things were the same as they had left them. He studied the outer office again, looking for anything of interest, anything he might have missed last night. Abstract soapstone sculptures, books about financial markets and planning, and empty vases filled the shelves with a spacious gracefulness found in empty houses staged for market readiness. It all made for a bland boring space. Completely sterile. Easily forgettable.

Hunter glided past them, leaning casually against her desk, arms crossed. "So, what exactly do we do now, detectives?"

"Let's review everything you did yesterday. From the time you entered the office until we spoke. We also want you to walk us through what would have happened on Wednesday night if you had been here," said Court.

"All right, then. I'm here to help best I can. I cared for Berkeley deeply and want to see whoever did this to him caught. And tortured in a very unpleasant way."

COURT HIT the record button on his memo app and went through the whole 'date, time, place, we're recording this with permission' spiel. "Starting with yesterday. Tell us exactly how you entered the office, and how you came to find the body."

Hunter stared at the recorder for a moment before

squaring her shoulders and taking her place like an actress on a stage. "I came in through the door and bent down to pick up the mail." She bent over, pretending. "I picked it up from the floor and walked with it to the desk, putting it here." Her fingers circled an area on the polished desk, indicating where she'd left the mail.

She tilted her head toward the door leading into the other room. "That's when I noticed the door to the other room was closed. I *always* leave it open. So, I thought someone might be inside. Then, I took off both my shoes. I dropped one by the desk." She paused and slipped off one of her flats, her hand wrapped around the inside so the heel was pointed outward. "I held it like this, with the heel outward, but it was a stiletto."

This explained the shoes. The long heel had been pointy and would make a hell of a stab wound. "They're both in evidence," Court said. "But, you're telling us you went toward a room where you thought there might be an intruder, the heel of a shoe your only weapon?" Either she was gutsy or stupid. He'd go with the former.

"Why didn't you back out and call 911 if you thought someone might be in there?" Ivy asked.

Hunter breathed out heavily. "The only reason I'm talking to you now is I have a signed document that lets me speak freely. Think about it from my perspective. Calling the police is the last thing I would do."

This was pretty true for any sex-worker. Cops were rarely their best friends. "Okay. I get that. So, you had the shoe in your hand and you were holding it up for protection. Then what?"

"I walked slowly over to the door and opened it. Then,

the smell hit me. It was so quiet. So still. It didn't occur to me someone might be inside. Then, I saw Berkeley. Hanging there…" Her voice trailed off and she closed her eyes.

She used Drummond's first name. It showed familiarity. Dominance. A relationship. One he'd had an uncomfortable glimpse of through their texts.

"How did you know it was him?" Ivy asked.

"I recognized him."

"Really?" Court asked. "He was facing away from the door."

"Yes. He has a mole on his left buttock. Those skinny legs? The calluses on his toes? The bony ankles? I know… knew…every inch of him."

"So, you enter the room. See him hanging there and know it's Drummond. And then what?" Ivy asked.

Hunter's eyes went distant as she relived the moment. "I circled around to his face. Then, I dropped down to look at him." She raised her hand, holding her canvas loafer in front of her. Her voice became wistful, monotone. "I still had the shoe in my hand, so when I went to touch his face, I almost hit him with it by accident. I tossed the shoe over my shoulder, and then I touched his cheek. I had to make sure he was real."

"Then what?"

"I came back in here. Sat down for a couple of minutes to think. I called my attorney. It took her at least fifteen minutes to call me back. We spoke for a bit, and she advised me to call 911."

"Why didn't you mention Drummond's name in the 911 call?" Ivy asked.

Hunter sucked in her lower lip. "Bernice suggested I

keep his name out of it. Sometimes people actually pay attention to those scanners."

"So, what did you do after you made the 911 call?" Court asked.

"I waited for the police. Talked to the cop that showed up first, and then was stuck out in the hallway and told not to move. You know the rest."

Her story aligned with what they already knew. Court checked the relief he was feeling. He didn't want her to be guilty. "How did he find you?"

"I have a website. He did a thorough background check on me. He admitted to hiring a private investigator to check me out before contacting me."

He opened the browser on his phone. "What's the address?"

"Of my website?" Her brow wrinkled as if she didn't understand why he would want it, but pulled a business card out of the top desk drawer. "I don't think you can afford me, Detective, but here you go."

The site came up quickly—a tasteful homepage with a photo of a woman's curvy hip and thigh along the length of the left side. Her arm held a whip dangling toward the floor. The site was a little out of date, and a large banner read, MISTRESS FIDELMA IS NO LONGER TAKING NEW CLIENTS.

"Fidelma?" he asked. "Like in the mystery series?"

Hunter inclined her head, the tightness across her face relaxing a couple of notches. "Very good, Detective. Not many people get the reference."

"A mystery series about a Mistress Fidelma?" Ivy asked.

"Not exactly. It's a series about a plucky young nun who

solves mysteries back in Medieval Ireland. Her name is *Sister Fidelma* in the series," he said.

"Sort of like the Brother Cadfael series? But with a nun instead of a monk?"

Hunter nodded. "Pretty much."

Karen Hunter aka Mistress Fidelma was nothing like the dominatrixes Court had seen in porn. On the other hand, he'd never found porn to be a match for reality. The photos on her website were more sophisticated and artsy than pornographic. None of them showed her face. They were all teasing images of her body tastefully dressed in lingerie or leather.

"Sort of a strange choice, isn't it? I mean, a mystery-solving nun as a stage name for a dominatrix?" he asked.

Hunter leaned toward him, her hair sweeping past her cheek and shadowing her face. Her eyes became smoldering coals. "In my profession, being a nun is sometimes rather appropriate." Her voice dropped into a low sultry purr and her eyebrow lifted slowly on the last two words. It was a subtle change, but it made all the difference.

The gentle caress of her words washed over him. He could get lost in her voice. He cursed his Nordic complexion as the rosy heat of a blush crawled up his neck toward his ears. Her sudden change in voice and appearance showed she was also a remarkable actress.

Court cleared his throat to break the spell and continue with the interview. "What did Drummond come to you for, specifically?"

"He's in this high-powered position. High-powered life. Über-stressed all the time. He adores his wife, but she's completely vanilla, and not interested in giving him what he needs." She paused, sucking in her lower lip along with a bit of air and squeezing her eyes shut before continuing. "Needed. What he needed. I helped him relax."

"You helped him relax. Interesting way of putting it. And exactly how did you achieve that?" Ivy asked.

"You know, I understand you want more specifics, but you need to have some respect here. He was very private, and he wouldn't want the world to know any of this about him. He wasn't exactly ashamed of what he was doing, but he knew most people wouldn't understand." She leveled her gaze at Ivy. "And you're like the rest, aren't you, Detective?"

"It's not exactly *normal*," Ivy said.

"Most of the time, people find out what I do and are freaked out or disgusted. Sexual domination is parodied in books and movies, porn makes a hash out of it, and it's totally misunderstood. It may not be something the majority of people need, but it's a lot more than you think."

Court had plenty of experience with people shunning things they didn't understand. Being a cop had made him a bit jaded, though. Some people practiced a careful BDSM lifestyle--Cami was a pretty good example of that. Court had also seen dozens of injuries and deaths at the hands hands of careless, drunk, or angry people. A spate of recent deaths stemming from people jumping into trying kink based on a popular novel was proof that most people didn't research safety properly.

He'd known plenty of strong and successful men who got all masochistic in their down time. The more successful their outside life, the wimpier they were in private. Court had always figured it was repression and conservative guilt that led most guys to seek out a dominatrix. He'd never have imagined it of Berkeley Drummond. He was all over the news for being a huge philanthropist. A total liberal. Maybe the total change in family politics went only so deep. Maybe Court needed to take a closer look at his own stereotypes. It kind of blew his mind. If the press got hold of any of this, it was going to be huge. Huge in a bad way. Scratch that. Not *if. When.*

"Okay," Court said. "Rather than starting with a laundry list of what you two did together, let's talk about the last few days. When was the last time you saw Drummond alive?"

Hunter relaxed a little. "Last week. We had a regular appointment on Wednesday evenings from seven to ten, though he sometimes stayed later to rest. Sometimes spent the night. But I haven't seen him since a week ago Wednesday. He left around eleven fifteen or so."

"But you had some texts in between?" Ivy asked.

Hunter paused, her eyes narrowing. "You've read them, haven't you? They were all on the iPad you took last night. So why ask? Are you trying to catch me in a lie?"

Court shrugged. "It's one way of figuring out what happened. To ask a question we know the answer to."

"I hate games, Detective. You ask your questions, and I will tell you the truth. And, one last time, I had nothing to do with Berkeley's death." Hunter's voice grew louder with each word. She took in some air and continued more quietly. "I am here because I want you to find the person who did this. I am here for justice for a man I cared deeply about."

Court believed her. For whatever reason, it was implausible she would kill anyone in such an obviously bad location. She didn't come across as a complete idiot. Unless it was an accident, and she was covering for a mistake. Or she had an accomplice. It kept coming back to that possibility, especially with the second card key in her name.

The most logical conclusion was that Drummond had come here for his regular appointment and things had gone awry. Whoever did this must have taken advantage of the sudden change in schedule.

Court held up his hands in a placating gesture. "Okay. Okay. Let's move on a bit. How do you think he got hung up that way?"

Hunter leaned back against the desk. "I don't know. I mean … he was tied up using knots I sometimes use, but not all of them. I rarely mix Western ties with Shibari style. And, I'm never that messy."

"Shiba-what?" Ivy asked.

Hunter turned her attention fully to Ivy and her speech picked up a notch in speed. "Shibari. It's a Japanese form of bondage. Google it sometime. It's beautiful and incredibly erotic. I tend toward more conventional ties because it's what I know best, and they are faster. But, I do occasionally use Shibari techniques for aesthetic reasons."

Court was pretty sure the internet would give him an eyeful on that particular search, but Ivy was focusing on the wrong thing here. "What do you mean, *messy?*" he asked.

"Oh, well, I am very meticulous with my rope-work. The knots along Berkeley's arms, for example, they were not exactly the same size, and they didn't line up perfectly. The rest of the rope, holding his weight and pulling his legs up, was dangling over him."

"Can you speculate as to why this was so messy?" he asked.

"I would have to say there are two main reasons. No one

would do this intentionally. It's ugly, and Shibari is Japanese and all about presentation. No. I would say the person who did this was either inexperienced or in a hurry."

"How long does it usually take for you to do something like this?" Court asked.

"I draw it out. An hour? Sometimes longer depending on the client."

There hadn't been enough time to do a proper job of it if the killer left half an hour after Drummond entered. So, he was in a hurry, then. But why? If the killer knew Hunter wasn't coming back, why rush things? Maybe to solidify an alibi while Drummond was dying?

"Were you planning on tying him up Wednesday night?" Ivy asked.

"Yes, I was. I purchased a new rope for him, and I had set up the workroom for our session. The purple rope on his body is the one I had put out with the other things. The black rope was his pelvic harness ... a sort of rope underwear made for him to slip on easily. It saves time." Hunter crossed her arms, hugging herself. "I didn't kill him. Intentionally or not. I haven't seen him since last week. Berkeley was a good client. My best client. He was responsive, kind, and always respectful. Yes, he paid me very well. Really, really well." Her eyes opened wide to emphasize the point. "It was more than the money, but I can't lie, the money was important to me. Why would I kill him? He pays ... paid ... the mortgage."

"Okay," Court said. "Let's shift gears and go through exactly what would have happened Wednesday night. Tell me what Drummond would have done from the moment he entered the office."

Hunter pushed herself off her desk and strode to the entrance, turned her back to it as if she were pretending to have opened the door and entered the office. "He would have come through here, because no one waits in this room. It's a sham front office." She walked across the room to the other door, demonstrating the most likely angle of approach. "This door would be open. The first thing everyone does is take off their shoes and leave them inside."

Court and Ivy followed her into the other room. The low, empty shelf showed a tag indicating something had been taken into evidence. Berkeley Drummond's shoes, no doubt.

Hunter paused, her eyes fixed on the empty space below the hook in the center of the ceiling. Court imagined she was seeing the same thing he was. Even though the body and all its entanglement of ropes had been removed, he could still see it exactly as it had been the day before. The floor had been scraped clean, the evidence taken to the lab. The remaining stain could be from something as innocuous as general water damage or a spilled cup of coffee.

Hunter pointed to the other two rooms. "He would go through the bathroom and then into the dressing room."

They followed Hunter as she led them through. They had searched all the rooms last night, but having her lead them through would be instructive and clarifying.

Hunter reached around and flipped a switch to turn on a torchiére in the corner of the dressing room. Soft yellow light gave the room a warm, cozy glow. "This serves as a dressing room as well as a recovery room. Sometimes a punishment room."

A narrow twin bed took up the corner opposite the door. To the left of the door was a large metal cage.

15

Ivy dropped to her haunches in front of the cage, opening and shutting the door. barely large enough for her to fit through.

Even a small person would be cramped inside. Court licked his lips, breathing in a couple of quick breaths. The only thing worse than being tied up was being crammed inside a tiny space. The metallic clank as Ivy shut it was jarring in an otherwise quiet space. "He would come in here, undress, and then what?"

"He would have folded his clothes and left them with his personal items on the bench." She pointed to the bed. "If I have an outfit for him to wear, I leave it on the bed for him. We were planning on doing some suspension work Wednesday."

"Suspension work? Is that what you call it when you tie someone up?" Ivy asked.

"No, it's lifting them off the ground, regardless of how much they are bound. It requires a lot of skill on the part of the Domme, and a lot of desire and strength on the part of the submissive. It can be strenuous and draining at the best of times. But, once accomplished, the submissive has an elated sense of well-being. The stress on their body varies greatly depending on how they are tied and how they are lifted. Once in the air, the Domme usually coaches them through the pain and pushes them further, either emotionally or physically."

Hunter's whole demeanor relaxed whenever she was talking about her craft. She switched into a lecture mode infused with excitement and a desire to share her knowledge.

"So, you would use things like nipple clamps and dildos on him once he was up in the air?" Court asked.

"Yes. Basically. Sometimes dangling an object that can cause pain in front of them and pretending I was about to use it would be enough. Withholding the use of something can be quite effective."

Teasing. Court could totally see her dangling an object in front of someone, her soft voice making false promises.

Ivy's lips twitched into a tight pucker. "Drummond was suspended and left for dead." She put emphasis on "suspend-ed," making it sound like a made-up word, and a dirty one.

Court diverted Hunter from Ivy by waving at the bench where they had found Drummond's belongings. "Drum-mond would have come in here, undressed and put his things on this bench. Since you said he was to be naked for the suspension thing, the bed would have been left clear of costumes for him."

"Yes. Well. No actually. I left his harness rope on the bed for him. It was the black rope around his hips and groin. Once he was naked he would have put it on and then walked

through the bathroom and into the therapy room." Hunter
spun to lead them back through the bathroom.

Therapy room. The way she talked about what she did
made it sound like it was some form of psychoanalysis.
Court could almost see it.

On the other side of the bathroom, opposite the
changing area, was another door, leading into the closet.
Hunter pushed the door open and ushered them in. "These
are all my costumes. Different outfits for different clients and
situations."

Three organized bays filled the space with enough room
for a person to turn around and access the clothing hung
there. One wall held shelving from top to bottom filled with
shoes. Spiked heels. Flats. Mary Janes. Boots. Every manner
and style imaginable.

Court pulled the least sexy shoe he could possibly
imagine off the shelf. "Uggs?"

Hunter laughed, grabbing them to put back on the shelf.
"You don't want to know. I think Detective Langston might
pass out. And, Berkeley Drummond had nothing to do
with them."

The rest of the closet was filled with enough to clothe an
entire cast of *The Rocky Horror Picture Show*. Things hung in a
rainbow of colors, neatly organized along the palette. The
children's song about rainbows started its little mind worm in
Court's head—Red, Orange, Yellow, Green and Blue, Indigo
and Violet, too.

And Black. Lots and lots of black. Textures of all kinds
leaked out of the folds of fabric. Organza, silk, lace, leather,
satin, shiny patent leather. He shook his head as he realized
his imagination about what a dominatrix had been rather

lacking at best. He'd never considered the wide range of costumes one might use.

He noticed a nun's habit and pushed the neighboring garment to the side so he could see the whole thing. "You weren't kidding, were you?"

"Like I said, 'Fidelma' has been quite inspirational." Hunter's forehead furrowed in thought as her eyes scanned the hangers. "Now hold on a second." She pushed Court's arms to the side and flipped through the hangers, shoving them from one side to the next. She paused and removed an empty hanger. A white index card dangled from a red ribbon attached to the neck of the hanger.

"This one. It's missing." She pushed aside a couple of hangers, fishing out a body suit. "It's a suit similar to this, but the missing one is all leather."

Wearing something like that would be uncomfortable. Suffocating. Court shuddered when he touched it. Latex.

He fingered the index card. "What's this?"

"I keep track of when I use a costume." She flipped it over and pointed to the last name on the list. "Rosie was Berkeley's code name. I used it last with him eight months ago."

Court snapped a picture of it. The card was nearly full, and the dates went back fifteen years. "You've been doing this for quite a while."

"Professionally, about twenty years. I did it for fun for a couple years before I went pro. I realized I didn't need to give away something men would pay a lot of money for." Hunter shook the latex outfit she was holding. "This is an almost identical shape. It was here yesterday morning."

"You're certain of that?" Court asked.

"Absolutely."

Ivy tugged at the chest and hips of the outfit. "Was it skintight on you? If you wear something like this, the leather must be tight like a second skin."

"The missing suit is a lot like this, but not exactly. Tight. Yes. But, the missing suit is a little bigger. I bought it while I was getting back into shape after having my daughter."

Court poked at one of the arms. "Do you think someone else wearing it could pretend to be you?" He pulled at the fabric. It didn't give much. "Are we looking for a woman? Would there be any way for a man to fit in this and still make Drummond feel safe?"

Karen paused before answering, glancing back and forth between Court and Ivy a few times before settling on Court. "When I wore an outfit like this, I usually bound my chest and packed."

"So, the killer could have been a man. A skinny man could get away with the deception, then." Court said.

Ivy dropped her gaze to Karen's crotch. "Packed? You would have been wearing prosthetic junk?"

"That's what packing means, Detective." Karen's voice was icy.

Ivy fingered the high Manchu collar. "What about his face?"

Hunter tugged a box off the top shelf. It tumbled open into her hands, empty. "This is where I kept my full face mask. It hid all my features and my hair. It's terribly trite. Exactly what you might expect in a bad porn movie

"The killer got inside, somehow. Then, they put on the missing outfit, waited for Drummond to show, tied him up and left. Taking the outfit with him. Or her." Ivy's voice was filled with skepticism.

"It would be hard to get off. He probably left wearing it." And, on Capitol Hill, someone dressed in a full body leather suit would hardly be noticed.

IVY CLAPPED her hands together and turned back to the large room where the body had been found. "So, let's go over this. Drummond lets himself in with his keycard, comes in through the area here, and proceeds into the bathroom and dressing room. He would come out through the bathroom, and then what?"

They followed Ivy back into the bigger space.

Hunter pointed to the spot under the hook. "I would have him kneel there. Where ... the stain is. He was to have his back to me, head bowed."

Court pulled a pair of gloves from his pocket and dropped them on the floor to protect his jeans. It was unlikely anything would get on them, but the idea of kneeling directly on what was left grossed him out. He dropped onto his knees. "Like this?"

"Yes, but your hands go behind your back and you can't slump."

Court rolled his shoulders back and put his arms behind him. He dropped his chin to his chest. "Ow. Don't like this much. How long would he kneel like this?" His knees were already aching. And he had pants on to cushion them. Doing this naked would suck.

"Depends. If he had been good the last time he had seen

me, maybe a minute or less. If I wanted to make a point, I would make him kneel longer. Sometimes, I would scatter rice on the floor while he was changing. He would see a plain floor when he entered and return to find the rice. Or lentils. Something small and painful."

Ivy coughed. "Okay, so he comes out this door, and kneels. Then, you come out of your closet wearing your leather outift?"

"More or less."

Ivy came up behind Court until she was close enough he could feel her slacks against his fingers. "And his back is to you? So he wouldn't actually see you coming?"

"That's creepy, Langston."

"Not as creepy as the fact you're kneeling directly under where someone had been hanging for hours. Not to mention you're right on the spot that was thick with excrement and piss."

Court shrugged, not wanting to admit it bugged him. "Everything goes in the wash in the garage as soon as I get home, anyway." He'd put a separate washer in his garage to keep crime-scene smells from getting inside the house. The rank air from the day before was greatly reduced, but he'd grown accustomed to it in the time he'd been here. "So what next? You've got Drummond here, naked and on his knees, ready to go. Then what?"

"I would come up quietly behind him and rub his head." She reached out and ran her fingers through Court's hair. "Lean over and ask him if he's been a good boy." Her voice dropped at this last the way it had when she'd teased him about being a nun.

The subtle shift as her voice changed and her touch sent

his whole body tingling. There was a raw sexual power in her voice, and he understood how she earned the big bucks.

He cleared his tightening throat. "Okay. Get past the preliminaries, we don't have to play out the whole scene." Court wasn't enjoying the pain in his knees, but he couldn't deny the strange appeal of what she was doing to him.

Hunter dropped on her haunches in front of him and cupped his cheeks in her hands. Her lips twitched upward into a mischievous grin. "Detective Pearson, I think you're right. If I were to go through a whole scene with you, your partner would probably faint from the shock of it, and you might end up a permanent client."

Damn. She was good. Amazing, actually. But client? No, no, and *no*. He could get into kink with a beautiful woman like Karen Hunter pulling that kind of shit on him, but only on rare or special occasions. He craned his head to see what Ivy was thinking about all this.

She stood behind him arms crossed. It wasn't shock he was seeing. It was unmitigated disgust. This case crossed into private-life issues. Issues about sex and sexuality. He'd never had a conversation with Ivy about anything remotely sexual. He'd assumed her being on vice would have inured her to almost anything people do to each other. Being used to something didn't necessarily mean you had to be cool with it. Court still found himself disgusted with the human race with every murder, so maybe sex was one of Ivy's hang-ups.

Hunter stood, and her warm scent whooshed over him. She must have put on perfume earlier in the day, and it had melded with her natural scent. He shouldn't be thinking about the way she smelled. But scent was the kind of thing he enjoyed about women. That mix of chemical and natural.

A hint of the real body beneath the veneer of makeup and perfume and deodorant.

Court stood up, shaking his legs out. He definitely didn't like the kneeling part. Relating to someone who wanted to be in that position was hard. Relating to wanting more of Karen Hunter? That was all too easy. And all too inappropriate.

He bent over, pretending to tighten his shoelaces so he could wrap his head around his reaction to her. He wondered at her ability to shift gears so fast, to go from mourning over a favorite client to being all domme-y. He was unnerved by her acting skills and even more so by his response to her words and touch. He'd crossed a line. He stood up, hoping the contradictions tumbling around in his head were not showing on his face.

"So, once he's on his knees, you tie him up and use the pulley system with the ropes to pull him up and suspend him?"

"That's pretty much it."

The pulleys were gone, but the hook remained in the ceiling, a permanent fixture.

"So, once he's up there, then what?"

Hunter pointed to the counter. "I usually put out an assortment of things. Dildos, ball-gags, whips."

Ivy's arms flew over her chest. "Nipple clamps."

"I'm surprised you knew what those were for, Detective."

Ivy gave her a withering glance. "Drummond liked getting his nipples pinched?"

"I would only keep him in suspension for ten or fifteen minutes during which time I would employ one mental tactic and use one item from the tray. Then, I'd let him down and we'd finish the session." She looked up at the hook. "I would usually build up to the suspension for at least an hour. The tie itself is key to the buildup."

Court stepped back and crossed his arms, the scene still vivid in his memory. "So, would Drummond have let anyone else do this to him?"

"No." She paused, her lips pursing together into a deep frown. "That's the thing. I've been trying to figure out how this all happened. I mean, he comes in here, kneels, but if I wasn't there to tie him up, I think he would have been freaking. He trusted me. I don't think he would have let anyone else touch him."

"But, if the killer had the suit and mask on, Drummond wouldn't know it wasn't you, right?"

"Probably not."

"What about your voice?" Ivy asked.

Hunter sucked in her lower lip. "It wouldn't be unusual for me to treat him with silence to begin with."

"Is there any possible way he did this to himself? Any way he knew you'd be gone and used it as a way to kill himself?" Curt asked.

Hunter spun on him, eyes wide. "What? Why on earth would Berkeley want to kill himself?"

A brief flicker of communication passed between Court and Ivy. Karen Hunter didn't know about Drummond's suicide plan. "Didn't he tell you about his medical condition?"

"Medical condition? What are you talking about?"

16

COURT SHRUGGED. "IT'S A HYPOTHETICAL QUESTION."

"There's something you're not telling me." Karen put both hands on her hips.

"We're covering all avenues. If he'd told you he had a medical condition, what would you do differently?" Court asked.

Hunter eyed the stain on the floor. "It would totally depend on what was wrong with him. You treat someone with diabetes differently than say, a broken leg, right?"

"There was nothing unusual about your interactions with him?" Ivy asked.

"No. Nothing. Well. He was more tired recently. He claimed he was working long hours and didn't want as strenuous a session. Maybe a little forgetful about things. But last week, he said he wanted this." She pointed at the hook.

Court got the sense she felt betrayed by it, as if the metal hook could hold some culpability for Drummond's death.

"Tells us how the whole card-key thing works," Court said, ushering them all back into the front office.

"Well, I don't quite understand all the technical details, but I have a program on the computer linked to the little box from Haubek. I put the card into the box then type the rules I want to set into the computer." Hunter stopped and pointed to the empty spot on the desk where the computer used to be. "You took the box and the computer. I signed a paper that gave you permission to take it. You already know."

"Tell us what we already know, Ms. Hunter."

"All right. Fine. Well, you would have found I give each client a code name—using a flower. Berkeley's was Rosie. Then, I set up a rule allowing each client access for ten minutes before his appointment time. I set up the limit because I don't tolerate tardiness."

"So, when you get a new client, how do you give him the key?"

"What do you mean?"

"I mean, if you have a new client, do you interview them out here, then give them a key while they watch? Or do you prepare the key ahead of time?"

"Hmmmm. I see what you're getting at. I never made their keys in front of them. I usually made a key ahead of a first full session. This would happen after an initial interview and discussion of how we would work together. After the completion of a successful session, I would reward them with a key programmed for their use."

"So they never watched you make their keys?"

"No."

"How many card keys do you have issued to yourself?"

Ivy asked.

Hunter stiffened and hesitated before answering. "I only have one."

"Are you sure?" Court asked.

"Yes. I'm certain. I have *only* one card key. Why?"

"And, who all had access to the coder box?" he asked.

She walked around the desk. She opened the door to a shelf and waved at the empty space. "It was here. Any of my clients could have come in and used it if I was busy in my dressing room—if they had the time and my passwords to my computer. You can't make a new card without the password. They all left before me, except for Berkeley when he spent the night." She lowered herself into the chair and stared at the shelf. "He would be alone here for hours. I suppose he could have made a copy, but … I have to log into the computer and I never gave him my passwords. I don't know how he could have done it."

Court didn't tell her that every one of her clients was a suspect. But, if Drummond had the most access, it was reasonable to assume he could have made the second key and given it to someone. But who? Audrey Drummond had said she didn't want anything to do with the dominatrix her husband was seeing. She claimed to have compartmentalized his relationship with the domme and put it on ignore. Maybe Drummond had a mistress who would join him after Hunter had left. That could explain the second key being used after Drummond's sessions on Wednesday nights, but not the other entries when he wasn't around.

"Your clients come from a variety of professions, don't they? Any computer programmers in the mix?"

Hunter leaned back against the chair, her eyes slightly

unfocused. "Yes. Several. But, I can't imagine any of my clients betraying me." She shook her head. "You have all their information if you've gone through my iPad. They're all there."

Ashena would have a list for them soon, but some of those numbers were bound to get them nowhere. "You've got everyone coded. Can you help us out and give us the legal names to go with the flowers?"

"Sure." She opened her eyes wide. "I'll hand over my whole confidential list and expect all my guys to be fine with it. Right."

"You do sarcasm well, Ms. Hunter," he said.

"Thank you, Detective."

He let it go for now. If Ashena couldn't back-trace all the numbers, he'd get the warrant. "How often do you review the system or how the keys were actually being used?"

Hunter shook her head slowly. "I don't. I figured, since everyone shows up on time, the keys are working the way they are supposed to."

"So, you're telling us you don't pull up the report and check it out from time to time?" Ivy asked.

"No. I suppose I should, but, I didn't see a reason to."

"Tell us about the reboot of the system eight weeks ago," Court said.

Hunter's head jerked up and her eyebrows angled toward the center of her forehead. "Oh ... the break-in." She shook her head from side to side as if clearing it. "Yeah, I had forgotten all about that. The reader box was smashed off the wall, and I had Haubek out to replace it. They wiped the system and told me to issue new cards to everyone. So, I did."

"Did you file a police report?" Court asked.

"No. They didn't take anything other than a little statue worth maybe fifty bucks. They left my computer. All the equipment in the other room."

"Did you ask yourself why someone would break in and not take anything?" Ivy asked.

"It turns out all the other offices were broken into the same night, but it was the psychologist down the hall who was the real target. Someone had taken several files from his office and broken the locks on the other offices as a cover. Little knickknacks were taken from everyone, but nothing of value."

The reports by the other tenants would be on file, and it would be easy to verify her story when they got back to the station. "Why didn't you file a report? You need a police report to file with your insurance," Ivy said.

"Insurance? I don't carry renter's insurance anymore. Weren't you listening earlier? I don't call the police because … they are *the police.* Look, four years ago, I was broken into, back at my old place, and I had ten thousand dollars' worth of costumes and equipment stolen. The police did nothing but make off-color sarcastic jokes about what I did for living. They told me I was lucky they didn't arrest me for soliciting. One actually felt me up."

Court bristled. There were bad cops everywhere, power junkies who got off on intimidating other people. He kept his distance from them. "Okay, you don't trust the police to take care of you. I don't think you're being fair. Most of us are good people. But, it explains why you didn't file the report."

Ivy opened the report Ashena had given them, placing it flat on the empty desk. "This is a printout of your card key report. There are two with your name assigned to them. Those highlighted in blue show your original key. The yellows are from a duplicate key assigned to you, but only in use for the last six weeks."

Hunter flipped back and forth between the pages. Her face drained of color. "I only have one key. And, the yellow lines show someone coming in when I wasn't around." She poked at two times stamps for 2:00 a.m. "I've never been here that late. Ever. Someone has been sneaking in and out of here for six weeks? Without me knowing it?" She slammed her clenched fist against the desk. "What the hell? Do I have a stalker?"

"We're thinking someone discovered your connection to Drummond, then planned a very meticulous murder," Ivy said.

"But, why?" Hunter gathered her hair away from her face and twisted it into a ponytail. "They would have no way of knowing when they could actually do something. My not being here Wednesday was a total fluke. I never miss sessions. It was the first time. Ever."

Court tapped the yellow lines showing entries late on Wednesday nights. "Can you tell us if Drummond spent the night on any of these evenings?"

Hunter examined the dates. She compared her calendar to the list and pointed out three of the days. "These. Oh. God. Someone was sneaking in here while Berkeley was sleeping in the other room?" Her voice had dropped to a whisper as it sunk in.

Ivy marked the matching dates. "So, the killer was following Drummond, learned where he was going on

Wednesday nights. Then, he figured out how to fake a card key, and spent the next few weeks working on a plan."

"Maybe, he was going to wait until the next time Drummond spent the night. When you canceled, he took the opportunity to kill him instead of waiting any longer," Court said.

"How would the killer know I had canceled?"

Court used a finger to trace along the last yellow line on the list: 4:30 p.m. Wednesday. "So, I'm the killer. I see you leave the building at four fifteen. I've been watching for weeks, so I know you don't usually go away. I wait fifteen minutes before coming up."

Court scanned the room again, trying to figure out what came next. "The desk. Your iPad was on the desk. You came back Friday to get it?"

She nodded and tapped the desk. "It was right here."

"Do you have all your devices on cloud messaging?"

"Yes. If he came in here and saw my iPad, he could have seen my message to Berkeley telling him I would be late. It would have been on the iPad, too."

"Okay, so he was inside here, poking around. He saw you were going to be late, and decided to stay. You told Drummond to come at his regular time and wait because the card key would only let him in at his usual time. The killer knew this and figured he had about half an hour to do his thing."

"But, why would Berkeley have shown up at all? I had canceled."

Court flipped to the transcription of the texts and tapped on the last one. "Because, Drummond turned off his cell phone at six thirty when he got in the car to come over here. He never got your last message."

17

COURT SCANNED THE STREET AS THEY LEFT HUNTER'S building. The sun didn't set until about six p.m. Someone sitting in a car on the street or standing around watching would have been able to see Hunter come out of the building. She would probably have come out of the private tenant parking, but the killer likely knew the make and model of her car and would have recognized her.

"Let's make sure we look at the garage surveillance beginning at three Wednesday afternoon," Court said.

Ivy checked her watch. "My husband and I have tickets to the ballet tonight. A babysitter and everything. I need to call him let him know what's going on."

Was she excited to have to cancel her plans? Maybe. It was her first official case. Ivy hadn't said much about her family. It made most people uncomfortable to think about having their kids healthy and alive, knowing that his had died. He wasn't anti-kid or anything. He had loved and lost a

child once. That had been even more unbearable than
Amanda killing herself. That had been a fuck-you move.
Bailey's death? It was every parent's nightmare.

"Yeah. I have plans tonight, too." They both pulled out
their phones. Ivy walked a few feet away while Court used
texts. Instead of canceling, though, he told his sister he'd be
on the late end. The party for his twin niece and nephew
started at five. There was no way he could make it by then.
He wouldn't tell her he wasn't coming until he was absolutely sure there was no way of sneaking out for a couple
of hours.

The teens across the street were in a single line, leaning
against the mini-mart's wall, taking advantage of the thin
line of shade. Court stopped Ivy from heading to the garage
and directed her toward the little café instead.

"Let's talk to those kids over there before we leave. They
might have seen something." He pointed to the sandwiches
in the front case of the café, holding up his fingers for six of
them. He grabbed six bottles of juice from the cold case and
handed them to Ivy, then stuck one of his cards in each of
the sandwich bags as the clerk rang him up.

The teens eyed them warily as they crossed the street and
approached them but didn't budge. A girl with stringy hair
and too much eyeliner eyed the bags with obvious interest.

"Afternoon, folks," Court said. As he got close, he noticed
plenty of gender-bending going on, guessing that saying
"Afternoon, ladies" would have won him more hostility than
anything. The leader took a step back as Court fished out his
badge and introduced himself and Ivy. "I've got some sandwiches and juice here. Anyone interested?"

The oldest-looking one, the one who had earlier waved

off the john in the car, stepped forward, clearly speaking for the group. "And what do you want in return?"

Court shrugged and passed out sandwiches, not waiting until a deal had been brokered. "Not much. I want to ask a few questions."

Hands reached for the sandwiches. Ivy handed over the juices, but no one opened anything. Their leader crossed her arms, refusing the proffered bag of food, eyes narrowing into slits. "What kind of questions?"

Court indicated the building across the street. "There was a death there on Wednesday night. My partner and I are trying to figure out what happened. Seems like you hang around here enough to maybe have seen something. We have no interest in anything you all are doing here. There's nothing wrong with hanging out, right? We need to know about anything or anyone you saw heading into or leaving from four p.m. onward on Wednesday."

The girl relaxed a fraction, her eyes flicking toward a slowing car.

Court followed her gaze. He stepped in a little closer and whispered. "There are a lot of guys around here needing directions, eh?" He wanted it to be perfectly clear there was going to be no repercussions on their other activities—not from him, and not at the moment anyway. He'd need to make a call to CPS later. He had at least three of them figured for under fifteen.

She nodded and reached for the last sandwich.

"Were any of you hanging out here on Wednesday evening?" Ivy asked, passing the last juice to the girl in charge.

"We were all here. Plus about, like, four others. But, you

know. We're staying at this shelter. And like, we have to be back there like by seven thirty for dinner. They feed us and lock us in, like prisoners, but, it's a place to sleep."

"If you were here until close to seven thirty, maybe you can try remembering anything you saw starting at four?"

The others opened their sandwiches, taking tentative bites. He saw two of them notice his card, flash him a look and stick it in their pockets. One looked at him, held the card up between a couple of fingers, and let it drift to the sidewalk.

"There were only, like, regular people walking around. Nothing unusual. Like, for around here anyway."

Ivy pointed to the spot where Drummond's car had been parked. "Remember seeing a green Audi parked there?"

As a group they all turned to look at their leader. There was no mistaking the sense of recognition these kids had for the Audi.

The leader's face softened, her eyes narrowing in concern. "You mean Mr. Drummond?"

They knew him by name? "Tell me about Mr. Drummond." Court was more than a little interested in what this group had to say about him. His late-night internet search had shown Drummond had a softness for homeless youth. Did they know about his foundation? Or, given how the one girl was checking out every car passing by, was there another, darker side to Berkeley Drummond?

The leader paused, sucked in her lower lip, gnawing at it for a few seconds before answering. "He's been parking there and going inside the building like forever. Every Wednesday. Like clockwork, ya know?"

The other kids gathered close, a supportive gesture, but Court could see the curiosity on their faces.

A blonde girl stepped up even with the leader. "Did he do something wrong? Is he okay?"

"Actually, we're investigating his death."

The leader of the group looked down, letting her sandwich slide back into her bag. Others stopped mid-bite. "He was here. He parked as usual and came over to say hello." Others nodded as if to confirm what she'd said, but no one else stepped forward to speak. "So, like, he came over, gave us each like twenty bucks, like normal. Asked us the usual. Went inside."

"What do you mean by usual? Did he do this every week?"

The girl glanced up at Court, her eyes glistening with pooling tears. She was having a hard time holding it together.

"Once, he brought us all some jackets. He makes them, you know? Jackets and pillows and shit. He said he was going to make sure we get new sleeping bags like next week."

According to its website, Colchuck Down made several products filled with high-quality goose down, most of it imported from China. The ever-increasing links between Northwest companies and China could not be coincidence. He would visit the company on Monday when it was open. Manufacturing or not, it was closed all weekend, and getting in touch with anyone from the company had proved futile.

"Okay. So, he comes over, gives you some cash and heads back over to the building. Then what?"

Leader-girl shrugged. "He disappeared inside. I've never, like, been inside that place. It's not teen friendly."

Someone behind her let out a derisive laugh. "Not street-teen-friendly anyway." It was interesting that the kid used the term "street-teen," not "homeless youth." Court would have to remember that one.

Drummond was kind to this group. They appeared willing, almost eager to help. "You never saw Mr. Drummond come back outside?"

The kids looked at each other, their heads shaking and shoulders shrugging. "Like I said earlier. We have to be back at the shelter before lockdown. We never saw him leave. His car is sometimes still here in the morning, like, maybe once a month? I figured he has, like, some sort of girlfriend in one of the apartments above."

"Can you all concentrate on Wednesday night? Close your eyes for a second and picture anyone coming or going from the building Wednesday evening. Anyone you've never seen before? Anyone unusual?"

One kid at the back had his eyes pointedly trained on his sandwich, but he didn't say anything. The others were unable to add anything new.

Ivy reached down to pick up a fly away napkin and stuffed it into her pocket. "Thanks, guys. If you can think of anything. If you remember anything new. Give us a call."

Court kept his eyes on the kid in the back who continued to studiously avoid making eye contact with him or Ivy. He was uneasy about something, but Court didn't think pointing it out in front of the gang would go over very well. The kid had his card.

BACK IN THE GARAGE, Court and Ivy agreed that Hunter was not a strong suspect. She had been obviously weirded out when she learned about the second key and its use. If she was involved, it was most likely via an accomplice. There was the fact Hunter was also a pretty convincing actress to take into account. The likelihood she would murder someone she considered her biggest client was pretty low, too. There was always the possibility she'd been hired by another client to make it happen. Maybe Ashena would have her client list all sussed out by now. It didn't sound reasonable, but then again, what was reasonable about killing someone?

Court leaned against the car after Ivy had climbed inside, lost in his thoughts. He wanted to take all the kids to a shelter, or put them up in a hotel for the night. The nights were getting cooler, and they would soon be fighting off winter. Court's stomach always flipped and churned when he encountered homeless youth—no, *street teen*s. Most were on their own because living at home was impossible for them. Some had mental-health issues; others were gay or queer. Some were runaways, but most were kicked out by parents who couldn't accept them.

He had been so lucky to have a family as accepting as his. He was seven when he had stood at the dining table after everyone's plate had been served and tapped his knife against his water glass the way he had seen his uncle do it at a wedding the previous week. The way it gained people's attention in a crowded room was very impressive. The whole family had turned to him. Even his little brother had stopped his incessant chattering from his high chair. He bowed slightly and said, "I would like you all to please call me

Court. No more Courtney. I am a boy named Court. I just wanted to make it official. Thank you."

He liked to think of the ensuing silence following his huge pronouncement as awe-inspiring. His mother though, who had already been calling him Court for at least two years simply said, "Court, honey, you know, this isn't exactly news to any of us."

He'd looked around the room, feeling a little foolish for standing up and being so loud about it. His mother reached over and patted his hand.

His oldest sister, Amelia, laughed and threw a roll at him. He reached for it and fumbled, flipped it upward, and caught with a wild gesture. She snorted. "You still catch like a girl."

Brittany clenched her fists and slammed them onto the table, on either side of her plate. "Mo-o-o-o-m. Can I go by Britt?" His two younger sisters and brother were too young to get it, anyway, and they were eating their supper oblivious to Court's big announcement. He'd never played anything but the boy in their games.

Court had a sense of love and belonging in his family that was rare and something to treasure. Acceptance. It wasn't until he was in college that he became fully aware of how incredibly lucky he had been--how few people had the same unconditional love and support from their families. Whenever he saw youth on the street and recognized any facet of himself there, he recognized how lucky he'd been. He'd never had to fight to be who he was on a personal level at home.

Ivy's quick tap on the horn brought Court back to task. He climbed into the car, and they drove back to the station. He called Stensland. When he told the lieutenant their next step was to pay house calls on the clients they could identify, the lieutenant demanded to know the names on the list before they proceeded. Court hung up with a growing sense of unease.

"Why did he want that?" Ivy asked. "Is he micromanaging us?"

"I don't know. Let's get back to the station and check out the list. Ashena must've made some progress while we were gone."

"Don't you think Hunter could identify all of them if Ashena can't?"

"Let's see what we have first, and get a warrant for the rest."

He spent the rest of the time in the car texting with Britt and Cami. Britt sent pictures of the cake she had made for the twins. She had made a pretty normal cake, but had written HAPPY BIRTHDAY M&M in the font used on the candy as a play on their names—Morgan and Mandy. The cake looked like a giant M&M as a result. It was pretty cute. He held it up for Ivy to see while they were stopped at a red light.

"This is what I'll be missing tonight. My niece and nephew's sixth birthday party."

"Cute cake. Six, huh? Doesn't that make them the same age as..." Her voice trailed off.

"Yeah. Bailey would have been six next week, too. My wife and my sister were BFFs. That's how I met Amanda.

Through my sister. As soon as Amanda got pregnant, Britt did too."

He touched the photo of the cake with his fingers. Maybe there would be a way for him to make it anyway.

18

ASHENA HAD LEFT A COLORFUL SPREADSHEET FOR THEM ON Court's desk. It listed the flower name assigned to each client, their telephone number and their legal name if she could find it. Of the eighteen clients, only nine were easily identified. One was Berkeley Drummond. The rest all used burner phones, or had a burner app running on their phone. They had the numbers, so, theoretically, calling them would be a first step.

The chance that someone owning a burner would answer the phone was approximately zero, and getting them to the point where they'd answer any questions about their secret activity was less than zero. Court was sure that if he had a secret phone dedicated to his dominatrix, and a number he didn't recognize called him on it, he'd toss it. No, he'd probably spray it and wipe it down, then toss it in the grossest garbage he could find. All, of course, after deleting the call history, pulling the SIM card, cutting it into pieces, and taking a sledgehammer to what was left.

Just as Court was about to text him, Stensland appeared at Court's cubicle. He was dressed in Saturday casual, looking like he was dropping in to check up on things. But Court knew it was most likely because the higher-ups were pushing.

Stensland looked at the list. "These are probably a waste of time. Still wouldn't hurt to call to see if anyone answers, tell them something has happened to Hunter. Maybe enlist their aid. As a matter of fact, I'm looking for something to do this afternoon. I'll take care of them."

This was bizarre. There was no reason for the lieutenant to step in and make the calls. "No need, sir. Langston and I are here for the evening. Doing our job. Besides, they might respond better if Langston makes the calls. Having a man call might throw them."

Stensland took the report, turning toward his office. "Not your decision, Pearson. I'm checking the burner list."

Ivy approached Court after Stensland had disappeared behind his glass walls. "What the hell is that about?"

"Politics. Let him call. Less work for us to do," he said. "Why don't you call these other guys? I am betting they'd talk to a woman easier than a man."

"Okay. Should I set up meetings with them?"

"Give them a story." In spite of the way Stensland had approached the calls, the idea of using Hunter as bait would go a long way. "Tell them that a crime was committed at Allegiance Investments and you need to know where they were Wednesday, Thursday and Friday nights. Keep it nebulous and check on their alibis for all three nights. Anyone who doesn't have something clean-cut for Wednesday, we should talk to face-to-face. Have them come in tomorrow morning. I don't care if it's a Sunday. I'm guessing some of them have wives who don't know anything at all about their relationship with Mistress Fidelma."

"Sounds like a plan."

Court flipped on the computer screen and found the phone number for Haubek, the company that had made Hunter's card reader. He called, but got voicemail. A deep baritone informed him Haubek would be closed until Monday. Further searching gave him no new contact info, no emergency contact numbers, nada.

Audrey Drummond had given them contact info on her husband's personal assistant, but her phone went to voice-mail, too. He left a message for her to call back.

Court spun in his chair to see what Stensland was up to. The blinds to his office were down, but not closed, so he could make out the other man on the phone. Stensland caught Court staring. Their eyes locked as Stensland stood, reached for the blinds, and snapped them shut.

Court dialed Karen Hunter's number. She answered on the third ring. "It's Detective Pearson. I have a few questions I hope you can answer."

Court kept his eyes on Stensland's door as he spoke.

"Can you make it quick?"

"You know your iPad gave us your whole client list, right?"

"Berkeley was my most important client. My favorite."

"Wouldn't you want to protect your other clients? Why did you so easily hand over the iPad like that?"

"What are you asking, Detective?"

"Is there a client on your list that you want outed for

some reason? A connection between Drummond and another client on your list?"

"If one of my other clients had anything to do with Berkeley's death, I wouldn't do anything to protect them."

"Is there anyone in particular we should be looking at?"

She didn't answer right away. "My business is built on personal referrals, detective. Very close friends share certain details of their lives with each other."

"I don't suppose you can make this a bit more obvious for me, can you?"

"Detective, if the information on the iPad I gave you doesn't help you, then you should be looking at a different profession."

The fact she'd signed over the computer and iPad so easily should have tipped him off earlier. She'd wanted the connection to be made. In the bargain, she'd sold out all of her other clients. "I'll take that into consideration, Ms. Hunter."

Court closed his eyes, and the pieces fell into place. He stood up and strode across the room to Stensland's office, opening it without knocking. Stensland looked up from his desk, pen in hand making notes.

"Who is it?" Court asked.

Stensland sat back against his chair, steepling his fingers as he considered Court with his cold gray eyes. "Close the door."

Court cast a quick glance over at Ivy, who was watching them as she talked on the phone. Court threw her an apologetic smile as he shut the door. "Who is it?" he repeated.

"I don't know what you're talking about," Stensland said.

"The only reason you'd be making these calls is if someone higher up the food chain asked you to."

"You, Detective, are jumping to conclusions."

"Ah, come on, Lieutenant. Drummond dies, his buddy calls and asks you to keep his name out of the investigation, I'm right, aren't I?"

"Tell you what, Pearson. I have taken care of all the numbers on the burner list. The ones that didn't answer are never going to answer, and the ones that did gave me their alibis. I've checked them all."

Court opened his mouth, but nothing came out. He ran his hands through his hair before planting them on his hips. His mouth had gone dry. "You're telling me that you cleared nine people for murder in the course of half an hour? Over the phone?"

"That's exactly what I'm telling you, Pearson."

Court looked away, trying to calm the burning flame building in his chest. He leaned forward, palms flat on Stensland's desk. "Someone in power is obstructing an investigation, and you are helping them. You think I can walk out of here without an explanation?"

"Again, you are making some pretty vast assumptions, Detective," Stensland said, each word clipped and enunciated. "You will officially remove all nine people from your list of suspects and drop the line of inquiry entirely."

"You're worried someone like the mayor or the chief seeing a dominatrix would cause a scandal, and that's more important than catching a killer?"

Stensland's lip curled up at one corner. "Pearson, get the fuck out of my office and find the killer. Not a word to Langston about your little whacko conspiracy theory, either."

"Seriously? You want me to go out there and tell my partner, the one person in this whole fucking department who is supposed to trust me, that you cleared nine people? Nine? And tell her what?" Court was almost yelling now.

"You tell her I've handled it. Cleared them, exactly the same way you would have. Focus on the others." Stensland spoke through gritted teeth, pointing to his door the entire time. "That is a direct order."

Court met Stensland's eyes until the other man looked away before storming out of his office. He rushed past his desk to the elevator, smashing the down button five times in quick succession. He thought better of it, spun around and returned to Ivy's desk. She smashed the phone against her chest, looking up at him as though he'd strangled a kitten.

"I'll be back later. I am going to my niece and nephew's birthday party," he said.

"Whoa, wait, what happened in there? Pearson, you can't leave." Ivy held up a stack of yellow sticky notes. "We've got all this…"

He held up a hand. "Look, you keep working on those numbers, I'll do something else to make up the time to you. I need to get out of here for a while. I'll be back later."

She glanced at Stensland's office before turning back to him. "What is going on?"

Court looked away, unable to meet her eyes. "Nothing. Stensland is taking care of the people with burner phones. I *need* to get out of here for a bit."

Ivy sank back against her chair, jaw open. "Fine," she said in a clipped voice. "You go do your *thing*." She spun her chair around away from him, the phone already back to her ear.

19

COURT RACED HOME TO SHOWER AND CHANGE. HE DIDN'T see the point in busting his ass and ruining his relationship with his family when his lieutenant was pulling maneuvers like this on him. He'd been ordered to be part of some sort of cover-up, but he wasn't about to take it lying down. He needed to wrap his head around it before bringing Ivy into it.

Was the chief or mayor one of Hunter's clients? He didn't think Stensland would go so far as to cover up a murder. He'd keep what happened with Stensland from Ivy until he was sure about things. The last thing he wanted was to drag her into something that could blow all their careers. If he didn't tell her what he thought was happening, she would have plausible deniability in any ensuing internal investigation.

Fifteen minutes later, he was shuffling an enormous stuffed pig from his right to left arm so he could swipe his Orca card through the Metro bus scanner. He was sitting on a bus with a pig twice the size of a queen pillow on his lap. With a bright purple ribbon around its neck. He caught his image reflecting off the window across from him and laughed.

Court shifted the pig to one thigh and let it sit there like an oversized toddler, petting its floppy pink ears. Whenever one of the children on the bus dared to take a peek, he lifted one of the plush pink arms and waved. It became a game, with children covering their faces with their hands and playing peek-a-boo with the pig waving in return.

Early in his career, he'd been told how important it was to keep ties to family and friends outside the blue fraternity. Once you surrounded yourself with no one but cops, your view of the world twisted and warped into something too black and white.

By the time he got off the bus near his sister's house, he was thinking only of Morgan and Mandy and how much they were going to love the giant pig. He normally got each a separate present, but Britt had been clear that she only wanted one giant stuffed animal in their room.

Cami texted him letting him know she was going to be even later than he was. He figured she would show up knowing Britt had invited another "friend" for him to meet. Cami had a strange need to know who Britt picked for him and why. It was like a game with her.

Loud pops filled the air. Court grabbed at his gun and came up empty. A second round of firecrackers went off and Court shrugged off the tiny rush of adrenaline and chastised himself for being so jumpy. His sister had made him promise to leave his gun at home when he came to visit. Even though he agreed to do it for her, he always felt underdressed.

Unprotected. He missed the reassuring weight of it against his back. Sometimes, he wished SPD had a twenty-four-seven rule about carrying firearms. He couldn't even use his job as an excuse to keep it on him.

Court found the stack of gifts in the living room. He perched the pig on top of a large box occupying half the coffee table. Court liked the way it slumped to the front, looking for all intents and purposes like a guard pig, keeping watch over the pile of presents.

He turned to leave the room, but stopped at the book-shelves. At eye level was a photo he hadn't seen in a long time. The shelf was usually empty. It was an eight-by-ten of him, Amanda and Bailey. He was sitting next to Amanda, their bodies merging into a singular form from the hips down. Bailey straddled each of them, one leg hooked over one of each of theirs. He and Amanda were leaning forward so their cheeks were pressed together, their chins resting on the top of Bailey's head. In the back, the magic castle at Disneyland loomed up and away from them. The picture had been taken a week after they'd learned about the cancer. Their initial response was to cram as much childhood into Bailey before it was too late. Before Court had understood what was to come. Before Court's world had been turned upside down. Before Amanda and Bailey had died. Amanda already had deep circles under her eyes—dark half-moons giving her a starved look. Bailey was the only one grinning ear-to-ear in the happiest place on earth.

"I miss them, too."

Court whirled around as Britt's voice caught him off guard. He hadn't heard her come in. He turned back, reached out, and traced the image of Amanda with his finger. "You snuck up on me. I didn't know you had a copy of this."

"I know how you feel, Court. I do."

"You don't know shit, Britt." He laughed with the unintentional rhyme. A bitter, harsh, choked sound.

He heard her come closer. Winced as she put a hand on his shoulder. He shrugged it off. His emotions had been on a roller coaster all day. He needed to get through the next few hours before he could return to work.

"Court, I know how I would feel if I lost Patrick, if I lost Morgan or Mandy."

He spun around to face her, his face flushing from chin to brow. Britt stepped back.

"No, you don't. You. Do. Not. Know. You can't. The pain starts the same every day. Every day I wake up, and I remember they're both gone. I go to bed at night, wishing it's all been a twisted nightmare. Then, I dream about them. Sometimes, I want to stay asleep and never wake up."

He turned back to the picture. Amanda and Bailey, captured forever in time. Never changing, one never growing old, the other never growing up.

"You have to move on, Court. You're stuck in a self-destructive cycle. It's been a long time." She stepped in close. Forced a hand back onto his shoulder.

"What exactly, Britt, am I supposed to do? To move on. Everyone keeps telling me to move on. Dad, you, everyone. *Move on, Court.* I've moved from San Francisco, to get away from all those places … all those places we ate, played, drank, lived. Loved."

Her hand on his shoulder was warm, gentle. He resisted the urge to shrug it off again. The truth was the touch was comforting and familiar. Not the kind of familiar he was craving or needing, but it was better than nothing.

"You don't forget, sweetie. I'm not telling you to forget. You've got to remember, acknowledge what you've lost and accept it isn't going to come back. Not like you had it before."

"Easy to say. Easy to think you could do it. If you lost them all, do you think you'd be able to *move on*?" He spat the last two words out. Saying them felt bitter in his mouth.

"I think I understand how awful it would be. Worse than losing Mom. Don't forget, I loved Amanda and Bailey, too. They were a big part of my life as well. You don't get to hog the grief all to yourself."

She always brought up Mom. Parents were supposed to die first. Losing Mom had been painful, but after having lost Amanda and Bailey in such close succession, in such terrible ways, losing her had been easy in comparison. He had known the stroke would repeat itself and take her. He had flown down to say goodbye. She'd held his hand and told him everything would be fine, and he'd believed her. And it was.

"Maybe I shouldn't have come today." He ran his hands through his hair.

They hugged until his brief anger at her melted away like it always did, turning into a burning shame for having yelled at her.

She held him at arm's-length, fingers tight on his upper arms. Britt and he had always been close. Closer to each other than to any of their other siblings.

"Nonsense. It's only through the happy times that we can

counterbalance the bad times. And, I'm going to apologize ahead of what's going to happen next."

"Oh, Britt, please, not tonight. I've had a shitty day."

"Yes, tonight. I've tried to get the two of you together for weeks. I didn't think you'd get caught into super sadness when you walked in the door. I usually hide the photo when you're coming."

"You mean you normally leave it up? You've had it for a while?"

"Ages. I hide it between a couple of books when you're coming over. I got too busy today and forgot."

"Leave it out then. Because that's sort of silly, you know?"

"Not if you're going to get all gloomy like that whenever you see it."

He took hold of her upper arms, leaning in to give her a kiss on the cheek. "I'll get used to it if you leave it up, but we need to talk about you trying to set me up all the time." She hid her anger well, but something had just clicked. Her attempts at setting him up were some sort of whacked-out punishment. She still blamed him for Amanda's death.

"We can talk next week sometime."

Court wrapped his arms around his sister. "You need to stop trying to replace Amanda. I'll find someone when I'm ready. Okay?"

Britt pulled out of his embrace, tugging at his arm to follow her. "Come on. Let's go into the kitchen."

20

COURT FOLLOWED BRITT INTO THE KITCHEN. TWO WOMEN he didn't know were chopping veggies at the professional-sized butcher block serving as the kitchen's central focus.

Britt's husband, Pat, had spent six months of evenings and weekends remodeling when they first bought the place. He was good with his hands, and it showed. They'd removed the wall to the formal dining room to create a gracious kitchen with a family-friendly nook.

"Court, I'd like you to meet Candace and Madeline. Candace's son is in Morgan and Mandy's class. Madeline works with Patrick." Britt sounded like Monty Hall announcing the choices behind various curtains on *Let's Make a Deal*. Except Britt would only be trying to hook him up with one person at a time.

The two women slowed their chopping to a pace safe enough to look up at him. It took Court about ten seconds to figure out which one had been promised an introduction. Candace's face bore the hallmarks of a tired mom—no makeup, untamed hair sticking up at funky angles, a few wrinkles at the lips. Her clothing was decidedly lumpy and frumpy. She was a pretty woman, but she also had the general aura of being settled into her life, happy, content, not *looking*.

Madeline, on the other hand, was dressed casually with enough detail that showed a level of interest without coming across as desperate. Her jeans fit snugly around her hips and upper legs. The camisole she wore under a tailored sweater showed the soft mounds of her breasts with a cleft of cleavage that required some major support. She wore a gold chain with a small key, a gold ring and a charm of a pair of little red socks threaded through as a pendant. Her long dark hair was pulled back into a messy bun that left free strands drifting around her face in a soft halo.

He shook hands with each of them as Britt pulled out another cutting board and handed him a knife. The smell of meat on the grill drifted into the room as Britt slipped outside.

Picking up a zucchini and placing it on the board, Court sliced into it and addressed Madeline. "So, did my big sister tell you she was going to introduce us today?"

Madeline let out a laugh-snort and moved a pile of freshly sliced carrots onto a serving platter. "She told me about you a long time ago, but said you were too messed up to date anyone. Then, last week, she invited us to the party, and casually mentioned you'd be here. That's all."

"She was that blatant, eh?"

Candace picked up the tray of prepped veggies from the center of the counter. "I think this is my cue to leave you two alone." She swept out of the room with a grin on her face.

Madeline started in on a tomato. "You know Britt better than I do. She told me to come to the party today to check you out. To see if I was at all interested."

"Wow. I feel the need to apologize for the way my sister does things."

"She's direct. I like her."

Court paused in his chopping so he could read her face. "Exactly how direct was she?"

Madeline tilted her head to one side considering the question. Her eyes rounded a bit, understanding the subtext in his question. "As direct as possible." She gave him a long head-to-toe inspection, her eyes lingering at his chest before swinging back up to meet his face. "I'm cool. If I get into a person, I'm into that person, ya know?"

"So, I pass the initial visual test?"

She nodded as she moved thin tomato slices to a tray. "I would be willing to go out on a date, see what happens from there."

"Are you asking me out on a date?"

They both laughed.

"I think so," Madeline said. "You like movies?"

Court paused in his chopping. Movies were one of the few diversions he indulged in. Most of his time off was spent in a theater or home alone, streaming video. Madeline asked it in a tentative, gently probing question, betraying an under-lying guilt she had for liking movies a little too much. The kind of guilt that had her afraid to bring up the subject lest she came across a bit freaky. The way people who used drugs ask around the question before offering any up for use so they come across as less addicted than they are.

"Don't tell me," he said. "You're some sort of movie buff

who tends to go on and on about a movie until your friends tell you to shut up already?'"

She stopped chopping and stood stock still. "Wow. Britt told me you were a detective, am I that obvious? I admit to having a thing for black-and-white movies."

"Did you know they're doing a Hitchcock triple header at the Egyptian tomorrow?"

A fresh smile lit up her whole face and made the blueness of her eyes brighten and sparkle. "I was planning on going."

"Oh." A sudden disappointment stabbed at him.

"Alone. I mean," she added quickly. "I was going to go alone, unless I could find someone to go with me." She looked at him through her eyelashes, making the invitation clear.

Disappointment shifted into something else as his insides tensed. Conflicting senses vying for his attention. This was a good thing. A common interest. "Sounds like a perfect first date to me." Had he actually made a date for tomorrow? This wouldn't go down well at work. He'd find a way to get away for the afternoon. A triple feature might be pushing it. For the first time in years, he was hoping an investigation would hit a huge wall.

He caught himself staring into the cleavage he'd admired earlier. She was an attractive woman. They'd found a common interest in record time and already made a date. Maybe Britt's aim was getting better.

THEY CARRIED trays heaped with chopped veggies outside and into the full melee of the party. Kids ran around the grassy area, tossing a Frisbee. The darkening fall sky and cool air didn't slow anyone. The sun had been out in abundance all day, and its intensity had infected everyone.

He grabbed two bottles of beer from the cooler, and handed one to Madeline. She took a long drink from it. He was about to ask her what it was like to work with Pat when a bright blue neon disc hit him in the thigh hard enough to bruise.

A little girl ran up to him, grinning wide with a gap-toothed smile.

"Sorry, mister. I am not so good at aiming yet," she said whistling on all of her 's's.

Glad he hadn't cursed up a blue streak, Court forced a casual grin and rubbed at his leg. "You sure have a strong arm." He handed her the Frisbee.

She grabbed it from him, spun around and threw the Frisbee backhand toward a boy. It went over the boy's head, landing in the tall shrub screening the yard from the neighbors.

Her hands flew to her head, grasping one beribboned pigtail in each. "Oh, that wasn't supposed to happen like that."

The boy jumped up, grabbing at the errant disc, but he couldn't reach the top of the greenery. Court put a hand on the girl's shoulder. "Don't worry, I can get it."

He loped across the yard, pulling the Frisbee from the shrub. He handed it to the original target before returning to Madeline. The little girl had moved in closer to her, and Madeline's arms draped over her shoulder.

"It's okay, sweetie," Madeline was saying. "Why don't

you get some punch and try again. It takes lots of practice to learn how to aim."

"But, Mom, I've been trying for ages."

Court stopped a few feet away as he heard them talking. Mom? It struck him as both absurd and logical at the same time. Divorced? Then he remembered the ring around her neck. Widow. Crap. Well, maybe he could focus on her baggage instead of his own. That would be moving on in some small way, wouldn't it?

He finished the distance between them at a slower pace, trying to figure out the best way to handle things. He breathed in and out slowly three times, letting it go for now. It wasn't like anyone Britt had set him up with had worked out. Except for Amanda.

"I never got good at throwing one of those things," he said as he approached them. "I was more a basketball kind of guy."

Madeline stepped back, her hands up in the air. "Basketball? Oh. That's incredibly cliché. Please tell me you are *not* vegetarian."

Damn it. She was funny, too. So simple, so perfectly on target. Maybe a date or two to explore the whole situation wouldn't be a bad idea. He held his elbow out to her in invitation. "How would you like one of Pat's famous burgers?"

21

THE EVENING WAS WARMER THAN USUAL, AND THE OUTSIDE fireplaces pushed out a lot of heat. Court went inside to toss his coat over a chair in the kitchen as Cami came in through the front door.

"You made it." He lifted his arms for a hug, and she gave him a quick one and a kiss on his cheek.

She peeked around his shoulder to make sure no one else was around. "Yeah. Sometimes I surprise myself. So, who'd she set you up with?"

"Someone named Madeline. We're going to the Hitchcock triple header tomorrow."

Cami gave Court two thumbs up. "Quick work, dude. Though, will you have time with the big case and all?"

"Can't do much during the weekend. Got a few things we can do in the morning, but I'm betting I'll be free in time." He pointed toward the back and tilted his head. "I think Pat's got a couple of burgers left. Come on out."

Court was surprised she had bothered showing at all. The party was already winding down, and folks with the youngest kids had already left. He checked his watch. Eight thirty. There was a lot of time left, but he didn't think Pat and Britt were night owls any more.

He grabbed two beers from the cooler and walked over to where he'd left Madeline. Her daughter was leaning against her, droopy-eyed, with her lips wrapped tight around her thumb.

He offered a beer to Madeline but she shook her head.

"Sorry, we need to get home. It's way past her bedtime." She kissed her daughter on top of her head and smiled at him.

"Hey, can I get your number? I'm working a case, and if something comes up, I might have to cancel tomorrow afternoon."

Madeline started to give him her number, but he realized his phone was in the jacket he'd left in the kitchen.

"Give me your number, and I'll text you." She gave him a deliciously wicked grin. "Read it later. And, I've already found a sitter for tomorrow. I'm looking forward to getting to know you better, Court." She leaned in and kissed his cheek before leading her daughter back inside.

Court put a hand to his cheek where her lips had caressed him. Wow. It had been a tiny peck, but so simple and sincere. So natural. He watched the two of them until they were out of sight through the kitchen and beyond. Cami passed them on her way to the grill where Pat was still holding court.

Britt came up from behind him, startling him a little.

Beer oozed over the top of the bottle Madeline had refused before leaving. He captured the foam in his mouth. Great. Now he was drinking two-fisted.

"So, brother dearest, what do you think?"

22

COURT FELT LIKE A SCHOOLKID WHO'D SKIPPED A COUPLE of periods before sneaking back on campus. Ivy was at her desk, chin on one hand, while the other worked her mouse. It wasn't like he'd been gone forever.

She didn't acknowledge his presence when he came up behind her, but kept her eyes focused on her screen. He waited patiently behind her until she was done, holding the paper plate with a piece of cake out as a bribe.

"Want to tell me what happened in Stensland's office?" She wouldn't face him.

"Yes," he said, not adding any more.

She spun her chair around, holding up both hands moving in a 'give it to me' gesture. "Well, come on, Pearson. What's going on?" She eyed the cake.

Telling her Stensland had sworn him to secrecy would only intensify her curiosity. By not telling her, would he become a deeper part of whatever it was? Not including her would keep her free and clear, even if it did piss her off. No doubt she would accuse him of paternalism, or some other misogynistic shit. "Stensland cleared all the mystery clients with the burner phones. We're to drop them from our list as completed."

She stood up, closing the distance between them planting her feet shoulder width apart, hands on hips. She studied his face for a long, uncomfortable moment.

"Please, Ivy, don't push me on this one." Court hoped Stensland was protecting someone out of misguided politics and nothing more. He liked to think he was working for someone who knew where to draw the line. Until he was sure, he wasn't going to compromise his partner, regardless of their personal relationship, or lack thereof.

She turned her head and considered Stensland's darkened office for a moment before reaching for the cake. "Okay. Okay. Fine. For *now*." She grabbed her yellow tablet and handed it to him. "I spent all evening following up on the nine people Ashena was able to trace. One was Drummond. The others had varying responses to my call, but none of them were particularly interested in talking to me until I got kind of pissy with them. Five gave me alibis for Wednesday night I have verified over the phone. This leaves us three suspects from her client list. If we're really assuming all nine of the others are clear."

She dug the purple fork into the thick frosting and chocolate layers, cutting off a big bite.

"For now, at least," Court said, hoping she'd let it drop. The yellow sheet was covered in notes, a chart with the name and number of each suspect in one column, the alibi given for each night in the next column, and the names and numbers of people she had called to verify the alibis in the last. This must have taken her the whole evening. He'd have to make it up to her in some way. Maybe he shouldn't have run off to the party. .

She tapped the cake with her fork. "Man, this is amazing. Your sister made this?" She shoved another bite in before continuing. "At the top is Carroll Mullins, a high-level executive at Microsoft. The second is Giovanni Duffy. He was the mayor's most recent campaign manager. He's working for a GOP Senate candidate now. Neither have answered their phones or called back. I left them messages giving them the choice of coming in or letting us pick them up from their homes sometime tomorrow."

"A choice anyone would love. What about this third guy? Jim Schorr."

She took her time scraping the crumbs off the plate before answering, wiping at her mouth with a tissue she'd pulled off her desk. "So … Jim Schorr is an ex-Amazon exec with a start-up in Fremont." She paused, sucked in her lower lip between her teeth and closed her eyes before continuing. "The problem is, I know this guy. He's a member of my synagogue. His son and mine were in the same cohort. I can't even begin to believe he's into this, or that he'd kill anyone. I'm going to have to have you follow up on him since I can't. Total COI."

Court's bullshit meter was tilting into the red. "So, I get the connection being a minor conflict of interest here. There's more to this than you *sort of knowing* him, isn't there?"

She looked away for a second. "I did everything else tonight, so you could at least pick up some of the work."

Court held up his hands. "Okay. Okay. I'll get to it first

thing in the morning. I came back to see where'd you gotten. We should both go home and get a good night's rest."

"Yeah, I'm too tired to think."

Court followed her into the elevator, but she ignored him. He probably deserved it. It was late enough the buses had stopped running, so he snagged a taxi home.

Once inside, he took off his jacket, hung it on the hook by the door and removed his shoes. Amanda had instituted the no-shoe rule early in their relationship. He changed into his plaid Haflingers. The ritual had morphed into something he did every day when he got home, like Mister Rogers donning his sweater at the beginning of every show.

In the silence of his home, he could no longer avoid thinking about the way Audrey Drummond had talked about her husband's planned suicide. She'd been so steady and unruffled. Classically black-widow-y. There had to be more to her story.

Had expecting her husband's death made his death easier for her? He had expected Bailey's death while hoping for a miracle. But it hadn't made the reality any easier on him. The way Drummond had described her husband practicing with his gun was distant, clinical. The fact she hadn't tried to stop her husband when he was practicing with the gun bothered him. Too many years as a cop thinking and training about stopping guns from being fired, maybe? What if it had been real and not practice? What if he had blown his head off in front of her, after she'd had plenty of time to stop him? So many "what ifs." And he wasn't Audrey Drummond. And Berkeley wasn't Amanda.

He shuffled into his bedroom and opened the closet. Shoving aside the hangers holding his trousers, he unlocked the safe, feeling around for the velvet bundle. He sat on the bed with it on his lap, stroking the rich fabric before unfolding it to reveal his first gun. The same gun that Amanda had used to kill herself.

For years, the gun was a natural extension of his hand. The heft of it, the size, everything about it was perfect. He'd babied it. Cleaned it, oiled it, cared for it like any other part of his body. It was unloaded, but habit had him opening it to spin its empty chambers before closing it. The affirmative click sent a familiar surge of warm excitement and expectation through him even though it was empty. He raised it to his nose and smelled. Simple gun oil. Nothing more.

Had she done the same thing as Drummond? Had she spent any time considering where and how to shoot? Had she planned it ahead of time and waited for the moment when Court stepped into the shower leaving his gun on the dresser like he always did? She had left a note, almost illegible in her drug-addled script. Or, had she scribbled the note and shot herself without thinking it all the way through? He'd never know. Enough premeditation to leave the note. To make it clear she'd meant to kill herself. The why had destroyed him.

He'd been placed on leave during the investigation, taking an extra two months off after he'd been cleared and her death ruled a suicide. It was bad enough after Bailey died. Co-workers didn't meet him in the eye for weeks, mumbled incoherent sympathies and empathies, grasped his arm gently without words. None had seen the loss of a child. His was a singular experience, and then Amanda shot herself. Her note was taken into evidence, along with the gun and many of their belongings in their bedroom. Her journal.

How many people had read her private thoughts? And cops gossiped. As far as he could tell, the gossip hadn't all made its way up to Seattle.

Once the investigation was over and he'd gotten the gun back, he'd been unable to use it again. Couldn't stand the thought of carrying it around. The thought of shooting someone else with it was sacrilegious. He also couldn't sell it or get rid of it. It had been an intimate part of his life, and the last thing Amanda had touched.

He ran his finger along the short muzzle and imagined her lips wrapping around it, swallowing it up. She had made the mistake many people make, and aimed too much upward and sheared off the front of her face. He fell back onto the bed, cradling the gun against his chest as he fell asleep.

23

COURT SPENT AN HOUR SWEATING AT HIS LOCAL GYM before heading into the station. During his cardio workout, he read the latest on the train wreck in the mountains. The news of twenty-three dead and fifty-seven injured eclipsed the news of Berkeley Drummond. The paper ran the promised obituary, quoting a vague "close to the family" source as stating the death was likely related to the brain tumor he'd kept a secret from the public. The article stated that SPD had yet to make any comment. Links to articles on Colchuck Down, Drummond's history with Montpelier, and cancer took up the sidebar of the page.

He was inside the squad room before the October drizzle began. It was disappointing to see gray clouds gather and hang over the city only to get a slow steady drip. Thunderous lightning storms were few and far between in Seattle. In the three years he'd lived here, there'd only been one thunderstorm. It would be nice to have some flash and crash every once in a while. Endless rain without the rest was ... boring.

Court cleaned out the sludgy coffee remains clinging to the bottom and made a fresh pot. The Sunday morning squad-room atmosphere was peaceful. He was alone, with nothing new on the docket. He and Ivy were still the on-call detectives through the weekend, and he'd been thrilled to not have to divide his time between cases. This one was enough.

While he waited for the coffee to drip, Court checked his phone and noticed the text Madeline had sent last night. It was odd it didn't show up as new. Had he been so tired he'd forgotten it? She'd wished him a good night and sweet dreams, ending by telling him she was going to think of him as she went to sleep. It was a nice start to whatever this thing with her was going to be. And he hoped whatever it was going to be involved sex. Steamy, hot sex with a gorgeous woman like Madeline would make his life a lot more pleasant. Her texts were gently erotic without being gratuitous. He could hardly wait for the afternoon to arrive.

Court turned to work, hoping to plow through what they had as fast as possible. He would wait until nine to give the Schorr guy a call. Give him a chance to be coffee'd up. He transcribed what they'd learned the day before into something legible for the Monday briefing. He spent some time searching for a few good pictures on the internet to put up next to each current suspect list. He put their code names next to their legal names, reconsidered and deleted the flower references. Didn't seem necessary to out them all so blatantly. Bad enough that everyone working the case would end up knowing these men were all Hunter's clients. The guys with the burner phones were getting off easy in more ways than one.

He studied the photo of Jim Schorr on his company's

home page. Short-cropped brown hair, dark skin, simple suit and tie. The internet offered up plenty of articles to read. Self-made millionaire yada-yada-yada. The image search came up with a ton of Facebook photos. One of Schorr at a Mariners game had Court stopping short. Next to Schorr were two kids. He grabbed the photo of her son's bar mitzvah off Ivy's desk and compared the kids side-by-side. Ivy's son was sitting next to Schorr's. No biggie. She'd said they were friends. Court sucked in air as he recognized the dark curly hair draped over Schorr's shoulder. Ivy had admitted to a conflict of interest. She'd been less clear on the details.

He put the picture back on her desk. It was time to call Schorr. His cell phone went to voicemail, so Court tried the home number. Voicemail again. Didn't anyone answer their phones anymore? He didn't leave a message. No telling who might be picking up those messages. There wasn't a reason for the whole family to be in on it. He tried the cell number again. This time, he left a message demanding a response.

24

HALF AN HOUR LATER, IVY SHOWED UP IN JEANS AND A button-down shirt. Something less casual than her usual, while still being appropriate for interacting with potential witnesses if necessary. Her hair was free of its usual confines. He'd gotten so used to the tight bun that kept her hair under control, he'd forgotten she even had long hair. The curls she sported in her wedding picture had been shortened a few inches, but still managed to not go to the curly-haired-lamp-shade effect. She appeared ten years younger than usual.

She held a travel mug letting people know she was the *Best mom in the world.* The accompanying drawing was of a stick figure family holding hands standing on top of a blue and green earth rendered in crayon. It was the kind of drawing only a parent could truly appreciate.

Court lifted his own department-issued mug, half full of lukewarm coffee, in greeting. "You seem relaxed."

Ivy scowled at him and shrugged, not saying anything.

Court put down his mug. She'd been so chill last night.

Eaten the cake he'd brought her like they were friends. It was like she was an ice cube left out for a while to melt a little bit, then stuck back in the freezer overnight for a new hard-chill the next morning. It was strange how she would be interactive and all talky when it came to specifics on the case, but a cold fish otherwise. There was something in her body language and the way she spoke to him, or, rather, didn't speak to him. Even though she had been in Vice until last week, it felt like she had always studiously avoided him. He hadn't gone out of his way to get to know her either. Now they were partners, he had to make an effort. This less-than-enthusiastic greeting tipped the balance over.

Ivy rolled her chair from her cubby to his so she could share the monitor he was working on. She plopped into it and took a long drink of her coffee.

Court inhaled a steady breath. "Ivy, we've only been partners for a week, but I'm wondering if I'm the only one feeling like we're not gelling."

She gaped at him like he was an alien who was talking in a language she didn't understand. "Don't know what you're talking about." She turned pointedly to the monitor again.

"So, this"—he wiggled his fingers between the two of them—"this kind of interaction, it's normal for you?" The word on her was that she was relaxed and cool, even though she had a prudish streak.

"Pearson, we've got a lot of work to do. Can we get to it, please?"

"No. I hardly know you at all, but I get the feeling you'd rather be working with anyone else."

She crossed her arms and pushed her chair back from him a few feet. "Pearson, I don't care who my partner is as long as we get the job done. We can't jump into being best buddies. Besides, I am pretty sure we have absolutely nothing in common, other than our jobs of course."

"How would you know? The only conversations you engage in with me are all work related. You shut me down any time I try."

"And I'd like to keep it that way." She met his eyes, speaking without flinching.

Ouch. "I'm not asking to be best friends, but you come across as pretty cold."

Ivy held up her hands as if she was giving in. "I know you do your job well. I know I will learn a lot from you, but, I don't need you as a friend. Besides, you're the one with the walls, Pearson."

"What? What walls?"

"You stormed out of here after your little tête-a-tête with Stensland. Didn't explain anything to me—*your partner.* You can't tell me there's nothing going on there. I'm supposed to *trust* you. You never do anything with people after work. You say no to drinks. You don't show up to parties. You ice *us* out. It's not the other way around."

Hadn't she let go of the Stensland thing last night? A lot of what she said was true, but it hurt to hear it spoken out loud. He had intentionally cultivated a friendly-outsider persona for himself within the department. He took great pains to be open, to be willing to do extra work even in the face of obvious belligerence from some of the older guys. Even in San Francisco, he'd held himself apart from groups, especially after he was alone. When he had Amanda and Bailey, they'd gone as a family to gatherings. Amanda had leaned on the other spouses for support. Being a cop's wife comes with unique and special challenges. She had lived for a long time in constant fear he would be shot while at work. The irony was a bitter pill.

He had never been comfortable in the LGBTQ groups in either city. He presented as a man who liked women, and he was often given heat for "passing too easy" by other trans-gendered officers. The fact that he'd had early hormonal support through puberty and had transitioned before college meant he hadn't suffered much through career loss or change due to his transition. He knew plenty of people who'd actually been demoted or forced out of their jobs.

Everyone in the department knew about his kid dying, his wife shooting her face off, and the fact that he'd been born a girl. As much as he would have liked to have left that info all behind him in San Francisco, there was no keeping secrets in the cop world—it was its own microcosm clearly delineated by an infamous blue line.

No one ever approached him to talk about any of those things. Most people stuck to work in conversation. Or sports, the universally safe subject. Court surveyed the empty squad room, picturing people at their desks. He got along with everyone else well enough. Sure, he wasn't best buds with anyone, but they were like a big semi-dysfunc-tional family, like any police department. He lingered on Flanagan's desk, and his wrists ached from yesterday's Krav class. He'd had the most issues with him. Nothing overt—that would be illegal, and Seattle PD was known for being one of the most gay-friendly departments in the country.

Ivy wasn't done yet. "Dude, you need to see a shrink. After what happened yesterday at the Drummond house, I'm not sure I can trust you to be there for me if some shit hits the fan."

She might as well have slapped him. Was she talking about the momentary phase-out when Drummond was explaining how her husband was practicing with the gun? In the twelve years since he'd made detective, he'd never zoned out during an interview before. It was a complete anomaly. Partners had to have trust in each other. Her telling him she doubted he would have her back made him sick to his stomach.

This whole discussion was not going the way he had planned it in his head. She was supposed to say she'd try harder to be more open with him, and he'd do the same, and they'd be able to work side by side as they got to know each other. This judgmental shit about him needing to see a shrink was crap. He was fine.

He didn't want to talk about himself any more. "Why do you think Stensland shoved us together?"

She sighed like a disappointed parent, her finger tracing the blue outline of the little earth on her mug before answering. "I don't know. Maybe it has to do with the fact your partner retired and they pulled me in because they needed a woman on the squad for *gender equality*."

The way she turned away from him told him she was not telling the whole truth. "So, he stuck you with me since everyone else was paired up?"

"Have you ever compared our résumés side by side?"

"No. What has that got to do with it?"

"Everything." She held up her hand, ticking off each point on a finger as she went. "We went to comparable schools, got similar grades and awards. We entered police academies at the same time, spent the same amount of time on beat patrol, climbed up the ladder the same way. Until it was time to make detective. You made it two years ahead of me. Then, you moved up from San Francisco and snagged the *one* opening in homicide. I got stuck in Vice another three years because of you."

Ah. This explained a lot. Court had figured she carried some sort of grudge over his transfer into the department. He hadn't thought about their comparable history at all before. Hadn't known about it. She had taken a close look at their histories. It was sort of creepy.

"Don't you see? The only *real* difference between our careers is that I am a woman, and you are a ... *man*." She laid into the last three words with such force it might as well have been a physical punch.

She was pissed he was ahead of her because he had "switched sides." He'd known staunch feminists who thought his very existence was a betrayal to everything feminine before. Christ, he had no idea she was one of *them*.

He raised his hands to his face and rubbed at his eyes, the bristle of his facial hair already poking through his morning shave. This conversation was so loaded with land mines that he didn't want to move forward in case he stepped into something more explosive. He had to work with her, for a while at least. The only thing he'd ever found to work was to be who he was and let people get to know him. When they came at him from this far-out "you've betrayed your gender" attitude, it was hard. Some women didn't like any male no matter what their history. Ivy was married, though, so he had hope.

He went for the only clear way in he could find. He

switched the focus of their discussion for a second time. "Did it ever occur to you I had different skills that were needed here? Even though we have a similar time line, we don't have identical skills."

She tilted her head in closer toward him, getting in his face. "That's not the point, Pearson."

He held his ground. "Yes. It is. Do you remember why I came up here to begin with?"

"The Sino-Trans Case." Her eyes narrowed into slits.

Court shuddered even though he had brought it up. Hearing the name spoken aloud brought back the clear image of the thirty-seven decomposing bodies locked inside a shipping container. Some things cannot be unseen. The case was connected to a bigger operation of a Triad-based human trafficking ring. The notorious Chinese Mafia had been smuggling workers into Seattle via shipping containers. They'd bungled a shipment, leaving only three survivors. Court liked to think his ability to get those three to trust him had made the case go smoothly, but the Triad had closed up the avenue and disappeared from Seattle's spotlight. "And, do you remember why I was called up for it?"

Ivy folded her arms, speaking through gritted teeth. "No one in homicide spoke Chinese."

Court had her now, SPD had wanted someone fluent in Chinese with homicide experience. They'd called on their sister city for some help. The only reason he'd come up to Seattle in the first place was because he spoke Mandarin like a native. An opening came up while he was working the Sino-Trans case, and he was invited to stay. As far as he was aware, they'd never even looked at other candidates, Ivy included.

"Are you fluent in Mandarin, Ivy?" He sounded more snide than he intended, but what the fuck? She was all crossed-arms-and-teeth-clenched bitch, so why not lay it out there?

She focused intently on her coffee mug. They sat statue-still in silence for what felt like forever—interrupted only by the gurgle of the coffee machine expelling its final drops.

At length, she let out a long sigh, crossed her arms and leaned back against her chair. "Okay, Pearson. How the hell did a *goy* like you get fluent in Chinese?"

COURT MADE IT BRIEF, giving Ivy the syllabus of Court 101. Having grown up with a Chinese nanny was one of the many lucky things in his life. He and his siblings used to speak Chinese to each other when they wanted to hide things from their parents.

Ivy admitted to hearing the gossip about Amanda and Bailey from department wagging tongues. He still wasn't up for giving Ivy the intimate details, but sharing that he had known he was a boy from his earliest memory lightened his heart. His last partner had made it very clear he didn't want to ever talk about "it." They had co-existed for a while, becoming close friends after a year of working together.

"My parents were such hippies that they didn't blink an eye about me being a boy—they always told me they knew I was a boy from toddlerhood. They had a lot more of an issue when I told them I wanted to be a cop. In my family, that was some *real rebellion*."

She considered him in unmoving silence before responding. "Well, that was on the verge of being TMI, but I think we should get through this case together and see where we land."

Court understood her hesitation to pledge to be best friends. A decent working relationship would do. "Fair enough. Let's get to work, shall we?"

He put the disc from the garage surveillance into the machine. They fast-forwarded through the images, getting through eight hours in less than two—two eye-numbingly boring hours of footage. It showed Hunter's green Subaru Forester entering the garage and leaving at the times she had told them. That part of her story checked out. The only other people using the garage were quick in and out stops, most likely to some of the small retail shops, all of which closed by seven p.m. Eighteen cars entered the garage after five p.m. before entering the tenant parking area. There was no other traffic within ten minutes of four thirty or six fifty.

"They didn't have anything from the street view?" Ivy asked.

"No cameras facing the building. The closest intersection is a half block away."

"Well, that was fun." Ivy stood up and stretched. "You think there's any chance our guy lives in the building?"

"There weren't many cars entering during our time of interest."

She held up a list. "Eighteen. I wrote down their licenses. Might as well check them out."

"Why don't you run them while I go through the site videos." There was always someone assigned to take videos of the crime scene and the area surrounding it. Sometimes a killer got off on watching the tumult following his crime.

Court slowed the video occasionally, zooming in on every person as they came on screen.

He had a good memory for faces. The video showed only a succession of curious faces checking out the scene briefly before turning away when it was clear there wasn't anything to see. Everything interesting was upstairs out of public view.

25

"THIS IS CAROLL MULLINS. I GOT YOUR MESSAGE ABOUT Allegiance Investments. Is … Mistress okay?" His voice was a whispered baritone punctuated by the crackles and pops of a bad connection made worse by Ivy's crappy phone. Court leaned in closer, but Ivy waived him back and punched the volume up.

"The crime we're investigating has to do with a death at her office, but Mistress Fidelma is fine," she said.

"Oh, thank God."

"Mr. Mullins, can you tell me where you were each evening last week?"

"Sure. Right where I am now. In Australia with the family. Coming home Friday."

Ivy scowled at the phone. "Thank you, Mr. Mullins. I assume you can verify your whereabouts?"

Court gave her a questioning look. It would be easy enough for them to check on an international flight. Maybe she was trying to rattle his cage a bit. Ivy shrugged.

"Of course I can. What's this all about anyway? Who died?"

"We'll get to that in a minute, Mr. Mullins. We are talking to everyone who is known to have a card key to the system at Allegiance Investments. Do you happen to know any of Mistress Fidelma's other clients?" she asked.

"Me? No. I haven't told anyone else about my involvement with her. No one knows."

"How did you learn about her, become her client?"

"I looked her up on the internet. About six years ago."

"Why use your regular phone to contact her? Aren't you worried your wife might notice texts or calls from her?"

"My wife? She would never see them. Hey, wait. What is this all about? Hey, you know, this *is* an international call. Can't this wait until I am back next week?"

"We're investigating the death of Berkeley Drummond, Mr. Mullins. Do you have any kind of business dealings with him or Colchuck Down?"

"Oh, wow. That's too bad." His voice was distant, distracted. "Berkeley Drummond? She saw him, too?" He sounded like a wounded puppy left out in the cold.

Court met Ivy's eyes over the phone. Was that all Mullins cared about, who his mistress was seeing? Ivy shook her head and made a face.

"Mr. Mullins, did you know Mr. Drummond?"

"What?" he asked, almost inaudible now. "No. No. I never met the man. He was in manufacturing clothing."

Court scribbled on a sticky pad. Ivy read it and nodded, getting the gist.

"You both gave large donations to the same candidates in

the last election. Perhaps you met up at political fundraisers or other political events?"

"No. Maybe. It's possible, but honestly, I am shit at recognizing faces. Detective, I know you have a job to do, but talking to me isn't going to get you anywhere. If you have any more questions, you can contact my office and get my attorney's information." The line went dead.

"Wow. That went south fast," Ivy said.

"Easy alibi to check."

"Clears him, too." Ivy tapped the screen on her phone. "Yeah. But why would he be calling me in the middle of the night from Australia? It's four thirty in the morning there."

"He said he was traveling with his family, right?"

"Oh, right. Not likely to make that phone call in front of his wife. Got it."

BEFORE SHE COULD POCKET her phone, it rang again. "Langston."

"Yes, hello? This is Giovanni Duffy. You called me last night. I don't appreciate being threatened with a visit like that out of the blue."

Ivy made a face at the phone. Her voice was sweet and without any hint of irony as she replied. "Thanks for calling me back, Mr. Duffy."

"Well, what is this all about, then?"

"We have some questions about your relationship with Mistress Fidelma," Ivy said.

There was a long pause. "I don't think I want to talk about this over the phone."

"You're welcome to come down to the station, discuss things here."

There was an even longer pause. "Fine. Give me directions."

This was surprising. Court checked the time and made some mental calculations. They could finish their report for the briefing tomorrow before Duffy showed up. That interview would take them through to early afternoon. If he was lucky he would still be able to make it to that triple feature with Madeline.

26

THEY WERE IN THE MIDST OF PUTTING TOGETHER THE smart board presentation for the briefing the following morning when Giovanni Duffy arrived with a woman dressed in a tailored business suit. Court wasn't at all surprised he'd shown up with a lawyer in tow, and in less than an hour. The guy had money. Court wondered what it was with rich men and dominatrixes. Maybe all men secretly harbored a desire for women to take the lead now and again, but only rich men could afford to go to professionals.

Court ushered them into one of the interrogation rooms while Ivy set up the recording equipment. He read him his rights and went through the whole recording-the-conversation spiel, wondering the whole time what they were likely to get from him under the circumstances.

"Thanks for coming in," he said as Ivy returned and sat next to him.

"Would you please get on with it?" Duffy asked. "I have no idea why you called me down here."

"Well, as Detective Langston informed you, there was a death at Allegiance Investments. We want to talk with you about your connection there." Court paused, hoping the other man would volunteer something. When he didn't offer anything up he asked, "What is your relationship with Mistress Fidelma?"

Duffy didn't even look at his attorney. "She is my dominatrix. I see her once a week."

"And?" Court prompted.

"And what? It's not like we're dating. She performs a service, and I pay her for it."

"What service would that be?" Court asked.

The other man sat back and crossed his arms. "Pretty sure specifics don't matter. The only thing you need to know is we don't have a relationship outside of our weekly sessions. We don't talk, we don't email, and the only time we communicate is to double check or cancel session times via text."

Ivy leaned forward, halving the distance between her and Duffy. "Tell us how you get into her office."

Duffy looked a little nonplussed, but he pulled out a card key identical to the one they'd found in Drummond's wallet, except it had a picture of a daisy on it instead of a rose. "I swipe it, and it unlocks the door."

"What else do you know about the system she uses?" she asked.

His eyebrows merged into a single thick line as he tried to figure out what Ivy might be getting at. "Well, it's a pretty normal-looking thing, as far as I can tell it's like any other card system out there. Don't know the brand, never thought about it. Looks and works like any other system as far as I know. What're you trying to get at?"

Ivy shrugged. "How well did you know Berkeley Drummond?"

Duffy blinked a few times, his eyes widened, and his mouth dropped open. It took a few seconds for him to gain control of himself. "Oh hell. Berkeley Drummond died in Mistress's office? Is she okay? She's n-n-not in trouble, is she?" He spun in his chair to face his attorney without waiting for their response. "Julie, if she needs an attorney, I want you to help me find the best one." He turned back to Ivy. "She's okay, isn't she? I mean, she couldn't have hurt him on purpose or anything. She's incredibly professional and careful."

"I asked you about Berkeley Drummond," Ivy said. "Can you tell us how you knew him?"

"Met him a couple times at Rotary meetings, I heard a news report about him dying." He stopped abruptly. "Oh. Wait. You're doing an investigation to make sure it was natural causes, aren't you? Mistress had him as a client, and he kicks it while with her? Well, you sure as hell better see to it that it's natural causes."

The attorney hadn't said much to this point, but now she reached over and put a hand on his forearm. "Giovanni," she said, "You need to be quiet now. I think we can all see you are very upset that your dominatrix might be facing criminal charges, but you need to answer the questions and stop jumping to conclusions."

So far, Duffy's response had Court thinking Duffy was in the clear, unless there was some connection between him and Drummond they hadn't found yet. Or, if their only connection was Hunter. Could there be some sort of personal battle between clients? The way Duffy was talking, though, made

Court pretty sure about one thing. "You don't know her legal name, do you? You only know her as Mistress Fidelma."

The other man's cheeks turned splotchy read. "No. I could have found it out. It wouldn't be hard to do a search on the lease situation, but I was told to not try. She didn't want me contacting her at home or knowing anything about her private life. I respected her wishes."

"Tell me about your relationship with Berkeley Drummond." Court said.

"We didn't have a relationship. I met him a couple of times at fundraisers. He supported the mayor in this last election cycle. We exchanged a few emails about campaign issues. I oversaw all the major donations to the campaign, so I saw his checks, wrote the thank-you letters."

"Where were you last Tuesday, Wednesday and Thursday evenings?" Ivy asked.

Duffy had to refer to the calendar on his phone. "Tuesday I was at a board meeting for my son's school. Wednesdays, I go to a club. Thursday … went out to dinner with the family, then came home, did homework with the kids."

"Which club were you at on Wednesday, Mr. Duffy?" Ivy asked.

Duffy closed his eyes and exhaled loudly, shoulders slumping. "Belle Nuit."

Court exchanged a glance with Ivy. "The private BDSM club? How often do you go there?"

"Every Wednesday. And sometimes on Tuesday afternoons." Duffy tilted his head up to the ceiling and rubbed at his face. "There's a new member orientation every Wednesday. I volunteer to help with the refreshments and small group tours."

A club and a private domme once a week? That must be hard to hide from a spouse.

"You can give us names of people at the school and the club who will verify this? Receipts for the restaurant?" Ivy asked.

"Yes. Of course, but the people at the club, they don't know me by my name. We all use different names there."

"And yours is?" Ivy asked, her pen paused above her tablet.

Duffy glanced over at his attorney. She nodded for him to answer. "Is there any way you can skip writing this down? I mean, if this ever gets out, it will be humiliating for me. Maybe even wreck my marriage. My wife has no idea that I go there anymore or that I saw Mistress. She would be more than devastated."

Court pointed at the two-way glass, reminding Duffy they were recording everything.

"Mr. Duffy, if you want us to verify your alibi for Wednesday night, you'll want to make that as easy as possible. I would imagine facing a murder charge would be even harder to explain to your wife."

Duffy shrank back against his seat, his face drained of all color. "You don't know my wife."

27

COURT AND IVY SPENT THE REST OF THE MORNING DOING paperwork and prepping for the briefing. They made a list of everyone in the apartments above Hunter's studio, correlating their cars. After putting together packets for the uniformed officers to use for interviews tomorrow, he called Belle Nuit. No one answered and the recording said they were closed for the day. No sense in going over there if no one was around. He left a message asking anyone who might be around to give him a call, but he didn't expect a response. Following up on Duffy's alibi would have to wait until tomorrow afternoon or evening. It was going to be a bitch of a day.

"I'm betting he's in the clear," Court said. "The way he reacted when he heard about Drummond? He was worried about Hunter and not himself. He didn't come across as guilty so much as embarrassed and worried what will happen if his wife finds out what he's up to on Wednesday nights."

Ivy put her hands to the back of her neck and rolled her head around as her fingers kneaded away. "Yeah. Hunter must have some power over guys to make them jump in to help like that. I mean, think about the money Drummond is leaving her. They're both super protective of her."

Most of the so-called paperwork was actually digital and stored in the nebulous "cloud." There were still forms to fill out, and they had plenty of documents to organize. Court scanned in his sketch of the crime scene, which had all the measurements written down without being proportional. He'd have to go in later to make a more accurate version if the case made it to trial, but this was all he needed to document for now.

Court added the photos he had taken on his phone to the official photographer's file and deleted them from his phone.

Ivy took over when it became clear her PowerPoint skills were way better than his. She had flow charts down to a fine art.

While Ivy finessed their presentation, Court worked through the contacts that Audrey Drummond had come up with. He completed the last call as Ivy pushed back in her chair.

"I'll write up the interviews with the kids and add it to the file."

"Learn anything from them?" she asked.

"Not a lot. Got the same story as we got from the mom, pretty much. All three were out of town on Wednesday. All three have alibis. All three have witnesses for their alibis. And, all three claimed to have known about the tumor. None of the three had spoken to him in the last week other than to confirm they were coming out for the weekend. Apparently, Drummond was planning a special family dinner on Sunday."

Court paused. It was inconceivable to him that none them had called their dad the entire week while knowing that each time they talked to him might be the last. Court talked to his dad at least twice a week, even if it was only for a half-minute check-in. The Drummond family might have plenty of money, but Court's had plenty of love. He shook his head. "Anyway. The daughter brought up Henri Montpelier as a possible suspect. Interesting, since Audrey Drummond was so adamant that Montpelier was not capable of hurting her husband."

"You think there's anything to it? Seems like a long time out for a revenge killing."

"Had to check it out. So I called the Montpelier house, and asked to talk to Henri. The woman who answered identified herself as Monica Montpelier, and then told me I'd have to wait another week to talk to Henri. He's been in Oregon for the last three weeks doing a silent retreat. At a Buddhist monastery."

Ivy laughed. "Seriously? So, did you get the number at the monastery?"

"I did. They're next on my list. But, I don't think anything is going to come of this. Unless he could sneak in and out of the monastery, drive five hours, kill Drummond, and drive back, with no one noticing."

"So, if they are under a vow of silence, do the calls go to voicemail?"

So there *was* a sense of humor in there somewhere.

"Good one, Langston. I'll call the monastery to complete the circle, but I think it's not going to take us anywhere."

She stood up and stretched, her t-shirt lifting enough to give him a peek of her stomach. Deep, angry silver lines ran up and down on either side of her belly button, testaments to her children who thought she was the best mom in the world. Women put up with a lot of shit when it came to their bodies. Ivy rolled her chair back around to her own desk. "I think we can write Drummond's kids off as suspects, too." She shrugged into her coat. "I'm out of here. My husband was more than a little pissed about me missing the ballet last night. He kept the sitter and went without me. Took someone from his office with him instead. A woman. Oy." She spun back around to grab her mug, actually smiling at him as she left.

When he called the monastery, the person answering the phone identified himself as a resident monk. He verified that Montpelier had been part of a ritualistic seventy-two-hour, Buddhist sitting-thing between Tuesday morning and Friday morning with another dozen people. He would have been noticed leaving. Court crossed Montpelier off the list.

Court finished the requests for the toll-bridge records for Wednesday evening. Staff at the Washington State Department of Transportation didn't work weekends, and Court didn't have access to their website the way he did the DMV's. By the time the briefing was over the next morning, he'd have confirmation of Drummond's bridge crossing time. He guessed it would be close to six thirty. Given there were several eyewitnesses who saw him minutes before he used his card key to enter Hunter's office at six fifty-five, it was more a formality, but Court wanted all the pieces in the timeline to be as accurate as possible.

He whipped out a bunch of warrant requests for the following day. He didn't want to hit Haubek or Colchuck Down unprepared. The judge on duty today was known for being signature-happy. They'd walk in with warrants in hand for both places. He drew a broad warrant for Colchuck. Given this was Drummond's business, it was a no-brainer. Almost any scrap of paper in the building would be up for grabs.

Getting a warrant for "everything" at the security company, on the other hand, might be a bit trickier, even with Judge Rollins wielding the pen. He asked for all records pertaining to the system at Hunter's office, a list of all clients using the same system, personnel records for all Haubek employees, and the physical components and software records of the system removed eight weeks ago. Maybe they kept the broken pieces.

The fact that Drummond's card key was used didn't mean he was the one to do the actual swiping. But, surely, one of the teens would have told him if Drummond hadn't been alone.

While he'd been on the phone, Drummond's personal assistant had left a voicemail. She was on her way back to Seattle and would meet them at Colchuck tomorrow morning. Any time after seven would be fine.

Court texted Mary Coleridge to see how things were going with the train derailment. She texted back giving him a tentative time of Tuesday morning for the autopsy. Court doubted it would give them any major surprises. He'd seen enough dead bodies to have a pretty good idea how Drummond had died. It would be nice to confirm he'd not been drugged and to set aside any doubt that Drummond had willingly allowed himself to be tied up. It wasn't like television, where magical forensic evidence would pop up with miracle answers. This case was going to take regular, normal detective work.

28

COURT PURCHASED THE TICKETS FOR ALL THREE MOVIES and leaned against the granite wall of the theater, letting the narrow burgundy tarp overhead shield him from the drizzle. Madeline appeared around the corner wearing jeans tucked neatly into leather boots and a Gore-Tex raincoat covering everything but the roundness of her face. He checked the sky, but it didn't look like it was going to start pouring any moment. She slowed her pace as she scanned the crowd outside the theater. When she finally found him, her lips whipped upward into a warm grin as she dodged around people to get to him.

He pushed away from the wall and held up the tickets.

"Oh, I'm glad I didn't buy them online after all. What do I owe you?"

Why did dating have to be such a minefield? If he offered to buy, was she going to be pissed or pleased? "Maybe you could get dinner." Her eyebrow popped up, so he added hastily, "Or popcorn."

She laughed. Court's heart leapt in his chest, feeling as though it stopped cold for three full beats. The harmonic cadence of her laugh was identical to Amanda's. The rhythm and key of it was different than Amanda's, but the intervals of her laugh moved up and down the same way.

"Popcorn it is." She turned toward the theater doors, assuming Court would follow.

He had to stop thinking of people in terms of how they related to Amanda. Stop comparing everyone he met to her. He caught up to Madeline in line, suddenly unable to think of anything coherent to say. He couldn't ask about her daughter because he couldn't remember the kid's name. With her braided pigtails and kaleidoscopic dress, she was a veritable Pippi Longstocking. Even though they had been introduced the night before, he couldn't dislodge "Pippi" from his brain.

"I'm glad I made it. Parking is a bitch around here. I don't know how you can stand it."

"I don't have a car. Parking is no problem."

"Well, I wouldn't either if I didn't have to schlep Lucy around to things. Metro would add a couple of hours onto everything we do. At least Boston had a decent subway."

Lucy. Pippi's real name was Lucy. Court thanked the god of small things Madeline used her name before it got awkward. "Boston ... explains the socks on your necklace."

She reached for the chain around her neck, sliding the charms and ring back and forth. "Originally, yes. I moved here after Jake died. I wanted to make a clean start. Away from ... places."

Court totally got that. He had moved from San Francisco for the same reason. Melancholy reared its ugly head, and he shoved it back down. Court decided to go for the deep conversation. Might as well figure out the extent of baggage they had going on between them. "So, how did Jake die?"

Madeline spun around to face him, but instead of shock or anger, she was smiling, looking bemused. "No one asks me about Jake like that. Most people usually pussyfoot around, hoping I'll tell them so they don't have to."

"Believe me, I am well-schooled in Avoidance 101. I'd have a master's degree by now if they offered one."

Her features settled into soft compassion. "I bet it's even harder for you."

Did she feel sorry for him? "Is any death easy to get over?" His words had come out harsher, more bitter than he had meant them. He dropped his gaze to his feet, trying to get a grip on the conversation, to prevent it from spiraling into the ground. "I'm getting the idea Britt has told you a lot about me. She hasn't been quite so forthcoming about you."

They made it to the head of the line and their conversation was interrupted by the kid behind the counter. When Madeline asked for extra butter and a box of Junior Mints, his dream combination, he felt a little weak in the knees. Hitchcock, buttery popcorn, Junior Mints. The triple crown of a perfect movie date.

They settled into *North by Northwest* as the first in the lineup. Their fingers occasionally vied for the same piece of popcorn, hers gently flicking him away, his following the drenched buttery bits with mock aggression. A couple of times, Madeline grabbed his wrist as the tension in the film ratcheted up.

A fifteen-minute break allowed them to hit the restrooms,

buy more food and stretch. By the time the second movie came on, the theater was filled to capacity.

As Grace Kelly first filled the screen in *Rear Window*, he heard Madeline sigh next to him as she leaned in close. Her lips buzzed gently against his ear. "I have always crushed hard on her. She was so gorgeous, and her clothes totally slay me. I wish we could dress like her, such class."

"You can dress like her any time you like. I know I wouldn't mind."

She laughed again, this time quietly against his ear. She nuzzled him with her nose before kissing his neck. The warmth of her lips on his skin sent an instant shiver of desire through him.

Was the kiss an introduction or an invitation? He turned in his seat to look at her, but she was already focusing back on the film. He settled into watching the rest of the movie.

During the next break he embraced her lightly as they stood to stretch. "What do you want to do for dinner?"

"Pick up some Chinese takeout and go back to your place. My sitter is spending the night at mine."

"Still want to stay for the third movie?" The promise of an overnighter was more than a little distracting.

Her eyes flashed with mock indignation. "What? Skip my favorite?"

He leaned in close, tilted his head to one side and paused with his lips an inch from hers, grazing her nose with his. "May I kiss you?"

"Oh, a gentleman who asks. Yes, I would like that."

He brought a hand up to her cheek, running his thumb across her lower lip. He kissed her tentatively, making sure of the angle before pressing in further, gauging her response.

The kiss was short, lacking the awkwardness so often found in first times. They parted with matching smiles, their noses circling around each other. As *Psycho* rolled onto the screen, Court put his arm around Madeline's shoulders inviting her to lean into him. Her head fell into the crook between his shoulder and neck. Court lowered his cheek to the top of her head, the warm lavender scent of her hair a refreshing and relaxing newness.

Amanda hated lavender.

<hr />

COURT CONVINCED Madeline to leave her car overnight where she'd parked it. They picked up takeout and walked arm-in-arm to his house. He talked her into the little Lebanese place that would serve up better food than anything Chinese in the area. She promised she would eat anything he ordered, so he ordered things previous dates had refused to touch. He wouldn't make it long-term with someone who refused highly spiced eggplant and kibbeh.

She leaned over the kibbeh, her eyes sliding over him suspiciously. "This is raw, isn't it?" she asked.

"It is. It's the national Lebanese dish. Highly prized, and this is the best in Seattle."

She took a tentative bite. "Lamb? Mint." She took more, closed her eyes. "Oh. Allspice, too." She swallowed and sipped at her wine. "So, do I pass?"

"Was it that obvious?" He wiped a crumb of bulgur from her lips.

She shrugged. "You picked the weirdest thing on the

menu? Had to be either because you wanted to impress me or test me."

"Maybe you should be the detective."

She laughed. "No, thank you. I'm happy with my crayons. But, since you brought it up. What got you into police work? Isn't it an odd choice for someone like you."

"Someone like me?" Court asked.

She colored. "I would expect you to be super liberal. Like your sister."

Nice save. "I am super liberal. Not every LEO is a gun-crazed Republican, you know?"

"Leo?"

"What we call ourselves. Law Enforcement Officer. Cops, FBI, SS, ATF, we're all LEOs."

"Oh. Okay. So what got you into it?"

Court wiped his fingers on a napkin. "Well, I used to watch a lot of TV. You know-- *Columbo, Cagney & Lacey, In the Heat of the Night.*"

"Wow, I haven't thought about any of those in years. I used to watch 'em with my dad. *Quincy, Murder She Wrote,* too."

"Loved them all. I was always figuring out the answer, sleuthing things out. Knew who did it before they did. Every time. Well, almost."

Madeline eyed him over her glass. "But, weren't they designed that way? So the audience had it figured out before the lead on the show?"

"I didn't know that at the time," Court said. "Anyway, when I was eighteen, I saw this woman get mugged. I didn't even think about it, I took off after the guy who'd hit her and snatched her purse. Threw him to the ground. Sat on him until the cops showed up."

"That's what got you into it? The chase?"

Court shook his head. "No. It wasn't the chase. It was the way she thanked me. She'd cashed her latest paycheck. She and her little kid would have been out on the street without the money in her purse."

She stroked his cheek. "I like that."

Court turned to kiss the palm of her hand. "That's what keeps me on the job."

"Does working homicide do the same thing?"

"When we solve a case, sure. There's something powerful about giving a survivor answers. When people die, their loved ones want to know why. How. Putting a murder in context helps them get through it."

"Do you still watch cop shows?"

"Sometimes. There are some good ones out there, but now I know the diff between TV and how things really work, I can't stand some of the crap that's out there. Like *CSI?* That show makes it look like test tubes and microscopes come up with all the answers. But, there are a few that have shitty science but are fun to watch anyway. You know, for the relationship drama. They're really soap operas with a thin veneer of mystery layered on top."

They ate in silence for a couple of minutes.

"Does seeing dead people all the time bother you?"

Now that was a loaded question. Court took his time chewing his shwarma before answering, trying to figure out what she was *really* asking. "It gets to me, sure. Doing my job means someone's dead. Often, it means they died violently.

Would I be happy if I were out of a job? Sure. The world would be a better place without killing."

There, the nice PC answer was out in the open. Might as well go on with the whole truth of it, show her his warts. "But, another part of me loves what I do. It's powerful. Finding a killer? Knowing you've *got* him. There's nothing like catching the bad guy. It sucks someone had to die first."

"Your world is kinda filled up with guilt, Court," Madeline said, stroking his cheek.

Court refilled their glasses. "Your turn. I asked you earlier about Jake, but you didn't tell me what happened to him."

Madeline's lips twitched into a partial smile. "He was a Marine. Killed in Iraq."

There was some competition he wasn't sure he wanted. "Have you always been drawn to men who have dangerous careers?"

"Yeah. I guess, maybe. I've always been attracted to strong, smart guys." She moved in closer, a finger dancing over his chest.

"Didn't Britt tell you how fucked over I am mentally?" Court asked, grabbing her hand to pull it against him, stopping her from tickling him further.

"Given what you do, what you've been through, the fact you're not under the table drunk every night shows a kind of strength."

He drew her into his arms, filling his fingers with her hair, gently pulling her head back into the perfect position for a kiss.

COURT'S ARM WAS NUMB. He'd forgotten what it was like to have the nerves pinched off long enough to deaden the feeling from shoulder to fingertips. He slipped his arm from underneath Madeline's head, wiggling his fingers and working through the pins and needles.

He sat up so he could see the alarm clock. It was only five thirty, but Court needed to hit the early Krav class before work.

He kissed Madeline's neck to wake her. Leaving her alone without saying goodbye was not an option. "Hey, you, I gotta get going. Big case and all."

She stretched her arms over her head. "It's not even six. Seriously?"

"Work. Six a.m. Krav class. If I run I can make it. You can sleep in, stay as long as you want. Food in fridge is all yours." They had managed to toss leftovers into the refrigerator before ripping each other's clothes off on the way to his bedroom.

Madeline sat up on her elbows, tilting her head back, her dark hair falling in luxurious waves onto the pillow. The sheet dropped from her breasts, pooling at her waist.

He reached over to cup her left breast with the palm of his hand. Rolled her nipple into hardness between his thumb and forefinger. "You're evil."

"I thought you needed to get to work."

29

Court ran the two blocks to his bus, waving the driver down to stop and re-open the doors. The driver gave him a fake stern expression as Court swiped his Orca card through the scanner. "If you didn't look like you were about to run down a bad guy, I might have kept going, Detective."

"Sorry, Maggie. I slept in." It was six forty-five, and he had substituted Krav with glorious morning sex. Madeline had been thoughtful and brilliant to make it so she could stay at his house. He wasn't late, but he had plenty to do before the briefing started.

The bus ride was long enough to help him transition mentally to work. Awesome as it was to start the day with sex, he needed to switch gears and stop grinning like he'd won the lottery.

It was finally Monday, a real workday, and they'd have access to the full departmental resources. The key people they needed to talk to at Colchuck and Haubek would be back at work. The standstill enforced by weekend hours was over. There were six other active homicide cases, a record in recent memory, but Berkeley Drummond would be up as prime. Newness and novelty would make his murder top priority with everyone. And Court was feeling it. For the first time in years he was eager to solve a case and not simply blindly fill his time with work.

Court walked by the main entrance to headquarters, noting the small gathering of reporters outside. He pulled his hood up to hide his face in case anyone noticed him sneak past toward the side entrance. The *Times* report had said there would be a press conference later this morning. Stensland, no doubt, had set this up without even consulting him. He raced into the squad room, relaxing when he saw only three others in house yet. It was early on a Monday, and things were a little slow to get moving. In spite of his lingering in bed, he was actually early. He dropped to the floor in his cubicle and did a set of fifty pushups to make up for skipping Krav.

He set his desktop computer up to share with the computer in the conference room, and had the tech working by the time the others trickled in with cups and mugs of coffee in hand. A few held purchased drinks from local coffee shops. Two women detectives held BPA-free water bottles— one glass, one metal. Three women in a sea of men. No wonder Ivy had been so prickly about her long-sought-after promotion. The word about Drummond's death had gotten around. People talked in excited tones as they waited for the briefing to start. As much as high-profile cases were a pain to work, they were exciting and made excellent gossip fodder.

Lieutenant Stensland walked in, waving the morning paper over his head like a lasso rounding people up. "We've got a front pager, people. Someone finally noticed Berkeley Drummond died. This means press, and press means stupidity, and everyone being followed for a juicy story." He pointed the paper at Court and Ivy before tucking it under his arm. "Before you begin, I want to remind everyone in this room everything you're about to hear is confidential. You must not leak anything said today to anyone outside this room." He looked over the top of his thick glasses, through his heavy eyebrow fringe at everyone in the room to emphasize the point. His gaze landed longer on the dozen uniformed officers he had brought in for some extra feet on the ground. Once the silence became uncomfortable, he gave Court the signal to start.

Court flipped on the smart board, starting with the crime scene photos. "This is Berkeley Drummond. The Lieutenant was able to get a generic press release out on Friday night, but once the word gets out that we're investigating this as homicide, it will immediately turn into the word *murder* in the press. We honestly don't know if this is ultimately going to be murder or manslaughter or even accidental. We can be reasonably assured it will be one of those three classifications, likely murder given the circumstances."

He told them about the brain tumor and the planned suicide. "The one thing we know for certain is Berkeley Drummond did not end up like this of his own accord. Our chief objective is to find whoever got him into this position and left him. Why, and whether it was accidental or purposeful will become clear when we find said person."

He put up a photo of Berkeley Drummond he'd pulled from Colchuck Down's site—the living, healthy looking entrepreneur he had been. The fact he'd been a big donor to the current mayor was well known, but the list of other donations he'd made in the last five years was a little more diverse, crossing traditional political party lines a good deal. He tended to play toward left-wing social politics and right-wing business interests.

He clicked on a photo of Hunter he'd found on her daughter's Facebook page. "This is Karen Hunter, AKA Mistress Fidelma." In spite of the innocuous and wholly boring clothing, a few catcalls and other appreciative sounds made him pause for a couple of beats before he continued. "Drummond was seeing her on a regular basis in her office, where she found his body. She was the 911 caller."

He ran them through the working theory about how the killer gained access, fooling Drummond into thinking he was the dominatrix. It sounded a little iffy, and Court could see more than one skeptical face in his audience. "We're pretty sure Hunter's in the clear, but there is a chance she was working with an accomplice."

He outlined the work Ashena had done with the card keys and how they figured into that theory. "We're about ninety-nine-percent sure whoever has the duplicate card key is the person of interest or let the person of interest into the office."

The next photo was of Audrey Drummond, in a sparkling evening gown taken at one of her many fundraising events. According to his internet search, it was all she did. With her kids gone, he wondered what else she had to do. Had she grown bored with giving money away?

"The victim's wife is a prominent socialite. She's an obvious suspect, and we're looking into her alibi for Wednesday evening. She said she was home all night, and her personal assistant backs that up. If Drummond did have the brain tumor, we can probably knock her off our list. It makes no sense to kill someone who is dying soon."

A few chuckles made him pause for a moment. Close friends and employees don't always make for the most reliable witnesses. Anyone who made it to Homicide had been lied to plenty of times. It made them all skeptical of everyone. Not exactly in a healthy way, either.

"We interviewed both the domme and Drummond's wife on Saturday. Both confirmed Drummond had an appointment to see the domme on Wednesday evening. The wife says she wasn't expecting to see Drummond home after his appointment." A hand shot up.

"You're telling us the vic not only told his wife he was seeing a domme, but she was *okay* with it. I heard that right?"

A buzz of concurring disbelief filled the room.

"Yeah, I know. I know. The wife told us herself she knew about the domme before we asked her about it." Court raised his arms overhead with his hands stretched out, waving them to silence. "Trust me, I was pretty dumbfounded by this, too. But apparently, it's good. We need to accept the fact Audrey Drummond knew about the domme. Whether she's as cool with it as she makes herself out to be is still in question."

He went to the next slide. "We're reasonably sure neither had a direct hand in the murder. However, we have some more things to look at before we can remove them from the list."

He put up a slide of the three Drummond offspring, their names and their current locations underneath. "As you can see, Katharine Drummond is local. However, she was in

Hawaii at the time of death. David Drummond lives in Texas, and he has a solid alibi with plenty of witnesses. Their youngest, you may have heard of him. He's Samuel Drummond, the civil-rights lawyer. He was appearing before the U. S. Supreme Court on Thursday and Friday. It's unlikely he could have been in Seattle on Wednesday night and still make an early court appearance across the country. Besides, we've confirmed he was out to dinner with Senator Murray on Wednesday in DC, so I think he's got a couple of pretty reliable alibis there."

More laughter.

"All of them had planned to be in Seattle by Saturday evening. All canceled their trips when they got the news late Friday night their father had died. All said they would come for the service next week instead of flying home immediately, with the exception of Katharine who returned home on her planned flight Saturday morning.

"They all thought their dad was stand-up. Samuel mentioned a huge shift in his dad's politics. Sounds like they felt pretty bad after Samuel's attack. Looks like they did an about-face when it came to gay teens, in particular." Court summarized Samuel's street history, his being kicked out of the house for being gay, his beating, Audrey and Berkeley's subsequent political shift, and their focus on street youth—a penance for their sin against their son.

"We've identified most of Hunter's clients. All but two"—he paused to give Stensland the eye—"are cleared as suspects. I've left a message with one, Jim Schorr, but he hasn't responded. I'd like"—he pointed to two officers—"you two to find him and bring him to the station sometime today for questioning. You can let me know when you've got him here."

Court forwarded to the slide of Giovani Duffy. "This is Giovanni Duffy. He came in yesterday and was fairly cooperative. He claimed to be at the Belle Nuit club Wednesday evening. Langston and I'll be checking it out tonight."

A few laughs, more catcalls. There wasn't much difference between a room full of cops and a room full of middle-schoolers when it came to anything sexual.

"Next steps…" He pointed to the remaining uniformed police in the back row. "You'll be interviewing everyone in the office building—all of the businesses sharing the same hallway are traditional nine-to-fivers and all the tenants of the apartments above Allegiance Investments. I want you to talk to everyone in the buildings adjacent, behind and across the street. Even the teens we talked to on Saturday should be questioned again. Langston and I will head over to Colchuck and talk to Drummond's assistant and other employees. We'll also hit Haubek to see what they can tell us about the security system and how the second key was made."

30

COURT WAS ADJUSTING HIS GUN INTO THE SMALL OF HIS back, getting ready to head over to Colchuck, when Ivy reappeared, waving a bunch of papers at him. "Is that the toll report?" There was an excited twinkle in her eyes he'd never seen before, telling him there was something more than what he had been expecting.

Almost every car owned by someone crossing the bridge on a regular basis had a little electronic sticker—a transponder—on the windshield that was scanned when it entered the toll zone. Court had found the system useful in more than one investigation.

Ivy spread the papers flat on his desk. Three lines were highlighted. The first indicated an Audi passing under the toll device heading Westbound on the I-520 bridge at 18:35:10 Wednesday. The second indicated a Mercedes passing under the same ticker at 18:35:24. The third indicated the Mercedes returning Eastbound at 19:43:22. Both vehicles were registered to Berkeley and Audrey Drummond.

"Shit. I knew she was lying about something."

Ivy tapped the paper for emphasis. "Fourteen seconds behind? She followed him in. Maybe even went inside with him."

"It only proves they drove across the bridge at the same time. She could have gone anywhere after that."

"Sure, but the fact she lied *and* said she was home all evening indicates she was trying to hide she'd come into town. If she'd come into town and wasn't following him, she wouldn't have lied to cover her tracks. She would have told us where she went."

"But those kids said they talked to him. They didn't mention seeing anyone else with him," Court said.

Ivy frowned for a second. "Doesn't mean that she wasn't there. She probably parked somewhere along the street, watched for him to go inside. Maybe she stepped into the café to wait for him while he talked to the kids."

That left about half an hour for her to follow him inside, tie him up and leave him hanging. Court let the implications sink in for a second. "Assisted suicide?"

"Makes a lot of sense."

"I don't know. Why would Drummond do something that would bring Hunter under scrutiny like this? Remember how Duffy acted when we brought him in? His first reaction was to protect her." Audrey Drummond had lied to them about being home all evening. He couldn't let that drop. "Let's see what she has to say when confronted with the log. Get her off her own turf, too. Let's bring her in."

IT WAS GOING to take at least an hour before Audrey Drummond could be located and brought in. They had time to get over to Colchuck Down and back. If she came in before they were done down there, she could cool her heels in an interview room like a normal person.

The morning commute was reduced to its usual midmorning trickle, and it only took them ten minutes to get to the Colchuck Down building. Decrepit buildings were the mainstay of the area, but the occasional company was coming in and buying up old and replacing it with new. Drummond had done this in 2009, when the real-estate markets across the country plummeted with foreclosures everywhere. He tore down everything on half a city block and replaced it with a white metal and glass structure. The press had called Drummond a leader in American industry, bringing manufacturing into the dawn of a new architectural era. The building's design had been hailed as a shining example of modernity and progressive pragmatism. Clean, well-lit, well-ventilated work spaces with an outdoor courtyard for breaks were touted as the new way of doing business. For workers, anyway.

Add in the fact Colchuck Down started pay at thirty bucks an hour for their lowliest workers, and the company employees were fiercely loyal.

They pulled up to the largest building on the block and parked in the space marked off for Berkeley Drummond. Large plate-glass windows across the entire front of the building gave them a view of a modern lobby sectioned off from the factory floor beyond. Large machines surrounded by people, their bodies moving in fluid synchronicity, took up the ground floor of the building.

It was hard to tell exactly what each machine did. Bolts of fabric were fed into one end of a machine, disappeared into its depths and were spit out at the other end in various shapes. At the far end of the floor, the process became more obvious with people sitting at sewing machines piecing long strips together. It looked like the entire factory was set on sleeping bag mode. Maybe they produced sleeping bags for a week then switched everything over to vests or jackets. Everyone on the floor worked with a quick precision Court would find boring after a day doing it. Centralized offices hovered over the factory in a dramatic yet not looming way.

They entered the lobby, a spare but clean space with no seating area leading up to a broad wooden desk. A woman in her late thirties sat behind the desk, her face splotchy and swollen. She did her best to smile at them when they entered. She waved to where they had parked. "I'm going to have to ask you to move. No one is allowed to park there." Her words were thickened by obvious grief.

Court pulled out his shield and one of his personal cards. "Sorry, but the space was empty."

She wiped at her nose with a tissue. "No respect for the dead. Are you here to see Ms. Mooring?"

Court nodded and the woman pointed to the door to the side as she buzzed them in. She directed them to a row of polished leather chairs within the inner door. "Wait there. I've paged her. She'll be down in a minute or two."

The steady thrumming, thumping and thwacking of the factory machines would give him a headache within an hour. Everyone working inside wore orange or red plastic earmuffs, which he doubted would cut all the noise. Being cooped up inside all day, every day, doing the exact same thing over and over was about as boring as anything imaginable. Being a cop was dangerous, but it wasn't monotonous, and it sure as hell wasn't boring.

A woman appeared around the corner, her quick step negating her heft with a surprising lightness. She was tall, wide and round all at once. Instead of a sweet cherubic face such bulk often conveyed, hers was angular enough to compete with the Wicked Witch of the West. Her eyes were bright, almost hawk-like in the way they stared at him. Unblinking. Critical. Court felt like he was a schoolkid at the principal's office.

"This way, then." Agnes Mooring guided them up, past an inner office sporting a desk with her name on it, and directly into Berkeley Drummond's office.

This was a large spacious room, but not beyond what might be considered simply "well-appointed." Its furnishings were high quality, but functional. It bore no resemblance to the Drummond home. The house and office were two entirely separate fiefdoms.

Agnes Mooring spun around, hands on hips, or at least where he thought there might be hips underneath the roundness of her flesh. "Now. Detectives. The news hasn't said anything of substance about his death. But you and I know Berkeley Drummond didn't die from his brain tumor, now did he?" The last two words were less a question than a scolding statement.

Court had wondered how open Drummond had been at work about his illness. "The media can't report on information they don't have. We'll be doing the autopsy tomorrow. Did everyone at the company know about his condition?"

She snorted. "The news often doesn't have any of the

details. I know more about glioblastomas than I ever wanted to." Her bright eyes focused on Court again. "Only the family and a few key people here knew about it."

She picked up a pad of paper and pen from the desk. "This is all the people at Colchuck who knew. We kept it quiet because news like that could affect stock prices. Not in a good way, I might add. His death has us down fifteen percent this morning."

Court watched as she made the list. Her writing was neat and refined, easy to read upside down. Her sausage-like fingers worked the thin pen in delicate strokes across the page with a grace defying their bulk.

She ripped off the paper, thrusting it at him. "Everyone on the list is either on the board or at a level with a 'need to know' kind of job. So, what *really* happened?"

"We'd like to see his official calendar," Court said.

Court could tell Agnes was not used to being put off, but she bucked up and waved at the computer on his desk. "He had dropped most of his work obligations. The last month he'd been coming in one day a week to guide us in operations. Mr. Greer, the current vice-president of operations, was going to be made CEO officially at this coming Thursday's board meeting."

She typed away, fingers moving with deft control, stopping abruptly after a few moments to stare at the screen with a furrowed brow. "This is strange." She clicked a few more times, shaking her head and harrumphing. "There's nothing on his calendar. Everything from Friday onward is gone. Even this week's board meeting. Not that there was much left on his calendar anyway. He had been handing things off pretty steadily."

"Did he shunt his appointments to anyone else?" Ivy asked.

"There weren't many left, to tell you the truth." Her lips twitched and she made a strange half-cough half-groan sound in the back of her throat. "It looks like he canceled everything. It's not like he *needed* to be here anymore, but it's odd. He didn't do any confirmation emails or anything."

"We'll need the details of your trip in order to confirm your alibi." Court said.

"My trip?" Her eyes widened as she figured it out. She shook her head with an aggression that would give some people whiplash. "I had no reason to kill the man I idolized. Besides, he was dying already. I was already freaking about how little time we had left." She waved her hand at the computer. "This tells me he was planning on not coming back."

"Had he talked to you about committing suicide?" Court asked.

Agnes fell back against the chair. Her lips twitched and curled into a snarl. "No. He'd never kill himself. Berk ... Mr. Drummond was a fighter. He would never give up without a fight. He was fighting his cancer with vigor."

"What do you know about Mr. Drummond's Wednesday evening appointments?" Court kept it vague on purpose. He wondered how a woman with such keen perception could not know about her boss's extracurricular activities.

She sat up, suddenly alert. "Wednesday evening. I think he spent them with his wife."

"Are you sure?" Court asked. "Mrs. Drummond informed us that he was otherwise occupied on Wednesdays."

"Ah. I see. I knew that he was seeing that ... that ... *creature*." She spat the word out. "But, I didn't know if Audrey knew, or what she might tell you. I ... didn't want to embarrass her. She's such a dear."

Creature? Someone had no love for Karen Hunter.

"What did you know about their relationship?" Ivy asked.

Agnes pursed her lips one shoulder shrugging into her dangling earring. "Not much. One day, about two years ago, I was clearing away some papers, and his phone was on his desk. He sometimes would leave it here while he went to the bathroom. He'd dropped it in the toilet once. Sort of awkward that way."

Each woman he'd talked to about Drummond had given him a different picture of the man. Audrey had painted a saint, Karen Hunter had portrayed him as tired and needy, and, now, Mooring was describing a kind-hearted klutz. He was, no doubt, all those things to some degree.

"Anyway," Agnes continued, "I saw a text from someone named 'Ma'am' telling him to...." She paused as she swallowed and shuddered. "She told him to shave." The frown of disapproval deepened the lines on her face as her eyes shifted into tiny slits. "You know. His private bits, but she used crude words and was very demanding about it. When the text popped up, I was so shocked, but couldn't help myself, so I read it."

Court could picture her standing there behind the desk, thumbing through his texts. "Did you ever talk to him about it?"

"No. It broke my heart a little bit, thinking of such a strong smart man like that, doing whatever it was they did.

But, he was always out of here by four o'clock on Wednesday afternoons, and I knew where he was going. I tried my best to not think about it. If I thought about it too much, I might have lost respect for him."

Ivy put her hand on top of the monitor. "Did you ever come across anything from this same 'Ma'am' again? More texts? Emails? Notes?"

"No. I did my best to not notice anything about her. There were signs, though, you know? Sometimes, he'd come in on Thursday mornings, and there would be red welts on his wrists, or he would sit down more slowly." Her eyes watered. "To need that in your life?" Anguish washed over her face and softened her sharp features.

Court had run into so much as a cop, he'd learned that people could get off on doing just about anything. He placed a hand on the woman's plump wrist. "Can you tell us who might have wanted to murder Berkeley Drummond?"

"Murder? So, it wasn't suicide? I knew he wouldn't kill himself." Her other hand went to her chest, pressing her paisley blouse against her freckled skin. "He was a good man, detectives. He was. But he wasn't perfect. There was the whole Montpelier affair. But that was years ago. Before Samuel. His poor boy." Her eyes widened as she spoke Samuel's name as if it were a top-secret code. "That woman."

It was a little creepy that she seemed happy he had been murdered. Was the taint of suicide so horrifying? Was suicide solely the responsibility of a single person? "We know about his son and about Montpelier. Is there more to it than the newspaper reported?"

"Mr. Drummond bought Henri out mere weeks before

stock went through the roof. Henri came back to claim that he was supposed to receive more for his patent than he had, but the courts ruled against him. He hadn't read his contract very closely."

"Was there something intentional in the way that went down?" Ivy asked. "Did Mr. Drummond force Montpelier out?"

"No. There wasn't anything malicious in any of it. But, Henri didn't take it very well. I think he and his wife retired out to North Bend or Snoqualmie. No. That's not it. Issaquah. They're in Issaquah."

"Didn't they get into a fight or something? At a Mariners game?"

Agnes let out a derisive snort. "That was an over-reported exaggeration. The press treated it like a drunken brawl, and it was nothing of the sort." She turned her watery eyes on Court. "Henri was an honorable man, and what people don't know is that Mr. Drummond has been paying him profit sharing ever since, even when he didn't have to, even after winning the case. Mr. Drummond felt bad about his old friend being shorted. He's been on the payroll as a consultant bringing in six figures, all because of Mr. Drummond's soft heart."

"If he'd stayed, what would Montpelier be making?" Court asked.

"More like millions. But, honestly, detectives, I don't believe there's anything there." She turned her gaze back to the monitor, clicked the mouse a couple of times and printed out contact information.

Though they'd already cleared Montpelier; Agnes's take on this wasn't exactly useless. It backed up Montpelier's story

and explained how he could afford to spend days sitting on
his ass in a monastery in Oregon.

She raised a hand, suddenly remembering something.
"You should talk to Mr. Wu about what he was up to last
week. Mr. Drummond was furious about something. He
called Mr. Wu in here and they had quite the row. After
yelling at each other for several minutes, they both got so
quiet I couldn't hear a word they were saying." Her words
picked up speed as she spoke.

Court wondered if she had been holding a glass to the
wall for the details. "Were you always in the habit of
listening to Mr. Drummond's conversations?"

Agnes flushed, pursed her lips. "They were rather loud,
especially at the beginning. They spoke more quietly for
upwards of half an hour. I don't have any idea what
happened, but Mr. Wu was upset when he came out of the
meeting, and Mr. Drummond even more so."

"What does Mr. Wu do here?" Court asked.

"He's a shipping manager. He handles all incoming shipments from overseas. Double-checks the stock and matches
them against inventory."

"When was their argument?" Ivy asked.

"Berkeley was only coming in on Thursdays. Had to be a
week last Thursday."

"And you have no idea what they were arguing about?"
Court asked.

"Nope. Their words were muted through the walls."

"We'd like to speak to Mr. Wu. Can you call him up
here?" Ivy asked.

Agnes' eyes narrowed, and she returned her attention to
the computer. She typed rapidly focused intently on the

screen. She raised an eyebrow and looked at Court with an "I-told-you-so" look. "Huh. Isn't this interesting? He's not been to work since Wednesday."

"Is there anyone here who is close to Mr. Wu we could talk to? Maybe they know more about the argument," Court said.

"There's a break in ten minutes. I can take you into the courtyard and introduce you to the people he works with most closely."

"Okay, let's do that. Meanwhile, let's talk a little about what we need you to do for us."

"Anything. I'll do anything if it will help you find out who killed him."

People were always saying that. They're willing to help, *to do anything.* Half the time it was an empty promise. In this case, however, he was certain Agnes Mooring would come through for them. She was invested in Drummond and the business. She'd be helpful. "I want you to go through the last week's emails, correspondence, files, anything in his desk. See if you can find anything that would explain the argument between him and Mr. Wu. Maybe Drummond wrote something down, made a note somewhere. Did he keep a journal?"

"No. He made notes on his calendar, sometimes. Is there anything specific?"

"We need anything that could explain what was going on. Make a timeline of all his activities from Monday morning on. Where he was, who he was with. No matter how trivial, you never know." He thought about her earlier obfuscation around the Wednesday night dates. "And, no matter how embarrassing it might be for Berkeley Drummond, we need it. If he's got another thing going, like the domme, we need to know about it. Okay?" Every time he heard a Chinese name connected with shipping, his heart rate went up a notch. His history with the Sino-Trans case would have him jumping to all the wrong conclusions if he wasn't careful.

Agnes Mooring flushed but lifted her bulk out of the chair. "I'll get you everything, uncensored, as soon as I can. Of course, I'll need a warrant. The board wouldn't look kindly on me throwing open our files to SPD without one."

31

"OKAY, PEARSON. FILL ME IN ON WHAT THEY WERE ALL talking about in there." Ivy buckled her seatbelt.

They got nothing out of the other employees. Wu worked at the loading bay as a foreman, checking in bundles from the shipping containers. He was in charge of opening and inspecting each shipment's inventory against the shipping labels. He had a team of six, all Chinese.

Colchuck Down grouped workers by language. The Mandarin speakers were in receiving and shipping. The Spanish speakers pieced together fabrics at the heavy industrial sewing machines. The Vietnamese ran the strange funnels that forced the feathers into various products.

Court finished typing Wu's address into the GPS. "Something is going on, but they are generally suspicious of cops. A few are illegal, and they didn't want to be caught. They know that Wu is off work due to an injury, but no one was willing to talk about it. They were being super cryptic, even though they had no reason to think I could understand them. They're uneasy about something. Maybe Mr. Wu will be more informative."

Court got Ivy going in the right direction before checking his voice mail. One was from the uniformed officer sent to collect Audrey Drummond. He had located her taking a mud bath in a private suite of a swanky Eastside spa. No one at the spa had enough of a spine to order Drummond out of her sloppy cocoon and so she had not yet arrived at the station.

A text from his sister reminded him about dinner. One was from Cami telling him she needed to talk to him in person afterward. Maybe she'd drive him up to Belle Nuit, too.

Madeline had texted four times. One was a selfie that showed a picture of her reflection in the full-length mirror of his bathroom. The room was steamed over, her naked body swathed in seductive clouds. A thick dollop of shaving cream sat on her sweet mound. She held his straight razor in her free hand. The text read, *Hope your day goes smoothly.* He let out a small groan. Whether it was from the bad pun or the smoldering desire to touch her, he wasn't sure.

"You okay, Pearson? You sound like you got hit in the stomach or something."

Court cleared his throat, looking for words. "Uh, yeah. It's nothing." He hadn't taken Madeline for a naked selfie kind of girl. Not that it was a bad thing. He didn't mind receiving them, but he hoped she didn't expect a response in kind. That was not going to happen.

32

BEACON HILL WAS ONE OF THOSE SEATTLE
neighborhoods with a real mix between the good, the bad
and the ugly. In one area were cohesive housing communities
working together on crime watches, block parties and trash
cleanup—both living and not. Other blocks were filled with
disparate low-income workers, families scraping by on jobs
that paid minimum wage—or less. On another street work-
ing-poor, law-abiding folks sequestered themselves from the
rabble.

Ling Wu lived in one of the latter neighborhoods. A
house where there might have been a happy *Father Knows Best*
sort of family when they were originally built in the 1950s
might today be filled with an extended, multi-generational
family. Maybe fifteen to twenty people sleeping crammed
together in rows across the floor of a bedroom. If Immigra-
tion wanted to do blanket raids, this is where they'd come.
Except the people living here were mostly Chinese, and

those anti-immigration prigs concerned themselves more
with Spanish-speaking workers.

Chinese people didn't bother them as much. Maybe the
image of people walking directly across the borders freaked
people out more. Maybe the fact it took more effort to get
here from China made people less wonky about Chinese ille-
gals. Maybe the Chinese hid themselves better.

As they got out of the car, Court and Ivy were greeted by
three sullen, droopy-eyed boys sitting on the front stoop of
the house. Court was well schooled in apathetic, bored kids.
He'd grown up around plenty of kids like this, and he knew
how to play them.

The porch was crammed full with worn out chairs and
was piled high with boxes. The lanky youths sat on the floor
of the porch, backs against the chairs, legs dangling down
toward what might have once been a flower bed, but was
now a scrabble-earth wasteland.

The oldest boy tilted his chin at them, the movement
throwing his sleek black bangs off to the side and clearing his
eyes at the same time. "Whatchya want?"

Court held his badge up close to their faces. "We're
looking for Mr. Wu."

"I'm Mr. Wu."

Court cocked his head to one side, his eyebrow shooting
upward with a clear "don't give me any shit" signal.

The teen rolled his eyes. "He's at work."

Ivy put a foot on the bottom step of the porch, leaning
forward on her elbows. She reached down and pulled a dead
weed out of the ground, tossing it at his feet. "He's not
working and you know it."

"He's sleeping then."

Court stepped into the empty flower bed and met the boy eye-to-eye. "Wake him up."

The smallest of the three backed away and ran into the house, all the while the one who had spoken continued to stare directly at Court. As far as Court could tell, there wasn't a lot going on inside.

"You must be good at poker," Court offered.

The kid broke a tiny bit. His eyes blinked, and he jerked a shoulder upward. "Not bad. Better at Mah Jongg."

"You and your grandma? You're too young for Mah Jongg."

Ivy moved up the steps and stood at the door, watching where the smaller kid had gone. He reappeared, holding the door open and beckoning them inside.

The house was tidy. A short Chinese "po-po" teetered in the kitchen doorway, hands on the frame for balance. Her white hair was parted in the center and pulled back behind her ears. Wrinkles lined her face from forehead to chin, testifying to a hard and long life. She wore an apron over a traditional high-collared silk shirt. Her shockingly small feet were clad in elegantly embroidered shoes. Bound feet? Here? How old *was* she? He'd never heard of anyone binding their feet in the United States. Not even eighty years ago.

Behind her, the kitchen counters were covered with bowls of chopped vegetables waiting to be cooked in the giant wok set on an improvised, and certainly illegal, wok rack. It sat on a large metal drum in a corner, with a hose running from behind to a propane tank on the floor. Aluminum foil was duct-taped to the wall behind the contraption. A thick layer of grease crusting the foil testified to the fact it had been used frequently and for a long time with no obvious explosions. A rice steamer blinked green, sending little aromatic puffs into the air. The familiar smells of bamboo shoots and Szechwan peppercorns vied with another familiar odor —incense.

Three glowing incense sticks stood in a sand-filled bowl in front of a fifteen-inch-tall statue on a tall wooden table next to the door. Court recognized the long glowing beard and fierce face of Guan Yu on the statue. The figurine held the customary halberd in his left hand. Plates with bits of food offerings and small scrolls surrounded it. Court's stomach did a triple flip before settling into a general flutter of angst. Crap. Maybe he was overreacting, but regular people—even regular Chinese people—did not put this kind of altar together out of a casual desire to appear traditional. This was a Triad family.

If Wu was Triad, there might be a connection between their argument and Drummond's death. A chill crept down his back as he contemplated the possible link between Colchuck Down and shipping containers. He should have known the Triad was merely laying low after the whole Sino-Trans thing had gone down. If Wu had been part of some smuggling operation, wouldn't the gangs unit have already gotten involved? Court ran over the scene earlier at Colchuck Down, but he couldn't remember recognizing anyone there.

The boy spoke to the old woman in rapid-fire Mandarin. The kid asked the old lady if they should be *doing anything*, calling *anyone*. The Po-Po told him to be quiet and show the cops into their father's room.

"What's this altar thing?" Ivy asked.

He needed to play it dumb until they got back to the car. "I don't know. Some sort of Buddhist-shrine thing?"

The boy grabbed him by the arm, pulling him toward a bedroom kitty-corner from the front door of the house. Court could feel the ancient woman's eyes piercing him between his shoulder blades.

A middle-aged Chinese man lay in the bed, with his foot up high on one set of pillows and another set propping him up at the back. He wore striped pajamas, something out of a Fifties television show. Except his were in color. The foot was covered in a towel, but the tell-tale signs of an ice pack were leaking out onto the pillows. A girl in her mid-teens sat on the far side of the bed, her hands in her lap. The boy who'd showed them the way climbed onto the bed, sitting cross-legged next to Wu.

After introducing themselves, Court waved at the others hanging about. "Maybe talking in private might be better."

Wu made a dismissive gesture with his hand. "I've got nothing to hide, detectives." His English was heavily accented.

"You were heard arguing with Berkeley Drummond last week. What was your argument about?" Court asked.

The old woman interrupted, shooing everyone else out with a bony hand, telling them in Mandarin to go outside and play before settling herself onto the chair next to the bed.

The man's face transformed into a smooth mask. A perfect poker face. "I wanted better hours." He held up his hands as if to indicate that was all.

"The argument you had was described as being very

heated. And lengthy. You expect us to believe it was about your hours?" Court asked.

Wu examined his hands. "What can I say? I wanted more hours, better hours, not only for me but for about twenty of us."

Wu had dropped his gaze. It was a sure sign the other man was not being completely honest. "And did Drummond give them to you?" Court asked.

Wu interlaced his fingers and laid his hands on his chest, affecting a nonchalant air. "He promised to listen to the union rep."

Wu was lying. His voice had risen in pitch, signaling the telltale signs of stress creeping in. Besides, Colchuck Down had a reputation for being more than fair to its workers. And why would Wu go around a union rep if he had one?

The Po-Po growled at Wu in Chinese, ordering him to tell the police to leave him in peace. She looked at Court, challenging him, chin up. "Hóng máo guǐzi. Gǔnkāi."

Court hoped his own poker face was working. She'd hurled the insult, no doubt to see if he spoke Mandarin. He pretended not to understand it. "What did she say?"

Wu responded with a curt, "My mother doesn't trust white people."

The old woman's lips turned white as they pressed against each other. She crossed her arms and returned to a sullen silence, her dark eyes narrow slits focused on Court. He wasn't sure she'd bought his feigned indifference to being called a red devil who should go to hell—about the rudest thing a Chinese grandmother would ever say.

Ivy plowed on. "Can you tell us where you were last Wednesday evening?"

"I was at home. With my family." He pointed at his foot. "After I had this seen to at the hospital. Why? What is this about, anyway?"

There were enough blankets obscuring his injuries that it was impossible to tell whether it was the foot or whole leg that was involved. "When were you at the hospital?"

Wu looked over at his mother. They conferred for a moment in Mandarin.

"I was there from about three until seven in the evening. At Harborview."

Court managed to withhold a groan. How convenient for Mr. Wu. It would be part of the Triad's MO to make sure an obvious suspect had an alibi while another member did a hit, however. What a mess. And two suspects at different hospitals at the same time? "You are aware that your employer, Berkeley Drummond, is dead, aren't you?"

"I saw it on the news. I had nothing to do with Mr. Drummond's death." His words were clipped. Deliberate.

"Do you know of anyone who might have wanted him dead?" Court asked.

Wu shrugged. "No."

"Mr. Wu," Court said. He paused, his mouth suddenly dry. He had to swallow a couple of times before continuing. "Mr. Wu, are you or anyone you know affiliated with the Triad?"

Wu's eyes widened. "Me?" He laughed. "Detective, you have an overactive imagination."

"Do I?"

Wu's face became a blank slate again. "Yes." He shook his leg and held up his foot. "I have been completely indisposed since Wednesday afternoon."

"What happened to your foot, Mr. Wu?" Ivy asked.

Wu and his mother exchanged a glance before Wu answered. He answered with a perfectly smooth poker face. "I dropped my garden shears on my foot and needed some stitches."

33

"GARDEN SHEARS, MY ASS." IVY SAID AS SOON AS THEIR car doors were shut. "Did you see that place? I took a peek out the window, and the back yard is as bereft of life as the front." She thrust the keys into the car's ignition.

Court waited until they were a block away from the Wu home to fill Ivy in on the details he'd gleaned from the sparse Mandarin. It wasn't much, but it was enough to make some assumptions. "The altar thing? Totally Triad. I bet the Po-Po is one of the enforcers or something."

"Po-Po," Ivy said, smiling around the word. "Does that mean grandma? And what did she say? Sounded like she was not happy."

"Po-Po means 'old woman.' Sort of generic. Did you see her feet?" Court ran his hands through his hair. "When I was in China, back in the late Eighties, I had a host grandmother with those things. God. What a fucking creep show. Smelled disgusting, too." He shuddered.

"Is that what that smell was? Looks painful, teetering around like that. What did she say to you, Court?"

"Oh. Doesn't sound half so bad in English. She literally called me a 'red fur devil' and told me to 'go to hell.' It's way ruder in Chinese."

"Huh, I guess some things don't translate well. So, how does this fit into Drummond's murder? I imagine there are hundreds of people working regular jobs and also in various gangs."

"The Triad is not just any gang. But, yeah, if his alibi checks out, it's unlikely he has anything to do with the death personally. One of his 'brethren,' maybe. Crap."

"I bet Wu doesn't even own a rake, let alone a pair of garden shears."

"Let's call Harborview and get the details on his injury. I've got a guy over there."

"Hold on, Pearson, what about HIPAA? They won't give you information over the phone. We'll need a warrant."

"Like I said, I have a guy over there. Fuck HIPAA. We'll go the legal round if we need it." It only took him a few minutes to get his friend to give him the lowdown. He turned off his phone, mopping at his forehead with the back of his hand. "Well, damn."

Ivy waved a hand in a circular "out with it" motion, keeping her eyes on the road.

"Looks like Wu's been to Harborview ten times in the last three years. Mostly minor injuries. A couple were work-related. He was there Wednesday night, but, it wasn't for some nebulous garden-shears wound. Someone cut off his toe."

Ivy sucked in her breath. "Oy. His toe? Did he think we

wouldn't check? Cut it off? As in off-off? I thought the Triad got all stabby with swords."

"That's true for bigger violations. They don't kill people until they've fucked up big time. Taking a toe is personal, more like punishment for failing at a smaller task."

"The thing about longer hours was all BS, wasn't it?"

Court fingered the window button and pushed it down a little bit, a small spray of cool mist hit him before he pushed the window back up. He scrubbed at his face with both hands. "Yeah. He had no reason to go to Drummond on behalf of other employees. That's union business. No. And, if you think about it, Agnes Mooring told us Drummond called Wu into his office, but Wu said he went to Drummond about hours. I'm going to believe Mooring on this one. Given that altar, I'm thinking Triad. Wu was in shipping, and Drummond was on to him about something. Drugs? People? Fuck all. This is getting complicated."

"I like complicated."

Court's phone buzzed with a new text. "Perfect timing, Langston. Audrey Drummond is furiously awaiting our arrival at the station."

34

COURT PEERED THROUGH THE OBSERVATION GLASS AT Audrey Drummond and Harlan Eccles. She could hardly sit still in her chair. She kept moving her hands between her lap and the table and looking around the room. Eccles put a reassuring hand on hers. It didn't stay long, and it felt entirely paternalistic, not the hand of a lover or close confidant. He and Ivy walked into the room with a pad of yellow paper and a clipboard holding the bridge-toll documentation.

Court sat across from Audrey Drummond while Ivy sat across from Eccles. He flipped on the tape and completed the recording ritual of introducing everyone and getting Drummond to acknowledge the session was being taped with her knowledge. "Do you know why we brought you in, Mrs. Drummond?"

Audrey Drummond nodded, looking down at her hands. "Yes, I do. I believe you've learned I crossed the bridge Wednesday night. Shortly after Berkeley did."

That was easy. Now, if only she'd drop a confession with as much ease. Court spun the report from WSDOT around for her to look at. "Thank you for coming clean so easily. Why did you lie to us the other day?"

Drummond looked down at the report's three highlighted lines. She had the decency to look sheepish. Eccles reached out to pat her hand. "It's okay, Audrey, you should have told them the truth the other day. Do it now."

She closed her eyes for a moment and breathed in deeply. "I lied because I forgot all about the toll on the bridge. I didn't think my trip in would make a bit of difference, so I lied to keep things simple."

Court could barely believe what he was hearing. Simple? "Being asked to come down here is less than simple, Mrs. Drummond. Were you trying to keep things simple, or were you trying to hide the fact you followed your husband into Seattle the night he was murdered?"

She shrank back, raising her hands in dignified surrender. "No. No. You've got it wrong. Yes, I followed Berkeley from home to Capitol Hill. He parked, and I parked down the street behind a minivan so he couldn't see me. I watched him get out to see where he was going. I knew who he was going to see, but I had never asked where this place was before. I had to follow him."

She clasped her hands together in front of her and placed them on the table. "When he stopped to talk to those kids, my heart wanted to break. Here he was, one of the richest men in the state stopping to talk to a bunch of homeless kids. I told you he was a good man, didn't I?"

Court sensed a theme. Everyone in Berkeley Drummond's family was taking great efforts to emphasize what a

230   LAURIE ROCKENBECK

fantastic man he was. It came across as *protesting too much*. Maybe Berkeley Drummond wasn't the saint he was made out to be. They'd have to dig deeper. The particulars of his death would shock and distance a lot of her friends. Audrey Drummond would end up a social pariah in Medina once the media got hold of the details. Or a laughingstock.

Mrs. Drummond wet her lips. "I watched him talk to those kids and hand them money. Then, he crossed the street and went into the building above the cute little café."

The same café where Court had purchased sandwiches and juice for the teens Drummond had been talking to. He kept silent, waiting for the rest.

"After he went inside, I sat there and waited for a while, trying to decide whether or not to go inside. I finally decided I would leave it up to him and left. I never got out of my car."

Court leaned forward, confused. "What would you leave up to him, Mrs. Drummond?"

"I wanted to make sure he told his dominatrix. About his condition." Her voice had dropped to a desperate whisper. She sucked in a bigger supply of air before blurting out the rest. "I wanted to make sure he had told her he was dying. I wanted her to know she needed to be careful about how hard she pushed him. I didn't want him dying in there. Not with her."

Audrey Drummond's coolness about the domme had some limits. She didn't want her husband to die with the other woman. Instead, he had died, probably alone, in the domme's studio, in a tangle of ropes on display for the world. If she'd followed him in, would her husband still be

alive? She must be asking the same question. He didn't see a
need to rub it in.

Her cheeks colored as tears trickled down them. Eccles
looked like he was about ready to jump in, but Court held a
hand out to stop him from talking. He pushed the tissue box
from the side of the table toward Drummond.

They weren't done yet. They had her at the scene of the
crime. The story might have been made up to gain their
sympathy. Or to cover up.

"So, let me get this straight," Court said. "You drive all
the way into Seattle to make sure the dominatrix doesn't hurt
your husband. Then you sit in your car for half an hour
while you think about it. Instead of going inside, you turn
your car around and head back home? Really?"

Audrey Drummond moved her head up and down,
looking more numbed and subdued than she had on
Saturday.

"Yes, Detective. That is exactly what happened. I never
got out of my car." She met his eyes with a fiercely
convincing sincerity.

Maybe he could shake her up by stretching the scenario
a bit. "Nice story, Mrs. Drummond. But what if I told you
those kids saw you follow your husband into the building?
What if they saw you come back out half an hour later
looking anxious and upset?" Court stood and leaned on the
table, over Drummond. He raised his voice. "You went in
with him. He told you how to tie him up, and you left him
there to die because that is what he wanted."

"No. No. No. It was nothing like *that*." She grabbed a
tissue out of the box and dabbed at her face. "I swear, I

never got out of the car. Whoever said they saw me was lying. Or, they saw someone else. I chickened out. I never went inside. I didn't want to meet her. I wanted him to be safe. Safe for the little time he had left."

Court had made up the kids seeing her, of course, but had decided to try the play to see what kind of response he got from her. There was a long heavy silence. Court gave Drummond some time to compose herself, before nodding at Ivy to continue with the questioning.

Ivy leaned forward, her voice smooth and gentle, contrasting with Court's harsh accusations. "Let's try this. Let's say we believe you. You were sitting in your car contemplating what you wanted to do. Maybe the killer walked by you while you were sitting there. Did you see anything? See anyone? Notice anything unusual?"

Sometimes getting people to talk about their story could trap them in lies. Ivy was going to try to trip her up by letting up on the pressure.

Drummond closed her eyes, let out a sigh of relief. "I don't know. I don't think so. Let me think." Her eyes moved beneath her lids. "There were about half a dozen teens hanging around outside the little store. And, there were lots of people out, walking."

Her fingers worked at her temples, massaging them. "Then, Berkeley went inside, and I sat there, staring at the building. A bunch of businesspeople came out."

"Think about all the people coming out of the building. Did you see anyone you recognize? Anyone who might have worked for your husband?" Ivy asked, stopping short.

Court could swear she was about to ask "anyone Chinese?"

Drummond closed her eyes again, shutting them tight. "No. People in casual business outfits. It was warm, so most people were carrying their jackets." She blinked a few times and lifted her head from her hands before sitting back against her chair, deflated. Then, she sat up, her eyes moving quickly back and forth, her hands up by her ears, fingers wiggling around as she pieced something together. "Wait a minute. There was something. It wasn't terribly odd, I suppose, but I thought I saw a priest come out as I was driving away."

She smiled broadly, pleased with herself.

"You saw a priest leaving the building?" Ivy asked.

"Well, sort of. I *thought* he was a priest because he had a high collar, black around his neck but with the white part missing."

Court had to work to not look at Ivy.

"Go on," Ivy prompted.

"Well … what I mean is I saw a man leaving the building, and he had a high collar on. You know, up around his neck. But, I decided he wasn't a priest after all. He was wearing a high-neck Manchu-style collar with a shirt over it. And jeans. It was…odd."

Court felt the tingle he got when a real clue was presented to him. He leaned in, breaking into the back and forth. "Can you remember what he looked like?" A high black collar would match Hunter's missing leather outfit. It would also give her story some weight because the only people who knew about it were Hunter, the killer, and the police.

"Well, he was white. Younger than I am, maybe thirty- or

fortysomething? I don't think there was anything unusual about him. I didn't pay that much attention."

"Think, Mrs. Drummond. Think hard, because it's very possible the man you saw killed your husband. You want to see him caught, don't you?"

Drummond clenched her fists together and put her thumbs up to her mouth. Her eyes were wild now, moving back and forth in a desperate search for details. "Yes. Yes, of course I do. I only saw him for a few seconds. It was Capitol Hill, for goodness sake."

Court caught Ivy's attention and held up his hands to mimic drawing on a pad in the air. She pursed her lips but stood up and slipped out of the room.

Court leaned forward. "Mrs. Drummond, you realize we could charge you with obstructing justice for lying to us the other day?"

Eccles held up his hand. "Look, Detective, my client is being very cooperative. It's got to be obvious to any sane person she had nothing to do with this death. She was a loving wife, and, with the brain tumor taking him soon anyway, there was no possible motive."

"We could make a case for assisted suicide." Court's voice was clipped, matter of fact. He watched Audrey Drummond as he spoke. She flinched, her face screwing up tightly, her lips drawing downward. Either she was a good actress, or she was truly shocked and disgusted by his suggestion. "You could be making this other thing up. Maybe you followed your husband inside, and he told you how to tie him up. You did it because you knew he'd die a happy man."

The color drained from her face. "Stop it. Stop it now. I

would never want to see him…" Her face twisted, lips pulled tight against her teeth. "He never wanted me to see him *like that*. We kept it separate. Out of our relationship."

Court opened the file he'd kept tucked under his notepad. He slid one of the crime-scene photos of Drummond's body across the table. She glanced at it. Covered her mouth, turning away, shutting her eyes tight. "I don't want to see it. I can't look."

Eccles put a hand on her wrist and leaned toward Court. "Detective, are you going to charge my client with anything?"

She was guilty of nothing more than lying about crossing the bridge. "No."

Eccles nodded with a small smile. "Thought not. It's time for us to leave."

"You can't leave yet." Court needed to follow up on the man coming out of the building. He had intentionally taken the questions in a different direction to get her rattled. Sometimes thinking too hard about something made it more difficult to remember details.

"I believe we can." Eccles stood. "Come on Audrey, I'll drive you home." He held out his arm to help her up from her chair. She looked back and forth between the two men, confused.

Court stood up. "We're not done here yet. Sit back down, Mr. Eccles. We could charge Mrs. Drummond with obstructing justice for lying to us. However, you and I both know you would make the charge disappear in the blink of an eye. It would be more trouble than it's worth to us. So, here's the deal. Mrs. Drummond is going to spend the next couple of hours working with our forensics sketch artist. He's going to have her sit down next to him and ask her a gazillion questions. And she's going to answer every last goddamn one of them until we have a picture of the man who killed her husband."

"LET'S HIT HAUBEK AFTER LUNCH." THE SECURITY company was south of the International District. Court was about to suggest lunch plans when his phone buzzed in his pocket. It was Agnes Mooring. "Ms. Mooring. You work fast."

Ivy sidled up to him and he put the phone at an angle so they could both listen. He didn't want this on speaker in the middle of the squad room.

"Well, Detective, like I said. I want to be of help. I am emailing you a spreadsheet. It will give you all the information you asked for, but I thought there was one thing worth calling about."

Court's heart quickened. "I'm listening."

There was a brief pause, and Court could hear the rustle of papers. "You'll find this on page four of my spreadsheet. But, what I found is three emails to different suppliers. Suppliers we have never worked with."

"And…" Court prompted.

"The suppliers are all for the same product. Down."

She said it with a grandiose finality as if it should mean something to Court.

"I'm sorry, but I'm not following you. He was looking for a new supplier of feathers? Why is this important?"

"Okay. Let me explain. We have several lines of products. Jackets, vests and sleeping bags. They're all filled with eider down, proprietary blends of cotton or poly compounds. That kind of thing.

"We've been using the same provider of pure eider down for years. It's a good-quality product, highly rated, and, at our last meeting, we confirmed we would continue with this supplier. There's no reason for Mr. Drummond to be sending these kinds of inquiries out to new providers. And, he's not copied anyone else on his inquiries."

"Okay," he said. This conversation was heading into uncomfortable territory.

"The current supplier is Yarong Industries. They provide Chinese down and ship out of Dalian, a northern Chinese port, but the queries that Berkeley was sending out were to Eastern European manufacturers. He was asking them very specific questions about production locations and their collecting practices. He wanted assurances there would be no Chinese or North Korean products of any kind in their shipping."

"His email specifically specified North Korean *products*?" There was only one thing Court could think of that North Korea was exporting. And it wasn't down.

"Yes. The emails were sent within an hour of his argument with Mr. Wu."

"Do you think Mr. Drummond would have filled you in on this given the fact he was stepping back on his duties?"

"Well, he probably would have once he'd made a decision about it. My guess is he was killed before he'd come up with his solution. It would have been more in character to not say anything until he had his recommendation ready. I suspect he caught Mr. Wu doing something illegal behind his back."

"Thank you, Ms. Mooring. I appreciate the call." Court hung up and turned to Ivy. "Shit."

"Drummond and Wu argue about some sort of smuggling. Then, Drummond starts searching for a new down source to cut out the illegal imports. Wu gets his toe cut off." Ivy put her hands on her hips. "North Korea. He must have gotten something out of Wu to come out with that."

"Meth is the big thing there, now, right?"

Ivy nodded. "Yeah. Supposedly the government destroyed all their official labs, to prove something or other to the U.S, but no one is buying it. We've been seeing a lot of it coming through Seattle the last couple years. It's the best on the market."

"You ever come across any from Colchuck Down? Heard of any connections there before?"

Ivy's lips puckered, moving side to side. "No. I didn't see anyone undercover at the factory earlier, did you?"

"No. Maybe Drummond stumbled onto something before we did?"

"You think the Triad would kill Drummond for closing down one avenue like that? It wasn't likely to be a big source yet. Especially if no one in Vice was working anything there."

"No. It's not exactly their style. Cutting off Wu's toe, I'd buy. A punishment for getting caught. But Wu wasn't giving us the whole truth. Maybe Drummond threatened to go to the police."

"That wouldn't get him killed. It's more likely the Triad would clean up all evidence at Colchuck and scoot. They aren't exactly chomping at the bit to be noticed these days."

"I'm with you on there. They've been keeping a low profile lately."

"So, what's next?"

Court pulled his coat back on. "Dim Sum."

THE JADE DRAGON SEAFOOD restaurant was nestled in between three other, more populated, Dim Sum restaurants. Court hoped to find Fang Zhao still working there. She was one of three survivors from the ill-fated Sino-Trans shipping container. They'd become close during the investigation, and she'd given him bits and pieces of information over the years since.

Lunch was in full swing with no less than four carts making their circuit around the room. The first stopped at their table, full of little bamboo baskets filled with steaming items, fragrant with delicately spiced pork and shrimp. The waitress automatically reached for the shu mai, but Court held up his hand and pointed to the sticky rice packaged neatly in lotus leaf, the fluffy white pork bao and the braised brown chicken feet.

She complied with the rice and buns. She shook her head, tapping the chicken feet. "You no like."

He spoke to her in Chinese. She bowed before giving them a full plate of the delicacy before scribbling on their card and moving on.

"What did you say to her?" Ivy asked as she picked up a piece of the chicken with her chopsticks. She held it in the air, twirling it around skeptically, inspecting it from all angles.

"I asked her to please allow us to eat the 'phoenix claws.' They don't call them 'chicken feet' when served like this. You can always gauge the quality of a Dim Sum place by this dish." He picked one up, sucking at the first claw. The black bean sauce was tangy with a bit of a kick.

Ivy copied him. Court wasn't a huge fan of chicken feet, no matter what they were called, but he always ordered them.

Ivy made a face, chewing experimentally. "You like these things?" She pulled the piece away from her mouth and inspecting it. "What is this?"

"It's cartilage or tendon." He scanned the room but didn't see Fang. Her willingness to talk to the police had gone a long way with getting her green card. He liked to think his sponsorship hadn't hurt, either. Fang meant "fragrant" in Chinese, but the connotations in English had been inspiration to the young woman. She had been barely eighteen when she was shoved into the shipping container bound for the United States. They were promised transportation out of China and jobs for a fee they could work off once they arrived. Fang had been one of the lucky ones. Her tenacity fit well with the American image she made for herself.

Ivy put her chicken back on her plate. "I'm sorry. I can't eat that."

"It's an acquired taste."

"I think the flavor is okay. It's the texture. I never liked fat or chewy things." She unwrapped one of the lotus leaves and inspected the rice closely. "Is that little pieces of pork?"

"Oh, damn. I forgot you don't eat pork. You can't eat these buns either, can you? They're filled with Chinese-style barbecue."

"It's okay. I think there are a few things coming around that I can eat."

Several carts came by before Fang finally appeared. She'd cut her traditionally long hair into short spikes set in gel. Last time he'd seen her, she complained about her job requiring her to look presentable. She railed against the old-country customs that she had hoped to escape by coming to America. When she got to their table, she smiled and took dishes off her cart.

"Look what cat drag in. Good see you Jian-Heng." She chided him. "This new partner?"

Ivy raised her chopsticks in greeting, snagging a dumpling out of the little bamboo steamer Fang had set in front of them once she'd confirmed it was stuffed with vegetables. "Jian-Heng?" she asked.

Fang smiled broadly. "His name too hard in mouth. I call him Jian-Heng. It mean he don't let go. He like pit bull." She mimicked biting the air, snapping bared teeth with a click. She bowed toward Court, smiling with obvious affection.

Court spoke quietly in rapid Mandarin while Fang marked their card. She reached over to snip one of the three sesame balls in half with her scissors as she replied. She marked their card and moved to the next table. A casual observer would only think she had served her customers.

Ivy leaned over her chili oil and soy sauce-covered plate. "Well?"

"I asked her what she could find out about any Triad links to shipments going into Colchuck Down. She'll get back to me in a couple of days."

"That was kind of tipping our hand, wasn't it? You were so specific."

Court sunk his teeth into the gooey exterior of the sweet treat, enjoying the subtle sweetness of the red bean paste. He had a momentary pang of concern. Fang had given him information before, but it had been more than a year since he'd done more than say hi and order Dim Sum. There was no telling who she was hanging with these days.

HAUBEK, INC. WAS SITUATED A FEW BLOCKS NORTH OF Colchuck Down. Their general proximity to each other was all the two had in common. From the outside, the building looked like it was about ready to be condemned. The signage was minimal--a single foot-wide plaque next to the door. The street numbers were cheap little ancient gold-and-black decals lined up along the metal frame of the door. Haubek employees must only make house calls. One look at this dump and anyone would question the company's credentials.

The light drizzle earlier in the day had become a steady, quiet rain. Court and Ivy dashed to the building, where Court pushed the glass door into the inner office open and held it for Ivy. He ran his hands over his head to sluice raindrops away.

The meager reception area was right out of the Seventies. Green vinyl chairs with fake wood armrests lined one wall opposite the desk centered in front of the back wall. A door to the left was labeled PRIVATE. Sitting at the desk, a youngish blonde blew a purple gum blob to its fullest potential before popping it and sucking the goo back into her mouth.

"Good afternoon. What can I do ya for?" She put down the bodice ripper she'd been reading. After they introduced themselves, the woman rose, a little flustered. "I'll go get Mr. Walker. He'll know what to do." She teetered on too-high heels over to the door marked PRIVATE and disappeared inside.

Court peered at the book cover. "I wonder how much she gets paid to read things like *Viking Love*."

"I can't imagine she has much to do. This place is not set up for clients. It's clear she didn't know what to do when we walked in."

"They say not to judge a book by its cover."

The woman reappeared with a balding man who was maybe in his early forties.

He took two large steps as he approached them, keeping his arms linked behind his back rather than reaching out for the customary handshake. "I'm Leland Walker, owner of Haubek. I understand you'd like to talk to me?"

He pushed the private door open. Behind the door, an expansive workshop spread out, rows of tables were covered in wires and electronic equipment. It was surprisingly bright inside given the cloudy morning, but the roof was mostly skylights, and there were plenty of task lights around the floor. Technicians dressed in khaki pants and navy company polos occupied nearly all of the tables. Court paused at one where a tech installed a standard security camera inside a utility box. Next to him, another fit a miniature camera into a wall clock. At another workbench, workers inserted cameras into large ceramic penguin cookie jars. Nanny cams? Haubek certainly had a wide variety of products.

Large cubicles lined the workshop in a U-shape along three walls. This part of the building told a different story than the neglected exterior. It was clear that Haubek didn't care about its outside image as long as the inside was kept state-of-the-art.

Walker led them into a corner conference room made of one-way glass on the interior walls. It afforded privacy for anyone in the conference room while allowing them to view the main floor. White boards covered with dry-erase marker drawings of squares, squiggles and equations lined the exterior walls.

Court and Ivy settled into chairs opposite Leland Walker, who dropped into a seat and placed his hands together on top of the table, the perfect picture of eager helpfulness.

Court opened his notebook. "We understand you installed the card-entry system at Allegiance Investments."

Walker paused. "I'm not willing to disclose any customer information."

Court wasn't surprised. If Haubek took security seriously, Walker would be unwilling to talk freely about a customer. "We're investigating a death, Mr. Walker."

Walker leaned forward, eyes narrowing in concern. "Oh, that's awful."

"Mr. Walker, here's the thing. Haubek installed the entry system at Allegiance Investments. Six weeks ago, a duplicate key shows up on the system without any history. Nothing on the log shows when it was created. We're trying to piece together how this could work. We're pretty sure Ms. Hunter, the owner, has no idea. She hasn't even accessed her logs in over a year. What would it take to make a duplicate card key? What kind of technical expertise? What kind of access? What kind of hacker are we talking about here?"

Walker stood up and made a circuit around the table. Court swiveled in his seat to watch his progress. There was a nervous energy about the man he attributed to the weirdness of geek-genius types. Walker had the thin gawky physique he associated with those guys who were losers in high school but grew up to make it in the real world. A stereotype, sure, but Walker came across as someone who hadn't completely outgrown his youth in spite of his receding hairline.

Walker stopped his pacing, facing them with hands on hips. "I'm afraid I can't answer any of those questions. Or, rather, I'm unwilling to do so without the presence of an attorney."

This didn't come as a huge surprise. Who would want to willingly offer up a weak link in their product? Court placed the warrant he had brought with him flat on the table, smoothing out the fold lines one by one. He could have played it first, but sometimes people gave up more information than a warrant stipulated. Warrants had to be detailed and specific.

"I hoped you'd volunteer information, but here you go, Mr. Walker. We'll wait while you collect the materials."

Walker sighed heavily as he sat down, donning reading glasses. He read the warrant line by line, one of his long bony fingers tapping the table-top in a steady rhythm. He paused and examined Court over the rim of his glasses. "Why would you want the names of every client with the same system? That's a little far-reaching, isn't it?"

"We're investigating anyone who might have had ties

with Allegiance Investments, the victim and knowledge of this card-key system."

Walker scowled as he read, his jaw working back and forth. At length, he folded the warrant into thirds, stowing it and his glasses in his shirt pocket. "Very well. I'll be back. Make yourselves comfortable. It might be a while. I'll have to have a chat with my attorney first."

After he left, Court stood up and found a place at the window where he could watch the employees. The techs working the center tables were focused on what they were doing, but also had a good deal of interaction. The general atmosphere was one of congeniality. He pulled up the company website on his phone, flipping through their online products. The cookie-jar-turned-nanny-cam was motion activated, remote controlled, and sold for two hundred bucks. The clock sold for a hundred bucks but was limited to still shots, and the customer had to remove its memory card manually to retrieve the photos. A small figurine was being sold as a "granny-cam" and touted as being useful in ferreting out abusive nursing-home workers. The copy in all of the product descriptions had a similar fear-mongering tone. Haubek also sold products with cameras in flower vases, stuffed animals, and fake plants. Court wondered how many people were spying on loved ones. The inventory being put together in front of him would suggest it was a lot.

The company's homepage described Haubek as one of the region's largest and most reliable suppliers to the local security companies. Haubek manufactured the hardware, and worked with various companies to install systems, but did not supply monitoring services. Haubek was happy to supply equipment to businesses on an à la carte basis.

"Can't blame him for not opening up to us," Ivy said. "If there was a glitch in a system they provided, his company could be held liable or something."

"Can you imagine feeling like you need to watch your nanny?"

"Actually, I've got one of those. Mine's a cat, not a penguin. Probably bought it online from here, now that I think about it."

"Do you use it?"

"Not anymore. I got it when we hired our first nanny. Used it for a month or two. It felt kind of weird. Like I was getting too paranoid. It's on a shelf in the garage."

Court's phone buzzed with another text from Madeline. He turned his back to Ivy for a little privacy. She was having a good day and hoping he was having a good one, too. It was followed by a selfie of Madeline holding a coffee mug declaring REVENGE IS SWEET AND NOT FATTENING—a famous Hitchcock line. It was a quote he'd always found a little disturbing if taken seriously. They'd talked about their mutual love of all things Hitchcock last night. He had one at home with another quote—TELEVISION HAS BROUGHT BACK MURDER INTO THE HOME—WHERE IT BELONGS. His mug probably came from the same website where Madeline had gotten hers.

In the background behind her, shelves were cluttered with figurines. He recognized some of them from movies and TV shows. There were more he didn't recognize than those he did. Above her head was a Lego space ship, which he tentatively identified as the Millennium Falcon. She followed it briefly with another text declaring the image "me at work."

She was an artist at the same company his brother-in-law, Pat, worked for. Court didn't own any game consoles and never played them on his computer, so whenever Pat talked about what his company did it flew right over Court's head. He'd toyed with a silly bird game on his phone for a while, but he wasn't into the games where everyone ran around shooting at each other. He experienced enough of violence in real life; he didn't need the pretend version.

He studied the picture of Madeline for a while, and then raised his phone to take a selfie. It showed him sitting in a plain chair with an empty white board behind him. Boring as all hell. He deleted it and slid his thumb up the text history with Madeline until he got to the steamy one she'd taken earlier in the morning at his place.

"Selfies, Court?" Ivy asked, interrupting his private moment.

He closed the message window and opened his email. "How long's it been, anyway? Maybe we should do something else and come back."

"Ten minutes, maybe. I bet he'll be back within half an hour. By the time we get anywhere, it will be ready for us. Besides, whatever he's got for us is probably our next best bet."

He scrolled through his email. "Nothing on Drummond's priest yet. If they can get a good drawing from her…"

"Yeah, don't count on it. You know eyewitnesses are almost entirely unreliable. Especially five days out?"

"Still. The collar. He's got to be our killer. It gives us some idea about his build at least."

"Hunter's size and general shape. Leather doesn't stretch much, does it?"

"No, it doesn't. There could be some variation in height, but the build would have to be similar."

"Even if they'd worn the suit so it was super tight, they'd still have to be similar in size. They could be taller. A skinny guy could fit in it with the hem of the legs hitting him above the ankles."

"Could have been a woman. Don't forget that."

"True. True. You think Audrey Drummond's about the same size as Karen Hunter?"

WALKER RETURNED HALF an hour later with a file three inches thick. "Everything you asked for is here."

"We'd like to look it over and ask you a few follow-up questions."

"I've complied with the warrant. If you want to ask me questions, you'll have to do it with my attorney present." Walker slid the file onto the table with enough force it practically flew across the wood to Court. "I'd like you to leave, now."

Court trapped the file with a firm hand, not sure where the outright belligerence was coming from. He remained seated, thumbing through the stack with deliberate slowness. There were several smaller bundles wrapped in rubber bands, each with a sticky note on top labeling them. It appeared to be pretty complete, though it was tough to know what they *should have* asked for but didn't.

"Hey, the warrant specifies the components of the system you removed from Hunter's office eight weeks ago. The old reader. Do you still have it?"

Walker's lips tightened. "No. It's been recycled."

"Thanks for all your help." Court tried to keep the sarcasm out of his voice. He stood.

Walker flashed a coffee-stained fake smile. "You're very welcome, detectives."

Court turned around at the door. "Oh, and that thing about answering questions? This is a death investigation. Come see us at eleven tomorrow morning, and bring your attorney. If you need a ride, I'd be happy to send a pair of uniformed officers to collect you."

37

COURT OPENED THE FILE ON HIS LAP AS SOON AS HE WAS belted in. The first bundle of papers was made up of work orders and invoices for Hunter's system. Haubek installed the original system three years prior. After the initial installation, there were two other system upgrades performed onsite that would have required Hunter to be present. The replacement on the entry and reboot a couple months ago was the only other work done on her system.

This was completed by two Haubek technicians—a J. Nolan and a T. Payne. The notes confirmed Hunter's story about the reader being smashed during a break-in. They wiped the system and told her to reissue cards to everyone who needed them. They also replaced the original card coder to accommodate software upgrades in the newer card reader. The last page included an inventory of returned equipment and how it was broken down into components for reuse or disposal. The usable pieces were wiped clean of all data before being sent back into the manufacturing line. It would be a mess, trying to locate the components of Hunter's system. And, if he was reading the notes correctly, there wouldn't be any data left on them.

Court flipped through to the list of identical systems, scanning their names for anyone he might recognize. There were over three hundred names and companies on the list, but he was only interested in a few.

"Well, look at this," he said. "Okay, don't look, you keep driving. Your friend Jim Schorr is also a Haubek customer. And, lookie here, so is Colchuck Down."

"You think that means he would be able to hack into Hunter's system? And wouldn't Colchuck have a much larger, more involved security system than Hunter's?"

"Yeah. It's still a connection. So, it looks like two techs worked on Hunter's system a couple months ago. An expert in the system could fake a card, right?"

"Why would a tech at Haubek be interested in Drummond?" she asked.

"Could be that someone was following Drummond, figured out he had a weekly appointment with Hunter, and bribed one of the techs to get access." Court flipped through the papers to the stack marked PERSONNEL. There were only three records, one for each of the techs who'd installed the new reader, and one for Walker.

"What motive would Walker have for offing Drummond? Unless there was some bigger thing going on with Colchuck security... Security and shipping logs?" Court tucked the idea away for now. "Let's hope this is not some larger Triad conspiracy with Haubek at the center."

"Oh, that would suck. And be kinda awesome at the same time, wouldn't it?"

"I can't imagine anything less awesome, Langston. Anytime the Triad is involved, things get nasty. I've had enough of them for one career." He took a deep breath. "Okay, so, here's Payne's personnel record. Not much to it. Shows he's a model employee. Given regular raises over the years, no complaints against him except once back in 2008. A customer called in about how slow Payne was being on some work. The notes say that Payne was given a warning and nothing more after that. Nothing else in here but a note about his mother dying. He initially took off two weeks, but called back in to give final notice after a week."

Back at his desk, Court pulled the DMV records on Nolan and Payne while Ivy pored through the Haubek paperwork. Court soon had phone numbers on both men. Payne's went to voicemail, but the message was from a woman with a different name. The number must have been reassigned.

Payne's DMV records showed the same address as in his personnel file from Haubek. If he'd moved recently, he might not have gotten around to updating his license information.

Nolan's personnel record was a bit sketchier than Payne's. He was chronically late. He had four warnings in his records over the last six months. Before that, he had been a model employee. There wasn't much else in the record. Court tried the number in the record for Nolan. He picked up on the first ring as if he had been waiting for Court's call. He politely informed Court that he couldn't talk to him over the phone or without an attorney present. Court told him to come to the station with his boss tomorrow.

"What can you tell me about Payne leaving Haubek?" Court asked, hoping he'd answer some questions anyway.

"I don't think that's a secret. His mother died about a month or so ago, and he quit. She left the house to him. He was going to sell it to pursue his dream."

"Pursue his dream? What kinda dream would that be?"

"You know, I'm not sure about that. Used to talk some about sailing, but he never invited anyone out on a boat as far as I know."

"You know how I can get hold of him?"

"Sure, it's still on my phone."

It was the same number that Court had already tried. If Payne's mom had died a month prior, how likely was it the house had already sold? Court checked the county tax records, but the home was still listed under Barbara Payne. So, if it had sold, it was recent enough that the database hadn't caught up with the sale. It was weird that the guy had disconnected his phone. Doubly weird since it was his cell phone and not a land line. Maybe his hunch had been right. Maybe Payne had been bought off by someone to gain access to Hunter's offices.

Court stood up and leaned over his cubicle to Ivy's. She had the Haubek file open out on her desk, and was scribbling on her yellow pad.

"Find anything useful?" he asked.

"Meh. You?"

"We need to go find this Payne guy. I have this weird feeling about him. His mom died a month ago, and he quit working at Haubek."

"So? What's weird about that? Lots of people lose it when their parents die. Maybe she left him some money and he could quit."

"Yeah, I know. Nolan refused to talk about anything

technical on the Haubek system, but he told me Payne's mom left him the house, and he was going to sell it to pursue his dream."

"Like I said, Pearson, it sounds like a totally normal thing to me."

"The thing is, people with 'dreams' talk about them a lot, don't they? Nolan wasn't even sure what this dream of Payne's might be. *And*, he disconnected his cell phone. Talk about bizarre. Who does that?"

"Seriously? You're not liking this guy for Drummond, are you? I mean, he's a tech who worked on the system *once*. What connection does he have to Drummond?"

"I don't know. Drummond has a Haubek system. We should see if he ever worked on that one. Maybe there was some connection over at Colchuck. It's more likely that the killer bribed Payne for access to Hunter's system."

Ivy breathed out heavily. "Those guys at Haubek are all licensed and bonded security types. I wonder how much it would take to get them to blow their careers."

Court shrugged. "We didn't ask for documentation on Schorr's or Colchuck Down's maintenance history. Let's see if either Nolan or Payne worked on them. If we can place either one with Schorr or Colchuck, it would make a connection to Drummond."

"I'll write up a warrant."

"We can stop by Haubek on our way out to Payne's house," Court said.

STENSLAND STEPPED out of his office, ordering them both

inside. He waved a meaty hand at two seats in front of his desk. Court dropped onto the edge of one, not settling in. Whatever Stensland had to say would be quick.

"Tell me about the visit you two made to a known associate of the Triad. What the hell is going on?"

It was disconcerting that they had been caught under someone else's surveillance. He was glad he was sitting as his legs turned to rubber. "Sorry, sir. We learned earlier today that Drummond had an argument with a man who worked for him." He filled him in on their visit to Wu's house and their subsequent trip to see Fang.

"And you didn't think to call Brody up in Gangs?" Stensland asked. "For either visit?"

Detective Trevon Brody headed the growing Gangs unit that was supposed to work in conjunction with other units— Homicide, Narcotics and Vice—to link all gang-related activity. In theory, close communication between everyone would make it easier and faster to solve crimes. When they'd been at Colchuck, Court hadn't seen any undercover cops. But, he hadn't been looking for them either. They wouldn't have signaled their presence. Not talking to Brody was a lapse in procedure, but not a huge one. Why were Stensland's panties in such a bunch?

Stensland pointed a finger at Ivy. "And you, Langston. You didn't either?"

Ivy sat in silence, her fingers interlaced over her stomach. The color had drained from her face. This was the first time she'd taken any heat from Stensland. She leaned back into her chair, crossing her legs at her ankles. She gave Court a "go ahead, you tell him" look.

"With all due respect, sir, we had no idea Wu was

involved with the Triad until we were at his house. We were following up on a lead," Court said.

"Wu? Who's talking about Wu? We're talking about Fang. She's one of Brody's informants."

Court fell back in his seat, jaw dropping. Fang hadn't given him any indication or hinted at being anyone else's informant. What the hell was Brody using her for?

"What am I supposed to do when my lead detective on a case isn't communicating the way he's supposed to? And his partner doesn't call him on it? The two of you are supposed to cover each other's ass and make sure all lines of communication are working."

Ivy leaned forward to say something, but Stensland cut her off with a wave of his hand. "I'm not done yet. You are going to include Brody on every aspect of this case. If the Triad is involved, he's got to be kept up to date and involved."

"Sir, was there anyone in Gangs on Colchuck Down?" Court asked.

"The point is, you can't go running into their territory. You might fuck up a concurrent investigation."

"I asked you if someone was already on Colchuck. Did we interrupt an active investigation? Or did we catch them with their pants down?"

Stensland's eyebrow twitched with a tic telling Court that he was pushing it.

"You need to report everything you touch from here on out to Brody. Let him know before you have any further contact. Got it?"

38

THERE WERE A FEW INQUISITIVE LOOKS FROM OTHERS AS they stepped out of Stensland's office, but Court ignored them as he made his way back to his cubicle and focused on his work. He printed out two copies of Payne's and Nolan's DMV photos while Ivy worked on the new warrant. The sketch artist's rendering popped up at the top of his email. He clicked the file and opened it on his screen. The most distinguishing feature the guy had was his balding head with a slim tonsure of hair circling the back and sides. He could be almost any white guy in his late thirties or early forties. The single definitive thing they got from the exercise is that he wasn't Chinese.

He flashed the printed copy at Ivy; she gave him a told-you-so smile. "To tell you the truth, I am hoping this has no link to the Triad—that could get nasty very fast. Whoever he is, he took the suit with him. Maybe he kept it as a souvenir so we'll have something tying him to the killing."

Court didn't like the sound of that. Killers who kept

souvenirs were not usually stable, regular folks. Most murders were crimes of passion. When a killer is confronted face-to-face, they usually break and confess. The serial killers of the world are the ones who don't break under pressure. They creeped Court out as much as they fascinated him.

"It's too bad the drawing is mostly useless. But I think we can rule out a Chinese hit man from the possibilities."

"The Triad could have hired him out. They could still be behind this," Court said.

"I hope not. After that scene with Stensland, I am hoping there is absolutely no connection with the Triad. The way Stensland was all quiet after you asked him, I'm betting Gangs had nothing going over at Colchuck."

Court checked his phone. It had only been a couple of hours, and he was pretty sure Fang had not had time to do any checking. "Here's hoping Fang can get back to me tomorrow sometime and clear it up. I'd be happy to cross the Triad off our list."

Ivy traced circles on her watch face. "If we leave now, we can go check on Payne's address and be back before traffic stinks."

They dropped the new warrant at Haubek. It took Walker fifteen minutes to comply, and they hit the road to check up on Payne. This time, Court drove as Ivy read through the file.

"Colchuck has a Haubek system, but the techs who have worked on it are all different. Neither Nolan or Payne are on the list. And, before you ask, I checked— none of the techs who have ever worked at Hunter's have worked at Colchuck Down."

"So no connection between Payne and Drummond. What about Schorr?"

She flipped through papers. "Nolan and Payne installed the system at Schorr's business. That's the only work done over there. But that was six months ago. That's a long time to make any real connection stick."

The ride out to Issaquah took them half an hour. Once they were off the freeway, it took another ten minutes to get through the main drag and south of town. "How does someone living out here work in Seattle? Wouldn't the commute totally suck?"

"It does. Did it for a couple of years early on. We moved into town when it was clear I was permanently SPD."

A group of paragliders jumped from the top of a small mountain as they passed by. The brightly colored gliders made swoopy circles before landing on a grassy field close to the road.

"Looks like fun," Court said, pointing up to where one tandem glider had floated off the rocky ridge above.

"Did it once. Right from there, too. Some of those jumpers are nuts, but it was fun. Once."

Court's estimation of his partner went up a notch. She had the balls to jump off a mountain. That was always a good sign.

They drove through several smaller developments surrounded by large trees. He liked hiking in the mountains, but living around trees made him feel claustrophobic. He preferred the smaller, manicured city lots and apartment-scape he was used to. The weather was barely cloudy, but the threat of rain hung over them as they wound through the streets. He couldn't see any distinguishing landmarks, and every curve blocked what might be ahead from view.

"You drive like my grandmother," Ivy said. "Can't you go any faster?"

"I only drive as far as I can see." He slammed on the brakes as a kid skated across the street ahead of them.

"I'm driving back."

Payne's neighborhood consisted of cookie-cutter houses and had a family-friendly vibe to it. Basketball hoops hung proudly from the middle of more than half the garages. Unlike the staid beiges and greens in most upscale developments, exterior paint colors covered the whole spectrum in this one. A purple monstrosity halfway up the block from Payne's house extinguished any question about the neighborhood's adherence to any covenants and restrictions.

Ivy parked right in front of the FOR SALE sign with a bright red SOLD banner nailed to it at an angle. The yard was well groomed, with a fresh layer of bark around the shrubs at the front of the house. Court took an information flyer out of the box on the sign. The house was a three-bedroom built in 1995 with an asking price of 642K. Payne would be walking away with a good chunk of change. The tax records had indicated Barbara Payne was the original and sole owner of the house. If it was free and clear, there'd be enough money to pursue all sorts of dreams.

When there was no answer to his knock, Court cupped his hands around his eyes so he could see in through the glass on one side of the door. There was some furniture in place, but it had the air of being empty and staged for show. He rang the bell again.

"We can see if anyone knows where he went. I'll take this

side." Court waved to the neighbors to the west of the Payne house. Ivy nodded and set out in the opposite direction.

The kid who answered the first door couldn't be more than eight and reached out to touch Court's shiny badge when he held it out for him. "You home alone?" Court asked.

"Nope."

"Did you know the people who lived next door?"

"Yes."

"What do you remember about them?"

The kid twisted his lips around as he considered the question and peered around the door to look at the vacant house as if to remind himself who used to live there. "I liked Timmy. He was nice. I didn't like Maw-Maw so much."

"MaMa?" Court asked, knowing he didn't have it quite right.

"Everyone called her Maw-Maw. She was old. She was loud. She died." He pronounced it more like the sound a crow makes.

"How well did you know Timmy. Was he your friend?" Court asked.

"A little. Maw-Maw used to babysit me sometimes, and I would play with his stuff. He had wires and things in the garage. He was nice."

"Do you know where Timmy went?"

The little boy shook his head. Court was about to thank him and leave when the boy added, "He pays me though."

"Pays you for what?"

He opened the door wider and pointed to a paper sack. "I get his mail after school."

"Did he tell you when he'd come get it next time?"

The boy shook his head.

Asking the kid to hand over the mail would complicate things particularly if there was any useful evidence in the bag. He weighed the options for a couple of seconds. "Can I take a look at the stuff in the bag?"

The little boy handed it to Court. He pulled out the small pile, flipping through it rapidly. Almost everything was addressed to Barbara Payne. Lots of flyers and coupon books. A couple of bills. There was one item addressed directly to Payne, a letter from Haubek. He put everything back in the bag and handed it back to the boy.

"So, you sure you're not alone in there?" he asked again.

"Yeah," he said, bringing the door in close against his face, making it hard for Court to see past him.

"All right then, thanks for your help."

"Hey mister," the kid said as Court turned away. "Is Timmy in trouble?"

"I don't think so. I need to ask him a few questions, is all." Court paused and pulled out card and scribbled a note on it. "Put that in his mail, will you? Make sure he sees it when he comes to pick it up."

With any luck, Payne would get his mail soon and actually call him. He wasn't going to hold his breath. He felt a little guilty about it, but dialed CPS to report an eight-year-old being home alone. The kid was probably okay, but eight was too young to leave without reporting it.

Three more interviews later, and Court was seeing a story take shape. Everyone he talked to knew both Paynes. The general picture of the mother was she spent a lot of her time in floral muumuus and curlers. She coddled her miniature poodle to the point of dressing it up with pink bows and carrying it in a purse while shopping. The others he talked to had all described a reclusive woman with a very nice son. A couple thought maybe she had a screw or two loose.

She was a heart attack in fuzzy slippers waiting to happen. No one was surprised when the ambulance rolled out of the driveway without the flashers and sirens. No one was shocked when the house was on the market two days after Barbara Payne had died, either.

The story was that she'd had Timothy when she was older. Her husband was already sixty when the baby came, and he'd died in a boating accident fifteen years later. Mrs. Payne and her son had moved in when the house was newly built in 1995. No one remembered her working a day. The gossip was that the husband's retirement fund or life insurance bought the house with plenty to spare. No one knew where Timothy had moved to.

Court met Ivy back at the car and compared notes.

"Bless those nosy neighbors and gossip," Ivy said.

She'd gotten a similar story from her side of the street. The most significant thing had come from the woman who lived right next door. There had been a loud fight between Payne and his mother the night she had died. When pressed, the neighbor admitted that fights between the two were pretty common.

Court dialed the realtor's phone number. His call went to voice mail, so he left a message. The realtor ought to know how to get in touch with Payne.

39

As they were pulling into the parking lot, Court got a text telling him Schorr was in-house. "You want to watch?"

"Yes, but I don't want him to see me. If he knows I'm working this case..." She shuddered and closed her eyes for a second. "Synagogue is going to be incredibly painful as it is. Me knowing he was seeing a domme like that? Him knowing I know is too much to contemplate."

"If he's got much to tell us, he'll find out. If he's guilty of something, he'll definitely find out."

Ivy closed her eyes and leaned back against her seat. "Yeah. I know. I would like to delay it as long as possible."

"He knows you're in Homicide, right?"

"Maybe. Not necessarily. It's not like I jumped up during service and let everyone know about my promotion."

Court made sure that Schorr was in the interrogation room before they entered the building. Court stood in front of the small window of the door while Ivy sneaked past to enter the one-way viewing room where she could observe them unseen.

Schorr sat at the table, hands folded placidly on top. Next to him, a short, barrel-chested man in a suit tapped his fingers against a folder in front of him. He stood and introduced himself to Court as Schorr's attorney, his thick smile warm and genuine all the way to his eyes.

Court sat across from the two men, read Schorr his rights and got their acknowledgement for the recording.

"Why didn't you return my phone call yesterday?" Court asked.

"Ignoring one's phone is not a crime," Schorr said. The attorney patted his wrist and gave him a warning look.

"My client is right. What's so important you send officers to collect him? If what you want is answers to questions, you need only ask. Mr. Schorr can be a very cooperative man," he said in a heavy Israeli accent.

"Mr. Schorr, tell me about your relationship to Mistress Fidelma."

He sat back, crossing his arms. "There's not much to tell. I've been seeing her once a week for the last four years."

"And where would you see her?"

He glanced at the lawyer, who held his hands open. Schorr let out an explosive breath. "Fine. She has an office on Capitol Hill. What's this about? Is she okay?"

Again, worry about the domme. Both Duffy and Schorr showed concern for her above themselves. "She's fine. Tell me about how you gained access to the office."

"What? At Allegiance Investments?" He pulled the cardkey out of his wallet and handed it over. "It's a card key, pretty much like any card key these days. She programmed it so I can use it at a certain time. If I'm late, I miss my appointment."

"And how old is this key?"

"She had to give me a new one after hers was broken. A couple months, maybe."

"And, how does this system differ from the one you use at your company?"

He shrugged. "I think we might have the same system, why?"

Court wasn't picking up any signals from this guy other than frustration and confusion. If Schorr had anything to do with the second key, he would have had a more telling response to the question. Court switched gears. "Do you know any of her other clients?"

"No. And I wouldn't want to know. It's bad enough knowing she *has* other clients. I have no desire to know who they are."

Jealousy? Could he have found out Berkeley Drummond was a client and offed him? "Who told you about her?" Court asked.

Schorr's mouth rounded as if he'd been sucker-punched. "A friend."

"A name, Mr. Schorr. Please tell me who hooked you up with her."

He looked at his attorney, eyes wide.

"I'm advising my client to not answer that question."

Court opened a folder and slipped Walker's photo out onto the table. "Do you recognize this man?" he asked.

Schorr's examined the picture. "That's the guy who owns Haubek, right? Walker?"

Court pushed Nolan's picture across the table. "What about him?"

Schorr shook his head. "Don't think I know him."

Schorr didn't recognize the man in the drawing or Payne, either. When Court pushed a photo of Berkeley Drummond in front of him, however, Schorr's jaw dropped open. "What? That's Berkeley Drummond. Why are you showing me his photo? Didn't he die a couple of days ago?"

"You recognize him?"

"Of course I do."

"How well do you know him?"

Schorr fell back against the seat, his hand flying up to cover his mouth, eyes blinking rapidly. "Oh, my god. You're investigating Berkeley's death? What does this have to do with Mistress?" His whole body deflated and he drooped into his chair, shoulders slumped. "He saw her, too?"

Interesting. He kept referring to Drummond by his first name. "How well did you know him?"

"Not well. We only know each other through Rotary. That's it. Worked on a committee or two together. We aren't *friends*." He paused, his eyes growing wide with understanding. "Did Berkeley die at Mistress Fidelma's? Is that why she canceled my appointment for tomorrow?"

Was that all this guy worried about? When he would see his domme again? Court dropped Duffy's photo onto the pile. "What about this guy?"

Schorr's face paled.

"Did Giovanni Duffy turn you on to the domme, Mr. Schorr? At a Rotary meeting, maybe?"

Schorr looked up at the ceiling. "Okay. Okay, all right. Yes. Giovanni introduced me to her. But I never mentioned

her to anyone else. Certainly not Berkeley Drummond."
Schorr closed his eyes, swallowing hard.

"Have you had any communication with Mr. Duffy in
the last two days?"

Schorr's eyes shot open. "What? Did you talk to him
already? Why didn't he tell me? Does he know you are investigating Berkeley's death?"

"I take it you are closer to Giovanni Duffy than you were
to Berkeley Drummond?" Court asked.

"Maybe not as close I as thought," Schorr said, bitterness
edging each word. His jaw jutted out as he looked past
Court's shoulder. "We are ... lovers."

Holy shit! This was getting more convoluted by the
minute. "How long have you and Duffy been lovers?"

"Five years. We've been very discreet," he said. "But,
you'd think he would have called me to tell me about this.
He could have warned me."

Court wanted to whip around to get Ivy's response to all
this, silently cursed the one-way mirror. He'd love to see the
look on her face about now. "So you were seeing Duffy and
the domme at the same time?" *As well as Ivy?*

Schorr became a statue, his voice strangled into tightness.
"What do you mean?"

Court cocked his head, considering the question, the way
Schorr was responding formed a whole new picture in his
head. "Did you go to the domme together? You and Duffy?"

He moaned a deep, mournful sound, clamping his eyes
shut. He rocked back and forth, whispering something in
Hebrew under his breath.

Court caught the attorney's eyes. The other man
shrugged and put a hand on Schorr's back. He leaned in

close, whispering into Schorr's ear. Schorr stopped his rocking.

"Can you answer the question, Mr. Schorr?"

He breathed in through his nostrils and out through his mouth, waving at his face with both hands. "Yes. Yes. Yes. Maybe four times a year. She would play us off each other. We would compete to be the better ..." He broke off, sudden tears streaming down his cheeks. "Look, I love my wife, I love Giovanni. I don't do monogamy well. If my wife..." He dropped his head into his hands.

Court gave him a minute before continuing. "Do you have any idea if Mr. Duffy and Berkeley had any sort of relationship?"

Schorr didn't move. He had drifted into another world. Court repeated his question.

Schorr spoke in a monotone. "I don't think so, but I'm not sure what to believe any more."

"How did you feel about Mr. Duffy going out to Belle Nuit once a week?"

He closed his eyes. "Annoyed more than anything. You wouldn't catch me dead in there, but Vanni felt like he was doing some sort of service there. Said he wanted to make a difference to newbies. Honestly, I think he went for quick pickups. I never saw him on Wednesdays. It's not like I would be jealous. We both have other things going on the side. Neither of us are good at monogamy."

"Mr. Schorr, where were you Wednesday night?" Court asked.

40

As soon as Schorr was gone, Ivy emerged from the observation room. "He was telling the truth in there. I don't think he had anything to do with Drummond's death."

"How well do you know him?" he asked.

She hesitated, focused intently at a spot on the ground so he couldn't see her eyes. "Not as well as I thought, maybe."

"Well enough that you're surprised he was seeing a domme?"

She kept her gaze lowered. "I thought I knew him better than that."

"I saw a picture of him on the internet. At a ball game. With your kid. I'm pretty sure you were sitting next to Schorr. Leaning against him."

Ivy cocked her head and met his eyes. "Yeah. So? We were friends."

"Close friends?"

"I can't believe he was seeing her the same time we were…"

She didn't need to finish the sentence. "Ivy, you should have told me."

She leaned against the wall, head back and eyes closed. "I haven't seen him in over a year, other than briefly at events. It was three months. We saw each other a couple times a week for three months. I guess this explains why he was usually available on Wednesdays. My husband and I were going through a rough spot."

Her conflict of interest was more than casual. "Look, I don't think he had anything to do with Drummond's death. We've got to check his alibi, but I don't want you working on anything to do with Schorr."

"Are you going to make that official?"

Writing up the details for the official report would mean everyone would know about her indiscretion. "No, I won't. I don't see a need to tell the entire department you had an affair. If it comes out later, we'll deal with it. But, if his alibi clears him, we can forget about your relationship. It's not likely to have any bearing on the case anyway."

Court's phone buzzed with a text from Mary Coleridge. The autopsy would be at eight in the morning. She was back from the derailment, but the staff was finishing the day with processing the victims they'd brought back with them.

He tapped his watch. "There's this family thing at seven. I gotta get a move on."

"Hold on. When're we hitting Belle Nuit? We still have to check up on Duffy's alibi?"

"Cami is a member there, I bet I could get her to take me up there after our dinner thing. You okay with me checking it out on my own?"

"You wouldn't mind?"

"Nah. All I have to do is flash Duffy's picture around, see if someone at the club remembers him from Wednesday night."

"Thanks, Pearson. I'll dive into that ream of Hunter's email Ashena printed out for us. It's something I can do at home." Ivy tapped a sheaf of papers to even them out and shoved it into a folder. She'd made an entire paper copy of the whole casebook, photos and all.

"You're a paper person, too?"

Ivy tucked the folder into her tote. "Yeah, I get screen headaches when I look at them too long. I like the way paper feels, too. I can draw on it, write down questions and take notes. I can cut it apart and make a different sort of timeline from statements. Add sticky notes. Still can't do that on a computer."

41

COURT FLIPPED HIS HOOD UP OVER HIS HEAD TO PROTECT himself from the brief drizzle. Britt had insisted on a second birthday celebration with family and close friends only. He thought it was silly to have two birthday parties, but he went anyway. Mostly for the pasta. Cami had readily agreed to leave as soon as they were done eating to take him over to Belle Nuit.

He filled her in on his date with Madeline.

"So what's the girl look like anyway?" she asked.

"Didn't you meet her at the party on Saturday?" Court asked.

"Can't remember. Got a photo of her?"

Court pulled up the selfie Madeline had sent him of her at work. Cami took the phone out of his hands. She let out an appreciative whistle. "She's hot. Wow. And you took her home with you last night?"

Was it only last night? Today had been one of the longest

Mondays of his career. Court grinned but didn't offer any
details.

"It's official. I no longer feel sorry for you."

"I figure I can stretch this out as long as possible. Keep
Britt off my back for a while."

"Or, maybe, it might actually turn into something more
than sex? Maybe Britt got it right this time."

Court wasn't looking for "right." All he needed was
company now and again. Sexual contact. Skin against skin.
He could live without a deeper connection.

Cami drove an ancient GM Roadster she tended like a
baby. It was only a problem if you were trying to have a
conversation while the engine was running. Court had to yell
to be heard. "So what did you want me to talk to you about
earlier? You texted me."

Cami didn't look at him but focused on the road.

Court was on immediate alert when she didn't answer
right away. Something was up.

She waved a hand around in the air. "I had a couple of
questions for you. But, I had to move on something. Got my
answers elsewhere."

Cami rarely lied to Court. The few times had been for
good reasons followed by excuses, apologies and explana-
tions. "You working on a new story?"

"Sort of."

Any prevarication on her part meant she was into something she didn't want to tell him. When she was digging into
something big, she usually got pretty mum about it. He
decided to not press it. He appreciated it when she didn't
push him for information, so he'd return the favor.

He had read a few of the stories she had published, but he didn't understand how she made a living at it. Come to think of it, there was a lot he didn't know about his friend. Cami had the physique and intellect to be some sort of government spook—CIA, FBI, Homeland Security. Journalism was a great cover. He had once joked with her about it, and her face had grown pensive and dark. She'd told him it would be better for everyone if he didn't ask so many questions about her job. He'd never figured out if she was serious or joking.

42

THERE WAS A SMALL LOT IN FRONT OF BELLE NUIT, BUT IT
was filled. They parked down the street, close to a popular
brew pub, and walked back to the club. The sign was
innocuous enough, simple blue neon letters surrounded by
three stars gave Belle Nuit an almost sophisticated air.
Nothing garish about it—the neon was understated, dark.
No flashing or blinking GIRLS! GIRLS! GIRLS! If he didn't
know what was going on inside, he'd assume it was a corner
bar like any other.

The few people standing in the covered smoking section
the requisite twenty-five feet from any doors looked like
anyone else stepping out for a smoke. Court was in jeans
with a sports coat, his usual work attire. Cami was dressed
vanilla for the birthday party—her usual leather and heavy
boots had been replaced with slacks with a tailored shirt
and tie.

The doorman did a quick double take at Cami. "Well,

look what the cat dragged in." He swung the door open wide for them.

The small lobby featured a series of coat hooks, most of which were filled. Music thumped behind a set of thick wooden doors across the lobby from the entrance. A woman in a tight leather skirt with an even tighter corset stood behind a podium that looked like any other hostess station in the city, complete with a little light over the pad on top.

She checked them out, her head jutting forward as she inspected Cami. "Whoa. I didn't recognize you, sir." She gave Court a cursory glance and winked at Cami. "Two for Monday Madness?"

"Actually, not tonight, Mac. This is my friend, Detective Court Pearson. I'm hoping you could help him out."

Court pulled out his ID, resting his wrist against the podium so she could examine it. "I'm investigating a homicide. I have a few questions about a member here."

Mac pressed her hands to her temples. "Not sure I can help." She turned to Cami with a disapproving glare. "You know the rules."

Cami held up her hands and shrugged. "I know, I know, but this is important, Mac. Talk to him. He's probably got a warrant tucked inside his jacket anyway."

"Cami," Court said, "I'm going to have to ask you to step out of earshot now, though."

Cami jutted out her lower lip in an exaggerated pout. "I'll go inside and see who's around. Mac, can I pop in for a bit?"

She opened the door leading into the main part of the club, slipping inside before Mac could protest. Laughter and music rippled out. Was that a scream?

Court hoped Cami would come back so he didn't have to go inside to find her. "I'm not asking you to break any confidentiality rules," he said to Mac. "He's already told me he's a member here. I need to establish whether or not this guy was here last Wednesday night."

"Our records are private."

"Your guests all have to sign in, right?"

"I can't have you looking at the guest book. You're probably looking for someone with their legal name, anyway. You know his scene name?"

"Let me make this easy on you." Court pulled out a small packet of papers and laid them out on the podium. "Here's a photo. He goes by Macbeth. And, here's a warrant to search for his activity here."

Mac whistled a low, breathy whistle. "Oh, I don't even have to look *him* up. He's here every Wednesday night. Checks in about five or five thirty. Leaves around ten. Every week."

Court was surprised at how easy that was. "You're sure? Was he here last Wednesday?"

"Yeah. He volunteers here during our new member orientation. He gets here early to set up the snacks and drinks. He was definitely here. I think he even gave the tour last week."

That had been easy. Maybe too easy. "Anyone else here who could confirm this?"

Mac jut out her lower lip, rounding her eyes. "You don't believe me, Detective?" She put a hand over her heart. "I'm devastated."

Court held up both hands. "Could be he called you to have you cover for him."

"Who me? Lie to such an adorable-looking morsel like you? No way, Detective." She held up the three fingers of her other hand, shifting the other from her heart to squeeze her breast. "Scout's honor. Macbeth was here last Wednesday, like clockwork." She tilted her head to the double-thick doors. "But, if you want, you could go check with Harry, the barkeep. He's here every Monday through Thursday, and he would know for sure." A smile played at her lips.

"Is it okay to go in there with clothes on?" Court wasn't sure of what might be happening beyond the doors. He'd never been inside before, but he'd heard plenty of stories.

"Of course, though not everyone inside will be dressed. And, there's likely some sort of spanking going on. Maybe some actual c-o-p-ulation?" She cackled at her joke.

"I think I can manage." He paused, pulling out the other photos he had with him. "Any chance you recognize any of these three?"

Mac leaned forward and studied the DMV head shots of Payne, Nolan and the drawing they'd gotten from Audrey Drummond's description. She tapped the drawing. "This is kind of useless, isn't it?" She picked up each picture and held them closer to examine them one at a time. "I don't recognize any of these. Not that I know *everyone* who comes in here. Have you shown these to Bam-Bam? She's been a member here longer than I have."

"Bam-Bam?" he asked before realizing she was talking about Cami. He looked over at the door to the inside. "Oh, right. I forgot. Maybe I'll do that."

"Anything *else* I can help you with?" The look she gave him made it clear she'd join him inside for something pretty kinky.

"That's it. Thanks for your help, Mac."

Court paused before pushing the doors open and stepping into the other room. His eyes took a minute to adjust to the dim interior. It was busier than he would have thought for a Monday night. He scanned the room for Cami, and spotted her on a sofa with another woman who was leaning in close, playing with her tie.

Half the people were dressed, the other half naked. Two women leaned over benches, their naked buttocks up in the air. A tall man in jeans and a crisp button-down shirt was spanking one of them with his bare hands, slapping against her pinkening skin to the rhythm of the music. The other woman was watching, wiggling her own bare bottom in anticipation. Court averted his eyes. Whatever went on in here was consensual, all adult, and none of his business.

He strode directly to the bar. "You Harry?" Court asked.

"Yup. What can I do for you, officer?"

Was it that obvious? Court spread the photos on the dark shiny surface. "Recognize any of these guys?"

Harry looked over the rim of his glasses at Court before shifting them up on his nose and examining the pictures. "Well, this here, that's Macbeth. He's here all the time. Well, at least on Wednesdays. Sometimes comes in Tuesday afternoons." He picked up Nolan's picture and shook his head. Same for Payne's. "Don't know these guys."

"Do you know if Macbeth was here last Wednesday?"

Harry rubbed his nose with a Kleenex and sniffed in heavily through his nose. "Last Wednesday? Let me think for a sec. I'm not sure I was here last Wednesday. Mighta been the day I was sick. Let me look." He examined his phone for a minute. "Yeah. I was out. So, I can't tell ya for sure. But,

Macbeth hasn't missed a Wednesday in years. He was probably here."

Court tapped the photos into a neat stack against the bar
top. "And Macbeth is the only familiar one of these?"

Harry shrugged. "None of them others look familiar.
Sorry. Want something to drink?"

"Thanks, but I'm going to grab Bam-Bam over there and
head out."

Cami had moved from the couch. She was standing at
the edge of another room watching a group play some sort
of game. Court sidled up to her to watch as six naked men
played a version of Simon Says with a domme at the front of
the room. She barked out orders, telling them to hold themselves, kneel, or do other things Court did only in private.
Instead of "Simon Says" she said "Mistress says."

He hovered near Cami for a moment before she realized he was there. "Dude. I didn't know you were inside.
Done?"

Court tore his attention away from the game. "Very
much so."

Cami laughed, lightly kissing the cheek of a woman
standing next to her as she turned to join him.

Court waved at Mac as he pushed the outer door open.

"Come back any time, Detective. But leave the badge
and gun at home so you won't be so overdressed." She
pursed her lips at him in a long-distance kiss. "And you," she
said pointing at Cami. "You look adorable all vanilla
like that."

"Bᴀᴍ-Bᴀᴍ?" he asked as he lowered himself into Cami's car.

She laughed. "Mac has a big mouth. Did you get anything from her?"

"What I needed." He pulled all the photos out of his pocket, handing them to Cami. "Before we get moving, take a look. You recognize any of these guys?" Mac had made a point about Cami being a longtime member of the club. Maybe she did know something useful.

She examined them under the streetlight coming in through the windshield. She held up Duffy's photo. "He's here a lot. Don't know much about him. He's a guy, and I tend to ignore guys. Unless they're being humiliated in public." She laughed, tilting her head toward the club. "The others are not at all familiar. Sorry." She handed him back the photos and cranked the engine. "So, Macbeth, there, I don't know him, but I think he's pretty stand-up. Is he a suspect in the Drummond thing?"

Had he mentioned Drummond to her at all? He was pretty sure he hadn't said anything at the bar Friday night. Saturday at the party? "Drummond thing?" he repeated.

"Relax, Court. I read the press release from this afternoon. You were listed as the lead detective on the Drummond death."

Court had forgotten Stensland's plans for the press release. "Right. Okay. So, yeah, I was here to clear Macbeth, so keep it to yourself, okay?"

"No need to lecture me, Court. The last thing I need is to be associated with leaking a member's identity from Belle Nuit. They'd never let me back in there."

"You go there a lot?"

"Used to all the time. I probably get there once a month these days."

"Why's that?"

"Remember that hot femme I found at Lez Brut a couple of months ago?"

Court did, except Cami had not mentioned her since. It was the last time they hit the monthly LGBTQ-friendly dance together. Court had gone home alone after Cami had been smitten by a younger, hot blonde femme. Court hadn't even got a very good look at her before Cami was spinning away out of the bar, a huge shit-eating grin on her face. "You still seeing her?" Cami nodded. In spite of the dim light coming in from the streetlights, Court could see the dark blush creep up on Cami's cheeks. "Don't think I've ever seen you blush like that before."

"Well, actually… she may be a petite girly-girl, but she's … a twisted, talented top."

Court twisted in his seat. "Wait. I thought you…." Cami a bottom? He couldn't imagine her playing the submissive to anyone. "No way."

"I know. I know. I used to be. But, we got into this *thing* a week or so after meeting. So, basically, I lost a bet, and I ended up subbing. It worked for me. It was the first time I'd ever let another woman take control in bed."

Court wouldn't have been more surprised if she had told him she was straight.

"Here's the thing. By having to do things for her, and get her off … she never *has* to touch me. But when she does? Man. I actually feel something. Physically. Like I never felt before." She wiped at some dust on her steering wheel with a finger. "I thought I was totally stone butch, you know? But I'm not. Not with her."

"Why haven't you mentioned her before now?" Court hadn't realized that Cami was capable of holding back on him. The smallest twinge of upset at the betrayal twisted in his gut. It wasn't a big deal, was it? He had secrets he kept from her.

"I was told not to tell anyone."

"Wait, she gets to tell you what you talk about?"

They were at a stoplight. Cami turned toward him and shrugged. "It's part of our agreement. If I decide I'm done with it, I'll be done with it. As it is, she's going to give me some shit for telling you."

Court tried to understand the appeal. Being married had been enough of a drain on his freedom. It wasn't that he didn't like it, or wouldn't want it back again, but it was a conventional relationship. He was expected to let Amanda know if he'd be late from work out of common courtesy; she would do the same. They each had their own friends. They each had their own lives beyond their marriage. There were more than fifty people at her funeral he'd never met before. Friends from school and work and *her life*. "She knows you hang out with me?"

"Yeah. And if she ever tried to control more than I want her to, I'd be out of it. It's not a big deal, Court. It's willing fun on my part."

Court felt a sudden urge to give Cami pamphlets on domestic violence. Abusers started out controlling their victims in small ways, gradually building their influence until they were completely in charge. He wondered what else Cami hadn't told him. "Are you living with her?"

"I still have my apartment."

"Keep it."

"Dude, you need to let up. This is all good. We're doing things safely. She's careful. I'm careful. Don't worry about me."

Court couldn't help it. It was in his nature to be skeptical. Of everything. He pointed to the side of the road. "Hey, drop me off here."

Cami pulled into the exact same spot where Drummond had parked his car the night he died. "Why here?" she asked.

"I need to look around."

"It has to do with the Drummond case, doesn't it?"

He didn't like the way she asked the question. It wasn't like her to ask about his work, and she'd already brought it up once. He'd opened the door by having her drive him to Belle Nuit. Maybe he should have taken the bus.

43

Court waited until Cami was down the block before going into the little market and buying a cold soda. He went outside to drink it where the teens had been hanging out the previous day. It was almost ten o'clock, but they were nowhere to be seen. The lower half of the building where Drummond had died was dark—the business and shops on those levels closed for the night. A third of the windows on the top two floors of the building still had lights on.

He made a full 360-degree turn where he stood, looking for anything he might have missed. The street wasn't far off Broadway, the main drag down Capitol Hill. There was enough traffic at any time of day or night, and he didn't think any one person would get much notice coming or going from the building. Add in the fact the area was famous for its colorful population of gays, drag queens, and artsy hipsters, it was even more unlikely anyone would have noticed anything helpful to their investigation. It made sense to Court the killer had left wearing the suit after killing Drummond.

He went back into the store to show the clerk the drawing and photos, including one of Berkeley Drummond. The clerk didn't recognize any of them, not even Duffy, who was in the neighborhood on a weekly basis. He left and meandered slowly in the direction of his home.

Court's usual routine had him riding past this very spot every day. He was seeing his neighborhood in a whole new light.

He saw Cassandra D., a hooker he'd run into a few times over the last three years, on the corner across from the mini-mart and checked his watch. She'd switched neighborhoods regularly. He hadn't seen her for at least six months. Maybe she'd been around last week. She was leaning into the open window of a red Suburban. Shaking her head, she stepped back onto the curb and waved the car away.

Court ambled over to her, not wanting to startle her. She knew he was a cop and had always kept her distance. He wanted to tell her that he wasn't the kind of cop who would beat the shit out of her "by accident." He wasn't the kind of person who would do that to anyone.

He approached with his hands buried in his pockets, hoping to appear casual and off-duty, not that he was ever completely off-duty. "Heya, Cassandra. Been a while since you've been around here."

She spun around, her eyes narrowing into tiny, wary slits. "Detective." She drawled out the word as if she was trying it on for size and not knowing how to make it fit.

The way she said it made him feel dirty somehow, complicit in the ways other cops treated those who lived or worked on the street. He lifted his chin toward the building across the street. "Were you around the other night?"

Her eyes followed his movement, and she blinked a couple of times, the heavy mascara on her lashes sparkling deep green. "And you think I can help you?" Her voice was deep and masculine.

He lifted the drawing so she could see it. "Ever see this guy around?"

She paused before bending over to look at it. She was at least six-four without her heels. In them she towered over him. She let out a snort of a laugh and leaned against the poster-littered telephone pole behind her. She took off a shoe that would have fit him with room to spare and rubbed away a piece of something Court couldn't see. "Looks like you."

Why did people keep saying that? "Okay, so what about these guys?" He handed her the photos of Duffy, Payne, Nolan and Drummond.

She studied them, looking bored while she did. She fanned them out like a deck of cards with Drummond and Duffy's images on top. "These two. They real familiar."

"Remember the last time you saw either of them?"

She held up her hands, her long nails glinting in the light from the overhead lamps. She inspected them as if there might be answers somewhere embedded in the specks of glitter. "Don't recall exactly."

"Don't or won't?"

"You know, you are taking up a lot of my time. I could be with someone right now. I saw three cars slow down already, just since we been talking."

Court gave her a twenty out of his wallet. "Maybe this will jog your memory."

She took the money and slid it into her bra. She tapped Duffy's photo. "I seen him. A few times, mostly at night."

"And?" Court prompted.

She let out an exasperated sigh. "I don't got more, officer. Look, I seen him a few times coming or going out of there. But I ain't keeping his diary, you know what I mean?"

"You ever talk to him?"

"No. That skinny white boy ain't having any part of this." She dragged her hands along her sides and shimmied.

"And the other?" he asked, tapping Drummond's face again.

"He's the dead one. I saw him come out of there a coupla times. That's it."

"Ever see the two of them together?"

Cassandra breathed in deeply, her eyes rolling upward in practiced exacerbation. "No. I don't remember seeing them together."

He handed her his card. "Call me if you remember anything else about either of them, okay?"

She took the card from him, smiling at him through her lashes. "Oh, you're giving me your number?" She held the card up to the light holding it out to read it. She slipped it in next to the money he'd given her. There was more than enough silicone to keep both in place.

44

THERE WAS NO WAY COURT COULD GO TO SLEEP AFTER
consuming the gigantic pile of spaghetti with browned butter
and mizithra cheese, even three hours later. The evening had
worked out rather well, all in all, but it didn't take much for
him to get distracted with the case again. He flipped on the
TV as he made himself an Alka-Seltzer to calm his pasta-
laden stomach, the old commercial jingle playing alongside
the fizzing in the glass.

As soon as the news came on, he was wishing he'd
climbed into bed instead. The local news was updating the
Drummond homicide. He turned the volume up, wondering
what news they could have after the press release earlier in
the day. Maybe it was a recap.

The perky blonde had recently taken over the second
chair on the local show. Something about her was familiar.
Maybe it was because all women news anchors sported the
same shoulder-length bobs and pasted-on smiles. She smiled
brightly before switching to a more serious face. She didn't

have quick transitions down quite yet. "And this just in. We reported the death of Seattle philanthropist and businessman Berkeley Drummond on Friday. Seattle Police Department has released a statement today telling us Drummond's death is being investigated as, quote, *suspicious*. Scott Ingram is here to fill us in. Scott, what's the story?"

The view switched to a man standing outside the building with a ticker across the bottom of the screen declaring it BREAKING NEWS, LIVE REPORT. The street address of the building was visible over the top of Ingram's head.

There hadn't been any sign of a news van when Court had been talking to Cassandra less than an hour before. They must have gotten there within a few minutes of Court's leaving or taped it earlier and were faking the live portion.

Ingram held his right hand to his earpiece and his microphone with his left. "Thank you, Tracy. The Seattle Police Department has been out in full force today, questioning the neighbors in the building where Drummond's body was found Friday afternoon in the building directly behind me."

The camera panned the area behind Ingram, and lifted upward to show the building's entire facade before returning to Ingram. "One witness, who wishes to remain confidential, told me the office where Drummond's body was found was, and this is a quote, 'all a sham.'"

Court sat up, stomach forgotten, sleepiness swept away. *Damn. Damn. Damn.*

"The original press release late Friday night says Berkeley Drummond died, and indicates the investigation was ongoing and the press would be updated when there was further information. Earlier this afternoon, the police issued an update stating the death is now being investigated as suspicious. They won't come out and say it's a murder, because even the police do not have an official cause of death. The autopsy has not yet been performed."

"Scott, isn't that unusual?"

"Tracy, it is, but the medical examiner's office was inundated with victims of the train derailment west of Wenatchee early Saturday morning. Berkeley Drummond's autopsy is scheduled for early tomorrow morning, however, and the Seattle Police Department has promised a statement with a definitive cause of death by tomorrow afternoon."

"Thank you, Scott. What else have you learned about the circumstances around Berkeley Drummond's death?"

Court bristled at their smiling faces, the way they used each other's names all the time. Why did they do that? The people watching them didn't care.

"Sources have confirmed Allegiance Investments is the front for a professional dominatrix..." The camera swung upward in a dramatic arc and focused on a window as he spoke "calling herself Mistress Fidelma. Sources say she keeps her private dungeon right here. And it was here that Berkeley Drummond's body was found."

Court pulled out his telephone and texted Ivy: *Channel 7, NOW.*

The camera panned back toward Ingram again. Court could see the excitement of a gleeful journalistic coup. Fuck. Reporters. This was fast even for them.

Ivy texted back. *Been watching. Tenants talking? Bound to come out, right?*

The screen switched to a photograph of the locked and taped office zooming into the sign on the front door. "This is the sham office. Behind this door is where Berkeley Drummond's body was found, tied in bondage ropes hanging from a hook in the ceiling."

Ingram looked into the camera with large sad eyes. "I have seen photos of the crime scene. The images are so disturbing we can't show them on the air."

Apparently, there weren't enough salacious details in the official press release for Ingram. He was bound to go digging on his own. That's what reporters do.

What made Court's stomach clench was his mention of the crime-scene photos. From the description he gave, he wasn't lying—he had seen them. None of the crime-scene photos had been released. Court was sure nothing about Drummond being tied up had made it out through official channels. But Ingram's description was too spot-on for him to not have seen them.

"The lead detective on this case has not returned any of my calls. We will keep you updated as this bizarre story continues to unfold. Back to you, Tracy."

"Thank you, Scott." She turned to stare back into the camera. "And in other news, you can expect some high winds and heavy rain to hit the Puget Sound by late...."

Court shut the TV off and flopped back against the sofa. He double-checked to make sure there were no missed calls or new messages. That asshole was claiming he had called him? Court had to keep himself from throwing the phone at the screen. His name and contact information had been part of the press release. He would have been easy to find. He dialed Ivy.

"D<small>ID</small> you put your tote down anywhere? Do you know anyone in the media?"

The closing of a door told Court that Ivy had moved from her bedroom into a different room. "No. Well. Yes, but, I don't see how anyone could have gotten into it. I had the tote with me at the bar, then left it locked in my car for ten minutes while I got some groceries."

"You left it in the car while you went inside the store?"

"My car was locked. No one broke in, I would have noticed. It didn't come from me."

His heartbeat had slowed down a little. "Okay, okay. So who then? We didn't give anyone access to the photos. They're all on the station computer or in your tote."

"Or on your phone. Court, you took pictures on your phone. Is there any chance someone could have hacked it? You use a screen lock, right?"

Court had a password protection on his phone, and he sure as hell hadn't texted any of the photos to anyone. "No. It's in my pocket all the time. Besides, I dumped them all onto the computer Sunday morning. My phone is clean. It's got to be someone in the department. Unless someone got hold of your files."

Ivy's voice sounded muffled, congested. "I honestly don't see how that could have happened."

"Langston, are you crying?"

"Fuck you, Pearson."

45

COURT YANKED THE DRAWER OPEN, SURE THE DAMN TIE clip should be in the front. He hated getting dressed up for five minutes of courtroom testimony. Lack of sleep and having to dig through his dresser put him in a foul mood. He ran through the day ahead as he hauled things out of the drawer and tossed them on top of the dresser. A screwdriver. Autopsy at seven. His last dead cell phone. Court at nine. A plastic hair comb he thought he had lost at the gym. Back to real work by ten at the latest. A wad of papers—old receipts and ATM slips. A pair of sunglasses he rarely used. He stopped short when his fingers touched the small blue box.

He examined it, noticing, for the first time, the box had several nicks and tears roughening its edges. He hesitated for a moment before opening it, knowing what was inside, but needing to see it again. He lifted the lid, picking up the thin silver chain. He held it, looped over his palm, the cold metal weightiness of it familiar. Its slinkiness made it slip down onto his wrist. The small metal circle with the letter A dropped downward and the chain tugged at his skin exactly as it had when he draped it around Amanda's neck the night he had given it to her.

They had finished making love, and he needed to dig it out of the pocket of the jeans he'd discarded on the floor. He rolled off the bed and onto his knees. She turned onto her side, her cheek rested on her hand, her elbow making a dimple on the bed.

"What are you doing?"

Court smiled up at her from where he knelt, kissing her while his hand fished around into the pile of clothing. He found the box he'd been carrying around for weeks waiting for an ethereal moment of "knowing" to come to him. That sought-after moment had arrived as they made love, though not for the first time. It had been different, though. They had shifted from the tentative, questioning and fumbling of new lovers into a comfortable couple where they could read each others wants and desires without hesitation. He palmed the necklace before breaking the kiss, keeping it hidden from her. "Sit up and close your eyes."

She hesitated for a second, but shifted into a sitting position. Her legs dangled languidly from the bed but open, making room for him to slip in between them. She closed her eyes, wrapping her legs around his torso, her heels pressing into his back. The scent of her, their sweat, everything mingling together made him want her again.

He lowered his head to kiss the top of her right thigh, worked his way up to her stomach, to her breast, to her collar bone. By the time his lips graced her earlobe, he was fully extended on his knees, her nipples dancing against his chest. He opened the chain loop, reached around to the back of her neck, and clasped it, her hair tickling his cheek and ear. He leaned back, sliding his fingers under the chain until they met the pendant.

An old-fashioned typewriter key with her initial, A, for Amanda, hung from his fingertips. He guided it to the cleft between her breasts and let it fall there.

She breathed in as it landed against her skin and shimmied her shoulders in an exaggerated shiver. Her lips broke into a smile and her hand flew up to touch it. "Can I see?"

Court rocked back onto his heels so he could watch her as she opened her eyes.

Her hair cascaded over her shoulders as she dipped her head to look at the pendant. "Oh, Court! You remembered," she said, her breath catching on the words.

Court let out the small breath he had been holding. He had known she would like it, but he hadn't been sure what she would say about him giving her something, especially right then. "Of course I did. You pointed to it and said," — here, he altered his voice into a falsetto caricature of hers —"*I love that little letter A, you can buy it for me as a present anytime.*"

She hadn't, of course, but she had oohed and ahhhed over it in the window of a little jeweler on Sutter Street in San Francisco. Several times. Even a dense guy like Court could get the hint.

She hit him on the shoulder, teasing, then leaned in to kiss him, pulling him toward her with her legs. The pendant swung forward and hit him on the chest, bouncing back and forth between them like a pendulum.

Amanda wore it every day, under her shirt with other jewelry or all by itself. It would swing down, hitting him on his chin when she was on top during sex. Over their eight years together, the back of the pendant was dulled from brushing against her soft skin. She wore it until the moment she had died. She took it off and put it with her note, explaining why she couldn't continue in a world without Bailey.

Court hadn't been enough for her. He shook his head to clear it all away. He didn't have time for this. He needed to focus. Testify. Get to work.

He dropped the pendant back in the fluffy white pillow of cotton lining the box and closed it. He swept everything else back into the drawer and set the box in the center of the dresser. He didn't know what he was going to do with it, he only knew he had to do *something*.

46

COURT COULD NEVER HAVE BEEN A PATHOLOGIST. IT wasn't the bodies or the job itself so much as the location. Morgues were windowless places. He always needed a window—a way out. Ever since he was a kid, he preferred being outside where he could be physical. He always got a little edgy when he spent too much time inside doing the desk part of his job.

Of all the clichés held up by television and movies, the deep dank nature of the morgue was one true to life—even if it had been recently remodeled into a modern wonder of stainless steel, brighter lights, and mildew-free tile. There was no changing the nature of a place dealing so intimately with death. King County's Medical Examiner office was located on the second floor of an annex to Harborview Medical Center—the same hospital where Li Wu had spent the evening of the murder getting his severed toe sewn back on.

Because of Drummond's close ties to the police department and political donations, the mayor, the chief, and Lieutenant Stensland were waiting by the time Court got there. Stensland gave him a penetrating look, but didn't say anything about the news the night before.

Two techs finished photographing the body and wheeled it into position. Mary began with an external inspection, hovering inches over Drummond's skin, speaking into the microphone clipped to her white suit. "The rope marks are clear. This indicates either willingness on the part of the victim to be bound, or that he was unconscious while he was bound. A struggle would have left more marks and bruising rather than a clean line that we see here."

She finished the external exam with a fluorescing light over the skin. Blots of purple showed up on his genitalia and on his face. She motioned for the photographer to take a picture of the pattern. "Both samples appear to be semen. The location on the victim's face, and the angle at which the body was discovered, indicate a second male in the room. That is, someone else ejaculated on the deceased's face. We'll send out for DNA testing."

Court took a peek at Ivy; they had already thought a man was responsible. It was nice to have confirmation. He resisted holding up a hand for a high-five from her.

Mary stepped away so the techs could get into the body and turned to her witnesses. "While they prep the organs, I think this would be a good time to clarify that it is possible that someone, anyone, could have squirted semen on the victim's face. However, I think the more likely scenario is that the victim was bound and pulled into position. The pattern of spray over the top of his forehead and nose indicate a male stood in front of him and ejaculated onto his face from slightly above. The pattern is more consistent with an ejaculate spray."

The techs had emptied the organs onto the cutting board over the sink. "Let's take a look at the parts here. There is a four-and-a-half-centimeter tumor in the brain, metastases throughout the brain, kidney, liver and lungs. He didn't have much time left."

She turned to the body again and spent a few minutes examining the neck and head. "The absence of congestion of face and neck above the ligature mark, lack of petechiae on the eyelids and conjunctiva leads me to conclude the cause of death was the obstruction of arterial flow to the brain due to backpressure on carotid arteries." She turned to face them. "In other words, the weight of the head against the rope was in itself, sufficient to occlude the carotid arteries and cause death. He got tired, his head went down, and he lost consciousness. Because his weight remained on the rope, he never regained consciousness and died."

Mary stepped back and crossed her arms, contemplating the scene for a moment before turning to the entourage. "All right, folks. I'm going to call this a definite homicide. His heart was fine. And, he most certainly did not do this to himself." Mary rested her chin in one hand, finger tapping at her lower lip.

"So," Court said. "Nothing surprising then."

"Had to look in order to be certain."

"It's possible that some freaky game went too far and whoever was with him ran when they realized Drummond was dead. Or tied him up and left him to die," Ivy said.

Court rubbed at his neck with both hands and turned to his boss. "Someone was with him, someone left him alone. It doesn't matter to our investigation if Drummond was alive or not when he got left. We're still looking for the same person, regardless of his intent."

Stensland took off his glasses and rubbed at the indentations left by the nose pads. "I'm inclined to agree. We can figure out charges—murder, manslaughter, whatever—when we find our killer. Honestly, I'm betting murder, but you're right. We just need to find him."

"Or her," Ivy added. "I know Dr. Coleridge said it looked like ejaculate, but a turkey baster could fake that pretty well."

Stensland looked at her as if he'd forgotten she was in the room.

"I can test the turkey baster theory if you want," Mary said. "If I can find a turkey baster that makes that kind of pattern, I'll be surprised. The one I have at home isn't forceful enough to do the kind of pattern we see here."

Stensland shook his head. "We'll come back to that if we need to."

Mary bobbed up onto her toes and dropped to her heels. She was done with them and wanted them gone. "Anything else?" she asked.

"You think that tumor could interfere with his reasoning?" Court asked.

"It was interfering with all sorts of functioning. Reasoning, muscle control, memory. Do you have a specific concern?"

"Drummond didn't use a code on his phone. Kinda odd given who he was."

Mary shrugged. "Ask his wife about it. She's the most

likely to know that kind of detail about his condition. The day-to-day stuff. His memory could have been affected."

COURT GRABBED Ivy by the elbow and ushered her out of there as Stensland turned back to the chief and the mayor. They delved right into a discussion about how to handle the press, a subject Court didn't want to touch. Let Stensland handle all that shit.

"Walk with me to the courthouse. I have to be there in twenty minutes. It should take me maybe ten, fifteen minutes to testify and then I'll be back at the office."

"We knew it wasn't suicide all along. What did that tell us other than the person who did it was a man? Or maybe a woman who had access to semen and a turkey baster or an accomplice?"

"We'll get DNA from it. It will help at trial, at least."

"I'm back to thinking Karen Hunter is involved with an accomplice. She made a second card key, gave it to another of her subs—maybe Duffy, maybe Schorr even—and had him off Drummond."

Court didn't feel it. Unless it had been some misguided attempt at assisted suicide. Take him out doing something he loved. But Hunter had appeared stunned at the news of his cancer. And why would Drummond agree to a plan that would so obviously point directly at Hunter?

He filled her in on his trip to Belle Nuit the previous night. "I think we should get a sample from Duffy and Schorr to see if either of them matches the semen."

"So, maybe Duffy lied, and used his longtime history at Belle Nuit to cover?"

Court shrugged. Duffy wouldn't be stupid enough to leave his semen on Drummond's face, but maybe he didn't know he was committing murder. "If Hunter set up something elaborate with Duffy, she could have lied to him. Had him thinking he was in some sort of sub war with Drummond and she would be letting Drummond down."

"Duffy's not a huge guy. You think he could fit the suit?"

"If Hunter lied about one thing, she could have lied about the suit. Provided him with a whole outfit to fool Drummond. Hell, maybe they didn't even have to fool him. Maybe Drummond was in on it." Court's head ached from the possibilities.

47

COURT TURNED OFF HIS PHONE TO KEEP IT FROM distracting him while testifying. Judge Griffith was known for his hatred of anything electronic. A good number of cops had been held in contempt for their equipment beeping too loudly while they were on the stand.

The jury was attentive, and Court did his best to smile and meet their eyes often. Some detectives were known for being so condescending to juries they worked against their own testimony. Court was used to taking the extra effort to be the "nice guy," so it was easy for him. There was a lot of nodding of heads and note taking, anyway.

There was a much livelier buzz in the squad room when he entered. A lot of sympathetic smiles as he walked to his desk. If anyone had missed the news the previous night, they had caught up with it online this morning.

Stensland was standing in his doorway to his office, like a spider waiting for its web to jiggle. He jerked his thumb over his shoulder toward his office. "Langston, you too."

STENSLAND SHUT the door behind them with an ominous thud. No one sat down. Stensland faced them across his desk, hands bunching into fists against the wood, leaning toward them. The extra flesh on his cheeks slid forward as his eyes ground into Court's. "What the fuck happened?"

Court met his eyes, unwilling to take the fall for this bit of bullshit. "There was a leak. I haven't had any chance to look into it."

"You disappeared out of the autopsy suite."

"I had to testify in the Allegheri case at nine. I think it went well."

"It might be the only thing that goes well for you today, Pearson. Langston, you look like shit. Were you responsible for this disaster?"

"No sir." Her voice quavered upward in tone, making her answer more of a question. "I don't think so."

Stensland leaned further across the desk, his face mere inches from hers. "Think? You. Don't. Think. So."

She squeezed her eyes shut at the barrage, swallowing hard before she spoke. "I took some files home, but they were locked in my car or on my person the entire evening. There is no way anyone could have got hold of them. That's what I meant."

"Now, I'm going to say this once. You two are on the thinnest ice possible here. Not only did someone get a photograph of Drummond trussed up like a pig, they let out he was involved with this Mistress Fidelma person. I have a good mind to pull the two of you off this case. Photos? Case photos out to the fucking press?"

There was no way Stensland was going to pull them. He was bluffing. Court was sure he could solve the case. They were getting close, he could feel it. "Sir, the information about the dominatrix came from a citizen source, completely legally free to speak his mind."

Stensland grunted. He pointed a menacing finger toward the window. "I have to go out there and update the press later today. Now, instead of a simple piece on an ongoing investigation, I'm going to be attacked by a bunch of pinhead reporters trying to get the juiciest, dirtiest bit of gossip they can. They don't give a flying fuck that Drummond is dead, they want to know what kind of pervert he was. And the news we got from the autopsy is he died because of some rope around his neck. I am sure Ingram is going to have a field day with that. You tell me, Pearson, how the hell did Ingram get the photos? You and I both know those are all in-house."

Court didn't have a clue. "I'll get Ashena on it right away. If anyone can figure out who copied them off the system, she can."

Stensland crossed his arms, eyeing Court, then Ivy, with long appraising looks. "Give me a reason, any good reason, why I shouldn't pull you off this case."

Court held Stensland's gaze as an awkward silence fell over the room. He'd never seen the other man so angry before. "We have solid leads, sir. I think we're close, and if you take us off now, we'll lose the building momentum." He paused. "Of course, if we are forced to hand over the case, whoever takes it will have to review everything we've done. Go over all the possible suspects we've already cleared."

Court let the last words sink in. Stensland wasn't an idiot.

He had been angry and spoken out of turn. If he took away the case now, someone else would be asking questions about why Stensland had taken on calling the burner phones and be curious as to how he had cleared them all so quickly.

Stensland mimicked Court's posture, but his voice remained tight. "You need to figure out how Ingram got those photos."

"I'll do that, too. After I find the killer."

Ivy slapped the desk. "After *we* find the killer."

"Right. After Langston and I find the killer, we'll make sure we find the leak."

"You have until Thursday. I want this thing wrapped up before that goddamn conference opens."

48

COURT DROPPED INTO HIS CHAIR, SCRUBBING AT HIS FACE with both hands. Was it only Tuesday? It looked like today was going to be another long haul.

Ivy leaned against the wall of his cubicle, coffee cup in hand. "I think we should pull Karen Hunter back in."

"I know you do. Let's go back over your theory again." Court wasn't liking it, but he had to give Ivy a chance to make her case or she'd never let it go.

"Karen Hunter made the card key and gave it to an accomplice—Duffy, or Schorr maybe—who was waiting for her call. When her son got sick, she found the perfect opportunity. She called her guy and had him show up at four thirty to get ready. She texted Drummond about canceling after he would already be on his way, and she knew him well enough to know he'd turn off his phone before crossing the bridge. The second text was a cover."

This was pretty out-there, but Court needed to hear her out. He'd lost some objectivity around Hunter and needed to

tread carefully. Her theory almost made sense, if they had
some sort of motive for Hunter to kill her cash cow. "You
think Hunter had an accomplice kill one of her favorite and
best clients? The only evidence we have is there was semen
on Drummond's face. That could have been entirely
consensual."

"In what way is being killed consensual?"

"Not the killing. The ejaculation part."

"That's sick."

"Would you drop the judgment? Why can't you accept
the fact people get off in different ways? How did you
survive in Vice for three years?" He'd raised his voice louder
than he had intended.

She glowered at him, glancing around the room. "She's
the one who told us Drummond was her best client. But she
also has Duffy—he's got deep pockets, too. And Schorr. And
sixteen other clients. Maybe she didn't even need Drummond. Maybe they worked together on this, giving Hunter
the alibi while enlisting the aid of someone else. Let's haul
Hunter's ass back in today, put some pressure on her, and
suss things out. There's not always a logical motive. You
know that, Pearson."

She was talking so fast Court was having a hard time
keeping up. "You think Drummond and Hunter set this up
together with a *third* person?"

"Hey, don't rule it out as impossible. We know there was
another man involved. The most logical solution is that
Hunter made a key and wiped it from her logs. She says she
doesn't go into them, but she could be lying about that as
well as everything else."

Court didn't like this theory much, but she was right. It

wasn't *impossible*. Not very probable, either. "So, you're thinking they don't want Hunter getting into trouble, so they find an accomplice willing to do the deed? They wait until a tight and realistic alibi for Hunter comes up—lucking into her son having appendicitis. But why would he dress up at all if Drummond knew him?"

"I don't know. Maybe they set it up so that if anyone saw the guy leaving, there would be an obvious suspect."

"But the semen. The DNA is going to prove there was another man involved. Why would he leave that kind of evidence?"

"Pearson, the data bases aren't going to have everyone's DNA in there. If they found a guy without a criminal history, chances are there's no record of him. Or, as you said earlier, maybe he didn't know Drummond was supposed to die, or Hunter didn't know he was going to get off all over Drummond's face."

"I still think it was some guy who has been after Drummond for a while. Planning, waiting, and then acting on the moment. The card key was used for *six weeks* before his death. It indicates the third person was checking out the scene and making plans. You saw how upset Hunter was when she saw those extra entries. She didn't know about the second key."

"Or, she's a terrific actress."

"You really want to bring Hunter in?"

"Yes. You know as well as I do most people break when confronted. Let's hit her hard one last time. If she doesn't confess this time, I'll shut up about her."

The morning was moving on. Walker and one of his

techs would be arriving for their interviews any minute. "Okay. I'll call her and have her come in."

"No. I want to send officers to collect her. Get her a little rattled."

Court would normally have no problem with this tactic. Why was it making him so uncomfortable now? The answer was obvious. He was attracted to Karen Hunter in a way he shouldn't be. "Fine. Let's do this."

If Ivy wanted to hang herself, he wasn't going to stop her. Her argument that Hunter was guilty, that they had enough of a story to break her, could be substantiated with the right twist in the report. He decided to go along with it. If Ivy was right, then he'd have to accept it. If she was wrong, she'd accept it and they could move forward with the investigation. The truth was, most people wanted to confess when given the opportunity. A formal police interrogation was one way to help them do it. He pushed himself to keep an open mind. Maybe Ivy was right.

"Okay. Get the ball rolling on getting her in here. I'm going to check my messages," he said as they stepped into the elevator. Ivy looked pleased with herself. He had the feeling she was going to fall on her ass in the interrogation. "You get to take the lead on this one."

"You gonna hang out behind the glass or come in with me?"

"I'll come in with you, but I'll sit off to the side and be the good guy when you need it."

She nodded, grinning. "Hey, did you ever hear from Fang?"

Court held up his phone. "Forgot I turned it off before testifying. I'll know in a minute." He waved her away so he would have some privacy, spinning his chair away from the opening to his cubicle.

Eighteen texts, three voice messages. The texts were from Britt, Cami and Madeline. Cami was asking if he wanted to meet for lunch. He'd seen her more in the last four days than he had in weeks. He texted back he was busy and would have to see her later in the week. Madeline also wanted to know if he was free for dinner with an offer to cook. He would enjoy an evening with Madeline, and Lucy too, he assumed, but declined. She sent him a selfie of herself with another mug. This one read IF I WON'T BE MYSELF, WHO WILL?

Britt wanted to come over to his place to talk after the kids were settled. Whenever Britt asked to come over, it was about something serious. She would show up without the kids so they could have whatever discussion she was planning without them hearing it. She never wanted to be the bad guy when her kids could see it. She had been deliberately vague, so it could be anything from her displeasure at him showing up at the restaurant the previous night with his gun firmly tucked against his back to the fact he hadn't responded to Madeline's latest text. No telling what she was going to hit him with.

One voice message, from Fang. "Ni hao, Jian-heng. I ask around and got some small info but not tell over phone. Meet me in line at Salumi at eleven thirty if you want what I got." Court listened to the message a couple of times. Usually, she spoke to him only in Chinese. Maybe she'd switched to English because someone could hear her.

It was almost eleven. Walker and Nolan were due any moment. It would take ten minutes of walking at a fast clip for Court to get to the restaurant. Ivy and Ashena could take the Walker interview. Ashena would know what technical questions to ask better than he would anyway.

He ran upstairs to check in with Brody in the gang unit. He'd been none too happy Court had approached Fang at the restaurant, and Court had promised a heads-up on any further contact. Brody coaxed him into bringing him back a sandwich in return for not insisting Court drag someone from Gangs with him to the meeting. Court put on his still-wet coat and made his way outside, hoping like hell the rain was keeping the line at the restaurant short.

49

A CASUAL OBSERVER WOULD BE HARD-PRESSED TO SEE WHY people would stand in a long line for a place looking like it had seen better years. A simple orange fabric banner bearing only the word Salumi and a silhouette of pig hung above the mustard-colored painted brick of the building. The storefront window bore the same word without further explanation. The restaurant was a downtown jewel and no longer a secret to anyone with a web browser. Every bite of the in-house cured meats was worth the wait.

Court was relieved to see Fang already in line ahead of another forty or so people. He could see ten more in line ahead of them before it disappeared into the shop. It would move quickly, but the rain meant that he'd take his sandwich back to the office. Seating inside was extremely limited.

They spoke quietly so people wouldn't hear them even though they spoke in Mandarin.

"So, here's the deal. The Sanhehui were bringing in North Korean crystal hidden in down shipments delivered to

Colchuck Down. Drummond found out about this, and he was livid. The word is Drummond gave Wu a chance to make it right. If Wu made it right, if he ended the shipments, Wu could stay at his job."

"And, what was Wu going to do, do you know?"

She shook her head. "It doesn't matter. The thing you need to know is that Mr. Drummond was killed by someone else. The Triad had absolutely nothing to do with it."

"Of course the Sanhehui wouldn't claim killing him."

She grabbed at his arm, pinching him roughly. "No. Listen to me. The guy I talked to would brag if he'd killed Drummond."

He didn't think there was a Triad member alive who would brag about this killing. "You believed him? Why would he brag about it?"

The expression on her face darkened. "He always brags. You know." She turned away, her voice dropping to a whisper. "When he kills someone."

It took him a couple of seconds to get the full impact of her statement. *When he kills someone.* She said it as if it were a routine occurrence. Something she was used to talking about. They moved up a few places in the line. "And you think he knows what everyone in the Triad is doing? How would he know if someone else was given the Drummond hit?"

Fang shook her head. "Look, you're not getting it. This guy, he is *the* guy."

"And you know him personally?" Court realized she was shaking. "Are you in danger, Fang? I can help get you somewhere else if you are."

"I am not in danger unless you keep asking questions.

Please, believe me. This death has nothing do with the Sanhehui."

"Do you know if they ever use white people?"

She shook her head. "Sanhehui is all Chinese. They might hire white people for little things, like courier work. Maybe. But they only trust other Chinese for the heavy work."

It wasn't until they were parting outside, wrapped orders to go in hand, that he thought of something. "Hey, Fang, one more thing." He walked over to the nearby tree to shield them from the drizzle and pulled out a folded copy of the sketch and photos from his jacket. "Do you recognize any of these guys?"

Fang took the papers and studied them one by one. "No, Jian-Heng. But, you know, you white people all look the same to me."

WHOEVER FANG WAS HANGING out with was deep in the Triad. Which meant she was, at least peripherally, related in a way he hadn't known about. She had given him tidbits over the years, but never anything this close to the top. No wonder Brody had been all over Stensland.

But he believed her.

He ran up the stairs and gave Brody the promised sandwich and peace offering, filling him in on what he'd gotten from Fang.

"Drummond was taking a huge chance facing that kind of shit on his own," Brody said. "Sounds like a perfect motive to me."

"Is Fang under surveillance? Is that how you knew we met with her? Wanna fill me in?"

Brody considered Court for a while before spinning around and clicking a few keys on his computer. A photo of a Chinese man popped up. Good-looking guy with tattoo sleeves on both arms and a dragon circling his neck. "This is Ma Longwei. He's supposed to be the Triad's local top enforcer. Your friend Fang lives with him. So far, we haven't caught him doing diddly, but we've only been watching him for three months."

Court had never seen Longwei before. He hadn't been a player in the Sino-Trans case. Maybe he was new in town, maybe he was newly risen in the ranks. If Fang was living with this guy, she was in a whole different league than Court would've guessed. "So, if she asked him about Drummond…"

"She's too smart to ask outright. But, yeah, her boyfriend has a weird sense of honor and pride in his work. Her information is probably accurate."

Court felt like an idiot. He should have come to Gangs first to see what they had before putting her at risk. For whatever reason, it hadn't even occurred to him. "Shit. Come clean, Brody, what did you have on Colchuck before we got it?"

Brody leaned to the side. "Shut the door."

Court closed the door, leaning against it with arms crossed.

"We had nothing. Colchuck wasn't on our radar at all until you showed up for Dim Sum."

The other man didn't have to fess up, but Court was relieved to know they'd not compromised an ongoing investigation. "Thanks. I'll be happy to drop the Triad from our list. You can have fun figuring out the Colchuck Down thing with Narc."

He tossed a lukewarm sandwich at Ivy and unwrapped his own. He had tucked them inside his jacket so they'd stay warm, but the chat with Brody had taken a few minutes. The gamey smell of lamb and red pepper had him drooling before his first bite.

Ivy opened hers, sniffing at it warily. "You like some seriously weird food, Pearson."

"Lamb is not weird."

"Put Hunter in a room five minutes ago. We need to eat and get in there."

"Never hurts to let them sit for a bit. Get them a little on the anxious side."

"So, what happened with Fang?"

Court told her. The fact that Fang had become so close to the Triad's local hit man had loomed larger than the implications of what she had told him about the Drummond case.

Ivy sat back in her chair. "Man, I can't tell you how relieved I am the Triad isn't involved in Drummond's death."

"You and me both. Doesn't make our job any easier. Now fill me in on what you got from Walker."

"Not much. There are a few ways to make keys without direct access to Hunter's system. You need specialized knowledge and some other technical mumbo-jumbo I don't understand. However, putting Ashena in there with me was pure genius. She ended up doing most of the interview. Turns out, anyone with access to the right Haubek equipment, like a customer with the same system, or an employee, would be able to make a key."

"Basically, you're saying everyone we had on the table is still on the table."

50

KAREN HUNTER APPEARED TO BE ANYTHING BUT ANXIOUS. She was seated with her legs and arms crossed, back against the chair, and eyes fixed on the one-way glass across from her as they entered the room. She didn't return Court's smile.

"Why am I here?"

Ivy was several inches shorter than Hunter was when standing, but Ivy's chair was set four inches higher to give her the height advantage. She sat and read Hunter her rights.

"I waive my right to an attorney," Hunter said. "I have nothing to hide. Besides, I thought I was cleared. So what is going on?"

Ivy said, "Let's start with this." She put a DMV photo in front of her. "What do you know about this man?"

Hunter studied the photo. "He looks sort of familiar. He reminds me a little of a young John Lithgow, but I don't think I know him."

Ivy replaced the photo with another. "How about this guy?"

Hunter studied it, made a face. "He looks like the Unabomber. He seems familiar, but I don't know where from." She turned it in the light, reconsidered. "Oh, wait. He was with the other guy, wasn't he? Let me see the other photo again."

Ivy put them side by side.

Hunter held them up together, nodding. "Oh, now I remember. They're the two men who came from Haubek to reset my system after the burglary. Why are you asking me about them?"

Ivy didn't answer. She slid the photo of Duffy onto the table. "What about this man?"

"This is a client of mine. Giovanni Duffy." Her forehead wrinkled. "He doesn't have anything to do with Berkeley, does he? I'm pretty sure *they* didn't know each other."

It was subtle, but Court got the sense she was trying to tell him something. The hint she'd given the other day about a connection between clients had to do with the client who used burner phones. Maybe her confusion over seeing Duffy's photo would prompt her to elaborate. It nagged at him that Stensland had shut down that avenue. What if Stensland had missed something important while covering for whoever it was he was covering for?

"Tell us what you know about him," Ivy said.

"There's not much. He's a client. I can't imagine any possible scenario in which Giovanni has anything to do with Berkeley's death. The only connection between them I know of is me." She paused, her eyes widening. "He's okay, isn't he?

"He's fine," Ivy said, pushing the photo of Schorr across. "What about this guy?"

Hunter looked up quickly. "So, you figured out a connection between two of my clients. I told you some men talk to their friends. Why show me their pictures in particular?"

Ivy didn't answer, but pulled out the sketch of the man in the leather suit Audrey Drummond saw leaving Hunter's building. "Tell me about this man."

Hunter grabbed the drawing and held it so the light from the wall behind her illuminated it. She focused on it for quite a while before slowly shaking her head. "Are you serious? The only thing I can tell from this picture is he's a white guy. A balding white guy."

"Look closely," Ivy said.

Karen studied the drawing again, shaking her head the whole time. "So, it looks like the collar around his neck could be the collar of my missing suit—the way it closes is the same anyway." She paused, her eyes widening. "Does this mean someone saw a man wearing my suit leave the building?"

Court was impressed with her leap of logic.

"We believe he's the man who killed Berkeley Drummond," Ivy said.

Hunter jerked a little and scanned the image with a new intensity. "He could be anyone."

Ivy retrieved the sketch and laid it flat on the table between them. "We have a theory about what happened. We need you to fill in the gaps."

Hunter looked at the drawing, her mouth dropping open as it was snatched from her. "Gaps? What are you talking about?"

Court wondered how Ivy was going to continue. If Hunter had been working with Nolan, Payne or Duffy to kill Drummond, she would have blinked. Hesitated. Had some sort of tell. She was obviously frustrated that the sketch was devoid of anything recognizable.

She didn't have anything to do with Drummond's death. Court let Ivy continue, though. He wanted her to play her full hand so she could see it for herself.

"Let me lay it out for you," Ivy said. "Here's what happened. At some point after the burglary and reboot of your system, you issued a second card in your name and gave it to an accomplice. He spent the last six weeks working with you on the best time to pull off the murder. He let himself in —coming and going multiple times—mostly after Berkeley Drummond's Wednesday-night visits. They correlate almost one hundred percent. You taught him how to turn down the lights, gave him a suit that would make him look as much like you as possible. You planned and waited until the time presented itself. Last week, your son's emergency gave you the perfect alibi. You contacted your accomplice before rushing off to your son. What you didn't know was he was going to have a little extra fun while he was there."

Ivy pulled out the photograph showing the blue-light photo of semen on Drummond's face. Hunter recoiled.

"He left us some nice, uncomplicated DNA. So, we'll be able to prove whoever did this when we get our DNA results. This would be the perfect time for you to tell us who the other man was. If we have to wait until for DNA results, the district attorney will be a lot harder to deal with."

Court admired Ivy's bluff. They would still need a suspect's DNA sample to prove the connection.

Hunter sat back in her chair, mouth dropping open, head moving slowly from side to side, her eyes blinking rapidly as she took it all in.

Ivy kept pushing. "We'll make a deal with you." She tapped the sketch. "If you tell us who this guy is, we'll make sure the DA goes easy on you. Why'd you have him do it, Ms. Hunter? That's what we'd like to know."

Usually at this point, Court would see a flicker of resignation in a guilty person's face. Confronted by murder allegations, most people crumble under the weight and guilt of it. Hunter was full of confusion bursting into outrage.

"Oh. My. Fucking. God." Hunter's voice bounced off the walls. She leaned forward in her chair, getting her face up in Ivy's. "This is unbelievable. I don't have any idea who killed Berkeley. I had no reason to kill him. None at all. Zero. Zip. Nada. And, I sure as hell didn't help anyone do it. This is insane." She swiped at the pile of images, sending them off the table.

Hunter had been so calm and reserved, in control up to now, it was a relief to see her lose it. The fact she had blown up was a classic sign of innocence.

Ivy leaned in closer so they were almost nose-to-nose. "Not even compassion?"

Court was impressed at Ivy's nerve. She had gumption, even if she was dead wrong.

Hunter leveled her gaze right back at Ivy, fingers whitening as they clenched the arms of her chair "Compassion? What was compassionate about the way he died?"

Ivy patted the file on the table. Her voice became a whisper, a confidence-inspiring lull. Her head moved in a slow nod as she spoke, a gesture to induce tacit agreement. "You had a motherly attitude toward him. You couldn't stand to see him in pain. When he told you he wanted to kill himself, you worked together to cook up this plan. But you couldn't go through with it yourself, so you hired someone to do it for you."

Court hated he was following Ivy's twisted logic. It made sense in a tangled way even if it was utter crap. The way she was working this was pretty damn good work, too.

Hunter twisted her upper body in Court's direction. "This is bullshit and you know it. What the fuck is going on here?"

Apparently, Court was now playing the good cop to Ivy's bad cop. He maintained his casual stance against the wall. "Look, Karen. You don't mind if I call you Karen, do you?"

She nodded as she took a deep breath, obviously trying calm herself down. "I don't know what she's talking about. I had nothing to do with Berkeley's death." She spoke in a slow and calm voice, emphasizing each word with clear diction.

Hunter hadn't slipped, had no tells, got angry when accused. Time to move on, tie up some loose ends. He met Ivy's gaze; she shook her head and looked away, defeated.

Hunter's eyes filled with tears. "I found him. He was already dead, and I called the police. Who are, as usual, treating me with suspicion solely for what I do."

Ivy broke in again. "Oh, not exactly. He was found dead in *your* office. Tied to *your* ceiling. With *your* ropes. It's not like we chased you down for being some random dominatrix."

51

COURT GUIDED KAREN OUT OF THE BUILDING. "I'M SORRY about all that. At least you are officially cleared, now. I can stop reading you your rights every time I see you."

"How comforting," she said.

"I can get someone to drive you back or hail you a cab."

"I'll take the cab. Having the police show up once in my neighborhood is enough. I'm sure the busybody across the street is already wagging her tongue."

Court fished out some money and handed it to her. It wasn't the way they were supposed to do things, but he was happy to eat a few bucks.

She strode off with confidence without looking back. While he was focusing on the dignified swaying of her hips, his skin broke out in goosebumps. He spun around, certain someone was watching him, but he couldn't make anyone. Did Brody have someone tailing him? He massaged his neck with both hands before going back inside.

Ivy sat in her chair, flipping through the file, her elbow

on her desk and her chin cradled in her hand. She only moved her eyes to look at him, and her voice was slow and monotone. "What? You look like you got something."

The apathy in her voice burned him. Now her pet theory was dead, she'd lost the wind in her sails.

"Come on, Langston. Buck up. We'll figure this out soon enough."

Ivy crossed her arms. "What about the burner phones? I want to know why Stensland took them over and we had to drop it. There was something about what Hunter said in there about Duffy and Drummond not knowing each other, like she was hinting at something. It sounded like she knows another of her clients did know Drummond."

Court cast a quick glance at Stensland's office. He had been told Ivy was brilliant. How she put together what Karen had said with Stensland's bizarre behavior was a little beyond him. He wasn't sure he would have connected them. But, he wasn't about to tell her about a cover-up he couldn't prove. "Look, I need to figure some of that out before I share with you. If it is what I think it is, you don't want to be part of it."

Court was back at his desk, getting ready to call Payne's real estate agent for a second time when his phone rang.

"This is Karen Hunter."

Her tone sent shivers up his back. "What's going on?"

"I got back home. And, there's this letter. I think it's important for you to see it." Karen's phone voice was warm and rich. She could make a mint at phone sex. "It's from the killer."

An adrenaline rush hit him. Something clicked. They were about to break the case. He jumped out of his seat and over to Ivy's cubicle, tapping the speaker button on his phone. "What kind of letter, Karen?"

"It's something out of a made-for-TV movie. It's letters, cut up out of magazines and glued to the page."

"What makes you sure it's from the killer?"

"He admits it in the letter. Tells me it's my fault. He didn't mean for Berkeley to die."

Court squeezed his eyes shut, imagining Hunter's finger-prints all over the letter. "Try not to touch it any more than you already have. We'll come over there to collect it."

"You know what's freaking me out? It wasn't mailed. It was taped to my front door."

52

Karen Hunter lived in a neighborhood across the lake from Seattle, on the Eastside but in an area vastly different from where the Drummonds lived. It was typical suburbia built in the mid-Seventies. The houses were mostly split levels with a limited variety of styles all originally built by one contractor with various modifications over the years.

"It's awfully convenient this letter came in now, don't you think?" Ivy asked. "I don't like her."

"You sure it's her you don't like or is it what she does for a living?" Court was not sure what to think of it himself. He wondered if her job had ended her marriage. What kind of man could be married to a professional dominatrix? He didn't understand why he kept focusing on Karen when he'd had one of the best dates of his life with Madeline. Their texts were playful, teasing. Every time his phone buzzed against his thigh, he grabbed for it, eager to read whatever she had to say. It was unusual for him to be attracted to more than one person at a time. Confusing, too. "Besides, we cleared her, remember?"

They parked in front of Hunter's house. The flowerbeds in front displayed the ubiquitous rhododendrons, azaleas, and ferns of the area. A clipped grass lawn filled the space on either side of the walkway to the front door and along the sidewalk.

Every house in the neighborhood had large fir trees looming overhead. A big greenbelt stretched behind the houses on Hunter's side of the street. Something about it wigged Court out. Too much ground to keep an eye on? Too many gigantic trees? How could anyone live out here?

As they reached the front door, rain fell in large, heavy, loud globules of water coming down with a shy hesitance, like each drop was looking for its own dry spot to invade, before shifting into a downpour.

Ivy pushed the doorbell and an electronic version of Big Ben sounded inside, fake and loud.

Hunter answered the door right away. She had changed clothes since their interview. She was now barefoot and in jeans. A light green button-down oxford fell over her hips, giving her shape a more nebulous sensuality.

Karen guided them into the kitchen and introduced them to her daughter, Sophie, before sending her to her room. "I have something private I need to talk about with these detectives."

The teenager scowled before scooping up her homework and stomping down the hallway. She wore her long dark hair straight down her back like her mother.

There was a pitiful howling sound from outside.

"What's that noise?" Ivy craned her neck to look out the window into the back yard.

"It's a dog, one that doesn't sound too happy out there," Court said.

Karen reached above the refrigerator and retrieved a large metal bowl. "I put the letter where the kids couldn't see it." She handed over the bowl. "Excuse me while I bring the dog in. Poor Aspen is a wimp when it comes to rain."

An envelope and letter were inside the bowl. Ivy pulled on a pair of gloves, and picked up the letter, holding it so they could both read the choppy blocky letters cut from magazine headlines:

HE DIED because you weren't there to save him. He wasn't supposed to die. He was supposed to deliver my message. And now it's your fault he's dead. YOUR FAULT. You should have been there. You were supposed to save him.

"SHE WAS RIGHT, looks like something from the movies," Ivy said.

Court pulled two plastic evidence bags from his inside jacket pocket, one for the letter and one for the envelope. The only thing on the front of it were the words MISTRESS FIDELMA written in thick black Sharpie with a neat hand.

Court leaned over the sink to get a good view down into the yard below. An enormous yellow lab with her tail tucked between her legs looked balefully toward the house. As the sliding glass door swished open, the dog perked up, tail-

wagging as she lunged for sanctuary. The cooing of Karen's
warm voice drifted toward him from the downstairs room.

"See," he said to Ivy. "She's not all that bad."

"Everyone loves a dog, Pearson."

KAREN APPEARED at the top of the stairs with a mostly
recovered lab hovering close to her legs. When Court whistled softly the dog padded over, sniffing at his outstretched
hand. The dog shrank from his touch.

"Oh, you don't like the gloves, eh?" Court peeled them
off. The dog came in for a good scratch. "So, this was
attached to your door while you were with us?"

"Yeah. I was gone, what, maybe two hours?"

He dropped to a squat and continued to pet the dog,
giving special attention to the ears. "Was anyone at home
while you were gone?"

"Both the kids. Sophie's old enough to babysit Brian."

"But you had a nanny when you went out for work?"
The dog turned to lick at Court's face.

Karen reached out, pulling the dog back by her collar.
"Aspen," she said in a chiding tone, running her hands along
the dog's neck.

"She's fine," Court said. "I like dogs. So, your nanny?"

"Right. When it was my turn with the kids, I didn't like
them being here without someone late at night. I have a
college student who likes to do her laundry while she's here.
Comes over from the university, and often spends the night
in the guest room. I didn't have her come today. It was only a
few hours."

"When it's your turn?" *Finally, some information about the father.* "Your ex takes them part time?"

"Actually, when I have the kids, I stay here. When he has the kids, he stays here. We both have apartments nearby when we aren't with the kids. It's easier for us to move back and forth than disrupt their lives."

Court had heard of such arrangements, but had thought it exclusive to the rich. This house didn't scream money. Living on the Eastside could be spendy, but this was not one of those exclusive fenced-in neighborhoods. Even if Drummond had been her only client, she could be bringing in over two hundred thousand a year. With sixteen clients, she had to be making more like five hundred a year. Where did it all go? He stood up and wiped his hands on his pants.

"So, any idea who wrote this?"

Karen sucked in her lower lip between her teeth for a second before exhaling with a slump of her shoulders. "Okay. Here's the thing. I have this feeling. More of a hunch. I haven't seen him in years. But, there's this guy I knew a while back, he was creepy and sort of stalker-like. I'm pretty sure it's him."

"You look disappointed," Ivy said.

Karen crossed her arms. She leaned her back against the counter. "Yeah. If I'm right about this, then yeah, it totally sucks. Having Berkeley die in my studio is horrific. If he had been killed because of who he was, you know, some business deal gone bad, or some bizarre revenge thing, that would be bad, but this? If the guy who sent this note is the person I think he is, then it puts everyone in the kink community in the spotlight."

"The fact Berkeley Drummond was found in your studio

the way he was is already going to do that. Protecting the killer isn't going to change that."

Karen's jaw dropped open. "I am not protecting him. I called you, didn't I? I'm just voicing the concern that this kind of thing makes it even harder for the regular people who are into kink. It's a hidden community filled with regular people."

Court understood the whole thing about being hidden. More than Karen Hunter probably could guess at the moment. He held up his hands, fingers played wide in a calming motion. She was kinda preaching to the choir but he didn't want to get into that at the moment. "There's not much we can do about that. The press has already leaked the fact he was in a dominatrix's studio. Karen, if you think you know who the killer is, you need to tell us. Now."

Karen ran her hands through her hair, gathering it into a ponytail low against the back of her neck. "There's a problem. It won't help you much. I only knew him by his scene name."

"Which was?"

"Jarvis."

"Jarvis? That's a strange name."

"Yeah, most kinksters put a huge effort into their scene name. It can be a very cathartic tool. Jarvis means 'servant with a spear.' He got all excited about how his name was a metaphor for his little penis… Like I said, he was weird."

"Did you just say 'little penis'?" Ivy asked.

"Yeah. That's why I remember what Jarvis means. His was small. *Really* small. He wanted to be taunted and humiliated because of it. It was only about two inches fully erect. And, he got off on being shamed for it."

Her eyes were focused inward as she mined her memories. It was hard to tell if she got any enjoyment out of the interplay, if she was grossed out by the small dick, or if she was a pro searching for an angle on a John. Court wasn't about to ask. "And where did you meet him?"

"At Belle Nuit. It's a club…"

Court interrupted. "We know about it. I was there last night. Go on."

"There's not a lot more to tell. He saw me at the club and did the thing subs do. Hang out close by, waiting to be noticed. I finally agreed to do a session with him."

"So, this guy, Jarvis, you saw him for a while?" he asked.

"Not long. A couple of months at most. It was years ago."

"And you wore the leather suit for him?"

"Once. I think it was only once."

"What ended it?"

"He started topping from the bottom, telling me what to do. He became ultra clingy and super whiny when I played with other subs. He would sit outside on his knees, begging for attention when I was done with someone else. The kicker was when he got extra pissy at my other boys. Actually threatened to beat one up. Jarvis was the reason I left Belle Nuit. I was planning on going pro, but I couldn't stand being around him any longer."

"A little pissy? Pissy enough to want to humiliate one of your coveted and favorite clients someday?" Ivy asked.

Karen leaned back against the counter, using her palms to support herself. "But why? It's been years. Why would he do something *now*?"

"I don't know. Sometimes people's psychosis takes a while

to develop. Maybe he's always been fixated on you. Maybe he's been with someone in between. Maybe some big event, like losing his job, broke him."

Ivy had been pretty quiet. Court hoped she was over her initial dejection at failing to pin Karen to the crime.

"Karen, do you ever look at the folder on your email, the one you call 'when hell freezes over'?" he asked.

"No. I don't. I set up a bunch of rules. Most emails go directly to that folder so I don't have to read them at all."

"Langston, you remember anything from a Jarvis in her email?"

Ivy shook her head. "Doesn't mean anything, though. There was a huge amount, and I only got through about a third of them. It was all on paper. We can have Ashena do a keyword search on his name now that we know it."

Karen hugged herself. "I wouldn't necessarily have seen it if he had written me. I mean, if it went to the hell folder. I shunted anything not from a client over there."

Court could make a good guess about where her thoughts were taking her. She was probably worrying she had missed something beforehand, something that would have prevented Drummond's death if she had seen it before. "Don't go there," he said, resisting the urge to reach out and comfort her.

"It's hard not to."

"What specifically made you jump to this Jarvis guy?" he asked.

"It's a little woo-woo sounding, actually. I haven't thought about him in years. When I read the letter, this image of him popped into my head."

"We can't act on hunches, and it'll be close to impossible

to find a guy you knew briefly over a decade ago only under a scene name. Is there anything else, anything at all, that you remember about him?" Ivy asked.

Karen looked up at the ceiling. "I don't think so."

Ivy waved the letter in its plastic bag between them. "Okay, so we sort of know who we're looking for. He says he didn't intentionally kill Drummond, but he had to have missed that second text and left thinking you would be back. How did this Jarvis guy get a key?"

"He must have some connection to Haubek. It's the only thing that makes sense," Court said. "Did we ever ask if Schorr had a scene name? We know Duffy goes by Macbeth."

Karen shrugged. "I never talked to them about their activities at Belle Nuit. I went by a different scene name back them, and I didn't even want any of my clients to make the connection."

"Mom?" Sophie interrupted them, poking her head around the corner.

All conversation stopped as they turned to look at her.

Karen thrust a finger out, pointing down the hallway. "I told you to stay in your room."

Sophie didn't move. "I'm sorry, but, Mom? You really need to look out front."

They rushed to the front of the house. The rain had stopped as suddenly as it had begun. The sun was streaming out in individual wide rays behind a foreground of thick clouds. The water gleamed on the wet pavement, but that wasn't what Sophie was talking about. The KILO news van was out in the street and Scott Ingram was setting himself up in front of a camera with Karen's house as his backdrop.

Court snapped the curtains shut. "Ah, shit. How did he find you?" He spun around. "Someone leaked your info." Someone must have been watching him earlier. He hadn't even thought to check if anyone was following him. "They can't actually come on your property with their cameras, or block your garage. At least they parked so you can get out. Whatever you do, don't talk to them about anything. Not a word." He pulled the curtain back at one corner, taking a peek. "Langston, call for some uniformed officers. I want some protection out here, now."

"Mom? What's going on?" Sophie asked.

Karen sat on the sofa, pulling Sophie onto her lap. "It's to do with my friend's death. I told you about him the other day. Well, some people think I had something to do with how he died."

Sophie cuddled into her mom. "How do we go anywhere with them out there?"

There was something endearing seeing a big teenager lean into her mom like a toddler. Court had thought unabashed cuddling died out at puberty.

"Pearson, you better not be planning on going out there and talking to them," Ivy said. "That would blow Stensland's gasket big time."

"Stensland can go…" He broke off, eyeing Karen's daughter. "Stensland will understand, eventually. I'll try to call them off. Let's get back to the station and find this guy." He turned back toward Karen. "We'll have uniformed officers out here in the next hour. We'll make sure someone is here twenty-four-seven until we get Jarvis. Better yet, I would suggest you get out of here. You can get a hotel room, or go to a friend's where he won't know to find you. We would get some people on you wherever."

Karen kissed her daughter's forehead. "No way. I'm not going anywhere."

It was unlikely this Jarvis guy was going to show up with a news crew out front and three cops hanging around. Betting on *unlikely* didn't sit too well with him.

Uniformed officers from Redmond PD arrived fifteen minutes later. *Must be a slow day.*

Court broke off from Ivy before they got to their car, storming toward where Ingram stood finalizing the angle of the shot with his cameraman. The cameraman was standing lower on the street and shooting upward so Ingram's face was in front of the house. The wind had picked up a little making the trees sway dramatically overhead.

Ingram smiled at him, obviously recognizing him. "Detective, can I get you on record?" He nodded at Ivy, who had followed close behind. "Your new partner, eh?"

Court didn't bother with an introduction. "On record? How about you admit you never tried to call me about this case. The way you lied about not getting a hold of me. On record."

Ingram snorted. "Oh, come on, Detective. You shouldn't hold that against me. What could you have said anyway?"

"You need to pack up and leave. You can't harass these people."

"It's not harassment. I'm out on the public street making a news report. All I want is for the domme to come out and talk to us. She can tell us all about Berkeley Drummond's pathetic sex life. Then we'll leave."

Ivy put a restraining hand on Court's arm. Ingram made

a gesture with his hand. The cameraman aimed the lens directly at Court. Fine. So be it. Court shrugged Ivy off and composed himself. He wasn't stupid enough to get caught on film while attacking a reporter. "Karen Hunter is a valuable witness in an ongoing investigation. She is not a suspect in any crime at this time."

"We heard otherwise. We heard she's a prime suspect in the murder of Berkeley Drummond. Are you saying this is not true?"

"She is not a suspect. You should leave. You're wasting your time."

"And you are willing to verify Karen Hunter is the real name for the dominatrix known as Mistress Fidelma?"

Court shook his head and moved toward the car with Ivy, Ingram following them hurtling questions to their unyielding backs.

53

Court phoned Ashena as they were crossing the bridge back into Seattle. The roads were wet and slick from the rain. It wasn't officially afternoon rush hour yet, but traffic crept along slowly, partially blinded by the setting sun.

By the time they got back to the office, Ashena had Karen's latest emails up on her screen. She was scanning them to see if there were any clues to Jarvis's identity. Eighty new messages had automatically split off into various mailboxes. Karen would have said something if there had been anything in the ones she read in her client folders, so they concentrated on the list set aside for creepers, the one labeled WHEN HELL FREEZES OVER.

Court and Ivy crowded in close, eager to help. Ashena flicked her manicured nails at them to back off. They gave her a little space.

He ran his fingers through his hair. "Damn it. You know, she asked if she might have a stalker, and I blew her off."

"We blew her off," Ivy said.

Ashena spun around, pointing a finger at them. "You both need to be quiet. I can't work with hover bees all over me. Now get back to your desk before you drive me crazy. I'll come get you when I have it all."

"I need something to pick me up," Ivy said as she bypassed her desk for the coffee room.

Court followed her, watching as she poured a cup of what looked like fairly fresh brew. "At least we know what happened. This Jarvis guy lets whatever happened years ago stew. It grows and morphs into something huge. Something collapses in his life and triggers his obsession for her. He goes after her. He figures out who her best client is, the one she spends the most time with. The one to be most jealous of. He sets out to teach them some sort of lesson. He takes his opportunity when he sees her leave early. He goes inside, and sees her iPad on the desk. He sees the first message and decides to take advantage knowing Drummond will be there. He gets everything set up, changes into the costume he associates with his best time with her, and waits for Drummond."

He grabbed the pot and poured himself a cup. "Once Drummond shows up, he waits for Drummond to take his position on the floor, coming up from behind. He uses what he knows from previous visits. He's probably picked up on some clues about what they've done together by prowling around. He starts with Drummond's arms and then gets him into the air. Then, he steps around and…."

He dumped in three packets of sugar and stirred it with a wooden stick. "He steps around and masturbates until he ejaculates on Drummond's face. Given he was getting jealous of other subs, I'm betting it was a sort of 'fuck you' move on his part, not something meant to please himself or Drummond. Drummond struggles, but there's nothing he can do. Jarvis delivers his message and leaves thinking Karen would be there any minute. He pulls off the hood, tosses his street clothes on over top of the leather suit, but the collar sticks out above the neckline, making the black-collar priest effect Audrey Drummond saw. He leaves, thinking the guy he's degraded and humiliated is going to be released. But, what he doesn't know is he has missed a second text, and she's not coming."

54

"YOU'RE GONNA BE SO HAPPY WITH WHAT I FOUND."
Ashena waved two stacks of papers toward them as they
returned. She held out the first stack. "This is a series of
emails speaking of perpetual servitude and eternal devotion,
if only Mistress Fidelma would heed his humble requests."

Court reached for the packet, but Ashena thrust it
behind her back, teasing him with it.

"But wait, there's more." Ashena's face broke into a big
grin. "Eternal Devotion Boy is not your man. Him? He's
here." She held up the second packet of papers. "The first
email came eight weeks ago. The latest one was yesterday.
Practically a confession."

Court's heart was thumping harder, and the surge of
adrenaline that came with closing in on a killer was coursing
through him. Eight weeks ago. It kept popping up. It was not
a coincidence. It was a link. "Show it to me."

She held onto the papers, and instead of handing them
to Court read the last message aloud. *"Mistress, Please ma'am. I*

cannot take your silence any longer. I need you to know it was a mistake. I didn't mean for him to die, I wanted him to be the messenger. I am not a killer. Why don't you answer? Please respond. Tell me how you will punish me. Please. I do need punishing." She paused, a triumphant grin on her face. "It's signed Jarvis."

They had their man. Sort of. Jarvis was more worried about Karen getting his message and punishing him than about a man dying. And his latest letter, the one taped to her front door, was stalker crazy. It was a good thing they'd posted protection at her house.

He reached for the papers and looked at the email address. Jarvis wasn't part of the email account. It was from TinyTim. His mind almost exploded with the revelation. He thrust the paper at Ivy. "Look at the email address."

"I don't get it," she said.

"We've had him in our sights the whole time. TinyTim. Tiny fucking Tim."

55

Ivy's eyes grew wide. "Tiny for his small penis? Tim. Timothy Payne? The Haubek tech? No fucking way." She grabbed the paper from Court, her jaw dropping open as she re-read the address.

Court let out a hoot. "We're almost there, Ivy. We're almost there."

"But, wait a second. We showed Hunter photos of this guy, why didn't she ID him?" she asked. "Why didn't she recognize him when he was at her office fixing the card-key reader? Isn't that kinda weird?"

Court paused. He pulled out the DMV photo of Payne and the artist's sketch. Payne sported a thick beard. The sketch was of a clean-shaven man. The only thing they had in common was their receding hairlines. "I bet Payne looks different with a shaved face and head." He tapped the license photo. "This was taken a year ago when he renewed his license."

He whirled back to Ashena. "Ashena, can you do some

magic and figure out exactly where this was sent from? A physical address? We need to find this guy. All we know is he moved, but we don't know where to."

"Give me a few minutes, and I'll see what I can find. But, if he's at all tech savvy, he will have covered his tracks."

"If he wasn't planning on killing someone, he probably wasn't even trying to cover his tracks."

Court was distracted by Stensland waving them into his office. "News update. That Ingram fellow is getting out of hand."

"We've got an ID, sir. We know who killed Drummond."

Stensland snorted, but pointed to the television on his wall. "Great. Perfect timing."

Ingram had his usual smug smile on his face as he launched into his report. "Behind me, hiding in what looks like a normal home, is the dominatrix who owned the lease to the office space Berkeley Drummond was found dead in last week."

The camera zoomed in on the house, showing Court and Ivy coming out of the front door. "Earlier today, I spoke to Detective Court Pearson, the lead investigator on the case. He stated the Seattle Police Department is not considering Karen Hunter, also known as the dominatrix Mistress Fidelma, a suspect in the killing."

Court's stomach roiled. He looked awful on camera. And he hated his voice. He looked away until Ingram brought it back to the live footage.

"Meanwhile, Seattle Police are focusing their attention on the Chinese gang known as the Triad. Here is Seattle Police Department's Lieutenant Stensland earlier today in a press conference." The screen switched to an image of Stensland in front of half a dozen reporters.

"What the hell?" Court asked. "You chose to let out we are investigating the Triad?"

Stensland shrugged. "Triad makes for a better story than 'We have no fucking clue'. And, I should remind you, we *were* investigating the Triad until about five minutes ago. You should know the drill by now, Pearson."

Ingram continued with his newscast. "Even though the police have said they no longer consider Karen Hunter a suspect, they have placed policemen at both doors to her house. There has been no comment as to why. I'm Scott Ingram for KILO news."

The image returned to the blond at the desk. "Thanks, Scott. Now for some breaking weather. Some of you may remember the Hanukkah Eve Storm back in 2006. Well, forecasters are predicting much worse to hit the Seattle area in the next twenty-four..." Stensland clicked off the TV. "So, who's the killer?"

"Timothy Payne. He goes by Timmy or Tim or ... Tiny-Tim. In this case, we found an email to Karen Hunter pretty much confessing to everything."

Stensland shuffled to his chair and sat down. "I can't believe it's only five o'clock. It feels like ten." He pointed to the door. "Better hurry and find Payne before things get wild outside."

"THE IP TRACE bounces all over hell and gone. No way we're going to find him that way."

Court and Ivy stood behind Ashena, looking over her shoulder at the list of numbers. Court didn't understand all the technology involved. He took her word for it. Payne had sent the email through a series of relay-like things making it impossible to trace back to his IP address. Court barely understood how IP addresses work, but he knew his phone always traced back to the closest cell tower serving his phone. Court's home IP always had the same number, linked to his FIOS cable company. He'd asked Ashena to check it out a few months back. There was some protection on the web, but putting his IP address in the tracer put a bright red mark right on his house. It was kinda creepy. He rarely used email from home.

"Would his work computer help?" Ivy asked. "If they still have it."

"Won't help with locating him, since everything on that machine will be traced back to Haubek. But, we might be able to find out information about him on any email he left or internet searches he did. It's been a couple of weeks, so they might have wiped his computer for a new employee."

No one was completely untraceable anymore. It would require some effort, but since 9/11 no one could go completely under the radar for long. "We'll get it. We need to hit Haubek and see what the people there know about him. Maybe he's stayed in contact with one of them. In the meantime, I want you to find all his credit cards, banking, cellphone information, use anything you can think of to get a current address. Someone is going to have it somewhere."

Court and Ivy hightailed it to the motor pool. "I'll get a warrant for the computer while you drive. I am betting Walker won't let it out of his hands without one. Also, I'm going to get some extra help out there to interview his co-workers for anything useful on Payne."

"Nolan wasn't particularly helpful the other day. I'm betting if the guy he worked with the most didn't know him well, other employees won't have much more."

"If Walker was reluctant before, he might be even more so now that we know it was one of his employees."

"That's why we have warrants."

56

Six uniformed officers showed up at Haubek at the same time Ivy pulled up in front of the dilapidated building. Traffic had been on their side for once, and they'd arrived before Haubek shut its operations for the day.

They gave the officers a basic script to follow, and they all went inside at once. A show of force could sometimes knock reluctance out of people.

Leland Walker's brows knit together as they filled him in. "I can't believe it. He was such a quiet guy. Not some raving lunatic or anything like that. When he was here, he did his job and did it well."

Payne's cubicle hadn't been taken over by a new employee yet. Walker read over the warrant, reluctantly leading them to the small six-by-six bit of real estate where Payne had spent his in-house work hours. There was nothing left on the bulletin board behind the computer. The drawers were empty, and the computer had been cleared and prepped for the next user. Ashena told him there was a chance she could still get something off it.

Nolan crept up to the edge of the cubicle. "What's going on, Detective?"

Court directed him back to his own cubicle. "Look, Mr. Nolan, we need to find Timothy Payne. As fast as we can. We think he might be intending to harm someone. Do you have any idea where he might be?"

"No. We weren't close. I told your partner everything I knew yesterday."

"Maybe something has come up over night? Some new detail? Anything, Mr. Nolan."

Nolan shrugged, held his empty palms out as if for inspection. "Nothing, I'm sorry."

"Langston, did you bring the service record on Hunter's office?" he asked.

"In my tote," she said poking her head out from under the desk.

Court opened her tote and found the original file from Haubek. "Look at it again, Something might jog your memory."

Nolan reluctantly took the folder and read through the notes. "So, Timmy did the writing on this..." He paused part way down and put his finger on the page. "This is probably how he did it."

Court leaned over and looked at what Nolan was pointing to. "You think that when you replaced the coder, Payne stole it?"

Nolan nodded. "One way to know for sure is to check inventory. But, it's the way I would do it. We take turns loading equipment in and out of the van. Sometimes we let stuff pile up in the van for days before we bring it back inside for recycling."

The fact Payne hadn't bothered to wipe the system that logged his comings and goings supported his assertion in the letter that he'd never meant to harm Drummond. Maybe he knew Karen never checked the actual card usage on her system, and that she'd never notice the extra access to her space.

"Did Payne ask the owner any questions that seemed odd to you?"

Nolan thought for a moment. "Well, not unusual questions, but we often ask clients how often they review their system for security reasons. She sort of blew him off. To tell you the truth, she acted like she didn't want us in her space. Wanted us to be in and out as quick as possible."

"How did he respond to her being aloof like that?"

Nolan shrugged. "He wasn't much of a talker, you know? He tended to keep quiet unless it was about work stuff."

Court shifted gears a bit. "Did Payne always wear a beard?"

"Uh, yeah. I think he was compensating for going bald on top. He usually wore a company baseball hat to cover up."

"And you never saw him clean-shaved?"

"Nope."

Ivy stood behind them, dusting off her pants. "Well, the computer's ready to go."

By seven o'clock, they had a statement from every Haubek employee who had ever worked with Payne. The consensus was that he was a quiet, but normal enough sort of guy. Two of the women reported feeling weirded out by him, but the word Payne was being sought for murder had gotten out.

People generally felt sorry for Payne when his mother died, but also a little jealous that he could leave his job. He hadn't been back to visit. He had never made any real friends at Haubek, and none of them knew where he was living or anything about his plans.

He wore plain clothes, usually Dockers and the company shirt. Nothing unusual. He didn't eat lunch out with his co-workers. He brought his lunches from home, and talked about cooking dinner for his mom. Everyone had the impression they were very close.

57

ALL THE PIECES WERE FITTING TOGETHER. COURT DREW A timeline on the white board to make it clear in his head. Eight weeks prior Payne showed up on a repair call and saw the woman he'd been fixated on for years. She'd hidden herself with a new identity so he couldn't find her, but, suddenly, there she was.

Two weeks went by without any activity. Maybe he was biding his time, or fantasizing about what to do next. But then, he started making visits in the middle of the night. Wednesday night in particular. This went on for a couple of weeks, and then his mother died from a heart attack. Maybe their arguments had gotten heated after he started paying extracurricular visits to Hunter's office.

Payne started visiting Hunter's studio more frequently, snooping around after she left for the evening. His fixation grew into full-out stalker mania. Maybe it was because his mother had died, and he no longer had a strong female to control him. Maybe it was something darker than that. Had the argument with his mother been intentional? Something to push his mother into heart-attack territory?

Payne came and went at odd hours, doing whatever it was he was doing in there, without being detected by Karen. Then Wednesday, everything changed.

Payne must have seen Hunter leave early and gone inside to investigate. He saw the text about her being late for Drummond's appointment. He put on the leather bodysuit and waited. What did he do in the two hours between the text and Drummond's arrival? Court put a circle with a big question mark during the two-hour interval.

Drummond arrived and went into the changing room. Put on his harness thing, came back into the main room, and knelt. Payne, dressed like a woman dressed like a man in the leather suit, entered from behind and tied Drummond up. Drummond didn't notice that whoever was tying him up was not Karen and didn't struggle.

Payne finished with some sort of statement, maybe said something to Drummond. Was his message simply to subdue Drummond and ejaculate on him? Or, had he given Drummond a more complex message, something to relay to Karen? The note only referenced the message. Too bad he hadn't repeated it.

Payne threw his regular clothes on over the suit because he realized he was out of time and left Drummond alone, expecting Karen to show up within minutes. He must have taken the mask with him. Payne didn't even know he had committed murder until the news reports of Drummond's death. He freaked out. His psyche wasn't strong enough to take the responsibility for what he did. He stewed, and blamed Karen Hunter, turning his anger at himself on her.

Court stood back from the whiteboard and looked at it. Everything fit. Now they needed to find Payne before he got to Karen.

58

HE WORKED WITH IVY FOR ANOTHER HALF HOUR PUTTING together warrants on all of Payne's credit cards. If he had a new phone, they couldn't find it. Payne's real estate agent wasn't returning Court's calls, either. Court left a curt message, threatening the woman with arrest for obstructing justice if she didn't get back to him ASAP. Payne's last paycheck had been mailed to the house, and he hadn't given Haubek a new address, not even for his income-tax papers for the end of the year.

For all intents and purposes, it looked like Payne wanted to slide off the face of the earth as soon as his mother died. It could have been a coincidence, or it could have been a more calculated effort on his part to hide himself. If so, why? Was he planning on some other deluded scenario with Karen?

Their only hope was for more information on the credit cards or his computer. Ashena was surrounded by components when he went to check in with her. She didn't even look up from what she was doing as he hovered nearby. "This is going to take a while. You might as well go get some rest, 'cause I'm betting you're going to have a lot to run with when I'm done."

Ivy suggested they go home, take showers and nap until Ashena was done, whenever that would be.

It was late, and the weather had an eerie quiet calmness to it. He got off his bus a stop early to pick up some dinner. What he loved about Dick's was the lack of choice. The burgers came the way they came. You either got a burger, a cheeseburger, or a deluxe, and you couldn't ask for changes like "no mayo." There were three kinds of shakes and the menu never changed. He got a Deluxe, a strawberry shake, and fries. Simple, uncomplicated. Freeing.

He needed the fat and carb fortification to face whatever Britt was about to lay on him, and the long night and day ahead. By the time he had eaten his fill and walked home, her car was parked in his driveway.

She was leaning against his front door reading email or Facebooking or something on her phone. When he got to her, she leaned forward and kissed him on both cheeks, European style. "Ohhhh ... you're eating unhealthy. I can smell the grease on you, Court."

"You saw the cup in my hand." He held it up and wiggled it at her.

"You got me."

"You'd make a good detective." He unlocked the door and ushered her in.

He slipped off his shoes and put on his slippers, motioning for her to do the same. She selected one of several extra pairs he kept for guests, making herself at home while he went into the kitchen to grab her a beer. He was hoping he would get called back in soon and kept to his milkshake. It had finally melted enough to suck through the straw.

"So."

"So," she repeated.

Awkward conversations with Britt had become the norm, so he waited for her to take a drink and launch into whatever it was she was here for.

"Remember when you and Amanda got into that fight? The mondo one before you tried that treatment with Bailey?"

Court couldn't forget. Wouldn't ever forget. It was like being hit in the stomach when she brought it up, completely out of the blue.

She didn't wait for an answer. It was a rhetorical question. "So, Amanda came to me when she left you that night. I don't think I ever told you this before, but she... She told me some things that made me hate you for a while."

Court sat back in his chair. None of this was a surprise. Why dredge it up now? Why now after she'd told him to get a life three nights ago?

"Amanda convinced me you were wrong to push for the treatment. That your pushing for the treatment is what killed Bailey."

This was old news. Bailey would have died without the treatment. That was one hundred percent certain, and he'd taken the slim odds that the experimental procedure would give them all more time.

It had been Amanda's mantra for weeks before she blew her face off. If he hadn't pushed the procedure, Bailey would have lived longer. "Why are you bringing this up now, Britt? Why today?"

She downed half her beer before answering. She wiped the foam off her lips with the back of her hand. "I've been blaming you for all of it. Bailey's death. Amanda's suicide. I've been telling myself it was your fault you left your gun out. I've been telling myself it was your fault. That you forced Amanda into allowing the treatment. That it was *all your fault*. But it wasn't. I abandoned her when she needed me most. I couldn't stand to be over there with my kids. She looked at them like they should have died too. She hated me for having healthy children. I should have known it was her depression talking. If I had listened better. Hung out with her more, held her hand tighter...."

Court's heart ached with a ferocity he had forgotten. Seeing his sister tearing herself up over this, with as much anger as he had aimed at himself, was gut wrenching. She had been talking to herself on Saturday. Not just him. He grabbed her hands. "Britt. You were right the other day. We need to move on. Both of us do."

She shook her head. "I know. I give you shit for not moving on, and then I got a good look in the mirror." She wiped at the tears on her cheeks. "Look, I've come to apologize. I get that it wasn't your fault."

"You don't need to apologize, Britt."

"No. I do need to. It's long overdue."

"Why tonight?" Court asked.

"One of the kids at school has a little sister who was just diagnosed with rhabdomyosarcoma. They asked me what I knew about it. I guess they'd heard about Bailey through the grapevine. I spent hours reading about the newest treatment options. And the one you chose? It's working. I know it didn't work for us, for Bailey, but in the last three years, they've fine-tuned the combination of surgery and radiation and medications. I honestly don't understand it all, but it looks like what they were doing four years ago was the beginning of a new protocol that *is beginning to work.*"

Court felt the pressure that usually hit him before he cried building behind his eyes and clogging his nose. He didn't want to cry any more, not for Bailey or Amanda. Something about the way Britt said it knocked something loose in his heart. Even if it hadn't worked for Bailey, the protocol worked for others. He focused on the art deco chandelier over his dining table. He willed away tears. He needed to be done crying.

"It's little comfort to know what you lost is helping others, Court, I know, but I felt I had to tell you. And, well, Amanda, she did what she did out of anger at herself as much as at you. It's her family that carries the depression gene."

"Did she tell you that?"

"A couple weeks before she died. I wanted to be angry at someone, so I chose you. Your gun."

"I shouldn't have left it out. It made it too easy for her."

"It doesn't matter. If it wasn't your gun, it would have been pills. Or something else. When Amanda put her mind to something, she always carried through with it." She paused, smiling. "I miss her. But ... well ... I wanted ... needed to apologize."

Enough. This was as much as he could deal with in one night. Change the subject, get her talking about something else now. "Does this mean you're going to stop setting me up with all the wrong women?"

Britt wiped at her face with her shirtsleeve and stopped, blinked and shook her head. "I don't know what you're talking about. What wrong women?"

Court stood up and walked to the fireplace, pretended to study the Klimt print Amanda had bought him for their first anniversary that hung over it. "Seriously? Ever since you came up here, you've been trying to set me up with the women who are totally not my type."

She jumped up, edging herself in between the mantle and Court, forcing him to face her. "I've introduced you to a lot of nice women, but, Court, you've been the one sabotaging things."

Court half-laughed. "Right. Let's see. Cami?"

"She's your best friend."

"Yeah, but she's a kinky butch into femme women."

Britt waved away the protest. "Okay, fine. Maybe you're not into each other, but you both like feminine women. Everyone else had possibility."

"Oh, like Vivian? She took me to a Renaissance faire. She made me wear tights. And elf ears."

Britt giggled. "Did you get any pictures?"

"Like I'd show you. There was Debbie, Carina, Helen, Margo, Jamie, Emily, and Roberta." He counted them off on his fingers, one by one.

"Hey, every one of them is a nice girl who liked you, Court."

"Right. Debbie wanted to have sex in yoga positions. Carina wanted me to become vegan. Helen wanted me to go Paleo." He stopped, seeing a theme. "All of them wanted to change me in one way or another. Margo wanted me to embrace my feminine side, Jamie wanted me to stop being a cop, Emily wanted me to give up all my worldly goods to travel the world, and Roberta." He stumbled on Roberta and had to think for a second to remember what had been Roberta's bugaboo. "Oh, right, how could I forget? Roberta wanted me to become a queer porn star. She said I could make a ton of money with my 'super-hot body.' Okay, that one actually appealed to me for about ten minutes."

Britt was laughing hard now.

"I'm glad to see you find the humor in it all," Court said, his voice heavy with sarcasm.

"Oh, Court, you should have told me some of this before now. I only got the story from their side, and I have to say you came across as kind of a jerk." She grabbed his chin in her hand. "It was pretty much a consensus. All you wanted from them was sex."

"Really?" But she was right. He had wanted sex. He had gotten it, too. But after you've gotten physically intimate with someone, they usually wanted the other kind—the emotional kind—something he wasn't able to give. He could see that now.

She nodded. "Can't say I blame you. Companionship feels good, no matter who you're with in the short term."

The truth hurt. "Yeah, well. They were right. I don't think I can handle much more than sex."

"Still?" Britt asked. "I got the feeling you and Madeline have clicked pretty well."

A warm fuzzy tickled him when Britt mentioned her name. "Okay, maybe. She lost Jake to gunfire, so it still remains to be seen if she can handle a cop in her life. But yeah, I like her. A lot. A lot." Court's pocket buzzed. "Hold on, we're getting close on this case."

It was a text. He held the phone up for Britt to see. "Your latest endeavor," he said. "She wants to know if I am free to talk."

"I like Madeline, Court. You'd make a good couple."

Court pulled Britt in close for a hug. "As long as she doesn't ask me to wear tights or pointy ears."

AS SOON AS BRITT LEFT, Court returned Madeline's call. Britt and he were forging a new way forward, but he doubted her ability to stop playing big sister. Court wasn't big on small talk, but he spent half an hour on the phone, mostly listening to Madeline. She had a pleasant, warm voice. She wanted to sign up for a dance class with him. She offered to sign them both up, but she had no idea if he could make a regular Tuesday night work.

"I don't know if I can make anything regular, ever, but if I don't try, it will never happen," he said. "I'm going to be coming off this case tomorrow or the next day. When's it start?"

"It starts in three weeks, every Tuesday for six weeks."

Was he committing to a nine-week relationship? He paused for a long moment. "Can we sign up next week still? I'd like to give it some thought."

He could hear the disappointment in her silence.

"Madeline? I'm totally focused on this investigation, and I'm exhausted. I need some time. The way my life works, I have a hard time imagining being available on a regular basis."

"Sure, Court. No problem. Stay safe chasing down the bad guy, will you?"

He knew he'd hurt her, that his pause had stung. Still, he wasn't sure he was ready for such a commitment. Not yet. He needed more time to get to know her.

Throughout his conversation with Madeline, he kept thinking about calling Karen Hunter to update her. As soon as he said goodnight to Madeline, he dialed her.

She picked up before the second ring. "Detective? What's up?"

Her voice sounded keyed. Anxious. "I wanted to fill you in. We figured out who Jarvis is."

"What? How'd you find him?"

"We didn't find him, we only know *who* he is."

"Well? Who is he?"

"There were a few emails from him this week. He signed them Jarvis but the email user name is TinyTim."

There was a pause on the other end of the phone. "Tiny-Tim, like in *A Christmas Carol*? So, how did that help you? Did you trace the email somehow, like where he sent it from?"

"No, but this TinyTim guy had sent you several emails you ignored. He was getting more and more upset about you not responding, so he put that note on your door. But what put it together was what you told me about Jarvis having a small penis. Tiny. And we had this guy from Haubek on our radar already. His name is Tim. TinyTim. Gotta be him. Anyway, we don't have a professional profiler like they do on TV shows, but I get the sense he has some screws loose and is going to come after you. Some people get angry at the focus of their addiction, and when it's a person that anger can turn into an attempt to kill that person."

"Wow. That's *just great* news," she said, her voice dripping in sarcasm. "After all that time fixating on me, do you think he'd actually try to hurt me?"

"No telling what he might do, but, in my experience, when people lose it like this, they often lash out. He very well might attempt to harm you or your kids. I know we talked about this earlier, but you ought to reconsider your decision to stay."

"You've got three people watching the house. I feel safe enough here."

"We don't know what this guy is capable of. We know he tied Drummond up and left him to die. If it were me, I'd be clearing out of there."

"Look, this guy used to worship me, I can't imagine that he'd really try to hurt me. I doubt he'd go after my kids either. And, if what he said is true, he didn't intend to kill Berkeley."

"I can't force you out of your house, but this guy is not the same guy he was twelve years ago when you knew him."

"I refuse to be bullied out of fear. You have armed officers here guarding us. And, I don't want to disrupt my life any more than it has been."

Court hung up feeling uneasy. The house backed onto a greenbelt. Lots of trees and shrubs created a pretty good hiding place. Still, three trained and armed police officers against one guy should be no problem.

It was late, but Ashena still hadn't texted back. He took a shower and dived into his bed for a nap. He put his phone by his head for easy access through the night. He could be back at the station in five minutes when he needed to. He worked through half a dozen meditation exercises he'd learned from one of the Britt's failed picks before he fell into a deep sleep filled with nightmares. Bailey and Amanda danced around Berkeley Drummond's hanging body chasing each other in circles and laughing as they sang *Ring Around the Rosie.*

59

ASHENA TEXTED HIM AT FIVE THIRTY IN THE MORNING, followed by Ivy. He hopped into the shower to wash away the nightmares and perk himself up. He was instantly deluged by a torrential rain as he stepped outside. He rushed back in and grabbed a couple changes of clothes, an extra coat and a few protein bars, stuffed them in a bag and waved down the first taxi that came by.

Ivy jumped onto the same elevator a split second before the doors swished shut, and they rushed over to Ashena's desk without even stopping at their own. Ashena stood up when Court and Ivy approached her desk, coming around so she was in between the two of them. Court could see this was going to be a short discussion by the small sheaf of papers she had in her hands.

"Here's what I got. His work computer was wiped clean. But, the good news is, it was wiped with the idea someone else was going to come in and use it, not to hide something major. I managed to recover a lot of his deleted data. There isn't much to go on, but he was doing searches of apartments in Redmond. He might not have talked openly about moving there, but he wasn't trying hard to hide it."

She circled a list of addresses with her long fingernail. "Here are six apartment complexes that he spent a lot of time on. Or, at least, he clicked on all their pages, some of them multiple times. Below those are four more where he only looked at the home-page. I'd start with the first six. I even put them in order of highest number of clicks to lowest. I didn't find any email correspondence, so he probably called or visited them."

Ten apartment complexes Payne visited on the internet. Could be worse. They could have been handed a blank slate or a hundred places to check out.

Ashena turned to the next page. It was a map high-lighting the apartments she had identified. "And, take a look at this. The apartments are all in close proximity to Karen Hunter's home."

"So, he was trying to find a place close to her. Why her home and not her studio on Capitol Hill?" Ivy asked. "Or the separate apartment she keeps when her ex is with the kids at her house?"

Court had forgotten about Hunter's apartment. He'd call her later to find out its location. Maybe Payne had found a place in the same complex. "Stalkers like to be close to their prey? His work computer showed him looking at apartments before his mother died. After he got the card key, but before he actually used it. He was planning on moving out. Maybe that's what he and his mother were arguing about the night she died."

Ivy put her hand on Court's forearm. "Do you think he

intentionally picked a fight with his mother, hoping she'd pop?"

Court forced himself to not look at Ivy's hand on him. Had she ever touched him before? It was a subtle sign she was getting used to working with him. "They argued right before she died. We'll have to see what the sheriff's report has to say about it."

Ashena shook the papers. "Okay, back to this. Then you two can go off and make your conjectures, okay? His credit card was switched to a P.O. box in Redmond, before his mother died."

Ashena did her job with a brisk efficiency and stuck to the facts at hand. Both shut down discussions that were about the "what ifs" of a case. Hitting all ten apartment complexes might take a while, but, if Ashena's hunch was correct, they'd find him in the first six.

Ashena flipped through to the next page. "The credit report came up with one Visa card. This is a list of the purchases he's made in the last thirty days. All from the same general area in Redmond, not far from any of those complexes."

"No purchases in Seattle?" Ivy asked.

"Nope. But, hold on a second... I saved the best for last. He never got a Good To Go pass for his car. Driving from Issaquah to work wouldn't need one. He does have an Orca card, though." She flipped to another table. "Look at this. On the day of the murder, he gets on the 545 from the Bear Creek Park and Ride at 2:30 in the afternoon. The 545 is a Sound Transit bus, so he has to swipe his Orca again once he hits the Metro system. Don't know where he gets off, but he switches to the 8 at Denny and Stewart at 3:30."

Court grabbed the packet from her and tapped his finger at the next line. "And here he's taking the 8 back downtown, swiped in at 7:46. Plenty of time for him to leave the building, be seen by Audrey Drummond and walk to the bus stop." The next entry showed him getting on the return 545 at Denny and Stewart. A complete reverse route.

They had him in the vicinity on the day of the murder. Evidence, circumstantial as it was so far, was syncing up to make the whole story work. All they needed was to find Payne. Court guessed he was the type of man to confess when everything was laid out in front of him. The fact he'd left a hefty sample of his DNA would make this a slam dunk. They didn't even need the DNA results in hand. All they would need to do is confront Payne with the fact they had it, and he'd be begging for a deal in no time. "You're the best, Ashena."

She looked over the rims of her glasses at him. "If you want to thank me, I'll take a tall macchiato, extra hot."

COURT AND IVY took the information they'd gotten from Ashena and spread it all out on the table in the conference room. The morning briefing was an hour away.

He opened a map and marked out the apartments Payne had been researching. Ivy added all the bus routes and shops Payne had used.

Ivy tapped her finger on the closest three sets of apartments on a major arterial running North-South. "If he picked one of these, he could walk to the park-and-ride. They're all pretty convenient to it."

Ivy traced her finger up the arterial to a cross street near Hunter's house. "Looks like the 221 he was using went this way. Goes right past her cul-de-sac. And, he uses the 232 Southbound off of Avondale. That would take him to the grocery store, the Panera, the Starbucks." She tapped each of the places where his charge card had been used. It ranged further west into Redmond proper, but the bulk of his purchases were closer to the set of apartments off Avondale.

"And look at this." He tapped the star marking Karen's house. Then, he drew a line running almost directly south to three of the apartment complexes. "Any of these run into this park." He tapped the small green square labeled NIKE PARK. He ran his finger along the trails going north out of the park. They ran in a direct path through the greenbelt behind Karen's house.

"Any one of these three complexes leads toward that set of trails. At the most he's half a mile away from her."

Court studied the map. "Oh, man. He's totally been stalking her." It was one of the first things Karen had asked about when they showed her the key log. It had been there all along.

"You think he'll make a move in this kind of weather?" Ivy asked.

"Anything is possible."

"Now that we know a general area, I think we should get a BOLO out on him. His mother's car is still registered under her name. Maybe we can find him through the license plate on that."

"I think we have enough for a warrant," Court said. "Get everyone in Redmond and unincorporated King County looking for him. At least one of these on the list is outside of

Redmond. I'll get dispatch to link it to his DMV photo as well." His phone vibrated as he stood up. It was an Eastside number he didn't recognize. "Hello?"

The voice was rough, sounding like a man who'd been smoking for his whole life. "Detective Pearson? This is Roy Swanson over at King County Sheriff's Office. I got that report you asked about. I didn't get your email address right. It bounced back to me."

Court gave him the right email. "Can you give me the gist while you have me?"

"Not much to say. Barbara Payne died from a massive coronary. There wasn't anything unusual about it. She was overweight, had clogged arteries, untreated diabetes. Perfect candidate for dropping dead. No bruises, nothing that would indicate any sort of physical confrontation. It was determined to be death by natural causes."

Court thanked him and hung up the phone, feeling somewhat deflated.

"Maybe he didn't kill his mother," Ivy said after Court filled her in. "We know he's good for Drummond. You can't tell what brought on the heart attack. Neighbors said they fought loudly less than fifteen minutes before the ambulance arrived. Maybe he did it intentionally to get her upset enough she'd blow. Maybe it was an accident. Maybe he's feeling some guilt over his mother dying on top of what happened with Drummond. Once we get him in a room we'll let him think we're charging him with the death of his mom as well as Drummond's and see what he does."

The whole picture was clear to him now, and it was not a pretty one. "Payne does the deed Wednesday, he finds out Drummond is dead from the news report on Friday or Saturday. He's sending threatening emails by Sunday and leaving freaky notes on her door by Tuesday? Yeah ... he's going downhill fast. He feels guilty over his mom—accident or no. Then, he refuses to take responsibility for Drummond's death. He's blaming Karen for who he's become."

Ivy gathered the papers together into a pile and tapped them into order against the table. "Oedipus, meet Hamlet."

60

PEOPLE WERE BEGINNING TO FLOW IN FOR THE MORNING briefing, but it was quieter than usual and a lot of people were missing. Stensland waltzed in with a determined grimness and took center front.

"We got a triple over on Beacon Hill. Was called in an hour ago, Flanagan and Graham were up, so they're on it. I want all extra personnel to head over there and give them support. There's going to be a ton of witness statements to get."

He turned to Court and Ivy. "You two have anything interesting to say?"

Court stood up. "Sir, we've got significant leads on Payne. We've issued a BOLO with his mother's plates and his DMV photo. We need a couple of officers to help go through this list of apartments he was looking at on his computer before he left his job."

Stensland shook his head. "No can do, Pearson. You're

going to have to follow up the leads on your own. We need all available personnel to work this fresh triple homicide."

It was only then that the mention of Beacon Hill hit him. "Sir, any news on who the victims are?"

"Three men, Pearson. You can relax on that one. Your little Chinese girlfriend is safe."

After the briefing was over, Court and Ivy organized everything they would need. The sky had darkened to a near black and the rain was coming down in a relentless torrent, and the region was on high alert for a major windstorm.

"Let's grab a bunch of food before we go," Ivy said.

***

WATER POURED out of the sky in a steady deluge. Ivy grasped the steering wheel hard enough to whiten her knuckles as she fought against the pull of the high wind as they crossed the floating bridge. White-capped waves battered against the few remaining boats still on the lake.

Behind them, the city was hidden behind dark gray and black clouds. It was early in the afternoon, and there was nothing but roiling clouds ahead. The only thing he could think of that was worse than chasing down a killer in Redmond was chasing down a killer in Redmond during a flood without any power. Maybe they'd get lucky and the storm would die out soon. Better yet, they would find Payne curled up on his sofa with a book.

The first apartment on their list was a straight shot across the bridge to the end of the freeway. Court sat back in the seat of the car, glad Ivy was happy to always take the wheel.

"This is the worst I've ever seen it. Nothing like this the last three years I've been here."

Court's phone buzzed right as they were crossing the mid-span. It was Madeline. He turned his upper body away from Ivy and leaned into the window for some semblance of privacy.

"Hey Court," she said, her warm voice sending glimmers of happy desire through him in spite of where he was heading. "I was wondering if you might be free tonight."

"Tonight?" Court snuck a glance at Ivy. She was shaking her head like she couldn't believe he'd even answered the call. "Not likely. What am I going to miss?"

She laughed that harmonious laugh of hers, and a wave of longing for her hit him, surprising him by the intensity of it. It had only been a couple days since he'd seen her, and he wanted more.

"Oh, I scored a couple of tickets to a play at Seattle Rep. It's not good for kids, but I thought you might enjoy it."

Court was feeling optimistic about getting Payne sometime during the day, but it would be impossible. The hunt and eventual arrest and all its paperwork would take him late into the night, even if they caught him in the next hour or two. He'd be in Redmond until Payne was in custody, no matter how long it took. "Can't. Working late tonight."

"You're not driving, are you?"

Was she worried about him? "Nope. Keeping it safe. Gotta go."

"Girlfriend?" Ivy asked.

Court couldn't call someone in her late thirties a girl, but *woman friend* was awkward and "significant other" was way too premature. He liked Madeline. Liked how it felt to hear her voice. Liked how it felt to be touched by her. To touch her. "Something like that."

Ivy sucked in her lower lip. "Can I ask you a personal question?"

He ignored the little knot in his stomach. "Sure. Go ahead."

"When you were married, you had a wife. And a kid. So, I'm trying to figure out how that worked. You know?"

"Not sure what you're asking. Are you asking about how my wife and I had sex? Or are you asking how we had a child?"

Ivy kept her eyes on the road ahead. "Sorry. That was too personal. Forget I said anything."

He'd been compensating for the noise of the storm, so his words had come out harsher sounding than he'd intended. She was right. It was a little too personal. He had no desire to share that level of detail with her. Not yet, and maybe not ever. They sat in silence the rest of the way.

They took the freeway to the end as it turned and onto Avondale Road, and headed north to the initial set of apartments on their list. At first neither of them got out. They both sat there watching the rain blowing at them at a near-ninety-degree angle, the car rocking gently in the wind.

"You think he's going to make his move in this?"

"Maybe. But, we can't wait for the sun to come back out to do our job." Court tucked the picture of Payne into his jacket and zipped up his coat. He nodded his readiness and they bounded out of the car and raced to the leasing office.

It was a short visit. The woman who greeted them was in her late fifties, dressed in an Eighties-era power suit, and very sure of herself. She took one look at the photo of Payne and shook her head. "I've been checking out every new tenant for the last six months. I know everyone who lives here by name and on sight."

Water ran in gushing rivers along the curbs, flooded the streets. Not wanting to kill the engine, Ivy straddled the highest part of the street behind other slow-moving cars, windshield wipers at full speed. A bright flash of lightning was followed by a booming crash and then an explosion. The stoplight they were approaching blinked out, and the buildings around them disappeared into darkness.

Wind and rain continued to whip at the car as they played the four-way-stop-light-stop-sign game with other drivers who had forgotten what to do when the lights go out. Ivy cursed as she proceeded across only to have a car turn left in front of her. The other driver flipped her off.

The second apartment complex was only a few blocks north of the first, but they had to turn left into the lot without a light. The slow-moving oncoming traffic was reluctant to let them across, but finally someone paused long enough for Ivy to turn into the driveway. The entire complex was out of power.

The woman behind the desk in the office was staring at the screen of her computer. Her face was scrunched up as she looked at it. She appeared to be unaware that the problem was the power, not the computer. She kept hitting the power button on her screen. Hadn't she even noticed the lights were out, along with everything else electrical?

"Excuse me," Court said, when she didn't look up as they entered.

She startled and shook her head, glanced up at them but

returned right back to the screen. "I don't know what's wrong with the computer."

Her low voice and words slurred by a thickened tongue hit Court like a baseball bat. It was dark, so he hadn't seen her features. That would have clued him in faster.

An older man bustled into the room. His pants were baggy around his waist and held up by suspenders. His button-down shirt was tucked into the trousers, but there was an overall thinness to him. His cheekbones stuck out and his eyes were large, sunken into his head almost. It was impossible to tell if he was a cancer survivor or anorexic. Either way, the bones on his wrists and arms were clearly outlined in his flesh.

He put his hands on the woman's shoulders and squeezed them gently. "I'm sorry. Serena, honey. Daddy needs you to go play."

She grinned broadly up at Court and Ivy as she got up and left the room.

"Sorry, folks. My daughter is visiting from her group home, and she doesn't quite understand how everything works." He grinned, showing wide yellowing teeth, and clapped his hands together. "Are you two looking for a place to rent?"

Ivy coughed and pulled out her badge. "No, sir. We're looking for someone we think might live here."

Court placed the drawing of Payne face up on the desk. "Do you know this man?"

He picked up the drawing and angled it toward the window to capture whatever light he could from outside. "Oh. Mr. Payne? Yes, I do. Is everything okay?"

That was easy. Second stop and they'd found him and

he'd rented under his legal name? They'd been lucky in their apartment lineup. It set Court on edge. The lights flickered back on, and the computer beeped and rebooted. The printer on the desk made loud churning sounds as it reset itself.

"We're in the middle of an investigation, and we need to speak to him." Ivy said.

"Oh, well, I don't know if he's home right at the moment. He does come and go a lot, but his car is parked in his space. Doesn't mean a lot, though. He takes the bus most of the time. Or walks."

The man walked them to the door and pointed to a building to the left. "That one there. Apartment 32C. You're welcome to go over there."

Court glanced at the business cards set in a small holder on the desk. "Perhaps you can come with us and bring the extra set of keys, Luke."

The other man stopped short and held up his hands. "You can go knock on the door and see if he's there. If he invites you in, that's his business. Unless, of course, you have a warrant. If you have a warrant, I'll be happy to grab the keys."

NOW THAT HE knew the address, Court was able to add the information he needed and text it to the judge, who'd refused to issue warrants without the specifics. Ivy kept her eyes on the parking lot and Payne's apartment door. She was shifting her weight back and forth at an increasing rate. "Let's go see if he's there while we wait for the warrant."

"You nervous?" Court asked as they ran from the covered walkway near the leasing office to one on Payne's unit.

She ignored him as they ran up the steps to the apartment.

Ivy pounded hard on the door. "Police, open the door." There was no response.

Court looked in through the window near the front door and saw only a pitch-black interior. They'd have to wait.

Ivy leaned over the railing, looking in toward the office. "Old Luke is no longer watching. We could pick the lock and take a peek."

Court stiffened, his back against Payne's door. Had she meant it, or was she joking? If he knew her better he wouldn't have to think twice about it. "If only I'd brought my picks with me today, we could be in there already," he said, using a tone that could only be taken as sarcasm.

He couldn't tell if she caught the sarcasm or if she was reconsidering her suggestion based on his response. "We should be happy we have electronic warrants, and the power is still on in Seattle, eh? I can wait another fifteen minutes."

They moved the car into an empty space where they could see both Payne's car as well as the apartment door. As they parked, there was another huge clap of thunder, followed closely by a flash of lightning. The power blinked off again.

The rain turned the windshield into a blur. Ivy turned the ignition back on. "I think we should call Redmond PD and ask for some backup."

Court made the call, but the storm was putting strain on the locals already sent out to manage traffic around downed trees and power outages. There wasn't going be any help from Redmond. Court didn't want to wait for the warrant, but he wasn't about to cross that line. Especially not with Ivy. Not yet. If he'd been alone, maybe he would be inside already, taking a preliminary peek around.

Ivy turned the key in the ignition and put the wiper blades on their fastest speed. It was barely enough. "Payne's probably en route to Karen's house. We should go there and wait for him."

"Shut down the wipers. They draw attention." Court looked up at the apartment. He wanted to get a feel for what they were dealing with before approaching him directly. It wouldn't take that long to get a preview into Payne's private life. "Nah. Let's give it a quick cursory search. We don't have to do a fine-tooth comb. I just want to take a look. You know what I mean?"

"Okay. Five, ten minutes, then we get the hell over to Hunter's."

Court's phone buzzed. The warrant was ready.

61

COURT TURNED THE KEY IN THE LOCK AND THRUST THE door open, holding his gun in front of him. "Police, don't move."

Nothing stirred. The darkness created by the power outage and blackened sky made everything as dim as full out night. The only light came from a laptop sitting across the room, sitting open with a ball bouncing around the screen.

As they turned into the hallway, the sound of something breaking against tile drew them to the first door. His heart raced as he moved forward, kicking it open with a single blow, gun at the ready. A cat jumped off the counter, streaking past them, a flash of orange, mewling and hissing as he went. It disappeared around the corner into the bedroom at the end of the hall.

Ivy let out a nervous laugh.

"Christ. That was cliché. Let's finish this," Court said. His heart hammered against his chest as the adrenaline flooded his body.

There were only two other doors off the hallway. They moved with quick efficiency to clear the rooms. Payne wasn't there. They put their guns away and slipped on latex gloves before doing a more thorough search.

The room across from the bathroom stank. Not with the sweet sickly scent of a dead body, but of human sweat, piss, and moldy leather. The window was covered in thick brown paper and taped around the edges with duct tape. It was neatly done, the corners of the tape mitered in perfect angles like a picture frame.

Payne had replaced the carpeting with bamboo flooring almost identical to that in Karen's workspace. The smell from the room was coming from a dark mound in the middle of the floor. Court dropped to his haunches to examine it. The light wasn't helping, and the reeking mass was thick and dark. He didn't want to disturb it before forensics got there.

"What is it?" Ivy asked squatting next to him and adding her light.

"Hell if I know. It smells like he pissed on whatever it is."

"Smells like rotting leather."

It clicked. "Someone in forensics is going to have fun with this. I'm betting it's the body suit."

"Dude's more than a little pissed, isn't he?"

Ivy stood first and motioned to the closet. Court added his light to hers. The entire inside of the closet was covered with photographs. A quick count showed about sixty photos. Each showed a man, his eyes carefully blotted out with black ink, in one submissive position or another and Karen Hunter standing over him. The implements she held in her hands varied as did what she was wearing and what she was doing to each man.

"Good thing Karen Hunter got that deal, eh? We'd have her on several charges in Vice based on these," Ivy said.

"Nope. Every one of these men would say it was consensual fun and free. No one would testify to paying for it. No one would press charges." Court studied the pictures, aiming his light on each one in turn. They filled the closet, and it was clear they had been taken from exactly one angle. He groaned. "He put a camera in the clock on the wall. Shit. I can't believe I didn't even think of that even when the clocks were being put together right in front of us."

"Payne was going in there to collect images. He went in to switch out the memory cards. Man. She was a busy lady if this was over six weeks' time."

Court was surprised that a full third of the images showed Karen wearing normal clothing, not the outrageous costumes in her closet. One man was not naked, but wore female lingerie in each of his images. The four shots showing Karen in shiny black thigh-high boots and tight corset were with a man that was familiar to him. The blacked out eyes were larger, covering up glasses, but thin metal temples glinted at each ear. She obviously catered to individual desires.

There were more photos of her with Berkeley Drummond than anyone else. Even though the eyes were blacked out, Court recognized him. "What's with blacking out the eyes?"

"I have no idea. I can't wait to see what the psych report shows on this guy. Lives with his mother until he's thirty-five. Has a long-term obsession with a dominatrix. Goes apeshit after his mother dies. Accidentally kills a guy in the domme's studio, and then … what? He's blaming the domme for all of it?" Ivy poked at the guy in the glasses. "These look familiar."

A tree scraped against the roof. They both looked up even though there wouldn't be anything to see. Court focused his light on the glasses guy.

"Definitely a cop. I'm sure I know him," Ivy said. She lifted a hand and peeled at a corner of one photo with a fingernail.

The photo didn't move. Court waited to see if she would work to rip it off the wall. She didn't. She dropped her hand, leaving the photo on the wall. He'd been holding his breath the whole time and let it out slowly. And recognition came to him. The man with the glasses was the man on the burner phone list that Stensland was protecting—Stensland himself. No wonder he'd stepped in to make those calls.

Court felt a wave of nausea flood over him. If they left the photos, there was sure to be a shit-storm in the department when people recognized him. If they took them, they would leave obvious holes in the order on the wall. Besides, if they were here, they would probably be on Payne's computer as well.

"He'll have to live with whatever happens next," Ivy said. "We should call in forensics and lock this place up."

Court decided the best course of action was to pretend he had no idea who was in the photo. Let it come out and watch as Stensland's career crashed and burned. He scanned the floor, but there was nothing there. The shelf above the clothes rack only had a thin layer of dust. The photos lining the interior of the closet were it.

"But the eyes. That is totally creepy,"

He pointed his light at the images one last time, settling

on one in the center. Berkeley Drummond knelt in the center of the floor facing the camera. Right under where he died. Karen stood behind him, one hand on his shoulder the other reaching around to cup his cheek on the other side as she leaned in to whisper something in his ear. Her long hair cascaded over his neck. It was an intimate moment, and, even with the eyes inked out, there was no mistaking Drummond's expression of calm bliss.

THEY TOOK another run through the apartment, careful to not touch anything. The lab team would be very thorough in collecting evidence. Whenever that would be. Word was the storm had picked up and the 520 bridge was backed up do to a major multiple injury collision. It might be hours before they got there.

The bathroom would yield a toothbrush, a comb and hair samples. He had no desire to screw up the backup DNA they might need if Payne disappeared.

"Nothing in the kitchen," Court said as he flashed his light over to the laptop. The ball continued to bounce its silent way back and forth across the screen. Court tapped the mouse square to wake it out of sleep mode and slammed it down shut when the password request box popped up. It figured.

He was about to suggest they get the hell over to Hunter's house when he saw a familiar black pouch sitting next to the computer. A gun bag. It was so dark, he could easily have missed it. Inside was an opened box of Magtech .45 auto bullets. The gun was gone.

62

IVY OPENED THE BOX OF AMMO AND COUNTED THE EMPTY slots. "He's got a big caliber with thirteen in the magazine."

Underneath the ammo was a receipt dated the day before. Court pulled out a plastic evidence bag and slipped the receipt inside. He did the same with the ammo and the empty gun bag. "Might as well since we're here."

"We've got two people over at Karen's. I'm feeling more uneasy about this. It looks like Payne has some sort of plan with the gun."

They sealed the apartment door with tape and a lock box. They put a boot on Payne's car. If nothing else, it would keep him on foot or bus. Court guessed that Payne was in Karen's neighborhood, and they needed to get moving. Who knew what he was likely to do next?

As they were pulling out of their parking space, a man wearing a dark green coat and carrying a Safeway bag crossed in front of them. His hood was pulled down far enough to cover his face. He paused and studied the boot on

Payne's car. He lifted his head slowly, looking up at the apartment. Even from this distance, the yellow tape down the sides of the door was easy to see. Ivy had already turned the car toward the exit. "Hey, hey... Stop the car," Court said. "We gotta check this guy out."

The man turned to look at the car as Ivy put the brakes on. He backed away from them and dropped the Safeway bag in the middle of the parking lot. He took off running toward the cluster of dark, brooding trees of Nike Park.

"Fuck, that's Payne right now. He's heading to the greenbelt. You take the car and get to Karen's, I'll go on foot behind him."

"You'll get lost."

"I took a good look at that map. I'll figure it out." Court jumped out of the car and pulled his gun from where it sat snug between his belt and his back. The wind lashed at him, but he threw up his hood and yanked on the cord to pull it close around his face. He almost tripped on the bag on the ground. Inside were cans of cat food.

He saw Payne disappearing into the path leading into the park. Court would have yelled for him to stop, but his words would get eaten up in the roar of the wind.

Court followed him onto the path, but couldn't see him anywhere. The canopy of tall trees would provide a cool comforting shade on a hot summer day. But now, with the storm-darkened sky, it looked like he was entering a tunnel that waved and shimmied with the wind. The ground was slick, and any footprints were nebulous pools of stone and mud.

The thick branches overhead swayed and creaked loudly, wood rubbing against wood. It competed with the rushing of the wind. The trees shielded him a bit from the swath of rain, but their needles made up for it with prickly darts against his exposed skin.

The path from the apartment complex ran north toward Karen's neighborhood, but there were several forks along the way. If he remembered correctly, he could follow it to the right until he got behind her house. There was a trail in the greenbelt behind her neighborhood that connected with this one.

He heard a large crashing in the woods off to the left. Maybe Payne had his own way through or had gotten off the path for better cover. He might have used it dozens of times since moving in.

Court followed the noise onto a smaller path through the ferns and Oregon grape. The wind was definitely less intense inside the cover of the trees. He tried calling out. "Payne! I know you're in here. Show yourself before it's too late."

Even with the help of the flashlight, it was tricky navigating through the tangle of roots and shrubs. He followed the sound of wood snapping, moving away from him to the west. Or, at least, he was pretty sure it was from the West. Mostly. Damn. There was nothing to orient himself on. No landscape, no mountain, no house. It was all dark.

He was getting closer. A louder snap and shuffling of the bushes a few feet ahead of him. He raised his gun at a shadowed figure coming toward him.

63

It was a deer. Great. Court lowered the gun. Now he was lost in the woods, and he'd lost Payne. He pulled out his iPhone and studied the map, grateful for technology. He found the trail he'd gotten off and decided he was pretty close to the abandoned Nike missile site for which the park was named. His GPS was sluggish, showing him half a mile from where he actually was.

He dialed Ivy. "I lost him. Where are you?"

"Almost there. There're branches everywhere. At least two trees on the ground over power lines. It's an obstacle course out here."

He could barely hear her over the storm. He raised his voice. "I'll be coming through the back..." and then his phone died. He tried dialing back, but he was informed the network was too busy. The wind must have knocked out cell towers in the area. He stuffed it in his pocket and thrust his gun back into his belt.

Within a couple of minutes, he found himself on the

edge of the woods facing military-style fencing with barbed wire coiling across the top. He turned to the right and followed it along the edge until it met up with the backyard of a house. He couldn't see anyone else along the space between the greenbelt and the fences of the yards.

Even out in the open, it was dark as night. Occasional bursts of lightning lit the sky and let him see his surroundings. Karen's house was the last house on the east edge of her little cul-de-sac. He would need to follow this row of houses to the end. The heavy rain made the ground underfoot slippery. He picked his way along while searching for Payne. A branch snapped overhead and landed right in front of him, its outstretched arms scraping across his face. It was big enough that moving it would be difficult, so he went around it into the embankment between the houses and the greenbelt. The ground underneath sank under his weight and he felt the ooze of cold mud fill his shoe.

Court had to grab the shoe with his foot to release himself. He worked his way back to the top of the embankment after getting stuck another two times. This was slowing him down. Once free of the mud, he ran, caution taking a back seat to urgency. Payne was probably already at the house.

64

CRACKS AND POPS FROM BREAKING WOOD COMPETED WITH
the shriek of the wind. Tree limbs swayed drunkenly, like
outstretched arms reaching for balance. More branches the
thickness of his arm snapped off and fell to the ground,
thudding to all sides of him.

He finally came to Karen's house. He hoped he had
gotten the map right. It looked like the right place. A
wooden fence blocked the back yard from the greenbelt. The
gate in the middle was shoved open into the slight uphill
slant of the grass.

They had managed to talk Stensland into setting up one
officer in the back and one in the front of her house with the
third on foot in a circuit around the area. He didn't want the
guy in the back inadvertently shooting at him. Court edged
his way slowly around the gate, his badge leading the way,
ready to identify himself.

His eyes were adjusting to the dark, but every flash of
lightning made him pause and take stock. The shape of the

house ahead was dark on dark, but visible. A dim greenish light glowed around the edges of a curtain in a room to the right and through the kitchen window.

He couldn't see anyone moving around inside. The guard wasn't where he was supposed to be. Court ran across the yard toward the sliding door and tripped over something. No, *someone*. He caught himself on his hands and knees, his legs draped over the soft form of a body.

One of the uniformed officers was unconscious on the ground, face turned to the side. Court checked for a pulse. Found it strong and steady. The cold rain had already soaked the other man through. Court lifted him by his underarms, dragging him off the grass and toward the cover of the back porch. He tore off his coat and covered the officer. He had no way of calling for help or backup right away, but at least he'd be out of the cold rain.

Court launched himself toward the sliding door, and pulled at it. Locked. He felt his way along the outer wall of the house until he came to a window. It was closed against the weather. He shoved at it, but it was locked, too.

He dropped to his haunches and felt around. Picking up a large rock, he hit it hard against the window near the handle. Even standing right next to it, Court had barely heard the crash of the glass. He pulled out thick spiky shards of glass and reached inside to grasp the handle.

The window opened to the outside and it took some gymnastics to climb through. He tumbled to the inside onto a sofa pushed up against the wall. He rolled off, dropping deftly to his feet as he oriented himself to the darkened basement.

His soaked and mud-caked shoes squelched and slurped

against the linoleum floor. He stopped to free his feet from his shoes and socks. Then he pulled out his gun.

He flashed his Maglite around the room but didn't see anyone. A trail of mud and water led from the sliding door to the stairs. Payne had tossed his coat at the base of the stairs.

A trail of wet mud led upward. How much time had Court lost by chasing down the deer and getting stuck in the mud? Court tiptoed on bare feet toward the stairs.

A banging boom, like a gunshot from behind him, exploded in his ears.

Court spun around, ready to shoot.

He was alone.

A rushing whoosh and explosive earthquake-like sound had him drop to his haunches. Art popped off the wall and slammed to the floor around him. Thumps from overhead. Outside, the thick trunk of a fir tree stretched across Karen's back yard, its branches missing the cop on the ground by inches. A tree had fallen on the house.

Screams. Shouting from upstairs. The dog barking.

Court crouched low, climbing the stairs, his heart pounding. The stairs split halfway up, turning at the front door landing. He paused, listening. Karen spoke, urgently, in a low voice. He couldn't make out the words over the weather and the barking dog.

A green glow cast shadows everywhere. He couldn't see anybody at the top of the stairs or in the kitchen. They all had to be in the living room, to the right. He could only get so far up before he would be seen unless he crawled the rest of the way.

A gunshot. The barking stopped.

"No one move." Ivy's voice cut through the din. Calm, commanding, clear. "Drop the gun."

65

COURT STOPPED TWO STEPS BELOW THE TOP, WHERE HE could still be on his feet and crouch low, yet not be seen. He peeked around the half-wall to check out what was happening in the living room, holding his breath, hoping Payne wasn't facing his direction.

Payne stood with his back to the stairs, his left arm outstretched, his gun still pointed at the dog. Court let out his breath, long and slow. The dog lay on its side, his chest heaving up and down in labored breaths.

He could barely see Ivy. She stood directly opposite Payne. She faced Court, but kept her eyes pinned on Payne. Karen knelt next to her daughter, whose legs disappeared underneath a bookshelf. It must have toppled when the tree crashed into the house. A Coleman lantern was on the ground, tipped over and casting fractured shadows around the room.

Court knew this scenario all too well. It was the coward's way out. Payne was forcing their hand. That had been his game all along. Coming in, shooting the dog, waving his gun around. Hoping they'd end his agony for him.

But why hadn't Ivy already shot him? At less than ten feet away from Payne, she had a perfect shot at him. His grip was shaky.

Court stood up from his crouch, moving with the speed of a sloth so Payne wouldn't notice him. He had a clear shot, it would be easy to justify. He took careful aim, moved his finger against the trigger and stopped.

He didn't want to give this man what he wanted. An end to his pain and suffering—things he'd brought on himself? A need to take Payne alive filled Court with an urgency unlike anything he'd ever felt before. Suicide by cop? Not gonna happen. Not by his gun. Court pulled back, putting his gun away. He had to end this a different way.

Ivy saw him and gave the slightest shake of her head. She made it look natural, like she spoke only to Payne, but the movement made him stop in his tracks. "Put Brian down, Payne. You won't get out of here alive if you don't drop the gun."

A movement between Payne's legs caught Court's attention. A pair of feet dangled between Payne's legs. Small feet. Brian.

If Court had taken his shot, the bullet would have killed both of them. So close. Sweat or water trickled down Court's cheeks, tickling at the point of his chin.

Ivy kept Payne focused on her, giving Court a chance to get closer.

Karen held up her hands in a placating gesture. "Jarvis, let him go. You and I can go talk this over." Her voice shifted into a calm, persuasive deep alto. "We can work through this. No one else needs to get hurt."

Brian repeated Aspen's name over and over, sobbing in between breaths. The dog whimpered in response, lifting her head, trying to rise, but collapsing back to the floor. Krav techniques spun through Court's head. His fingers practiced in miniature movements.

Payne pointed the gun at Karen, his hand wobbling with the weight of it. "You are the one who brought me to this. It's your fault I've become a killer." His voice was rough. He was crying. "You destroyed me."

"Let me fix you," Karen said.

Payne's hand wavered. The gun drifted down and off to the side for a moment, and then he whipped it up again. "No. No. No. I can't listen to you anymore."

His shoulders rounded with a sudden firmness as he aimed the gun at Karen.

66

COURT SHOUTED. A PRIMAL GUTTURAL TARZAN-LIKE yowl. It worked.

Payne spun around, firing his gun in reflex as he moved. The bullet pinged against the fireplace and zinged across Court's shoulder.

Payne's gun arm swung around toward Court. He reeled Brian away from him, directly at Ivy, as he spun to face Court. Ivy had no choice but to catch Brian or have him knock her backward to the ground.

Court ignored the searing pain in his shoulder and launched himself at Payne. He used a two-handed twist to knock the gun out of Payne's hand, kneed him firmly in the groin, and twisted his arm with a swift cracking sound. Court had Payne face-down on the floor in less than three seconds.

67

COURT SAT ON THE EDGE OF THE AMBULANCE AS AN EMT applied some butterfly strips to hold the wound on his shoulder together. "This is the best I can do here, but you'll need to get over to the hospital and get some stitches, antibiotics, and a tetanus shot if you haven't had one lately."

Court winced as the tech applied some pressure. The wind continued to blow, but the rain had stopped. Emergency standalone lights flooded the area. The top of the fir tree extended beyond the roofline of Karen's house, its tip hanging over the front yard.

Crews of news reporters pressed in against the yellow ribbons marking off the scene. At least the other ambulances had taken off with the injured cops and Karen's daughter before they'd showed up. The storm, which had subsided as soon as Payne was in custody, had delayed them from getting prime shots of Karen and her kids.

Court groaned when he saw Stensland lift the tape and enter the area.

The tech working on his arm stopped. "Are you okay?"

"I'm fine. My boss just showed up."

Stensland scanned the entire scene until he located Court. He strode over in long officious strides. "What's this make? Twice now? You've been shot twice in three years."

Is that what he was going to focus on? Court didn't need a lecture. "I'll survive. I'm barely nicked. Maybe I'll need a few stitches. Got our guy in the process so it's worth it."

Stensland leaned in to examine the wound. "Lucky you. I've got a dozen news people out there wanting to know what went down here."

As he explained what happened, Court sensed Stensland's disappointment. He had been hoping Drummond's death was Triad-related to refuel the department's fight against them. Drummond's death being an accident was a major letdown.

"Get his confession, get him processed, then go home. Take tomorrow off."

Court lifted two fingers to his temple in a salute as Stensland turned to talk to the news reporters. Stensland paused and returned to him. "You ever figure out the leak?"

Court shook his head. "Still working on that one. But, I think you'll want to give the deputy chief a call. Give him a *personal update.*"

Stensland leaned in close enough for Court to smell his coffee breath. "Your conspiracy theories are getting old, Pearson."

Court made a note to never play poker with his boss. "It's his glasses. They showed up in some photos. You have some ass-covering to do, Lieutenant."

68

COURT ROLLED HIS SHOULDERS AND NECK, TRYING TO relieve the tension that had grown in them over the last couple hours. The ride back into Seattle with Payne in the back of the car had been uneventful. The storm had cleared, and the bridge reopened to traffic. The continued darkness created by widespread power outages made the city appear like a post-apocalyptic ghost town. Lights, most likely lit by personal generators, dotted the landscape all around. The streetlights in downtown were not even flashing.

The department had generators, so getting Payne to talk on videotape went as smoothly as it could. He had become a weepy mess. By the time they were done, Court almost felt sorry for him. Payne's mother had a heart attack during their argument, and he Payne blamed himself for that. He confessed that he also blamed himself for his father's death during a boating accident when he was only fifteen. It sounded to Court like it was more likely the typical self-centered loathing found in a lot of teenagers, but they wouldn't know for sure until later. Court was pretty sure the psych evaluation was going to make Payne out to be an abuse victim, but that wouldn't keep him from going to prison for a long time. He confessed to everything being his fault in the end. Begged to know if he'd killed the dog, too.

As they left him for processing, he turned to Court, his eyes swollen and cheeks tear-streaked. "Please. Can you make sure someone takes care of Higgins? I'm all he had."

"Your cat?"

"Yes, please. It's not his fault. He's a good cat. He even fetches."

Court couldn't quite believe it. The man had tied up Berkeley Drummond, ejaculated on his face and left him. And now this? "Don't worry about your cat," Court said, wishing already he hadn't.

"Thank you."

Court had forgotten to ask about a detail, he put a hand up to the officer who was leading Payne away. "Why'd you turn up the heat?"

Payne looked at him, confused. "The heat?"

"In the studio, when you left Drummond."

A sad little smile creased his cheeks. "He was naked. I didn't want him to get cold while he waited for Mistress."

IN THE WRITTEN REPORT, Court made a point of documenting Payne's stalking behavior. He had to have known that her leaving early was unusual, and by not staying around to ensure her return, Payne's leaving Drummond alone to die was intentional. He wanted the prosecutor to bring down first-degree murder charges. He made a good case for stalking, harassing, and kidnapping to add to the package.

At eleven, he switched on the news out of curiosity. Storm damage took top billing. A third of the city was still without power, there were half a dozen mudslides being reported, and the flooding along the rivers wouldn't peak for a few more hours. They brought Ingram in with his hot breaking news as if he was reporting live action. Ivy came over from her cubicle to stand next to him, looking up at the TV mounted on the wall.

The footage showed the chaos outside Karen's house. First, it panned across the whole scene showing flashing ambulance, police and other emergency vehicle lights. It zoomed in on Karen as she climbed into the ambulance, Ingram's voiceover narrating the scene.

"Berkeley Drummond's dominatrix is seen here climbing into the ambulance with her son who was held hostage before the police were able to subdue the man."

Then, it zoomed in on Court. He looked in fascination at himself, his shirt off and his wound being tended to. His sense of time looping around to hours before was disorienting as he stood there watching himself in a previous moment.

"Lead detective Court Pearson was shot as he grappled with the suspect."

Ivy elbowed him. "Man, you have some muscle on you, don't you?"

Ivy was actually being friendly?

Stensland appeared on the screen. "While I am not at liberty to discuss the particulars, we are confident we have the man responsible for the death of Berkeley Drummond in custody. His name is Timothy Michael Payne. Unfortunately, I can't share any details about his motives in the Drummond killing."

The footage switched to Ivy directing a handcuffed Payne to a car and pushing him in. "Glad I remembered to put my hand over his head. Looks better than bashing it into the car, eh?"

Ingram had gotten this part of the story pretty much right. All but the part about the hour-long kidnapping. Payne had only been a couple minutes ahead of him. And, it couldn't have been more than a minute from the time Aspen got shot to the time Court had Payne on the floor.

When Ingram finished his report, the camera zoomed in on Tracy's face. "Thank you, Scott," she said.

For a moment, it was as if Court was in a little bubble with her, as if she were able to see him on the other side of the lens.

How had he missed this? Holy hell.

"Oh, fuck," Court said falling back against his chair, struggling to breathe. His throat felt like it had a rope around it, tightening, squeezing it shut.

"What?" Ivy asked.

Court couldn't say it out loud. *I'm the leak. I'm the fucking leak.*

69

COURT DIDN'T CARE HOW LATE IT WAS. HE POUNDED ON Cami's door.

She opened it partway. "Oh shit." She stepped back, refusing to look at him as he entered. She was dressed in cutesy pajamas covered in neon-colored owls. The kind he would never have guessed she would wear. He'd always pictured her in leather, even while sleeping.

He brushed past her. "Why? Why did you do it? Is she here?"

Cami closed the door, leaned against it still not looking at him. "What are you talking about?" She looked like a dog who was sitting with a chewed-up shoe in her mouth still trying to get away with it.

Court didn't have the energy for prevarication. He spun around, getting up in her face. "Seriously? You really want to play it that way?"

She sucked in her breath, slipping away from him, scuttling to the overstuffed armchair that took up most of her tiny apartment. She pulled her feet up to her butt, hugging her knees to her chest. "I'm sorry, Court. Are you in trouble?"

"It's nice of you to worry about me." His anger deflated a little at the round wetness of her eyes, her near-fetal position. Of course he was going to be in trouble. "You used me. Our friendship."

She pressed her forehead against her knees burying her face into the flannel owls. "I'm sorry. I needed the money. Tracy told me she could pay me for juicy stories. I could get paid a lot if I could find good information."

"How did you know what I had on my phone?"

"I didn't. You told me you had a new case Friday night at the bar. Then, Saturday, I heard the news report about Drummond dying. I put two and two together."

He'd never seen her look so vulnerable. "You went through my photos at the party on Saturday." He hadn't dumped the pictures until Sunday. The text Madeline had sent at the party hadn't shown up as new because Cami was going through his phone at the same time she'd sent it.

She lifted her head. Her eyes were red and tearing over. She nodded. "You left your phone in your coat pocket. It was hanging on the chair in the kitchen, and I heard it beep. A text or something. So, I … took a quick peek."

"You know my PIN?"

"Yeah. You're always checking your messages when you're out with me. You're not the only one who can read upside down, Court."

"You followed us to Karen Hunter's house on Monday, too. I felt you watching me when I walked her out of the station."

She looked away.

He walked to the door, yanking it open. "Was it worth it, Cami?"

"Court, don't go. We can talk this out, can't we?"

Court paused. If he tried to talk it out with her now, he'd say nasty things. Things he would regret. Things he couldn't ever take back. "No. We can't. Not now. I needed to see you deny me to my face. I'm gonna go. I'll call you when I'm ready to talk to you again."

"Court, please."

"Don't hold your breath."

70

COURT WAS STEPPING OUT OF THE SHOWER READY TO FALL into bed when his doorbell rang. He looked at the clock. It was almost two. He was in no mood for Cami's apology. He wrapped the towel around his waist trudging to the door.

It was Madeline. She looked up at him, her lower lip sucked in between her teeth. Her face scrunched into a giant question mark. "I saw you on the news, and I thought this was worth more than a text."

Court stepped aside to let her in. "Where's Pippi?"

"Who?" She slipped off her shoes.

"Sorry. Lucy. She had pigtails the other night. I named her Pippi in my head."

"You're sweet, Court. She does look a little like a Pippi, doesn't she?"

She reached out to touch his shoulder, her fingers gently tracing the outline of his bandages. "How many stitches?"

"Seven. Just got home a little while ago. It's been a crazy night."

"Can I stay?"

He put his hand on hers. "I'm not going to be much fun."

"I want to be with you. You shouldn't be alone."

He brushed a stray hair out of her face, tucking it behind her ear. "Okay. I plan on sleeping. I'm almost asleep on my feet."

"That'll be fine. I'd like to stay next to you, keep you company."

She took him by the hand, guiding him to his bedroom. She pulled the comforter and sheets back for him. He dropped the towel around his waist and climbed in naked. She removed her outer coat to reveal bright turquoise pajamas with kittens all over them. Owls and kittens. What was it with pajamas these days? Court traced one of the kittens on her shoulder after she settled in next to him. "Cute," he said. It was the last thing he remembered before the smell of coffee woke him the following morning.

71

COURT LET HIMSELF INTO BRITT'S HOUSE. THE PHOTO OF him with his family at Disneyland was sitting in the same spot on the shelf as last week. His chest felt tight, but it was a different kind of ache. Amanda and Bailey were captured forever at age two and thirty-seven.

Britt came in slowly, peeking around the door into the living room as if she was expecting an intruder.

"Court," she said, opening her arms, running toward him.

He held her close. "I'm okay. I'm fine."

"You could have texted. Called. Anything."

"I'm sorry. I was distracted. Hey, come sit with me a minute will you?"

He dragged her over to the overstuffed sofa, patting the cushion next to him. He slipped two fingers into his shirt pocket and pulled out the little blue box. "You remember this?"

Britt took it and lifted the necklace out of its cotton bedding. She traced the letter A with her fingernail. "Of course I remember this."

Their eyes met for a second. Court nodded, wanting her to continue.

"She wore it all the time. She told me she had pointed it out to you a couple of times. She didn't think you were even paying attention. When you gave it to her? That's when she fell in love with you, you know?"

"Are you saying she wasn't in love with me before I gave her the necklace?"

"I'm saying that's when she really fell in love. She knew, but she wasn't sure. Do you get what I'm saying?"

Court ran both hands through his hair and laughed. "Oddly enough, I do. I want you to have it."

Britt clasped her hand around the necklace, leaning forward to kiss him on the cheek. "Thank you, Court. But, why not keep it yourself?"

"I can't wear it. It's too girly for me. And I don't want to drape it over a photo or something like some sort of altar." He shrugged. "I don't want it hidden away and unused. I've kept my memories of Amanda and Bailey squashed down for too long. I want to look back and think about the good stuff. I can't do that if I bury everything in drawers. You were best friends, and when she died, I was too wrapped up in my loss to see how much it hurt you."

Britt put the necklace on. "I'm sure people will wonder why I'm wearing an A around my neck, but then, it will give me a chance to talk about her, too."

Court wrapped his arms around her and his head

dropped to her shoulder. They sat there, quietly holding each other until Morgan and Mandy rushed inside. They held up the newspaper with Court's picture on the front and demanded to see his stitches.

72

COURT KNOCKED ON THE DOOR OF ALLEGIANCE Investments. Karen opened it right away; he had texted her from outside the building he was on his way up. She looked past him, scanning the hallway for curious lurkers.

"You have people giving you a hard time?" he asked.

"One of my neighbors has been hanging around his door a lot. Asked me for a tour this morning."

"Would that have been the psychologist on the corner?"

Court could see how men would pay for the privilege of making her smile.

"How'd you guess? Come on in."

There hadn't been much to pack up to begin with, but the shelves in the front office were all empty of their little statues and books. Four neatly labeled boxes sat on the desk ready to go.

"Come on into the studio. I'm almost finished."

Four huge wardrobe boxes were stationed under the hook in the ceiling; her costumes were shoved in tight. She had thrown shoes in around the base and sides, filling up the bases.

"How're the kids doing?"

Karen pulled one of the plastic bins out of an upper cupboard and placed it directly in a box, labeled it with the code name on the bin. "Brian is anxious. He's old enough to know what's going on. It's going to take some time to forget some crazy man trying to shoot him. But, I actually think he's more upset about Aspen getting shot. Sophie's broken leg will be out of its cast in a few weeks." She closed the flaps over the box, deftly pulling tape across the top. "I think I'll be spending some money on therapists. But, we'll be okay."

"And Aspen? She looked pretty bad."

"Oh, that dog will live forever. She's going to be fine. She'll have a limp." She shrugged. "As a parent, the worry over a pet isn't as heart-wrenching as it used to be."

"Do you want his cat?"

Karen stopped what she was doing, looking at him as if she hadn't heard him right. "Jarvis's cat? *Seriously?*"

Why had he asked her like that? It was a stupid idea, but it had popped out without much thought. "I told him I'd find him a home."

"*Hell no.* I don't want anything to do with him, ever again. And I'm definitely not taking care of that man's cat."

"He's cut a deal with the prosecutor. No trial in exchange for a life sentence."

She crossed her arms, studying him for a few uneasy seconds. "You're a kind person, Court. I'm surprised he didn't go the insanity route. I'm disappointed. Audrey Drummond doesn't get to face the man who killed her husband?"

"Nope. But, I think justice is being done. He's a messed-up guy who's taking blame for more than he probably actually did. Once we got him inside he totally broke down."

He pulled the stack of checks out of his shirt pocket. "I got clearance to give these to you. Should help your ... transition."

Karen shuffled through the checks, shaking her head. "What was he thinking?"

"Mrs. Drummond thought maybe it was his way of taking care of you. He wasn't planning on coming back after last week. His family was expecting some huge gathering on Sunday. He was going to kill himself."

Karen stuffed the checks into to her purse. "He was one of the gentlest men I had ever met."

Court picked up one of the flat boxes and formed it into shape, taped the bottom and flipped it over ready to fill. He repeated the maneuver with three more boxes.

Karen dropped a plastic bin into one of the boxes he'd taped together, the tell-tale redness around her nose and eyes the only proof she'd been crying.

"What are you doing with your ... practice?" Court wasn't sure what to call her business. It was sort of therapeutic, what she did.

"I like that. Practice. Half my clients fired me. I told the rest I'm retiring." She used the tape gun to indicate the space they were in. "There is no way I could work here again. Not after seeing Berkeley..." She shuddered and closed her eyes, breathing in deeply. "Besides, that idiot at News 7 gave everyone a very clear view of what building I'm in, my legal name, and showed everyone my house. No anonymity left in this location. Not with my face being all over the news."

"Are you moving away?"

"No. I think I'll be looking for something else to do. Go back to school, maybe. I've got considerable savings and the cash Berkeley left me."

"What about your house? The damage the tree had done must be expensive."

"Insurance will cover it. We're moving into the apartment I normally use while Robbie has the kids. They'll move back and forth for a few weeks until the repairs are done."

They worked together in companionable silence, filling and taping boxes in a steady order. After an hour, they were done. Court looked around the room, now stacked with neat boxes ready to be hauled to somewhere new.

He held out his hand to her. "There's no trial with the guilty plea. So, I think this is it. You don't have to ever talk to me again."

She side-stepped his hand, slipping in to hug him. "I've been trying to find a way to thank you for saving my life. But, the only thing I can think of is this."

She linked her arms around his neck and pressed her lips against his. A simple, sweet kiss to start. When she leaned back, asking with her eyes, he didn't step back or try to disengage. Her breasts pressed into his chest as she kissed him again.

He held her close, shifting the kiss into a need-driven exploration. Their tongues danced in each other's mouths, testing and probing with the delicious freshness of someone new. He pulled away before he got in so deep he wouldn't be able to remove himself.

"You're welcome?" he said, dazed by the sudden and unexpected interaction. He tucked a hair that had come loose behind her ear.

She chuckled softly, putting a hand against his cheek. "Would it be wrong of me to ask you out? Now the case is closed?"

There was something incredible about the way she looked at him. The feel, the touch of her. It was always a self-esteem boost to have a gorgeous woman come on to him. It wasn't something he let happen very often; he never got this close to a woman without giving her some clue to what she was getting into. The vibe he was getting from her was one of pure interest. One of pure attraction. Physical attraction. To him. Nothing complicated about it. Not on her end, anyway.

Madeline. Karen. So many issues with both women. Karen was a professional dominatrix—a sex-worker. He'd seen the photos on the wall, and there were some things he wasn't sure he could handle.

"Not wrong, but I have to decline. You're a beautiful and fascinating woman, Karen, but…" he turned her hand palm-up and kissed it gently, already feeling like a heel for his judgmental crap excuses. "I don't think it would work out. You're…business…I'm a cop. It's complicated. I'm seeing someone." He ended with the lamest excuse in the book, his voice trailing off.

She obviously didn't buy it. Karen placed her hands on his shoulders and squeezed them, one delicious eyebrow lifting in obvious amusement. "Let me know when you change your mind."

ACKNOWLEDGMENTS

I'd like to thank everyone in my life who has supported me through the process of getting *Bound to Die* into the world. Friends and family have heard me talk about this book for a long time, and their encouragement has buoyed my spirits through some hard times.

My beta readers and my writing group have read any number of versions of this book over the last few years. Thank you all for your fine attention to detail, your inspiration, and your unfailing honesty--Patrick Callahan, Jayson Caracciolo, Sandy Esene, Michael Gooding, Heidi Hostetter, Bridget Norquist, Ann Reckner, Emma Rockenbeck, Heather Stewart McCurdy, Elizabeth Visser, Charlotte Morganti, and Terri Thomas. Your insights, questions, and willingness to thwap me upside the head have helped make this a better book than I could possibly have done on my own.

My editors Jason Black at Plot to Punctuation, Jim Thomsen Creative and Margy Rockenbeck have helped me plug plot holes and repair structural damage. Without them, this book would have been a complete mess. Thank you for your fine attention to detail!

Many thanks to Scott Driscoll, Kathleen Alcala, and Pam Binder for their teaching and mentoring. My craft would be crap without your coaching and support.

The folks at TCOPS international answered tons and tons of questions—not only about what it might be like to be a transmale detective, but general police procedure. TCOPS International supports transgender police who suffer unique challenges as they transition—at home and in the workplace. Thank you, thank you, thank you.

Lee Lofland and all the instructors at The Writer's Police Academy—your willingness to open up the cop world to writers is awesome. A special shout-out to ex-ATF agent Rick McMahan for answering all my gun questions. Jeff Roberts, thank you for taking me to Wade's and letting me shoot all your guns. It was a blast.

Finally, my family gets the biggest hugs. Margy and Dave, my in-laws have donated their time-share many times to provide me a space for mini writing retreats. They've been there for my kids while I was away—feeding them, driving them, and doing whatever I wasn't doing because I was writing. Bill, Emma, and Eli—my husband and children--have supported me through this journey and put up with many night classes and my being away for days at a time. They're probably sick of Court and Ivy and all of it, but continue to cheer me on. I love you all.

ABOUT THE AUTHOR

 Laurie Rockenbeck was raised a Navy brat and moved around a lot as a kid. She lives near Seattle with her family, two cats and three chickens. She graduated with a degree in journalism and quickly learned that writing fiction was a lot more fun. With a grandmother who started every story with *This is a true lie...*, there is no doubt that story-telling and exaggeration are part of her genetic make-up. She is creating a mystery series set in Seattle. Rockenbeck has her private investigation license but prefers writing about made up cases to investigating real ones.

www.laurierockenbeck.com

CPSIA information can be obtained
at www.ICGtesting.com
Printed in the USA
FSOW02n0827071217
42145FS

9 781947 234031